HUNTING AND HERBALISM

BOOK TWO

HUNTING AND HERBALISM

BOOK TWO

Leif Roder

aka Synonymoose

Podium

This is a work of fiction. Names, characters, places, and incidents are either products of the author's imagination or used fictitiously. Any resemblance to actual events, locales, or persons, living, dead, or undead, is entirely coincidental.

Cover design by Jason Nathaniel Artuz

ISBN: 978-1-0394-7498-7

Published in 2025 by Podium Publishing
www.podiumentertainment.com

HUNTING AND HERBALISM

BOOK TWO

CHAPTER ONE

Cormaine

Zalia

Stretching out before Zalia was a hellish landscape of strangely formed leafless trees and other plants. The air was slightly red, colouring everything in a crimson hue. In the sky above, vaguely humanoid figures floated through the air, letting out dull croaks and cries. She realised that there was no sky at all, only the ceiling of the giant cavernous space she was now in.

Zalia noticed a sharp twinge in her leg and looked down to see Boreal latched onto her with claws out. She felt a twin pain in her mind as what had been a dull discomfort began to rise. She fell to her knees, holding her head with both hands as the pain increased. She could feel a similar sensation through the bond with Boreal and instinctively began focusing her healing on the both of them. Immediately, the pain lessened to a dull throbbing in her temples, and she began observing her surroundings once more. The air had a sulphurous taste to it, the ground beneath oddly squishy, like the mud of a swamp. She spotted something she did recognise, a body lying unconscious on the dirt underneath one of the warped trees.

Zalia knew what had happened to her. The last time she had a similar experience, she'd been brought from her world to the one she now resided in. Well, used to reside in, anyways. Now she was in a new world, and she had a sinking feeling she knew where: Cormaine.

She crawled over to Juniper's still form and nudged her, trying to figure out if she was actually unconscious or dead. She seemed to be breathing, so Zalia took the woman's belt that had a sheathed dagger and pouch attached.

Should I help her? Zalia thought.

She stood, looking down at the woman. Flashes of all the good times, fond memories, and trust they had shared passed through her mind—then, the memory of Juniper sitting on the bench in front of their cell as they sat imprisoned. She looked up at the hellscape around her and then back down to Juniper.

"Not this time," she whispered. "You've lost the right to my kindness."

She picked up the struggling Boreal and began making her way through the warped trees, keeping to the shadows.

Zalia had no idea what the shadowy forms floating above were, but the constant croaks and cries made them sound like a chorus of tortured souls. She really didn't want to bring herself to their attention. Now that the initial adrenaline had worn off, her survival instincts took over. Emotions and thoughts could wait until later; for now she had to get safe. The very first thing she needed to find in an unknown and possibly hostile land was shelter. Food and water could wait, especially with her Survivalist skill. Getting away from the eyes of anything hostile and any dangerous weather was priority one.

She moved towards where a large pillar stuck out of the ground, reaching far up into the air before meeting the stone ceiling above. Far off in the distance she could see a large, floating shape, slowly moving through the sky. Noting it as something to possibly check out later, she turned her attention back to the pillar and made her way as quickly as she could manage while remaining stealthy. She didn't know why she hadn't gone insane or become corrupted like the men and women who had performed or seen the rituals, but she had an inkling it had to do with her Healing Presence ability. Previously, it had countered the strange aura that the corrupted deserter captain had emitted, and as she thought of that, she could feel that same aura here, only it didn't have an origin. It seemed to permeate the air, land, and trees around her, emitting a field of corruption that her ability barely managed to keep at bay.

Her Healing Presence had also managed to bring back the mind of the insane man within the rebels' war camp, if only for a moment.

I should have killed her, Zalia thought.

Leaving Juniper alive might have been a bad idea, but Zalia didn't want to risk turning around to finish the job. Considering the pain and blood loss the woman had inflicted on herself to start the ritual, in addition to the aura in this cursed place, she might be dead already.

Zalia reached the base of the giant pillar and began searching around its perimeter, eventually finding what she was looking for. A small cave sat nestled between two large boulders, with an opening barely big enough for her to enter. She set up some distance away, watching the entrance as she held Boreal close to her chest. The little feline seemed to be struggling more than she was, despite the constant dull throb in her temples.

> **Congratulations! Healing Presence has reached Iron 13.**

She hugged Boreal closer, keeping her eye on the cave as she settled in to wait.

It only took a few hours for her patience to run out. In a situation like this she definitely needed to be careful, but she also couldn't spend too much time waiting around. She steeled herself, not summoning her blade yet because of the dim light it emitted, and made for the cave. Nothing had come out of it in the time she had waited, so she didn't keep her hopes up.

Before she got too close to the entrance, she checked the sky again and saw the shadowy forms were still floating around. Their croaks and cries were constant, and yet she regularly felt the need to check if they had noticed her. She had a feeling they would be a little louder than they were right now if they had, though. She carefully moved to the boulder, shuffling sideways until she could peak her head around into the cave. She could vaguely see a small cavern with clumps of glowing, mushroom-like plants scattered across the walls. There was no creature that she could see within the cave but she didn't let her guard down just yet, as she spotted a small crack that led further in. The mushrooms could also be a threat, though her Flora Identification should have been able to tell her that.

Deciding to take the risk, Zalia summoned her blade just as she squeezed between the two boulders into the small cavern. As soon as she was close enough, she used Flora Identification.

> **? (Helpful) - Bronze rank - Use in a ritual
> to add an element of Shadow.**

Wonderful, Zalia thought.

It was a good start, at least the plant wasn't poisonous.

She carefully poked at it with her blade, but the sharp implement simply stabbed into the mushroom, eliciting no reaction. Satisfied for the short term, she moved to the side of the cave where she could watch both the entrance and hole leading further in, and sat down with her back to the wall. She gently put down Boreal, still holding her blade in the other hand. Noticing Boreal seemed to be struggling still, she brought out a little bit of Frozen Heart, the herb from the cold north of Endaria, which assisted with healing. She gently fed it to Boreal and was relieved to see she seemed to be able to breathe easier immediately.

As she looked around her cave and felt a remote bit of safety, she let the reality of her situation set in.

"Fuck," she said, feeling absolutely lost.

It wasn't the first time she had been sent to another world, but this place was meant to be, well, hell. It was essentially the Endarian version of hell.

Rather than let herself succumb to misery, she tried to think about it in a logical manner. Sure, it was hell. She had planned to go explore some really dangerous places after the war anyways so why not here?

She had already discovered one possibly useful thing here, it could be useful to find more as well. Deciding to try to maintain that mindset, though some horror and doubt resided in her mind still, she took stock.

She had her bow and sword, a combined, bound weapon that was possibly the greatest advantage she would hold here. In addition, she also had a small amount of each herb she was unable to replicate stored in her Stasis ability's spatial storage. Those would most likely prove to be invaluable in her first days in this new land. She didn't have her armour or spatial bag, having had both taken when they had been imprisoned. She had the dagger and pouch she had taken from Juniper and quickly opened up the pouch to see what was inside. It contained a small vial with a purple liquid, a few golden coins, and a scroll. She took the scroll out and read it over, finding descriptions and instructions for the very ritual that Juniper had performed. The ritual required many things that Zalia did not have, but it might just be her most valuable possession. It might be the only way she knew of to make her way home.

She carefully rolled it back up and put it back in the pouch, now much more protective of it. Her thoughts turned to the ritual that had brought her here and a vivid memory flashed into her mind. The sight of Zen on one knee, blade piercing through his torso. Her whole body shuddered and she told herself that he would be fine. She had healed him a little, and Ember was there too. If there was anyone she trusted Zen's life to when it came to healing, Ember would be the one.

If she even survived, Zalia thought.

Ember had been fighting another of the guards by herself as Zalia had disrupted the ritual, and she had no idea how that turned out either. She didn't even know if she had managed to disrupt whatever the ritual was meant to accomplish. She knew it was meant to open some sort of portal or summon someone from Cormaine because her reversal of it pulled her here. It was also part of a much larger and more powerful ritual. It was completely unknown to her whether her disruption during that one part had affected the whole ritual. For now, all she knew was she couldn't see any portal or effect that it had on this side, so she tried to stay positive.

Alright, back to the present, Zalia admonished herself.

The next thing she would need to do was find some source of food. She had the Water Lily stems that would hydrate and nourish her a little bit, but they couldn't keep her going forever. She hadn't seen any animals she could hunt on her way here, and she definitely didn't want to try eating one of the floating shades in the sky. She eyed the mushrooms suspiciously. Her ability hadn't told her they were poisonous but neither had it said they were edible or nutritious. Many of her herbs had a diminished effect when eaten directly, such as the Frozen Heart, so Zalia thought the mushrooms might do the same. What that would mean when the element they provided was one of shadow, she didn't know. She put it down on her list of things that might be worth exploring, along with the far-off floating island she had seen earlier.

She checked on Boreal, who had settled down and was in the process of cleaning herself thoroughly.

"Good to see you doing better," Zalia said, feeling relieved.

While she was quite alright being by herself, she had grown used to Boreal's company and didn't want to be in hell alone.

"What are we going to do?" Zalia asked.

All that Zalia received was an image of herself and the concept of faith. Boreal's faith in her.

That makes one of us, Zalia thought.

Zalia didn't quite have the faith that Boreal did, but surviving in harsh environments was her specialty, after all. She stood up and buried the pouch she had taken from Juniper in the corner of the cavern under a small pile of dirt and rocks. It would be better if that stayed where she knew it was and not where it could get damaged while she explored.

"Let's find out if we are going to stand a chance out here, shall we?" Zalia asked Boreal.

"Mreow," Boreal replied.

CHAPTER TWO

Caves

Zalia

Zalia considered her two options for exploration. The first was going back to the open land outside, the second was going further into the cave. Each idea had its merits, but Zalia eventually decided to check out further into the cave first. She still didn't know if those haunting figures in the sky were hostile or not, and she wanted to see if she truly was safe in these caves or if some unknown danger lurked further within. While her instincts told her that such good shelter would never be left uninhabited when possible danger lay outside, she didn't know if there were even any creatures here other than the shadows.

Standing before the dark hole in the ground, Zalia focused on her heat vision, compliments of her bond with Boreal.

"It doesn't seem like there is anything down there," Zalia said to Boreal as they both crouched before the opening.

Boreal was watching intently as well, searching for signs of life. Not that any life would necessarily even create heat, rendering the heat vision potentially useless.

"Wanna go first?" she asked.

Boreal looked at her as if she was crazy, then walked behind her, waiting patiently in line.

"Rrright," Zalia said.

She considered for a moment before summoning her bow. She shot an arrow through the hole and watched the flight of the dimly lit magical arrow. It ricocheted through the cavern before sinking into the stone wall some fifteen metres away. It looked like the tunnel was narrow all the way through, with jagged walls. She would have to crawl through the space if she wanted to fit and wasn't super keen about the idea. The arrow's light at the end of the space was slowly fading, so she made her move. Getting down on her hands and knees, she began crawling through the small gap.

"I'm really too old for this," Zalia complained as she scraped her barely protected knee on the floor.

Her healing ability was easily able to take care of the small scratch but it still hurt. Boreal followed behind, able to move much, much easier than Zalia could. Luckily for the feline, she wasn't fully grown yet and had quite a ways to go before she would be.

"One day you'll be big enough that I can ride around on you instead of having to carry you everywhere," Zalia muttered.

She smiled at the idea as she finally reached the end of the tunnel. It split in two different directions, one side looking like it widened out enough for her to stand whilst the other remained just as narrow. She summoned her sword to provide a little more light; the mixture of her Low Light vision and heat vision allowed her to see quite far with just the tiny amount it provided. The narrower path curved around out of view while the wider one started to angle downwards into a slope. Deciding to explore the more difficult path later, she started crawling towards the sloped path. She was thankfully able to stand hunched before long and with a straight back shortly after that. Boreal, who had grown so much she now reached Zalia's mid-thigh in height, followed along as easily as before.

The air started to cool significantly as she descended, to the point where a small frozen stream broke out of the rocks and followed alongside the path. It made the going much more treacherous, but Zalia and Boreal were well-accustomed to walking on ice. The narrow path widened out further as Zalia reached another cave. The space was similarly lit with the mushrooms she had found in the first cave, providing a dim, purplish glow to the whole space. The space was relatively large, the far end taken up by a half-frozen lake into the depths of which Zalia could not see. There didn't appear to be any way out other than where she had come from, and she looked around the space with a critical eye. In terms of a safe and hidden place to stay, this was probably one of the better places she could have lucked out finding.

Boreal carefully walked around, smelling the air and Zalia realised that the sulphurous smell from above didn't quite reach down here. The aura of corruption was also lessened, though not gone entirely. Boreal seemed to like the space, the ice likely reminding her of her birthplace. Though she didn't have particularly fond memories of the mountaintop, it was still her natural environment.

"What do you think, good place to set up?" Zalia asked.

Boreal meowed in what sounded like agreement.

"Alright, I'll need to go get that pouch, and we need to explore the other path as well, but it's a good start."

Zalia didn't really need a traditional fire to cook anymore, the use of her heat manipulation was all she needed to create a smokeless fire. She would have to test the water, but if it proved to be fresh then it could be a good source. If it wasn't, she might even be able to grow some of the Water Lilies in it as a method of purification. Now all she needed was a source of food.

Despite her ability to ignore having to eat for a few days, she hadn't eaten at all during her imprisonment and was actually starting to feel hungry for the first time in a long time.

"You don't think we can eat those floating shadows, can we?" Zalia asked.

Boreal gave her a look that told Zalia she thought her to be an idiot.

They probably didn't taste good anyways.

Zalia hadn't seen any tracks in the lands above when travelling here, so maybe her best plan was to find some sort of plant life to live off. Boreal would most likely need to eat some sort of creature though, being more of a carnivore than she was. Zalia pulled out some of the Water Lily stems, chewed one, and placed one down for Boreal. She didn't seem excited about the prospect of plant stem but ate it without complaint. Zalia sat down as far from the lake as she could get, eyeing the deep waters with suspicion. The deep ocean had been something Zalia had an interest in before she had moved far from civilisation back on her own world, and she knew what horrors could dwell in those depths. Especially when she was now in a magical world's version of hell.

Thinking back, the ocean might have been the start of her fascination with moving away from all civilisation to somewhere untouched and untamed by people. Thoughts of her childhood brought to mind her parents. She hadn't thought about or talked to them in many years and didn't plan to now. That way lay trauma and a whole host of issues she really didn't have time for at this moment.

Breaking free of those thoughts, she brought herself back to the situation at hand.

"Right, let's go see that other path!" Zalia said, standing up.

Boreal scrambled to her paws at Zalia's quick stand and followed along. They made their way back through the cave until Zalia had to crawl once more. She arrived at the T-section and moved past it towards the other path.

"This might get real old, real fast," Zalia grumbled as she crawled along.

It was one downside to staying here, but at least she would be somewhat safe. She hoped.

She moved slowly through the space, trying to remain quiet once more as she entered the unknown tunnel.

Does this place have night and day? Zalia questioned.

It probably wasn't the best time for such thoughts, but it made her realise that there weren't any stars either. No prayers to the starlight wolf would be heard here.

The tunnel finally changed, growing wider and taller, but as it did, Zalia felt something slimy on the wall. She stopped as her hand landed in the disgusting goop and looked down. She could barely see it with the lack of light but could definitely feel it. She looked back up and carefully examined every sight before her. As she inspected the walls, she saw a flicker of movement and looked closer. Further into the tunnel she could see a flat, stone-coloured creature hugging the wall. It had slightly jagged patterns across its back so it looked almost exactly the same as the wall on which it hung.

? - Iron rank

She got some relief learning it was of her rank, but that quickly faded as she started noticing more and more of them ahead. She slowly and very carefully backed up, shuffling quietly backwards until she reached the T-section once more.

"That could be a problem," she whispered to Boreal, who had turned back around and moved ahead after sensing Zalia's distress.

Boreal sent a questioning thought and Zalia tried to send one back. Most of the time when she tried to use their bond to communicate she just used words, but she now tried to send an image of what she had seen. The fur on Boreal's back pricked up a little and Zalia could see her claws extend.

Too many, she thought to Boreal, who looked like she might be getting ready to fight.

And while that was true, it was also promising. Those grey creatures could very well mean a source of food. She would just have to learn how to hunt them in the most efficient way. She eyed Boreal; the feline was small and fast enough to act as bait for a few of the creatures. She didn't like the idea of using Boreal that way but put the idea to the back of her mind in case it became necessary. Luring a few of them into a space where she could fight properly might prove useful. She would first have to learn if the creatures were predator or prey, or if they obeyed any of the traditional rules of wildlife that she had learnt at all.

I guess you can even find wildlife in hell, Zalia thought.

Despite the place being called that, so far it seemed more like just another world. It had a different atmosphere and wildlife. The corrupt aura permeating everything may well just have been another natural occurrence of the place. At first sight, it was definitely hellish to the standards of someone from a world like her own, but to the creatures living here it might just be normal.

What caused those men to go mad, then? Zalia wondered.

It was after rituals that the soldiers of Endaria's army had either gone mad or become corrupted, so if it wasn't the sight of the land that did it, what did?

She remembered the words the man had spoken over and over in his madness, back in the building within the rebels' camp. How could she forget them?

"Fire and death and fire, the lands below where they stir in their torment. Terrible, oh so terrible are the lands below. They speak in whispers and murmurs, murmurs and whispers, always in pain, so much pain," the man had whispered.

He had repeated the same words endlessly and she now thought she might know of what he spoke. Did he mean the shadows floating through the sky, croaking and crying until they formed a sound akin to a chorus of torment?

Well, the sight had not driven her mad but maybe her healing protected her mind as well. If it wasn't that then there was something else out there that could drive someone insane, break them so thoroughly they sat scratching at the walls muttering. Something that Zalia really did not want to meet.

She sighed.

Immediate problems first, Zalia, she scolded herself.

It wasn't something she could solve or do anything about right now.

CHAPTER THREE

Grey

Zalia

Zalia sat against the wall in her little cave, watching as Boreal dashed around the space. She was much larger than when Zalia had first found her. Back then, she had been only just below her knee in height, but it wouldn't be long now until Boreal outgrew Zalia in weight, though hopefully never in height. Boreal would be a truly terrifying sight then. Going by the size of Boreal's mother, that wouldn't happen, though. She would probably reach about mid-chest in height one day and not much more.

She looked back down at the purple vial she had found in the pouch taken from Juniper. It wasn't labelled, and none of her various abilities let her identify what it was. Glemp would probably have been able to find out without having to drink the whole thing.

She had brought the pouch down here and buried it in this new cave, thinking it much more safe than the last. She would need to decorate the place with something more comfortable to sit on than the stone and ice floor, though. She thought it would probably be a good idea to find a few safe places around where she could retreat if she ever needed to. One place was all good and well, but if she was too far from it, or it was discovered or destroyed, she'd be in trouble once more.

"Want to try and hunt those odd grey creatures?" Zalia asked.

Boreal cocked her head and gave Zalia an icy, predatory look.

"I'll take that as a yes. Any ideas on how to do that?"

Boreal, despite sometimes seeming otherwise, was actually quite intelligent.

I wonder, can I see her profile?

Thinking about it, she was awarded with a message popping up.

Profile - Boreal Taori
Health - Excellent
Mana - Full
Stamina - Full
Creature Type - Mountain Frostfang
Linked Attributes - Dexterity, Wisdom,
Resilience, Intellect (Beast Bond)
Active Skills
Cryokinetic Pounce - Iron
Blending Shadows - Iron
Cute Convincement - Iron
Passive Skills
Frost Adaption - Iron
Feline Eyes - Iron
Survivalist (Beast Bond) - Iron

What? "Cute Convincement?" Zalia asked.

Boreal looked towards her with wide, sparkling eyes and gave a little mew.

"Oh my god," Zalia groaned, rolling her eyes.

Whatever power created Zalia's messages apparently considered Boreal her child, as it had given Boreal her own last name, Taori. Boreal also apparently had an ability that was literally just being extra cute to convince people. It was a defence mechanism employed by the young of many different species to help them survive until an older age. After all, who wants to kill a cute kitten?

"Right. It looks like you actually got an extra linked attribute because of our bond as well, hey?" Zalia asked.

Boreal looked happy at that.

"Zalia strong," Boreal said.

Zalia stared at Boreal. "Two words!" she exclaimed, excited.

Boreal hadn't ever managed to send two words in a row before. She was getting better at the language, it seemed. The icy blue translucent shards on Boreal's back started to glow, and she jumped into Zalia's arms, coating her in a layer of frost.

"Oh, thanks for that," Zalia said, pretending to be upset.

The impact actually had a bit of force behind it for such a small creature.

It definitely had something to do with the ability she often used to freeze things she jumped at. Having a thought, Zalia decided to try and see if she could get a description of Boreal's abilities like she did her own.

> **Active 1 - Cryokinetic Pounce - spell - body enhancement.**
> **Tin - When charged, pouncing on something will**
> **cause it to be coated with a layer of ice and snow.**
> **Iron - When charged, your pounce will have greatly**
> **increased strength and weight behind it.**

"Makes sense," Zalia said, having a look at the rest of Boreal's abilities.

> **Active 2 - Blending Shadows - spell -**
> **channelled - body enhancement.**
> **Tin - You are able to blend into shadows,**
> **using their darkness to hide yourself.**
> **Iron - When blended in a shadow you can**
> **move directly into a nearby shadow.**
> **Active 3 - Cute Convincement - spell - targeted.**
> **Tin - You can use your cuteness to make**
> **others less aggressive towards you.**
> **Iron - You're able to slightly affect the actions**
> **others take in regards to you.**
> **Passive 1 - Frost Adaption - passive - body enhancement.**
> **Tin - You have incredible resilience towards snowy and icy**
> **terrain and environments. This includes ignoring the majority**
> **of cold and cold-based magic damage and walking easily on**
> **ice and snow. You leave behind a faint trail of icy footprints.**
> **Iron - You have a passive healing effect based**
> **on how cold the temperature is.**
> **Passive 2 - Feline Eyes - passive - body enhancement.**
> **Tin - The sharpness of your vision is dramatically increased.**
> **Iron - When activated, you may see heat in**
> **addition to your normal vision.**

"You little—" Zalia started saying after reading the Cute Convincement description.

It seemed like Boreal may have been manipulating her just a little bit since the very start. She looked down at the furry creature purring in her arms. *Didn't really need a spell to do that, did you?* Zalia thought.

Reading through the rest, Zalia understood why Boreal seemed much better down in these caves than she did up above ground. With the significantly colder temperature, she was able to gain a little passive healing. They also explained why even Zalia was almost never able to see Boreal when she activated her camouflage.

"You're pretty strong for someone with only one class," Zalia told Boreal.

"Mreow," Boreal said.

The sound meant something along the lines of "I know, and you need three to keep up." Or so Zalia thought.

"I'm pretty new to this world, you know, you've got an advantage on me there," Zalia protested, huffing indignantly.

Boreal just looked at her.

"And you're basically a child," Zalia interpreted.

She swore Boreal almost smiled before she jumped off and started running around the cave again with a pitter-patter sound. Sighing, Zalia went back to thinking about how they would hunt those stone creatures.

We just want to draw one or two out. I could use some Flame-root to burn them out, but I really don't want many to come out, or to burn them to a crisp. Damn, I just really don't know enough about them. Are they reactive? Will they chase? What do they eat? If they are predators, they seem more like ambush creatures with that camouflage, but they could well be a type of stone scourer, travelling along eating anything growing on it. It seems strange they don't come out of that tunnel . . . Zalia thought, before something occurred to her.

"Oh!" Zalia realised.

Boreal looked over.

"They might not like the light made by the mushrooms!"

It might have been completely wrong but was definitely something she could test. She jumped to her feet and left the cave, Boreal obligingly following. She went to the very first cavern that had the mushrooms and the exit to the lands beyond. Moving to the exit, Zalia peeked out towards the forest outside. She made a dash out to the first warped tree and ripped off a small branch, sprinting back to the caves. The dash might not have been necessary, but she wanted to stay out there for the minimum time possible.

Back in the cave once more, she looked around for the one mushroom she had stabbed earlier. Unfortunately, it had stopped glowing since then, so she chose another one and impaled it on her new branch. Pulling the mushroom off the wall, she went back to the tunnel and began crawling through. She went to the T-section and headed towards the stone creatures but stopped. Thinking better of it, she put down the branch and moved back a bit.

"Hey, Boreal, wanna take this branch down there and throw it towards the creatures?" she asked.

She felt bad asking Boreal to do it, but the feline could move significantly faster than she could. Boreal took up the branch and started moving through the tunnel, much faster and easier than Zalia. Boreal started sending flashes of images to Zalia so she could see Boreal's own vision like a slideshow.

Blink, darkness surrounded a purple glow.

Blink, the tunnel started widening out and the grey creatures came into vision.

Blink, the stick and mushroom flew through the air and there was a blur of movement.

Blink, darkness. Darkness, but still she could see as Boreal sent through the vision of heat. The grey creatures had swarmed the mushroom incredibly fast, smothering it, and she saw no more as Boreal ran.

Moments later, Boreal hurtled around the corner and came to a stop next to Zalia.

"Well, that didn't work," Zalia muttered.

She watched down the tunnel for a little bit with her sword in hand but the creatures didn't come.

"Hmm," Zalia hummed, thinking.

She stared down the tunnel for a few more moments.

"Ah, fuck it."

She used Preparation to turn some of her Flame-root into a fine dust and started making her way down the corridor. Getting to the point where the slime began, she could see that the creatures had returned to the walls, waiting. She threw the dust past the first few creatures and used the heat manipulation from Heat Resistance to set it ablaze. The creatures reacted in exactly the same manner, rushing the fire and trying to smother it. Zalia quickly moved forwards, able to stand hunched in the space. Summoning her sword, she impaled one of the closer creatures, dragging it over to the entrance with her blade. Boreal grabbed it and started dragging it down the tunnel, and Zalia quickly followed after.

Zalia and Boreal arrived in their cave, with Boreal's jaws still clamped onto the creature. Zalia came over and quickly dispatched the creature with Kill Shot as it struggled, ending the hunt. Boreal sat up, a strange grey ichor dripping from her mouth.

"Taste alright?" Zalia asked.

Boreal looked . . . unimpressed.

Zalia shrugged and used Preparation to start skinning and deboning the creature. Its anatomy was extremely strange and unlike anything Zalia had ever seen. It didn't have a heart that she could see or any other organs for that matter. As she used Preparation on it, a strange, almost clear goop separated from the body and piled itself to the side. Zalia inspected it and found it to be some revolting, smelly . . . discharge.

"This thing is disgusting," Zalia said.

Boreal seemed to agree, but they didn't have anything else to eat, so weird stone goop creature it was.

She started a small fire and cooked the few pieces of meat she could get from it, seasoning them with a little bit of Bitterbalm. She knew she would miss the couple other bits of seasoning she used to bring around with her and wished she had her bag and armour.

After she was done cooking, she held up a piece of the meat. It had remained grey despite being cooked to what Zalia could best guess was perfection.

"You want to try it first?" Zalia asked Boreal, looking at it dubiously.

Boreal came up and sniffed at it before politely sitting, waiting for her to go first.

"So polite," Zalia said sarcastically.

She ate, chewing the stringy meat. It wasn't terrible, the same way that she remembered waking up in the morning to go work a nine-to-five wasn't terrible. Despite the Bitterbalm, it was almost tasteless, the monotony of the extensive chewing required making her almost grow bored after a single mouthful. She swallowed and then waited. She had quite good Poison Resistance, in addition to her healing, so she wasn't too afraid of whatever poisoning she could get from an Iron rank creature. She observed how her Healing Presence was acting, and it didn't seem to be counteracting any poison. It was just protecting her outer body from the constant, corrupting aura of this place.

"Well, it seems alright. Your turn," Zalia said, holding up a piece for Boreal.

CHAPTER FOUR

Woodwork

Zalia

Boreal was finished chewing the piece of odd grey meat, enjoying it as little as Zalia was. Luckily, they wouldn't have to eat the stuff more than once every two or three days. When her Survivalist skill was much higher the number of days between meals would grow and grow until she didn't have to eat at all.

As they ate, Zalia's mind turned to some of the bigger issues she would have to figure out. The main one being that she was stuck in a very inhospitable place. That in itself wasn't actually a terrible thing; she was used to living in the harsh, snowy north of her own homeworld, but this cave might just be a tad too uncomfortable for her. Living in a hard place was fine, living in a hard place that was also the afterlife of another world was not.

That meant she would need to find a way out of here, or more accurately, find a way to power or fuel the ritual she had taken from Juniper. From what she had seen and the descriptions she had read, it not only required quite a blood sacrifice to enact the ritual but was designed to be used from Endaria, not Cormaine. She would probably have to alter it a little to account for that, but she had absolutely no idea how to. All of the ritual knowledge she had was from the innate information she got from her Herbal Magic skill, and that only gave her insight into rituals when using herbs and other flora.

She could theoretically find some kind of plant that gave an element of transportation or dimension, something like that. The issue was that something of the kind would most likely need to be very high-ranked to transport her across worlds in the first place. Juniper might have been able to find a way to fix the problem, but there was no way Zalia would have saved the woman. She'd made her decision and she didn't regret it.

She had seen vague silhouettes that might have been buildings atop the floating island, but she didn't know if she wanted to meet whatever creatures lived down here, if there even were any. Another of the issues was the ghostly figures floating around in the sky. So far they hadn't seemed to have taken notice of Zalia, but she didn't know what rank they were, if they were hostile, killable, spies, or, well, anything about them, really. She knew she would have to travel eventually if she wanted to find something, anything that could help her get out of here.

"Want to try and see if we can find anything up there?" Zalia asked Boreal.

Boreal looked up from where she had started chewing another piece of grey flesh and tilted her head quizzically. Zalia pointed to the entrance receiving a feeling of nonchalance, like Boreal didn't mind either way. They were fed and safe after all, no need to risk it. On the other hand, they might find something interesting to hunt.

Zalia sighed, looking down. She remembered the many other beams that she'd seen shooting into the sky when she had reversed Juniper's ritual. She hoped that her interference had caused some disruption to the kingdom-wide ritual that had occurred. She stood up, pacing around the edges of the room, still subconsciously keeping her distance from the half-frozen pool in the space. She was frustrated at her inability to do much about her situation immediately.

Knowing that physical activity, like going for a run, usually helped her think and cool off, Zalia decided to start heading up to the surface. Her sword wasn't quite a replacement for an axe but with its magic, her passives, and her enhanced attributes, she could probably take on a tree. She wasn't a furniture maker by any means, but she had some practice making the basics and decided to make herself a nice log chair. Her sword could be somewhat compared to a machete in its design as well. It was less broad in its width, yes, but it would do just fine.

She sent a thought to Boreal, letting her know it was fine if she wanted to wait in the cave, and she would be back soon. Boreal sent back a lazy affirmative, and Zalia smiled as she made her way up. She wanted to gather some of the wiry, vine-like plants she had seen around the place as well. A couple of traps to guard the entrance to her cave wouldn't be such a bad idea.

Zalia peeked out of the cave entrance to the 'surface' once more, looking up into the sky at the various shadows floating around. She realised that they actually held a similarity to the shade she had nicknamed Hidey.

Could this be where he came from? Zalia wondered.

He had once said that he wasn't sentient before Zayes had found him, only becoming so when the man had done something to form a familiar bond with him. Could these shades be the same creature? Could it be that Zayes had once been here and discovered Hidey's true name? Her other thought was much more sinister. That Hidey had come from here and formed a bond with Zayes on purpose, under the control of someone else who knew his true name.

Pushing the thoughts away, she slipped out of the cave and made her way towards the closest tree that looked thin enough to be cut but still thick enough to be useful. The wood itself was warped and twisted as all the trees were, but she might be able to whittle it down to something usable. She drew back her arm, summoning her blade, and swung into the tree. Her blade hit with a loud *thwock*, digging several inches into the wood. Zalia stopped and looked up, none of the shades reacting, to her great relief.

Alright, that's a good start, she thought.

She pulled the blade out and swung again, the impact rewarding her with another *thwock*. Checking the sky once more, the shades still did not react. She smiled and got to work, chopping quicker as her confidence grew.

Zalia eventually cut down enough of the tree for it to slowly tilt to the side and fall over. She quickly ran away and hid behind another tree out of the trajectory of the quickly collapsing trunk. It hit the spongy ground with a quite dull but still loud *thud*. The moment it did, the shades above finally reacted. The sound or movement was apparently enough to finally get the creatures' attention, and Zalia ran even further away, utilising her Stealth skill and ability to stay hidden. A magical darkness formed in the air as the screeches and cries of the shades grew louder. The darkness billowed towards the fallen tree like a pitch-black cloud, and she watched as it hit the floor and flowed outwards, creating a pocket of shadow she could barely see through. The ability reminded her greatly of what Hidey had done when they had been captured.

The shades eventually floated away back to their eternal screaming and the dark cloud dissipated. Zalia trudged up to the tree and inspected it. The shades hadn't done any damage, thankfully, so Zalia grabbed it and tried to pull it towards her cave. Failing completely, she realised she would have to cut it up into at least a few pieces and got to work.

* * *

Some time later, she had finished cutting it into large logs that she rolled one by one to her cave. Unlike the tree falling, the shades weren't attracted to the relative quiet of her chopping. It wasn't a large thing, maybe twelve to fifteen metres tall, but it still had a surprising weight to it. It also had no leaves, which only added to the impact it made when it fell. Something Zalia learnt in her many years living in the wilds was that trees actually fell slower when they had leaves, which acted like a million tiny little parachutes.

She finished rolling the last of her chosen logs into the first cave and looked towards the smaller entrance to her more private cave. She hadn't really considered how hard it would be to roll these things through there but a few would be small enough to fit. Others, she would have to chop up a little.

Before making her way down she also collected a few good, sturdy branches and a few lengths of the wiry vine. Eventually, she managed to get her collection of various wooden bits and pieces into the icy cave where Boreal was making a tiny ice sculpture. When she had looked at Boreal's profile it hadn't told her about any of the passives that the feline had, but she must have had her Cold Resistance in Iron, the ability allowing her to manipulate ice and snow to a minor degree.

Zalia stood proudly over her pile of wood, inspecting each piece once more, before walking over to see what Boreal was creating. It was a minia-ture icy recreation of Zalia, Zen, Ember, and Indis fighting the icy winged creature atop the mountain home of the Born of Heat and Stone. Boreal had also included the landscape, recreating the battle rather accurately to how Zalia remembered it.

"You're pretty good at that," Zalia commented.

Boreal looked up at Zalia, then back to her sculpture. Zalia noticed the larger dead Frostfang, Boreal's mother, as well as kitten Boreal hiding in her shadow in the sculpture.

I guess you have a pretty vivid memory of the battle too, hey? Zalia thought.

Zalia rolled the largest log to a good spot and laid it down flat. The surface wasn't super comfortable but she cut it as smooth as she could and put the hide of the stone creature atop it. Her temporary chair done, she pulled another log over and slammed her sword into the side of it so the weapon stuck upwards, providing a good, stable, and sharp edge she could whittle the wood against. The first thing she did was chop up one of the branches to make eight small wooden spikes. She used the tip of her blade to slowly carve a hole into the ends of each one. Tying a length of vine between two spikes and repeating the process, she ended up with four sets of vine with spikes on each end. She then took a bunch of splintered wood pieces and jammed them through the vine at different places along its length. It wasn't perfect but she was hoping her Trapper passive would make up for it.

She went to the entrance of the cave system and tried out her first trip-wire trap. As she had hoped, the second she slammed the spike into stone, instead of cracking or breaking, the wood buried into it. She slammed the spike on the other end of the vine into the opposite wall, and the vine tightened between the two, pulling taut. The splintered wood along its length multiplied, becoming smoother and sharper before the whole contraption faded into shadow, changing colour and becoming incredibly hard to see. Zalia could still make it out if she looked closely but thanks to her Trapper ability, it was pretty well hidden. She planted one more at the entrance to the first tunnel, another at the T-section in the tunnel, and the final one in the tunnel at the very entrance to their icy cave.

Satisfied with having at least a couple defences set up, Zalia turned her attention back to her other project. She had already made her log chair, a simple yet effective piece of furniture, but she also wanted to make some kind of stone tools. A hatchet and knife she could use to properly shape wood, maybe. She wasn't really a woodworker or toolmaker but now was as good a time to learn as any. Setting her blade up as a whittling surface once more, she got to work.

A few hours passed as she worked, slowly whittling and smoothing a piece of wood until she got it into the shape she wanted. It was just a small handle with a slit down half its length that she could shove a piece of stone into. Using some thinned vine, she could strap it to the wood and, hopefully, have finally progressed to the Stone Age. All she had to do now was find a piece of stone suitable for the task. Looking over at Boreal, who was playing around in a tiny snowfall she was apparently making herself, Zalia had an idea. Maybe she didn't need to use stone at all and something like ice would be suitable for the task. Usually, it would be a terrible idea, but she had her Cold Resistance at Iron rank, meaning she could manipulate the material.

Zalia held out her handle and started manipulating some of the nearby ice to flow up and form into a solid icy blade. She focused on compressing the ice as much as possible to keep any air bubbles or flaws from the material and eventually had what she wanted. Her sword was as sharp as she could ask for, but for a few parts of woodworking it just wasn't quite practical. Something smaller like this ice blade could be really useful for her, though she would definitely need to maintain concentration to keep it in good shape so it didn't end up as a useless, shattered clump of ice shards.

She worked for the next few hours again, using her ice blade and sword to create another handle. This one was longer and shaped like a hatchet's handle. Once it was done, she used her heat manipulation to dry the wood even further, not heating it too much or too little but allowing the wood to stiffen. She made the hatchet head out of ice and tested it on a piece of wood, finding it to work quite well. It was disappointingly not as good as her blade at cutting the wood, so unfortunately, the effort might have been a bit of a waste. She felt better for having been able to actually do something, though, so no harm was done.

Having finished her newly set task after a good few hours, she sat down on her log chair and thought about what she would need to do to escape once more.

CHAPTER FIVE

Exploring Hell

Boreal

Boreal watched as the warm one, Zalia, continued to shape the wood into whatever she envisioned. She was as impressed as ever with the skill Zalia used to manipulate things with her hands. Those appendages were far better and more diverse in their use than Boreal's own paws. Though her claws were much sharper, Zalia's hands were able to make and use tools that were arguably superior. Boreal looked down at her ice sculpture, willing the icy ground to shape ever closer to the memory that stuck stubbornly in her mind. Maybe if she pushed it into the ice, it would leave her thoughts forever?

Ever since the message announcing the bond she had formed with Zalia, Boreal found she didn't need to eat as much anymore. This was an excellent ability that greatly increased her survivability, yet she felt almost offended that she needed to spend what little appetite she had to eat the grey. The warm one did try her best but they would need to find something different to eat or Boreal might just lose her sanity.

Boreal knew Zalia was quite the observant one. She always kept watch on her surroundings no matter what she was up to, and even now kept her distance from the half-frozen pond in case it held danger. Despite this, though, Boreal didn't think Zalia had seen the small opening near the ceiling of their cave. It was only large enough that Boreal could barely squeeze through and she wanted to explore it.

Leaving behind her ice sculpture, Boreal padded over to Zalia.

"Mreow!" Boreal said, thinking about the tiny tunnel entrance and pushing the thoughts towards Zalia.

Zalia looked at Boreal, frowning. "What?" she asked.

Boreal moved under where the tunnel was and looked up at it, trying to show Zalia where it was.

"Are you sure? I won't be able to help you if you get stuck or something bad happens," Zalia said.

Boreal meowed her affirmation and Zalia sighed.

"Alright, just be careful."

Boreal ran to the wall and willed some of the ice coating the floor to follow her. The ice crawled up the wall, and she used it as purchase to begin climbing. Her sharp claws slid smoothly into the ice as if it were liquid, only getting stuck when she willed them to. She made it to the ceiling, and half upside down, pushed through the gap into the tunnel. She crawled along in the tunnel before it widened a little, allowing her to stand. The space was still small but more cozy than stuffy. She moved further into the tunnel and it eventually widened out into a room very similar to the one she had just come from. Drops of water fell from the ceiling into a tiny little pool in the centre of the circular room. It was quite comfy and a nice, chill temperature.

Boreal actually liked it a lot and decided it would definitely make for a good space to make her own room. She started forming her little patch of ice into a comfortable bed in the corner, slowly decorating the room with her sculptures.

Zalia

Zalia watched Boreal crawl up into the crack with a shake of her head. She had noticed it, of course, but hadn't really considered it anything other than just that, a crack. Boreal obviously thought otherwise, seeing the unsearched area as her own little adventure. Watching Boreal manipulate the ice into a climbing surface with such skill made Zalia a little envious and a lot proud. She didn't have that kind of control over it, but she could probably get there with practice. For Boreal, it seemed to come naturally as she explored her powers and their limitations.

Zalia sat back down and got to work.

Over the next week, Zalia started writing a list of objectives into the wall as she thought about everything that needed to be done and sorted to get her out of here. The list wasn't terribly long, as there were a few key things that needed doing before anything else could be decided.

In between the short brainstorming sessions, she worked on all kinds of different projects. Boreal had started using ice to grind and push at the stone forming the little crack she had explored, and Zalia eventually started to help out when Boreal finally told her what was up there. She started using her own heat and cold manipulation simultaneously to rapidly heat and then cool sections of rock until cracks and faults appeared, making it easy to smash them apart. Eventually, they reached a point in the process where Zalia could actually get up into their little attic as well; the space was a snug little bedroom they could hide in. Rather than having to haul herself up every time, Zalia stopped the expansion efforts to build a little rope ladder that led up into the room.

Along with the expansion, Zalia also made a little cot out of branches and vines. She padded the surface with more grey creatures' hides so it became something of a bed. They managed to fit it into the upper room as well, and though it took up most of the space, Boreal didn't mind so much, crafting her ice sculptures around it. Boreal hadn't stopped doing that, recreating various memories and sculptures, each one better than the last. Zalia hadn't been expecting to have her own little cat artist, but there she was and here they were.

They had perfected their method of hunting the grey creatures but each time took a little bit of Flame-root. She'd run out eventually, though she wasn't too worried about that just yet. She also transplanted a few of the glowing mushrooms around their cave, creating dim and even lighting that lit up the space purple. She planted a few of the Water Lilies in the bigger pond, hoping they would be able to survive off the purple light. They might be plants, but they were Bronze and Iron ranked, so it might be possible that they'd grow. Either way, she didn't take all of the ones she had stored out of Stasis, so she wasn't too worried if it didn't turn out.

She didn't explore any further out of her cave during the week and neither did she try to explore down into the watery depths of the pool in the main cavern. Despite that, she still managed to gain a few levels in skills passively and actively from practice.

> **Congratulations! Survivalist and associated skills**
> **have gained three levels, reaching Iron 16.**
> **Congratulations! Preparation has gained**
> **three levels, reaching Iron 10.**
> **Congratulations! Herbal Magic has reached Iron 11.**
> **Congratulations! Healing Presence has gained**
> **three levels, reaching Iron 16.**

> **Congratulations! Aura Observation has reached Tin 20.**
> **Congratulations! Aura Observation has**
> **gained two levels, reaching Iron 2.**
> **Aura Observation - passive**
> **Tin - You are able to identify what rank a creature is by**
> **sight, unless it has a method of hiding that information.**
> **Iron - You are able to identify a creature's**
> **general progress to the next rank.**

At the end of the week, Zalia finally made the move to mentally map out the area surrounding her cave. She wanted to find a couple of possible safe places around that would allow her to expand and travel further and further in each direction. It was definitely the long way of doing things but it would be much safer, and in an unknown world, safety was key.

Engraved into the wall of her cave was her list. Number one on that list was escaping this world, of course, but there were also a few more currently doable items. A major one was to investigate the flying island, another was finding a way to defend against, harm, or kill the shades. She had a few ideas around that already but would need to test them. The last, and one she was about to work on, was investigating the immediate area for safe spaces, possible dangers, and possible advantages.

And so Zalia found herself leaving her cave with Boreal in tow, moving outwards towards where she had first arrived in the world. She wanted to see if Juniper really had died when Zalia left her there, and wanted to check if there was anything she had missed in her rush to find someplace safe to compose herself. Arriving back in the open world once more, the corruption started pressing down on Zalia and Boreal again. She used her cold manipulation to purposefully cool Boreal, now knowing it would work to heal her. She kept her healing equally focused between the two of them as well, hoping to keep them both in good shape.

They travelled for a bit through the warped woods and found themselves right where Zalia had left Juniper for dead. Unsurprisingly, but still to her annoyance, there was no body to be found.

"Damn it," Zalia muttered.

She knew it had been a mistake to leave her alive—another idiotic decision on her behalf. As she was berating herself, she heard a quiet shuffling sound and saw movement out of the corner of her eye. Using her heat vision alongside her normal stealth techniques, Zalia immediately looked towards the sound and found who she was looking for. Shambling along looking gaunt and lifeless was Juniper. Her eyes held a vacant look, arms held limply at her sides, still marked with the cuts made from the ritual that brought them both here. She shuffled through the leafless and thorny undergrowth, aimlessly tripping and shoving her way around. Zalia sent a thought to Boreal and she stealthily moved off to the side, preparing an ambush. She had made the mistake of leaving Juniper alive and would fix that now.

Zalia quickly and quietly performed a few rituals, namely Dodge-vine to push away attacks directed at her, and then a Dodge-vine, Manifest, and Snow-leaf ritual she had recently discovered. One of her most complex rituals so far, it created an icy armour all across her form that she could manipulate with Cold Resistance to protect her from a range of attacks. She summoned her bow and stood, drawing the string as a starlight arrow conjured, already nocked. She released the arrow, aiming for Juniper's thigh to cripple her. At the same time, she applied Hunter's Mark and performed a Dodge-vine and Bitterbalm ritual around the woman that would draw attacks towards her. A swirl of different coloured dusts formed a glowing ritual around Juniper just as the arrow struck, lodging halfway into her thigh as she let out an otherworldly howl. She was definitely not herself anymore.

A radiant glow could be seen coming from the wound that Zalia left with her arrow but she didn't stop to admire it. Though Juniper might be severely weakened, this was still a Bronze rank enemy she was facing off with. Zalia released another two arrows; one was dodged entirely, but the other managed to scrape across the woman's side. Juniper approached with an eerie jerking motion that was much faster than it should have been— but was waylaid before she could reach Zalia. Boreal launched out from the woods, emitting a bright blue glow from the shards along her body, and landed against the same leg that Zalia had impaled. She landed with force and an explosion of ice spread across Juniper's leg, rooting her to the ground. Both Zalia and Boreal began expanding and thickening the ice as Zalia quickly performed the Dodge-vine and Dodge-vine, Snow-leaf, and Manifest rituals on Boreal. Swirls of glowing runes spread around Boreal as similarly icy armour, tailored perfectly to her form, appeared on her.

Now distracted from Zalia, Juniper turned to Boreal and began to try and attack. Due to the Dodge-vine ritual, Boreal's own speed, and Juniper's frozen leg, she fell just shy of hitting the feline, and Boreal sped back into the shadows, vanishing from sight once more. In the space of the distraction, Zalia managed to get off two more shots, one hitting Juniper's other leg in the calf and the other shot landing in the stomach. Juniper now glowed from four different wounds as her body was burnt up from the painful starlight Zalia's attacks applied.

Despite this, Juniper finally broke free from her icy cage and reached Zalia. Her bow morphed into its sword form and Zalia went on the defensive, waiting for the starlight and Hunter's Mark combination to damage Juniper. She was still actively spreading the ice across Juniper's body to try and slow her as well.

Despite it all, Juniper was still quick, and Zalia found herself giving ground. A particularly nasty hit shattered the shoulder section of Zalia's icy armour and left a deep gash. Luckily it was her left, and she still fought on with her right arm. Boreal jumped out at various intervals, spreading more and more ice across Juniper's body and leaving large gashes in other places. Still small for her species, Boreal was playing the hit-and-run tactic perfectly, letting Zalia keep Juniper's attention.

The fight went on for a few minutes before Juniper finally faltered. The buildup of ice and glowing starlit wounds became too much, and she fell to one knee. Without indecision, and all mercy gone from her mind, Zalia instantly beheaded the woman with one final stroke enhanced with Kill Shot.

Boreal came out from the woods and paced around the body, not letting down her guard until Juniper's body stopped twitching. Zalia dropped her sword, letting it dissipate into starry mist. Her healing was slowly taking care of the shoulder wound, which was taking longer due to having to also actively fight the corruption.

> **Congratulations! Kill Shot has gained two levels, reaching Iron 10.**
> **Congratulations! Hunter's Mark has reached Iron 9.**
> **Congratulations! Hunter class has reached Iron 9.**
> **Congratulations! Herbal Magic has gained**
> **two levels, reaching Iron 13.**
> **Congratulations! Healing Presence has reached Iron 17.**

Zalia quickly jumped back as a dark form slowly lifted from the body, floating up and away into the sky above to join the other shades in their eternal torment. She watched it go with mixed feelings of sadness and exhaustion. It needed to be done for the lives Juniper had ended, the misery she had brought. It was a mercy to the woman and justice to those she had wronged. As she gazed into the sky, she noticed what strangely looked like a crow sitting on a high-up branch of one of the warped trees. Noticing her attention, it gave a single hoarse, croaking *caw* before flapping up and away into the forest.

The starlight within Juniper's body slowly caused it to disintegrate while Zalia and Boreal watched. Eventually there was nothing left but a pile of ash, slowly being blown away by the gentle, sulphurous breeze. Zalia looked up to the warped and twisted hellish landscape around her and grimly set off to continue her exploration.

CHAPTER SIX

Crow

Zalia

Zalia moved quietly through the trees until she found herself where she was aiming to get. She had seen it from far off, a clearing after the forest that looked like the world just ended. Zalia now stood, looking out over a clifftop at the surrounding lands and realised that she was standing atop a giant island tethered to the ceiling with the many giant stone pillars.

Well, damn, Zalia thought.

This was going to make things a little harder.

She took a few steps back from the edge to think about what to do. It could be that the island was actually safer because of its relative isolation; maybe there really was nothing living here because it was so high up. Staring out over the land far below, she finally caught a proper look at the floating island far above her. It was like her own, tethered to the ceiling with the large stone pillars, though it hadn't seemed that way from where she had seen it before. Now that she was out of the trees, she could see that there were a few more similar islands far off into the distance as well, though too far away to be of any concern to her right now. She could see that the closest island did have buildings like she had expected, some kind of odd constructions that may have been natural, but that she thought to have been made by something or someone.

Zalia turned away from the edge and moved further into her island to continue exploring. Surely there was something here that she could use. She could float down to the real surface using the Zephyr herb but wouldn't have any way back up. She didn't want to do that; keeping access to the safe cave she had found was important. She added "finding a way down and back up" to her mental list, planning to add it to the wall list later.

She thought back to the fight with Juniper and wondered again what a crow was doing here and how it had survived the corrupting aura. She hadn't ever seen one in Endaria and had not seen one for a very long time in her own world either. To find one here, of all places, was strange. Deciding it was not only improbable but impossible for it to be a normal crow, she thought it must be some kind of magical creature. Maybe it was something from this world that had disguised itself.

She travelled all the way through the centre of the island to the other side, a feat that took her a good hour to accomplish even at her speed. She had just wanted to see how big the island was and the whereabouts of her cave. Now knowing it was somewhat central, she knew she could find it from anywhere on the island by looking up at the pillars that rose up into the sky, as she was able to identify the correct one to use as a landmark. Looking up into the sky, she thought about the person she had seen flying overhead in Endelbyrn and once again wished for a similar ability.

Mobility was close to Bronze ranked already, and she wanted to get it there soon to see if it would provide her with such skills. She doubted it would but it was worth a try. Then again she didn't really have any way of quickly increasing its rank other than her already existing daily routine.

As she travelled in a circular pattern around the island, Zalia found an old, decrepit-looking altar. It was hard to read what exactly was written on it or to discern what the carved pictures were, but she got a feeling of mystery from it. The altar was a small chunk of wood, the top split and curved up and outwards in either direction before coming back in to the sides of the altar. Each of the sections had what looked like feathers carved into them. Wings, maybe? It was hard to tell.

On the front, there were words written in a language she couldn't read, the majority of the letters so faded and torn by time that even if she did speak the language, she wouldn't be able to read it anyways. She brushed her hand over the top of the altar, feeling an instinct similar to when she had first met the starlight wolves in Endaria. She couldn't help but remember the crow she had seen and decided to pick up the small altar, taking it home with her.

She returned to the cave, pushing the small altar ahead of her through the smaller tunnel section before lifting it once more and bringing it into her new home. She thought about widening the passage to make entering the icy cave easier but decided it could be a good defensive measure if she were ever attacked by bigger creatures. She placed the altar gently on the ground and looked at it. She felt like she should try and fix it; some instinct was telling her it was important. She didn't really have the tools to do that, though, and so left it there to go explore some more.

She spent the next few days exploring but found nothing else of interest. Just as she had thought, there was no other life on this floating island, either due to the shades floating above or its isolation from the land below. She was about to give up on finding a way down without using Zephyr when, on the third day, she made a discovery.

She was sitting in front of the altar she had found on the island, trying to figure out the strange instinct she experienced when looking at it. She had tried all kinds of things, from cleaning the spongy dirt off it to performing a couple of harmless herbal rituals, but nothing changed. She read through all of her abilities and the description of Healing Presence caught in her mind. It allowed her to actually heal flora as well as creatures, so she tried pushing the healing into the altar. It wasn't flora, but it had originally come from a tree, so why not?

To her surprise, it worked and the small altar slowly healed. The writing and carvings on the front were repaired and roots grew from its base into the stone beneath. Finally, as her healing stopped and the altar stood reformed, she could see the depictions carved into it. The two pieces coming from the top and curving around it were indeed styled as wings. The front had depictions of creatures, objects, and mysteries clouded in shadow. Amongst it all, the recurring image of the crow appeared in different sizes and shapes, but it remained unmistakable. The wings were those of a crow; the creature showed up in the background of different images carved across the altar.

Zalia didn't understand who or what the altar was dedicated to, but she did know that the crow she had seen amongst the high-up branches of the trees couldn't have been a coincidence. A memory of something the starlight wolf had said to Zalia came to mind:

"My power has waned much since the days past, not many still revere the old gods. Those of us who remain wish to see nature preserved and you have shown yourself to be someone who would do such. Do I see wrongly, Zalia?"

Looking at the altar, she had a feeling that it was dedicated to just one such god of old. But why was it here? How could the altar of a god of Endaria come to be in Cormaine?

Cormaine was what many on Endaria considered to be the afterlife for those who were bad in life, a hell as such. She had never heard anyone speak of any comparison to something like heaven and she had a chilling thought. What if Cormaine was just where everyone went when they died? What if somehow this god had died and come here?

Maybe Cormaine wasn't even an afterlife at all, just some world closely linked by magic to the world Endaria sat upon.

Realising she might be able to help the growth of the Water Lilies in the pool, she started pushing healing into them as well. She turned away from the altar and gathered a bit of stone creature hide and some various herbs from her Stasis, then placed them at the foot of the altar. Boreal even made a little ice sculpture of a crow there as well. Once they were done she felt a hint of acceptance mixed with surprise. She couldn't explain where those feelings came from or how she knew what they were; it was just . . . instinctual.

She watched the altar but nothing happened. Shrugging, she walked off and left the caves once more, getting back to work. She had explored most of the island, but there was just a little bit left that needed to be seen. She didn't expect to find anything there but it was worth looking anyways.

As expected, there was nothing of interest there and she left, heading back home. When she arrived, she found Boreal playing with the crow from the treetops. They were running around, chasing each other, and being a general nuisance.

"Um," Zalia said.

The crow immediately stopped and Boreal crashed into it, bowling it over. Boreal got back up and looked like she was about to pounce again but saw Zalia and stopped as well.

"*Friend!*" Boreal said to Zalia.

With the word came images of the ice sculpture crow cracking and growing until it became the little creature Zalia saw before her now. The crow looked at her through one eye, its head tilted to the side. It let out a low croak.

"Hello to you too," Zalia greeted.

It hopped towards her, inspecting her inquisitively. Deciding she wasn't a threat, it went back to roughhousing with Boreal, the two of them rolling across the floor in a mock battle. Zalia shook her head and went back to her list on the wall. She thought about what she could do to get to one of the other islands, maybe even down to the ground. A rope or vine ladder was a bad idea since it was so far—making something would be hard and take forever. Let alone making something sturdy enough.

As she thought about it, something made her turn around to look at Boreal and the crow. The sound of their battle had stopped dead and Zalia saw why. Boreal was rearing up to jump on the crow as it lay on its back, yet they were both frozen, unmoving. With a twitch, the crow looked at her and spoke.

"To go across, look up, not down," it said in a hoarse, croaking voice.

In a flash, Boreal unfroze and they continued the fight. The crow didn't turn towards her or even seem to notice it had spoken. Boreal didn't seem to have noticed either.

What the hell was that? Zalia thought.

To go across, look up, not down. What did that mean?

Realisation struck.

"You're a genius! We can climb up the towers to the ceiling of the cavern and traverse along it to the other islands!" Zalia exclaimed, looking at the crow.

Both it and Boreal looked at her, confused, but Zalia was too happy to care. It might take a long time but it was definitely a more reliable way of getting to the other islands. She just needed to figure out an easy way of traversing the ceiling of the place. It was quite rocky with plenty of dangling spikes and other rock formations sticking out of it. She could probably find a path across using some Zephyr, her double jump, and the strength and dexterity she now had. Boreal could probably just use ice to walk upside down across the ceiling thanks to her strange wall climbing method.

Zalia looked at the altar in the room and realised whatever god it was dedicated to might not be as dead as she thought. It had just spoken through her and Boreal's new friend.

CHAPTER SEVEN

The Climb

Zalia

Zalia stood at the front of her cave, staring upwards at the stone pillar extending from the island to the ceiling far above. Climbing up the pillar with her increased strength and the help of the weight-lightening Zephyr herb would be easy. Somehow making her way across the ceiling of the giant cavern to one of the other islands would not. She'd had a few ideas on how to traverse the space between islands. One was to use the feather-fall effect and gusts of wind supplied by Zephyr rituals to float across once she had reached the top of the pillar. This held an obvious downside, namely, that she would run out of Zephyr quite quickly and couldn't even guarantee she would make it.

Another idea she had was to make her way across the ceiling by climbing across it in a similar way to Boreal, though she would have to practise the technique significantly to manage it. Finally, she realised that she was going about it in a stupid way. Because of her Iron rank Herbal Magic skill, she could replicate any Tin rank herb effect in a ritual without needing to use any of the herb whatsoever. Two of her Tin rank herbs were Manifest and Dodge-vine. She had used the combination of the two in many ways before, mixing them with Snow-leaf to make icy armour, creating shields similar to Protection of the Wilds, things like that.

There was no reason, however, that it couldn't be used to create a bridge across gaps. She considered just going straight across from her island to the other but thought better of it when she looked out at the hundreds if not thousands of shades floating around. Closer to the ceiling there weren't nearly so many of them. It seemed like the shades didn't like being near to anything solid, for whatever reason. The ceiling would also provide the fallback of being something firm to anchor her Dodge-vine and Manifest bridge on. The material created by the ritual was only temporary, and she would have to attach it to something every so often. The large stalactites growing from the ceiling would provide perfect points to do just that.

She had no idea if the other island would have dangerous creatures on it, but she had to have a look anyways. She was actually feeling a lot calmer here than she had back in Endaria. There were no politics, no deceit, betrayal, or, most importantly, people. Despite that, it was still not a very nice place to live. The red-tinged atmosphere, sulphurous air, and corrupting aura definitely lent motivation to her goal of leaving. There were much nicer places that shared this place's lack of people and politics.

She started climbing, Boreal following close behind. For the first part she just jumped nimbly from rock to rock, climbing with ease until the base of the pillar steepened into a rough rock face. At this point she started making a staircase circling around the pillar into the sky. They climbed the seemingly endless stairs as swirls of glowing herbs brought a viney path into existence in front of them, the plant withering and falling to dust not far behind.

Long ago, when she had first joined the Morning's Shade, Zalia had told Hildebrandt, Matthias, and Hidey that her Herbal Magic would become one of her most important and diverse abilities. Her words spoken then became true now. She climbed tirelessly until she reached the very ceiling of the endless cavern. She looked down across the land below from her new vantage point. She could see many other floating islands now, each of them suspended from the ceiling in the same manner. The ground below each island stretched endlessly into the distance, so far distant from her now that she couldn't make out any detail.

As she kept up the ritual beneath her, refreshing it constantly to stop it from decaying, she started using her rock shattering method to dig out a small place to sit. It took a long time to heat and cool the rock enough times to break off a section large enough for her to sit in, but it would be good for later. Having a space she could rest in up here might save her life down the line. Boreal helped by pushing ice into any cracks that appeared and expanding it, splitting the cracks further open until they were done. They stepped off the vine construct beneath them and sat down, Zalia letting out a sigh.

Congratulations! Healing Presence has reached Iron 18.

Another level closer, Zalia thought.

It wasn't long now until she discovered what Bronze rank would have in store for a few of her abilities. She summoned a piece of Water Lily stem and crunched it down, savouring the feeling of refreshment that it provided. She passed a little bit to Boreal, who seemed to enjoy the crunchy stem much more than she did grey creature meat.

Zalia looked out across the jagged ceiling, trying to plot as much of a path as she could from where she was. If she wanted to go back and forth from the other island, it might be worth trying to mark out a good path for herself. She just needed some way to go about doing that. She summoned her blade as an idea came to mind. The sword was extremely sharp and ignored armour quite well. While it couldn't cut straight through stone, it could definitely leave it marked without damaging the blade at all.

She resummoned the vine bridge and stepped onto it, stretching as she yawned.

"Let's do this," Zalia said to Boreal, cracking her neck.

She started moving as quickly as her vine ritual would allow her, zigzagging between stalactites and marking each with a slash of her sword. They made slow but steady progress across the gaping abyss below; she was not entirely worried, as she had the backup plan of Zephyr and her Mobility double jump, if necessary. Twice she had to backtrack as a passage led to a dead end, and there were no other outcroppings or stalactites close enough to bridge to. Each time, she slashed through her marks again, making a cross so she didn't go by that path the next time she made the trip.

Eventually, she reached one of the large pillars holding up the island that was her intended destination. She took another rest here, making a similar indent into the stone that they could sit in.

I really need to find a better way to dig through stone, Zalia thought, remembering Larel's ability to punch through basically anything.

The woman had made a new "doorway" in a wall by simply punching it, revealing the secret room that had held the first ritual site they had discovered. For the first time in a while, Zalia thought about that day atop the tower where everything had gone so wrong. She was still worried for Zen, but only now considered that Larel could have been in trouble as well. She had been fighting Hidey when Zalia was taken to Cormaine, after all. She didn't owe the woman any loyalty, but she had broken them out of jail.

No point worrying, Zalia reminded herself for the hundredth time.

Whatever happened had already happened, and there was nothing she could do or have done about it.

Zalia looked down at the island beneath her. Unlike the previous one, it wasn't forested whatsoever and held what looked to be the ruins of some ancient city. The buildings stretched across the entire width of the island, most of it crumbling but some in relatively good shape. Looking down, she could see movement here and there that didn't seem like the shades floating around. It looked like something or someone did live here.

She was really hoping they weren't hostile but didn't go so far as to believe they wouldn't be. Maybe they were a peace-loving people that lived in literal hell?

Getting down was going to be much harder; she would have to forgo using her bright, glowing bridge-making on the way down to avoid being seen. It was risky enough to have bridged here in the first place and it was possible she had been seen already. She lightened herself with Zephyr and started making the long, treacherous climb down. Boreal, for her part, just used her neat ice trick to provide herself with as many good holds as she could ask for, cruising down next to Zalia.

It took almost an hour and a half for Zalia to finally reach close to the ground. Blending into the stone with her Stealth ability, she waited for a good moment where she couldn't see any movement before lightly dropping down the last part and crouching amongst the rock. She didn't hear any calls of alarm or anger, so she probably hadn't been seen. Boreal was even stealthier than Zalia, able to move between shadows as if she was teleporting. She simply jumped into a shadow, then popped out of one further down before jumping through another to appear next to Zalia.

They peered over the rocks they hid behind, looking at the decaying city around them. The structures were definitely all built in a similar style, giving a sense of continuity through the city that made Zalia think it used to be host to a large population. She finally saw one of the inhabitants and her heart skipped a beat. The creature was of a race she recognised, one of the Bathar. It shambled through the city, its vacant eyes and stumbling gait reminding Zalia of how she had found Juniper. The best word she could find to describe how it looked was "undead."

She mentally cursed. It looked like the creatures here would be hostile after all, though they were at least thoughtless enough that evading them could be done with relative ease. She considered her next move thoroughly. She could go back with the information she now had, travel to another island with less danger. If she was going to find something helpful though, an old city might be a place where she could locate such a thing.

So, Zalia and Boreal started making their way through the city from shadow to shadow, ducking behind and into buildings. She searched a few of the more broken down ones first but found nothing of value. The buildings had mostly fallen to pieces, along with anything once held within them. To her relief it looked like most of the Bathar were Tin rank, with a couple Iron. She didn't see any that were Bronze but didn't find the possibility unlikely.

As Zalia exited the most recent ruin she had been exploring, she was a little careless. Boreal noticed the Tin rank Bathar before she did and immediately pounced on the creature. Despite her carelessness, she still reacted with speed, summoning her blade and slamming it into the creature's head as it dropped to its knees from Boreal's attack. Her daily practice lent her incredible speed, but before the Bathar died, it managed to let out a loud screech and a shiver made its way down Zalia's back.

There was a moment of silence, a pause as Zalia and Boreal waited. Her blade was still stuck through the creature's head as they waited in silence. She thought for a moment that they had managed to get lucky, but her hopes were dashed as she heard a series of eerie, high-pitched, yet hoarse screeches across the city. They both reacted immediately, with Zalia ripping out her blade as she kicked the Bathar in the chest, and Boreal beginning to sprint away. Zalia quickly followed and they made their way at speed through the city ruins, dodging a few of the slower creatures they passed. It felt like they had kicked an ant nest as hundreds of the Bathar exploded out of buildings, some rising from rubble or debris like they had lain there long enough to be buried.

Before long, they were surrounded and Zalia was forced to use Nature's Wrath. Hardy grasses exploded out of the paved streets and grasped onto the Bathar around her, forming soft appendages that caused the undead Bathar to scream when they made contact. A few of the lower rank ones immediately fell thrashing as they tried to fight off the odd grasping grass. An elemental ally ripped free from the stone beneath, immediately smashing its fists down on an unsuspecting Bathar. Nearby, some type of murky water feature exploded as a sludgy, amorphous water elemental overflowed its bounds and began submersing Bathar.

Using the two elementals as a distraction, Zalia ran into an alley and jumped, using her one air step to jump higher up to a wall. She then jumped off that wall and used another air jump to reach the roof of the opposite building. Boreal followed by swiftly climbing the side of the building with her ice. They began quickly fleeing across the rooftops, jumping from one to the next in a quick, aboveground escape. One Bathar saw them, but from the sky, their crow friend swooped down and slammed into its face, clawing at the Bathar until its foot slipped off the edge, causing it to fall. The crow flew back up into the sky and fled.

Further above them, sounds echoed of elementals fighting the undead Bathar. Zalia saw the shades above take notice and begin spiralling down in a cyclone of darkness. She didn't watch for long before beginning to run once more, searching for somewhere to hide.

CHAPTER EIGHT

City Guerilla Tactics

Zalia

Zalia exhaled slowly and quietly, watching from the small cubby she had hidden herself away in. She could see between two crumbling stones towards where the shades slowly floated back to their tortured existence in the sky. It had taken them a short time to make quick work of the two elementals she had summoned, and it seemed like they had left the undead Bathar in peace. She could tell that was the case by the flood of the creatures spreading out from the area with disjointed and agitated gaits.

I wonder how long they've been down here for? Zalia thought.

Ember and Indis once had an argument about the Bathar people, an argument about how the kingdom of Endaria had taken over the lands that were once theirs. Their race was now reduced to a tiny number, dwindling more and more by the year. She was a little curious as to how that came to pass because the city she saw, despite its current state, was quite advanced. Maybe they were a peaceful people once and it was the aggressive nature of the human race that let them conquer them.

There were many other explanations for how it could have come to pass, however. Something like an Emerald or even Diamond ranked person could have accomplished it by themselves, depending on how powerful the Bathar were. If the ranks of the undead here correlated in any way to what they would have been long ago, the average Bathar were anywhere from Tin to Bronze. That meant they probably had members of their society in the higher ranks as well, making that theory a bit less probable.

Her last idea was that it was something other than a hostile takeover, though that idea seemed ridiculous to her.

Now that she had woken the undead in the city, the once somewhat clear streets were filled with Bathar who had slept for who knew how long. She was going to have a much harder time finding her way back home now. She would only have to reach the nearest pillar thankfully, though it was somewhat far away. She had a look at the one message in her vision.

> **Congratulations! Nature's Wrath has gained
> two levels, reaching Iron 8.**

It wasn't much but it looked like the ability had managed to kill a good number of the Tin ranked Bathar. She had an idea at that thought, looking down to the street below. The Tin ranked Bathar only held danger in the fact they could call higher-ranked allies nearby if they saw her. They wouldn't be able to harm her unless they somehow managed to pin her down and overwhelm her. She summoned her bow and checked down below for a Tin ranked Bathar, and with a swift movement, drew, released an arrow, then ducked back down. She could see through the small gap in between the stone bricks as the Bathar dropped with a hole straight through their head. The flight of her arrows was so quick that the Bathar around her target didn't see where the shot had come from; it was milling around the dead one in confusion.

She knew for a fact by the fight with the undead Juniper that these undead were not intelligent in any manner. They walked around, heads jerking from side to side to try and catch sight of an attacker, with a vague awareness of a threat. After being unable to find any apparent attacker, they went back to aimlessly wandering the streets once more. She smiled, looking over at Boreal,

"Looks like we're in for the long haul," she whispered.

She began slowly picking off the Tin rank Bathar, now using Hunter's Mark on each just to help level the skill. She also began using Kill Shot—the ability added very little to the first shot but the time between shots allowed her to use it for each target. After twenty or so minutes, she finally finished clearing the majority of the Tin rank Bathar from the street below her cubby. It might have once been a covered rooftop balcony with a stone fence but one corner had collapsed, making it more akin to a piece of covered rubble.

Zalia used a Dodge-vine ritual, altered to protect her from sight rather than attacks, and began making her way quietly down from the building.

She swung from the fence into the open window below, landing in a roll to dampen the sound of impact. She paused for a moment in the small room, listening to the sounds from the street below. Thankfully there were no screams of alarm or anger so she kept moving. She moved through the rooms until she found a window looking to the building across the street. The opposite building had a similar window but the actual structure went much further down towards the nearest support pillar.

Measuring the distance, Zalia nodded to herself and looked over at Boreal.

"Think you can make it?" Zalia asked in a whisper.

"*Make it,*" Boreal replied, looking into her eyes.

Zalia reprimanded herself, she should have been using the mental connection to talk.

She backed up as far as she could for a run up. Then took off quickly, sprinting towards the window, using its ledge as a step up to throw herself across the street. She stepped on the air once in the middle of the jump, feeling it solidify beneath her boot before landing in another roll on the other side. She remained in a crouch, moving to peer through the window. Looking out, it didn't seem like the Bathar were aggravated; none of them were so much as glancing upwards. She looked across the street.

"*Your turn,*" Zalia said to Boreal.

She saw a small feline form shoot out of the window and immediately saw that Boreal wouldn't make it. She quickly leaned out of the window, catching Boreal as she fell barely short and pulled her in, stumbling backwards but keeping her balance.

"*Close,*" Zalia told Boreal, her heart beating quickly.

"*Didn't make it,*" Boreal replied.

"*No shit,*" Zalia said.

No sound of alarm came from below so Zalia didn't worry too much about it, continuing through the building. There were several patches that looked like Bathar had recently burst out after being woken by the racket she had made. She also found sections of rubble with suspiciously humanoid shaped holes in them, debris strewn across the floor or doors that had been broken down. A fate she would have shared had it not been for her passive healing. Even then, the ability at Tin rank wouldn't have been enough to protect her; it was barely able to now.

Boreal had her own passive healing, a combination of her control over temperature and her passive that healed her based on how cold it was. In fact, Boreal had actually gotten all of Zalia's passives associated with her own Survivalist passive as well. That meant she would have the Heat

Resistance, Cold Resistance, and Stealth and Trapper passives, though she probably had Cold Resistance and Stealth already. Trapper wouldn't be super useful unless she learnt to construct traps, but the passives were still a powerful addition that she hadn't considered before.

They moved through the length of the building, the layout reminding Zalia of some kind of hotel or apartment complex. She eventually reached the end of the long hallway leading down the length of the building. Finding nothing but a stone wall, she checked the two closest rooms and found one to have a giant hole in the wall where the corner of the building had collapsed. She inched along the wall to see out into a crossroad, both streets filled with the shambling Bathar. The intersecting street looked to be a highroad in the city, the distance between buildings far enough she wouldn't be able to jump it. That meant that they would need to go down to street level if they wanted to go further.

Zalia thought for a moment. Clearing out the Tin ranked ones again would be a good first start, though it might be worth looking further down to see if there was any cover she could utilise. Deciding on the latter, she climbed up onto a big piece of rubble and used her air step to get high enough to reach the edge of the collapsed roof. She hauled herself up and crawled across to the streetside edge of the building as Boreal stepped out of her shadow, getting low as well. She looked down the length of the street either way and saw that to her left an entire building had collapsed, strewing rubble all over the place. It was as good an opportunity as she would get to cross without being seen, so she started making her way in that direction.

They had to jump across to two other buildings, these having sloped rather than flat roofs. It was easy for them, the distance short enough that Boreal could jump over without trouble as well. They reached the edge of the third building and looked across to the next, the one that was just a pile of rubble spilt across the street. Luckily, Zalia could hide behind the edge of the sloped building to look across the street. She would definitely need to thin them out before crossing, moving across with that many Bathar there would be treacherous.

She summoned her bow and got to work.

It went pretty much exactly the same as last time, only getting a little scary when one of the tiles under her feet slipped, clattering to the ground below. She managed to keep her footing with a timely use of Fight or Flight to slow time to her perception. A few of the Bathar came investigating but weren't able to spot her from in the small alley between buildings. Soon enough, her work was done and the immediate street was left with a significantly lesser number of undead.

She snuck over the other side of the building and dropped lightly to the ground. She moved up to a large chunk of building and waited until it looked like the Bathar were looking away. She made a dash for her target, a big chunk near the middle of the street that might have once been a corner of the building. It formed a hollow triangle that she would be able to dive underneath. With light feet and as much speed as she could muster, she managed to reach the cover and dove under to safety. Boreal followed soon after, though she could hide behind many more pieces of rubble her size so was much less likely to be seen.

Only one particularly perceptive undead came to investigate, possibly having seen or heard something. Luckily, it didn't think to look under the rubble, only walking around it before walking off again. She could see by the feet that stepped past that it was Bronze ranked, a challenge for her on its own, even without the other Bathar. Wishing she had found some type of teleportation herb, Zalia eventually crawled out from under the rubble and covered the rest of the distance with another dash.

Much of the next few hours were taken up by periods of travel followed by waiting around, taking out Tin rank Bathar one by one. She killed enough of them that despite being Tin rank, she managed to level Kill Shot once and Hunter's Mark twice. Her Survivalist ability also ranked up once, gaining experience from her constant brushes with danger.

She managed to make it to the pillar without attracting another swarm, though there were a few close calls. Thankfully her Stealth ability kept her very well hidden against an enemy that wasn't too bright. She climbed slowly up the pillar, about halfway, using nothing but raw strength to accomplish the feat on the rough stone. She used her digging method to create a little spot where she could be safe for a time, sitting in it as she mentally recovered from the stress of the past few hours.

Breathing a sigh, she looked out over the city and saw a large building further out that she hadn't been able to see earlier. It looked like a keep with high walls and towers, the architecture like nothing she had seen before. Whoever built it had obviously been very familiar with the materials, fashioning a structure sound enough to survive a very long time. Unlike most of the other buildings in the city, it looked to be relatively intact. If there was anywhere she was going to find anything useful, it was likely to be there.

CHAPTER NINE

Infiltration

Zalia

Now that she had learnt the undead very rarely looked to the sky, she would have been comfortable using a little bit of the Zephyr herb to float down to the city. Unfortunately, there were still the ever-present shades floating through the air, letting out their cries of torment. The sound had faded to background noise to her now, always heard but no longer paid attention to. It could actually be helpful, in a way, as it was loud enough to cover the sound of her footsteps, much as a thunderstorm would.

Zalia climbed back down the tower and began making her way towards the keep in the distance. The going was slow but she eventually made it to an old, decrepit forge near to the high walls of the keep. The closer she had gotten to the keep, the higher ranked the Bathar were and the better the buildings were constructed. It did mean the numbers thinned slightly, but it also meant the fewer she could reliably kill in a single shot. She hadn't yet attempted to kill any of the Iron rank ones. While it was possible, the chance of discovery wasn't worth the risk.

She inspected the high walls from the window of the floor level forge. The room was filled with various pieces of rusted metal that may have once been weapons or armour, but were now useless to anyone.

Congratulations! Healing Presence has reached Iron 19.

Her heart skipped a beat as the ding resounded, announcing that her ability had levelled up. She hadn't been expecting it and the loud sound, only audible to her, fortunately, had felt like an announcement to the entire neighbourhood. Calming her breathing, she checked the high walls again. There wasn't anything patrolling the top of the wall, as far as she could see, though there were plenty of the undead along the path at the wall's base.

She knew the best way to get in would be to make a distraction to draw them away from the wall. Unfortunately, the same method would also bring a lot of the further away Bathar closer to the keep walls, making any escape harder. Weighing the options, she decided to wait the last half hour or so until Nature's Wrath was available for use again. Going in was worth the risk if she had her entire arsenal of abilities at the ready. Besides, she hadn't seen any of the undead above Bronze rank yet—what were the chances she did now?

The answer to that question, she knew, was very high.

While she waited for her ability to come off cooldown, she started setting up the distraction she had in mind. She ripped off a small section of her shirt sleeve, knowing the minor enchantments on the cloth would be able to repair it eventually. Rolling her shoulder as a dull ache pulsed in it, she pocketed the length of cloth and started to gather a few pieces of the heavy metal. She would need to find a way to suspend them from a high place, where they'd be held by the length of cloth. She could set a fire to slowly burn the cloth until the entire contraption dropped, hopefully making some sound.

She started heating bits and pieces of metal until she was able to bend them into a large ball, using what might have been an old sword's handle as a hook she could tie the cloth to. The entire thing looked like a misshapen mass of rusted metal with some cloth sticking off it, but it would work. Hopefully.

She managed to find some kindling from a desiccated bush near the entrance and brought it with her as well. Sneaking up to the roof of a tall, abandoned building that reminded her of a church, she laid down the kindling under a rooftop decoration. The metal decoration was a spike in the ceiling that split upwards into a Y shape, the two top ends showing broken décor that might have once been something tree-like. With the cloth now tied to the metal base and the metal ball hanging off the edge, all she would need to do was light the kindling and run for it.

Remembering that Boreal now shared her Survivalist passive, and so also shared the Heat Resistance passive, Zalia sent a thought to her friend. She sent short images of Boreal lighting the fire and then running away; the feline was much smaller and able to move stealthily at a higher speed. She also asked that Boreal wait until Zalia had a better head start, then moved back away towards the forge.

As she arrived, she turned to see a small flame begin flickering atop the church roof. She could see a slight shimmer as Boreal dashed away, teleporting through shadows to remain hidden amongst the streets. This was possibly the most dangerous part, as Boreal moved with less care than they had been since arriving. Luckily, Boreal arrived shortly after a loud crash, as the metal ball dropped an odd three or four stories to the pavers below. The Bathar immediately began moving in the direction of the sound as Zalia and Boreal waited patiently.

Before long, they saw their opportunity as the moving undead all passed by. Using her bridging technique, Zalia started making a ramp up to the top of the wall and made a dash for it. They made it to the top and vaulted the battlements, getting down into a crouch as they waited for the chaos outside to subside. Zalia began scanning the inner courtyard as they waited, noticing a fair few undead but significantly fewer than outside the walls. Inside the walls was a now dead and wilted garden leading to the still standing keep. That was where Zalia wanted to get to.

She was hoping that something inside that building had managed to withstand the test of time and provide her with some edge, some advantage in this wasteland. If there was nothing there, then she may as well abandon this island, as it was simply grounds to gain easy levels for her abilities. Clearing out a whole host of the weaker outer undead may have given her enough experience to level some of her abilities to Bronze. It would also finally give the Bathar the rest they deserved. She couldn't help but notice when she killed them that they didn't release shades like Juniper had. She thought it might have something to do with how corrupt they were when alive but didn't have any way to test the theory.

She considered her next move as she looked around the length of the wall. There were actually two undead on the walls; they'd most likely stumbled up the stairs along the inside. They were far enough away that they wouldn't be an issue, so she ignored them for now. Making her way through the Bathar in the courtyard would be easy enough—it was the inside of the keep that she was worried about. She had no way of telling what was behind the walls, and a surprise such as hordes of undead or the Silver rank she was dreading would not be ideal. She was far enough into the danger now that she would need to be real careful with how she acted.

She could have slowly culled the numbers of the undead over weeks or even months to get to the keep in a safer manner but was willing to take the risk in case there was something in there that could help her for the short term.

Her indecisiveness came to an end when she noticed that a central part of the keep had a glass roof on it. That would provide her with insight into what the inside of the keep looked like, in terms of how many undead there were. All she had to do now was get on top somehow.

She went to the nearby set of stairs and slowly moved down them, entering the withered garden below. Using the emaciated plants as cover, she carefully made her way past all the undead in the garden. There were a few close calls, as the Bronze rank undead were slightly more perceptive than the Iron or Tin ones outside. Luckily, she hadn't yet seen any Silver undead and so kept moving.

She made it to the keep's wall and began scaling it slowly and carefully. It was harder than she would have thought, even with the abundant wall reliefs, but something about the design of the keep made it innately difficult. It could have been some kind of latent magic that went into the making of the structure, but she made it to the top anyways, with Boreal close behind. Safely above the undead, she walked over to the glass-topped room and was able to see down into a kind of feasting hall that was on the top floor.

It was heartening to see that some of the furniture had managed to survive its time in Cormaine; even some of the cloth was intact. There were a few banners along the wall that she didn't recognise except for one. It was the same Y-shaped logo the metal decoration on top of the church had been, though she could see the treetop shape that the two top prongs of the Y were intended to be.

She could also see that there were indeed undead inside. Thankfully, it looked like there were significantly fewer than even the courtyard. While she couldn't see their rank, she couldn't help but feel encouraged. Looking around, she noticed that one of the nearby spires had a balcony that she would be able to reach. It had a door that was very slightly ajar, a perfect entrance for her. She moved up to the door, using her bridging ritual this time, and inched towards it to peek inside.

Through the door was a bedroom, though much different from what humans traditionally used. The bed was sloped inwards so that it formed a kind of nest in the middle that almost reached the floor. Lying motionless in the bed was an undead Bathar, though it was small enough that Zalia thought it may have been a child. For some reason, the sight brought her a level of distaste the others had not. She wondered, not for the first time, what had happened to bring this place here. Was this how the Endarian kingdom had taken over? Some sort of ritual to disjoint the Bathar cities into Cormaine?

Putting the thoughts aside, she was close enough to see that despite its motionless form, the undead was not dead. It still displayed a rank—Iron, thankfully—where dead creatures did not. Well, properly dead creatures at least. Moving quietly, she slipped into the room. All of a sudden the howling and crying of the shades outside instantly stopped. She quickly jerked her head around to look outside, but they were not reacting whatsoever. It was like the building somehow muted the sound.

While she had grown accustomed to the noise, she didn't realise how unnerving it would be for the sound to stop so suddenly.

Fucking hate this place, Zalia thought.

It was, well, it was hell. She wanted to go back to the frigid north she called home, where it was silent and calm, free from both most life and undeath. Boreal caught on to what she wanted to do next without a word spoken or thought. They moved towards the Bathar in unison, Zalia summoning her blade as they attacked in sync. Boreal jumped at the creature's legs, pinning them to the bed with a layer of ice that began immediately spreading up its body. Zalia stabbed her sword straight down through its throat, cutting off any sound it could have made. She left the sword impaled there, pinning it to the bed as Boreal began tearing at the creature's torso.

Using the Iron rank of Cold Resistance and Heat Resistance in unison with Boreal's help, Zalia began pulling heat from the creature's lower body and surrounding air and bringing it to its head. Before long, a fire engulfed it and the undead only managed to let out a quiet croak, trying to pull her blade from its neck. The fight was over before it began and Zalia doused the fire with her heat manipulation, letting the sword dissipate back into its spatial storage.

CHAPTER TEN

Keep Time

Zalia

Zalia quickly went across the room to the other exit, dropping the bar across the door as she left. The fact that even the bar mechanism was intact gave her more hope for the state in which most of the keep's internal decorations lay. She looked a little closer around the room, trying to find something that would give her a hint to its purpose, but it just looked like a normal bedroom. There were some knickknacks she couldn't discern the use of, but overall, they seemed underwhelming.

She gently raised the bar and pulled the door open, the hinges making a slight creak in the silence. Past the door was a staircase, spiralling down into darkness, far beyond the dim, sourceless ambient light of the caverns of Cormaine. For some reason, the fact that even the accursed light of Cormaine did not reach into the depths of the keep was a little unnerving. Steeling herself, Zalia began the descent into the stairwell anyways. She was able to see in the darkness perfectly fine, so the lack of light wasn't any kind of impairment for her.

The stairwell came to an end and another door lay in front of her. She tried listening closely with her ear to the door, trying to discern if there were any sounds of shuffling on the other side. She couldn't hear anything but that didn't necessarily mean the room was empty. It could simply mean the occupants were asleep.

**Congratulations! Survivalist and associated
skills have reached Iron 18.**

The notification sound made Zalia jump—again. She wasn't used to her abilities randomly levelling all the time; the situation she was in constantly gave good experience to Healing Presence and Survivalist.

She pushed open the door gently, peeking around to see into the next room. Through the door was a corridor, off of which she could see several doorways and an open, squared stairwell leading further down. Thinking logically, she was probably in some kind of housing or bedchamber section of the keep, somewhere visiting nobles and their retinue could stay. The room up above had held someone when the city had been brought here, and that meant there might be others in these rooms as well. She assumed her reasoning about what the next rooms might hold was sound—it wasn't always.

Zalia and Boreal slipped out of the door into the corridor beyond, moving quietly down the hall until they reached the next stairwell. Looking down, she couldn't see any undead on the floor below, so she decided to check out the rooms in the hallway. Each door had a keyhole on it, something she could utilise if she managed to find a key. Maybe she could even break the locks with some ritual or ice manipulation. Thinking about it, she didn't know if the undead even remembered how to use doors at all, if there were any inside.

The first few rooms she carefully opened held nothing inside—they weren't small bedrooms like she had thought. They were significantly less well-appointed than the one upstairs but still nice. In one of the rooms closest to the stairs heading back up was an undead sitting at a small writing desk, head lying on the desk where an inkwell had spilt across a piece of parchment. It seemed like the Bathar had fallen asleep and never woken up again.

What the hell happened here? Zalia thought.

It was as if the entire city had fallen in an instant, no alarm or reaction quick enough to save the people asleep, walking the streets, or otherwise.

She eyed the undead warily; though the furry, desiccated corpse didn't so much as twitch, she still didn't like the look of it. The Bathar had probably been Bronze rank in life, a fact she could tell since her Aura Observation had detected the undead as the same. Fighting the Bathar here could be disastrous; she wouldn't be able to keep the Bronze ranked one silent as she had the Iron one back upstairs. Instead, she left the room and closed the door, using heat manipulation to superheat the handle. After a minute of working at it, she managed to start melting the metal inside until she could no longer turn the handle.

She wasn't too happy with the temporary solution, knowing that the undead could probably break through the door with ease. Leaving behind such a high-ranked creature was risky here where it wasn't outside. Out there she had many avenues of escape, in here she only knew of one, and she was leaving a Bronze rank along its path.

She continued on anyway, finding each of the other rooms empty. She then made her way down the next stairwell. There were two floors she could go to: one was a door that led further into the keep somewhere, most likely the keep proper. The other was the ground floor, from what she could tell. Looking around the corner, she could see the entrance to the keep as two armoured undead stood still, slumped against the wall to either side. She could also go the right rather than straight ahead; the corridor led deeper into the ground floor of the keep.

She decided on the right path on the ground floor. She was looking for a treasury or armoury of some sort, hoping to find some armour that might fit her. She didn't think she would find anything that fit well whatsoever, but armour was armour. The path led her down to a T-intersection, and the left path had a large, arched doorway set within the wall. Two more guards were slumped asleep against the wall there too, intended to watch over whatever lay further inside. She had a feeling that in there would be the armoury. She just had to find a way to get past the Bronze ranked guards.

Congratulations! Healing Presence has reached Iron 20.
Congratulations! Healing Presence has reached Bronze 1.
Healing Presence will not gain further levels
until all classes reach Bronze 1.

Zalia froze.

Passive 1 - Healing Presence - passive - aura
Tin - Your very presence grants life to all around you. You,
nearby allies, and any flora and fauna you so choose within
your aura are affected by a heal-over-time effect. The heal-
over-time effect heals for low health every second.
Iron - Healing Presence now heals the most grave injuries first
and you may focus it onto a single target, increasing that target's
healing while reducing the healing other targets receive.
Bronze - Healing Presence now attunes to the specific needs of
each individual target within your aura. It adjusts its healing
output based on the severity of injuries or ailments, offering
targeted healing to each person or creature accordingly. You

> **may still change this manually, if you wish. Additionally, once every twenty-four hours, when you or an ally die, you are instead cocooned within a protective barrier made by Protection of the Wilds and made invulnerable to most damage for six seconds.**

She breathed out silently as she read over the new effect. She now had another way to survive death; the Protection of the Wilds barrier was a counter-execute heal, meaning it healed based on missing health. She wasn't quite sure how that number worked, but being within an inch of death meant it would be at its most potent. Protection of the Wilds also let her enhance the shield with any herb replicable by Herbal Magic. Her abilities were becoming more and more synergistic, pulling effects from each other in a long chain that made all the abilities more powerful. When Protection of the Wilds eventually reached Bronze, the effect gained then could boost Healing Presence's new effect significantly depending on what it was.

Having the second chance ability also gave her a little bit of breathing room right at this moment as she stared down not one but two Bronze rank enemies, with more still behind her. Feeling more confident, she thought about how she could get past those two guards. A loud distraction was off the table—waking and drawing the attention of every undead in the keep was not an option she was willing to consider.

In the end, she decided to just try and walk past them. None of the other sleeping undead had reacted when she had walked past or moved near them, only hearing the alarm call of another Bathar or being stabbed in the neck had done so thus far. Using a Masking ritual that used Dodge-vine to protect her further from being discovered, Zalia crept towards the guards.

Her plan worked, and the two slumped and unconscious undead didn't react as she moved past them into what she had correctly guessed was the armoury. Inside were various racks of armour and weapons, but what interested her most were the bodies inside. Unlike the undead around her, one of these bodies was actually fully dead, with a greatsword impaled straight through its head. It was unmistakably a Bathar, though smaller than usual for its race. What interested Zalia was the armour it was wearing.

It had heavy leather armour, thick and sturdy. There were no metal plates on this set like her old one had, but it looked just as if not more tough. This set had a helm where her old one hadn't; the headpiece featured two ribbed horns branching out from each side of the head, curving down, then forwards.

There was other armour around the place but this set was small enough it might actually fit her. Creeping forwards, she got close enough that her Aura Identification was actually able to pick something up.

Duskwraith Armour (Heirloom) - Iron rank.

Tempted to let out a whistle, she held back on making any sounds and got to work taking the armour off the corpse. It was morbid work but would be worth it for another heirloom. Indis had her own set of heirloom armour—well, robes—and Zalia was more than happy to have her own. Duskwraith didn't really fit her style, whatever that meant, but if it gave her some kind of stealth ability, she wouldn't say no. Besides, if it was anything like her bow, then it had the opportunity to change and grow as she used it.

Eventually, she managed to carefully extract the armour from the body and placed it down in pieces on the floor. Remembering how she had bonded to her bow, Zalia began by examining the entire set, trying to remember the features and thinking about where it had come from. She vaguely remembered bonding with the bow after learning some of its history.

After a little bit, she began putting the armour on piece by piece and found it shrinking and molding to her shape. When she put on the final piece, the helmet, a message popped up.

Congratulations! You have equipped 'Duskwraith Armour' in a ritualistic manner. The item is now bonded to you.
Duskwraith Armour (Heirloom) - Bonded Iron rank.
Tin - Wearing the armour applies Shadows' Veil to you.
Iron - Shadows' Veil gains a new effect called Partial Intangibility.
Shadows' Veil - Shadows' Veil suppresses the wearer's aura and magical signature, making it challenging for magical beings or entities with heightened senses to detect their presence.
Partial Intangibility – Shadows' Veil grants the wearer partial intangibility, allowing them to phase through thin barriers or objects, such as walls, fences, or closed doors, as long as the barriers are not too thick or magically protected.

It did indeed give her better stealth abilities, but not how she was expecting. Hiding her aura like Hidey did would mean some people wouldn't be able to detect what rank she was. That could come in handy later, as well as provide a measure of stealth for a different type of vision. The Partial Intangibility ability she was much more excited for. It would let her pass through various obstacles, maybe even non-magical weapons would pass through her. She would have to thoroughly test that before letting herself get stabbed though, it hadn't seemed to have protected the last wearer who now lay dead with a greatsword through their skull. Inspecting the weapon, she could see that it was magical in some way though. She would have liked to take it but having no storage or use for the weapon, decided to leave it behind.

Standing up, she began to search the rest of the room.

CHAPTER ELEVEN

Death Comes

Zalia

Once she was done searching the room, Zalia was left feeling a tiny bit disappointed. There wasn't anything else in the room except for a lot of very basic equipment. While it was most certainly worth a lot, with no storage or manner of transporting it all, the hoard was basically useless to her. There were some shields and various weapons, but she didn't use a shield and had all the weapons she needed.

Her disappointment faded away as she tried pushing her hand into the wall for the hundredth time. The wall was too thick for her intangibility to allow her through; it was a feeling like pushing her hand into jelly. As she pushed her hand forwards it got harder and harder to move it through until it was stopped completely. She had discovered that with a thick enough wall she could basically hide in it entirely if she stood in it. She also discovered that the only thing stopping her from sinking into the floor was that she didn't want to. Willing herself to do so, she could sink up to the middle of her shin.

This is so weird, she thought.

She had tested moving her arm through a spear and it had passed straight through the weapon without trouble. Having a thought about what counted as magically protected, she picked up a sword and tried to wave her arm through it. It didn't work and upon putting it down, she found it worked when not held. Her sword proficiency passive increased the durability of the sword she was wielding, which was her guess at why she couldn't pass through it. A better description of magically protected would then be something with magic imbued into its structural integrity. She didn't know exactly how that worked but didn't question it too much; she wasn't some magical scientist after all. She just needed to know what worked and what didn't.

Deciding it was too much of a risk to ever allow an attack to pass through her defences, she gave up the idea of dodging attacks by phasing through them. If all someone needed was a simple proficiency to counter the ability, it would be useless against most enemies. That wasn't to say it wouldn't be useful in combat. Being able to pass through all kinds of barriers could be useful at just the right time if an enemy didn't expect it.

She didn't dally in the armoury for too much longer, leaving when she noticed Boreal getting restless. Boreal messing around out of boredom was the last thing she needed right now. They slipped past the front guards again, a task she only dared try in the first place due to the lack of Silver rank undead around so far. She could go either left or right from the armoury—the left path looking like it looped back around to the entrance. Deciding to take the right, she moved slowly, trying to drag her hand through the wall while she walked.

She found that her hand wouldn't sink into the stone, which made her realise it was probably one of the outer walls. It seemed like they had some kind of structural magic which explained the relatively good state the keep was in. It may even have something to do with the sound blocking magic that the keep had. Well, whatever had caused the sound from the shades above to cease.

She followed the corridor, finding a large kitchen with not a small number of unconscious undead. Past the kitchen was a courtyard with a covered walkway leading around its edge, nothing but a small fence separating the two. Within the internal courtyard, two possibly once well-dressed people sat unconscious on a bench. The now undead Bathar were still seated in rest however many years after they had first sat down on that bench. She wondered if either of them had thought their lives would end on that bench. Probably not.

She walked around the edge of the courtyard, keeping a wary eye on the undead and the shades, she could see above the ceilingless space. Despite there being no roof, she still couldn't hear the cries of torment let out by the shades. The soundproofing was an incredible display of magic, if anything else.

Arriving around the other side of the courtyard from the entrance, she stopped mid-step as she noticed the guards at the doors up ahead. These were not unconscious like the others, and stood at attention two-a-side by the door. She couldn't tell their ranks from here but something about them sent a chill down her spine. She immediately turned around and went back the other way, making her way to the original set of stairs she had come down. Finding those awake guards signalled the end of where she could explore on the first floor.

Due to the location of those awake undead, she was pretty sure they had been guarding the entrance to the banquet hall she had seen from above when looking down through the glass. Knowing that there were also some undead in that room meant it was definitely a no go. That way lay death.

So she started exploring the second floor. She poked her head around a corner in the long corridor to see another door guarded by an awake undead. She quickly backed up and moved away. It seemed like this was the end of her exploration of the keep for now; she didn't want to risk being caught by any of the undead in such a confined space where others all around her could wake up too. She went back up the long stairwell into the tower, closing and barring the door behind her.

As she entered the room, she heard the flap of wings as their crow friend came to rest on the floor. She smiled at the crow but the expression was wiped from her face as it spoke two words,

"Death comes."

What? she thought.

She quickly went to the balcony door and peeked out to see outside. As her head left the keep, her ears were bombarded with sound as the cries and moans of the shades had turned to agitated screams. She winced at the sound but refrained from retreating back to the comfort of silence, watching to see what the crow had meant. Finally, she saw it.

Flying towards the keep on giant bat wings, cloaked in a dull, dark red fire was a horrifying creature fit for the hellish environment around it. It had four legs that ended not with hands or feet but razor sharp spikes. Each of the limbs were shaped not unlike a spider's, yet muscled, rather than covered in a carapace. At the centre of the four legs was a thin and warped torso, thousands of eyes covering the twisted mess. Rather than a head atop the torso, it had a gaping maw.

It flew across the island with its four legs hanging, the sharp tips pointed to the ground. Carefully, Zalia retreated back into the keep and closed the door with a soft *click*.

Oh hell no, Zalia thought.

The image of the hellspawn was burnt into her mind, the sight so horrific as to almost cause pain. She sat down on the floor, pulling Boreal to her arms as the corrupting aura all around grew steadily stronger with its approach. Her newly Bronze Healing Presence was significantly greater in its healing ability than previously, yet it had to work overtime, keeping both her and Boreal safe from the corruption. Still, it grew stronger as the creature flew over the keep. The crow didn't seem bothered by the corrupting aura, simply preening itself in total relaxation.

The very air seemed to vibrate as the creature finally flew overhead, thankfully not landing as the aura began weakening once more. It slowly faded back to its previous strength and Zalia felt like she could finally breathe again. She let out a gentle sob as a shiver wracked her body. She had seen some terrifying things in her lifetime, many in the past few months in this world, yet that monster was the first to truly bring her terror. Most of the things she had faced were scary in their own way and usually held some kind of danger to her, but that thing . . . that thing seemed antithetical to life itself. The maw of that monster was where the soul went to die.

Zalia didn't know how long she sat there, holding Boreal as the feline shivered against her chest. It was probably the first time Boreal had ever even shivered, considering her natural protection against the cold. This was a different type of cold though, a chill in the bones that couldn't be shaken. A chill that no warmth would cure.

She had started growing somewhat comfortable in Cormaine, confident in her ability to stay out of the reach of shade or undead. The illusion of her own ability shattered—she was only alive now because she hadn't been outside when that monster had flown over. She had a feeling that it was quite a high rank, and only the newly acquired aura masking and magical protection of the keep had kept her hidden.

The crow sat there watching her as she held onto Boreal for any comfort she could get.

"W-what was that thing?" Zalia asked.

"Death comes," the crow repeated.

Zalia shivered again.

I wonder if my presence drew it towards these islands or if it was just flying over anyways, Zalia thought.

Her mind was shifting into thinking with logic, trying to explain what she had seen to itself. She knew her brain was doing that but didn't try to stop it.

"It must be some kind of warden for Cormaine," Zalia murmured.

"Mreow," Boreal said, conveying a sense of terror as she did.

Zalia stood, still holding Boreal. She wanted to get back to her cave as soon as possible. She needed the safety and protection it provided her. The only problem was that she would have to traverse the large gap between islands with that *thing* flying around out there. She didn't know if it would come back or be able to sense her from this close. No, no, she wouldn't go back just yet. For now, the proven safety of the keep, despite the lesser threat of undead, would do just fine.

She took out a little bit of Frozen Heart and started chewing it, giving some to Boreal as well. The herb had some healing properties she hadn't yet learnt how to use to their full potential, but the feeling it provided when eaten was comforting nonetheless. Her entire situation here had just changed. She no longer felt comfortable taking her time to find a way out. She would live in fear of that thing while she remained here.

If that was the type of creature those rituals in Endaria were trying to summon, she was now really hoping they had failed. Thinking about that and Juniper, she wondered if she would be able to find Zayes down here. Juniper had said he was in Cormaine, but whether held hostage or dead, she did not know.

She also thought she might know what had happened to the Bathar. Some of the destroyed buildings around the city held a more sinister meaning now; the collapsed sections were possibly created by the spiked legs of that monster. Anyone without her type of healing would fall to that corruption in seconds, if not instantly. Others could have fought back but . . .

She put the thoughts out of her mind and tried to figure out her next move.

CHAPTER TWELVE

Flight and Frogs

Zalia

Zalia stood at the door to the tower, hyping herself up to make a move. She couldn't wait here forever. Eventually she would need to go outside and get something done. She didn't really have a plan on what to get done other than get back home and figure out her next steps. She took a deep breath, exhaling slowly as she built up confidence. She had felt no change in the aura of corruption since the creature had first flown over.

Zalia gently pushed the door open, the hinges giving a quiet creak as the view of the outside appeared once more. She kept her eyes cast away from where she had last seen that monster, checking around the rooftop for undead by habit. Finally, she moved her gaze to the sky where she had seen it and . . . it was clear. Her heart began slowing down from its panicked beat and she let out another deep breath. Who was to say such a creature would take notice of her anyways?

She stepped out of the door onto the balcony and the background cries of the shades reached her ears once more. They were back to their normal moans—tormented, yet not agitated like they had been not so long ago. Squaring her shoulders and steeling her mind, Zalia set off from the balcony using the Manifest ritual spiced with Dodge-vine, which she had decided to name Structure Creation. It was a simple name she could use to describe her bridging technique.

She made her way down to the rooftop, Boreal close behind, and looked across the city. The undead outside the walls were in chaos, many sprinting around at speeds she hadn't seen before. It was like they had gone into a panic, maybe at a surfaced memory of their last moments in life.

How the hell am I going to get through that? Zalia wondered.

Maybe the chaos would cover her movement and any sound she made, but that was doubtful. She would have liked to walk through the walls of the houses with her new armour but was not about to leave Boreal behind to find her own way. Maybe a sprint through the horde would be possible. She and Boreal were definitely faster than even the Bronze ranked undead at their full speed, so the idea wasn't necessarily a bad one. It would have been if she were trying to get to the keep, but trying to flee the island entirely? Not so much.

Besides, she had this new armour she needed to test out a little. Being an heirloom item, it would repair itself slowly over time if damaged, so she wasn't worried about breaking the new shiny armour she had found on a corpse. A thought occurred to her, and her Herbal Magic ability confirmed it. It did things like that, only giving her the intuitive knowledge about ritual possibilities, when she thought about them. Zephyr gave the element of air where Manifest gave the element of, well, physical manifestation. Using the two of those together was a natural combination to create wings.

She tried the ritual and it worked, summoning a pair of translucent, wispy wings over her shoulders. She could feel them like two new limbs, the experience extremely odd. Despite the fear in her mind at even the thought of the monster she had seen, and the horde of agitated undead beneath her, Zalia was excited. She had been wanting to figure out some sort of flight for a while and could have had it long ago if she had properly examined each herb combination. Now that she had discovered this, she would need to go try every combination she could later.

For now though, she looked over to Boreal and used the same ritual on her, adding a little bit of Snow-leaf for effect. Similar wings, only frosted with ice, appeared on Boreal's back. With the wings, Boreal reminded Zalia even more of a mythical creature from her homeworld. Boreal mreowed in surprise, hopping around with little flaps to test out the new limbs.

"Wanna try fly over that?" Zalia asked, pointing towards the milling horde.

Zalia and Boreal jumped from the keep roof, flying low over the wall and then dipping down towards the street. They were somewhat clumsy as they got used to the flight. Because of their Iron rank dexterity and intellect stats, they were soon swooping over the horde, out of reach. They stayed quite low to avoid being near the shades but still high enough to be above the undead. It was a sweet middle ground that allowed them to move through the city at speed.

Zalia refrained from whooping in joy, keeping their passing as quiet as she could. Despite the sense of freedom and happiness in the flight, the lingering horror and fear of what lay just beyond sight in this place remained in the back of her mind. Still, she allowed herself to feel some joy. Letting fear control her was a surefire way of remaining stuck here forever.

They soon reached the pillar and began flying up and around it in a spiralling ascent. She noticed that the crow had joined them as well, weaving around Boreal. The crow was much better than them at flying, which was to be expected with a lifetime of experience. More, maybe, due to the semi-godlike nature of the animal.

They made it to the ceiling and began the long glide across the distance, as the wispy translucent wings behind her held her aloft without difficulty. With the crow nearby, she couldn't help but notice that she had fashioned her wings in a style resembling the crow's. The difference being the translucency, and that the trailing edge of the wings blurred as if her eyes could not fully focus on them. They left a light misty trail that lasted barely half a second before dissipating.

They dove when they reached Zalia's own island, circling the pillar as they fell in a controlled manner. They landed before the cave entrance, and the wings dissipated entirely at Zalia's dismissal. She would have to be careful using that ability, as the amount of Zephyr it used was costly. She would have enough to use it maybe three more times on both her and Boreal before she was out.

Congratulations! You have learnt the passive skill 'Flight.'
Flight - passive
Tin - Your maneuverability is increased and your
air resistance is reduced while in flight. This scales
based on the rank and level of this passive.

Zalia smiled. The passive wasn't strong as usual but it could provide her with some nice things later on.

Congratulations! Herbal Magic has reached Iron 14.
Congratulations! Survivalist has reached Iron 19.

The two skills had increased over the course of her flight. She was getting real excited to see what Survivalist would give her at Bronze. Historically it had given her two passives and reduced her reliance on some general needs like food or sleep. She wondered if it would reduce her need to breathe or even slow her ageing.

She slipped into the cave, Boreal and the crow following her. If the crow was going to stick around she would need to name it. She just needed a good name to give it.

She crawled through the smaller section of tunnel, walking through the larger one before entering her home. She froze as she entered, seeing a very small frog-like creature sitting on the ice by the deep pool. It was small enough to fit in the palm of her hand, and had a soft, pastel-coloured body in shades of pale blue and lavender, reminiscent of icy landscapes. Its belly was a shimmering white, almost like the glistening snow. It had large, round eyes with a beautiful iridescent sheen, like tiny frozen sapphires. It noticed her enter and jumped quickly back into the pool with a soft plop.

Boreal immediately bounded over and stared down into the depths of the pool, touching a paw to the icy water.

"Get away from there, Boreal!" Zalia hissed.

Boreal reluctantly backed away, though she didn't seem concerned.

To be fair, the little frog had seemed more scared of her than she was of it. It was most likely not some kind of predator, though she didn't doubt it had some type of self-defence. She exhaled as she watched the pond, glad that the worst thing that had come out of it was a cute little frog. She was already collecting half a zoo of animal friends and she most definitely wanted to add that frog to her group if she could. She moved up to her and Boreal's small sleeping spot and lay down to rest in the crude bed she had made.

Her eyes closed as a troubled sleep overtook her, and Boreal nestled in next to her to rest.

CHAPTER THIRTEEN

Chances of Survival

Zalia

Zalia awoke what felt like minutes later, sitting up sharply with a gasp and throwing Boreal off the bed accidentally with the movement. Her heartbeat slowed as the nightmares of demonic monsters faded from her mind. She held one hand to her chest while her breathing calmed, and she smiled apologetically at Boreal, who was lying on the floor looking a little dazed.

"Sorry," she murmured.

She rolled her right shoulder, feeling an ache deep in the bone. Swinging her legs out of the bed, she picked up Boreal from where she lay and put her gently back into the spot of warmth she had left behind. She climbed down the little ladder leading up to their bedroom and dropped the last length to the floor. She heard a *plop* and turned to see a small disturbance in the water of the pool.

Hanging out again, were you? Zalia thought.

She would have to make a plan to befriend that frog at some point, but for now she had a little bit of experimentation she wanted to do. Her Herbal Magic ability allowed her to intuitively use any Iron and Tin rank herbs in rituals at this level. She hadn't been diligent in experimenting with each available combination, so she wanted to try and see what she could find now.

Her Tin and Iron rank herbs were Snow-leaf, Bitterbalm, Dodge-vine, Manifest, and Zephyr. She decided to go through the list with each. She knew that each ritual she had used so far tended to have a main component and a modifying component, for dual ingredient rituals at least. Using three or four ingredients was an entirely different matter, but she could experiment with that later.

With Snow-leaf as a base for the ritual, she knew how it interacted with Manifest to create ice, but hadn't really tested it out with much else. Focusing on the other Tin and Iron rank herbs, she felt that using Bitterbalm as a modifier would alter the element made by Snow-leaf to lava. When used as a modifier to rituals, Bitterbalm tended to reverse effects, something she had used to good effect many times. Using Dodge-vine as a modifier would put an effect on her that slowed attacks coming her way, and finally, mixing it with Zephyr would create a localised ambient temperature drop. She could innately tell what they would do if she actually focused on them and chided herself for not doing so earlier.

She herself had spoken many times about how versatile and useful Herbal Magic was, yet hadn't put in any time to study possible effects. So, she sat and consciously thought about each combination, trying to remember all the possibilities. This was something she should probably add to her daily routine, and what time was better to start than the present.

After she spent about half an hour thinking about her possible combinations and trying to push her ability to design new ones, she started her usual routine. Boreal finally got up and joined her as she began running around the cave in circles. Usually she would do the run outside but she didn't feel too confident going back out there just yet. She had a few skills she should be able to level up here with relative ease.

After her routine was done, she checked over her messages.

> **Congratulations! Herbal Magic has reached Iron 15.**
> **Congratulations! Mobility has reached Iron 18.**
> **Congratulations! Weapon Proficiency - Sword has reached Iron 9.**

Slow and steady progress, Zalia thought.

She was looking at her Survivalist ability. When that finally reached Iron twenty and tipped over to Bronze, not only would it gain a new ability but four passives would level at the same time. The possibilities for what she could gain from five different abilities reaching Bronze were too good to ignore. Thinking about what had helped level Survivalist in the past, Zalia looked over to the pool in the room.

Usually, it levelled faster from moments of danger, but surviving generally also worked. Her time here in Cormaine had levelled it quicker than anything she could think of back in Endaria. Preparing to do something stupid, Zalia took a deep breath and calmed her mind. Then, she stepped forwards and dropped straight down into the pool.

She sank quickly as bubbles rose around her. She could see the roots that were beginning to sink down into the water from the Water Lilies above. Looking down she could see nothing but darkness as she sank a little farther. Not knowing how deep the pool was, she was surprised when she very quickly hit the bottom with a muted *thump*. She was surprised she sank so easily while holding her breath, usually she should have floated.

Wondering where the frog could have gone, she felt around her until she found one of the walls wasn't a wall at all, but a passage. She started walking into it, feeling her way forwards until she saw a light ahead. Despite being underwater, she almost gasped as she saw an entire ecosystem appear before her. As the light became clearer, she saw a beautiful underwater scene lit in shades of blue and purple. The light was coming from many strange glowing creatures she could most closely call jellyfish. There were many gently floating through the long flowing tendrils of a plant growing from the floor beneath.

She noticed that some of the jellyfish had small objects in them and looking closer, realised they were the frogs. It seemed like they had a type of symbiotic relationship beneath the caves of Cormaine. She was awed and joyous to find such a calm and beautiful piece of nature hiding in the depths of a place such as this. Down here, the aura of corruption was so weak she could barely feel it. She heard a notification pop up but ignored it, mentally pushing it away as she watched for a little longer. Soon though, she had to return to the surface—she felt her breath running out. Reluctantly turning back, she swam back up the tunnel and burst into the open air of her cave home. She pulled herself out of the water and sat dripping on the floor. She started using her cold manipulation to freeze the water before willing it to flow away as ice. As she did, she read the message that had popped up into her view.

**Congratulations! Survivalist and associated
skills have reached Iron 20.
Congratulations! Survivalist and associated
skills have reached Bronze 1.
Survivalist and associated skills won't gain further
levels until all classes reach Bronze 1.**

**Survivalist - passive - body enhancement
Tin - The body of a Hunter shall not fail easily. Gain the Heat**

Resistance and Cold Resistance passive skills. They level alongside this ability. You are able to survive with less nutrition.
Iron - Gain the Stealth and Trapper passive skills. These also level alongside this ability. You require less sleep.
Bronze - Gain the Physical Resistance and Mental Resistance passive skills. They level alongside this ability. You are able to survive with less air.

Stealth - passive
Tin - Normal vision as well as sight sight-based skills and abilities have a harder time detecting you.
Iron - Other senses are also inhibited and you blend with your surroundings.
Bronze - When still, you become invisible to the eye, only becoming visible again when you move. Certain perception types can see through this.

Trapper - passive
Tin - Your traps are magically hidden from sight.
Iron - Your traps are magically enhanced.
Bronze - You are able to magically fabricate basic traps you have been able to make before in an instant without materials. You are limited in how often this ability may be used.

Heat Resistance - passive
Tin - You take reduced damage from high temperatures and heat-related magics.
Iron - You may manipulate fire and heat to a minor degree.
Bronze - You are able to channel heat from the environment to minorly boost yourself or allies.

Cold Resistance - passive
Tin - You take reduced damage from low temperatures and cold related magics.
Iron - You may manipulate ice and snow to a minor degree.
Bronze - You are able to channel cold from the environment to minorly heal yourself or allies.

Physical Resistance - passive
Tin - You receive reduced damage and effects from

> **physical attacks and physical related magics.**
> **Iron - You may manipulate earth and stone to a minor degree.**
> **Bronze - You become harder to move by force.**

> **Mental Resistance - passive**
> **Tin - You receive reduced damage and effects from**
> **mental attacks and mind-related magics.**
> **Iron - You may perform minor telekinetic feats.**
> **Bronze - You may mentally communicate with**
> **creatures capable of understanding language.**

Zalia breathed out as she read the host of messages before her. It was a lot to take in, especially considering the extra two passives she had also gotten from the rank up. She read over them once more, looking over to Boreal. It looked like Boreal was also trying to absorb all of the information from the newly ranked ability. Zalia wasn't the only one due for some experimentation.

Being able to minorly manipulate the earth and stone was an excellent skill she was glad to receive. Shattering stone by her usual method worked but wasn't quite as efficient. Again, it seemed like the rank up of her ability was strongly affected by her situation and mental state. She'd gained an ability to breathe less and she could rank it by swimming; she could use Mental Resistance when she was struggling to deal with fear, and had an improved ability to manipulate stone when she had been using a roundabout method to do so.

She was starting to wonder if abilities really were strongly motivated subconsciously by the wielder. Being able to fabricate traps instantaneously would prove very useful, bringing that ability from something she had to set up to something she could use in an instant. She also was able to stealth significantly better when standing still, something probably motivated by her recent tendency to sit in one place shooting undead.

The two additions to Cold and Heat Resistance were most interesting to her. She could feel the very minor healing added by the coldness of the room she was in—an ability that Boreal shared and now doubled down on. Using heat to minorly boost the effects could also come in handy as an extra bit of speed or power in the right moment, capable of changing the course of a fight. All in all, the ability gave her increased confidence in her own survival by giving her a variety of useful abilities. Survivalist indeed.

Thinking again of the frog, Zalia realised being able to hold her breath and communicate telepathically might just be able to help her in her quest.

She also wanted to explore that underwater ecosystem a little, hoping to find some type of flora she could use with her Herbal Magic.

Speaking of, Herbal Magic was the next ability she wanted to get to Bronze rank because the Iron rank ability allowed her to recreate the effects of herbs of one rank lower than the ability, rather than one rank lower than Zalia. That would mean she could freely recreate any Iron rank herb once it was Bronze. That would eliminate her need to use any Bitterbalm, Snowleaf, or Zephyr, all of which would run out in the near future if she wasn't careful. It would also allow her to use a variety of Bronze ranked herbs properly by using the intuition from the ability.

So, she sat back up, got comfortable, and began pushing her ability to analyse her herbs effects.

CHAPTER FOURTEEN

Frog Contact

Zalia

Zalia spent most of the rest of what she thought to be that day practicing her Herbal Magic. She only gained one level, bringing it to Iron sixteen for her efforts, but at least it was one closer to the eventual goal. She stood up, feeling restless, and glanced at the pond again. She wanted to go down there and explore its depths again as she had done quite a few times in between her meditative practice. Boreal had gotten extremely bored as well, going so far as to leave the cavern at one point, and coming back with one of the grey creatures she had apparently hunted on her own.

Zalia didn't tell her off for doing that but neither was she happy about it. She would have to let Boreal be independent eventually as she grew bigger and stronger.

"Want to go for a dive?" Zalia asked.

She hadn't yet tried to communicate telepathically with her new Mental Resistance passive but wanted to try with the frog friend. Well, soon-to-be frog friend, hopefully. She was a little worried about trying to interact with them because as of yet she had simply watched from the entrance to the little ecosystem. She didn't know if they would become hostile if they knew of her presence or if she tried to talk to them. Since they weren't a source of food, however, they may as well become a source of companionship. Not that she really needed to eat much these days anyways.

She might have just left them be and explored the surface more, maybe hunted down more of the undead to gain some easy levels. Unfortunately, she was still worried about the demon she had seen and wanted to wait a little longer before making the journey back to the other island. There were also the few sections of the keep she hadn't been able to get into that she wanted to explore, but getting past the Silver rank guards would be no easy feat. She might well have to be entirely Bronze rank before she attempted as much.

Taking a deep breath, she dove into the pool right after Boreal, who had run across the room and jumped straight in. She swam down, able to see the walls now that she had figured out how to interpret the heat vision underwater. Before, it had been a confusing, swirling mess that she hadn't been able to figure out, but with a little work it became natural once more. The water acted a little differently than air in the way heat transferred, but it didn't take her long to understand it.

Boreal made a little ice sphere, manipulating the material expertly until she floated along in a bubble controlled by her magic. Envious of the display of natural expertise, Zalia swam alongside the sphere until they reached the bigger space. Keeping her nerve, Zalia reached out to talk to one of the frogs with a telepathic connection.

"*Hello,*" Zalia sent.

A sound like distorted feedback bounced into her mind and she winced, holding the side of her head. The distortion slowly began clearing into words, but she wasn't so much focused on that at the moment, as she saw some of the glowing jellyfish that the frogs called home slowly approaching. She could finally hear a word through the distortion.

"*Gr—in-s,*" said a hundred different voices.

It was like she was hearing many of them all at once, rather than just the one she had spoken to.

"*I come peacefully,*" Zalia said.

There was a pause as a sort of confused humming filled her mind. Boreal joined the conversation, sending the frogs a feeling of peace and trust in the way she had done many times with Zalia. She was much better at that than Zalia was, having had much more practice.

"*Peace,*" came the reply.

"*Are you native to this world?*" Zalia asked.

The confused humming began once more but Boreal quickly translated.

"*Native . . . Yes. This . . .*" said the collective, pausing.

What came after the pause was the idea of the pond they lived in, along with an image of it.

"*I mean this world; we are from another,*" Zalia said.

Boreal somewhat deftly explained that they were from an entirely different world, sending the memory of their transportation.

"*Ah, the air above. Yes, this is our world. Memories from the . . .*" the collective replied, sending the idea of age, and ancient creatures. Their ancestors? "*Their memories show of such places.*"

What followed were images and memories of a lush world filled with life. Many other conversations they once had and sights they had once seen. Memories passed down through the ages to those in front of her now.

But that's not what this world looks like, Zalia thought, trying to process the blur of thoughts placed in her mind. "*That is not what it looks like up there*," she said.

Boreal followed up with images and feelings of their memories of the surface, the twisted trees, sulphurous air, and shade-filled sky.

"*This is not the ancestors' world,*" the collective replied.

A single voice came from the collective. "*I will explore.*"

A ponderous hum filled Zalia's mind.

"*One of us will join you to explore this surface. Will this be acceptable?*" the collective asked.

She noticed they had very quickly figured out the language she spoke. A quirk of being a large gathering of minds able to communicate directly, maybe. It could also be something to do with the unlisted translation power she seemed to have, or a combination of both.

"*Yes,*" Zalia replied.

She was starting to run out of breath despite the new power. She was able to hold it for about three minutes now while sitting still, probably less if she was actively swimming. A small, light blue and purple frog jumped from their jellyfish home into the water and swam over. Zalia gestured for it to follow and began swimming back to the surface, with Boreal trailing along in her little ice vessel. Zalia surfaced, taking a deep breath and wiping the water from her eyes. As she blinked, she saw the crow up close, staring straight into her eyes.

"Gah, what the hell," Zalia exclaimed.

"Caw!" the crow replied.

She pulled herself out of the pool as the crow hopped away to a safe distance from the dripping water. As soon as the frog surfaced, the crow hopped forwards again like it was about to attack.

"Hey! Hey now, none of that," Zalia scolded, holding her arms out to block the crow.

The crow let out a croak that sounded . . . questioning or confused.

"That's a friend, they're going to be travelling with us for a little while," Zalia explained.

"*Why did you volunteer to travel with us?*" Zalia asked the frog.

"It is a great honour to bring back new memories for the collective. Many have tried to reach the surface over the cycles, yet never have they returned. The risk is worth the reward for being the one to achieve this goal," the frog explained.

"Right. Frog, this is crow, crow, this is frog," Zalia introduced.

"Do you have a name?" Zalia asked the frog.

"None that you could pronounce in this primitive language. You may choose one if you so wish," the frog replied.

"Hmm, got any good ideas for names, Boreal?" Zalia asked.

Boreal tilted her head, looking thoughtful as the frog walked over to the water's surface and tapped it with its little hand. The water rippled, and Zalia swore she could see images appearing and disappearing quickly on its surface. The crow walked over to inspect the images and Zalia stood above them, watching the flickering surface.

"What are you doing?" Zalia asked.

"Seeing," the frog replied.

"Delphi," Zalia said.

"Delphi?" Boreal asked.

"It was the name of an oracle from a mythology in my world. The frog can be called Delphi," Zalia explained.

"This is acceptable," Delphi said.

"Excellent, now we just need a name for you, crow," Zalia added, turning to the crow who was still watching the images in the water.

Zalia couldn't make heads or tails of them, only catching a slight glimpse, but the crow seemed fascinated.

"Friend," Boreal said.

"Yes, I know the crow is a friend, but that isn't a name we can give it. It's gotta be something unique," Zalia explained.

Boreal looked like she understood but wasn't happy about it.

"Do you have a name?" Zalia asked the crow.

The crow didn't respond, captivated by the flickering water.

"Alright, let's go to the surface then shall we?" Zalia asked, finally catching the attention of the duo staring at the pool.

"I believe it is safe to do so," Delphi said, hopping over.

Zalia looked down at the tiny frog.

"Want to stand up here? You won't be able to keep up, I fear," Zalia said, patting her shoulder.

"This is acceptable," Delphi replied.

Zalia wasn't so much scared of the one small frog by itself, since it was only Iron rank. She felt like the entire collective together would be a formidable foe, however, possibly having some way of combining powers for devastating effect. There had to be a reason they had survived here so long.

"You said earlier that for many cycles you have been trying to reach the surface. What exactly is a cycle?" Zalia asked.

"*It is a measurement set by the ancient ones many, many cycles ago when the collective left the surface to live in these caverns. The ancient ones set the cycle as a way of measuring time and ever since, a cycle keeper has been ever counting, passing the title down to the next as they age. It is a position of great honour in the collective,*" Delphi explained.

"Do you remember . . . why? Why your people came down to the caves?" Zalia asked.

"*We do not. It is one of the many memories lost to time,*" Delphi replied, sounding mournful.

"You seem to cherish memories more than even your own life, from how you speak of them. Why is that?" Zalia asked.

"*If one should die, our memories continue on in the collective. If a memory should die, it is gone forever,*" Delphi replied.

It made sense, in an odd way. As a culture, they just cherished different things due to their nature.

"Let's go get you some new memories, then, though I can't promise they will be good ones," Zalia said.

"*All memories are good, even the bad ones warn future generations of their peril,*" Delphi explained.

Zalia took that little piece of information in stride and headed out of the cave.

"You said it would be safe to go to the surface. Do you know that because of whatever you were doing with the water?" Zalia asked.

"*The collective is able to peer into the past, present, and future. It is not always accurate, and simply knowing these things can change events, due to our actions. However, something such as this is simple enough to divine,*" Delphi replied.

"Hmm, I'll take whatever assurance I can get, even if it isn't entirely reliable," Zalia murmured.

They finally reached the surface and Delphi began making a low croaking sound in their throat.

"Everything alright?" Zalia asked.

"*This place is wrong. So, so wrong,*" Delphi whispered.

"It's not the best, no," Zalia agreed.

Zalia made sure to allow her healing to include Delphi, not wanting the significantly stronger corruptive aura here to harm them. She also constantly cooled herself so she could funnel the healing from Cold Resistance to wherever it was needed.

"Do you need to stay hydrated at all?" Zalia asked in a whisper.

"*I will be able to manage,*" Delphi said.

"Well then, where would you like to go first? There is this entire island, but it's pretty boring and empty. I've been to another island across the way that is covered in the ruins of an old city filled with undead. There could be something interesting there for you to find," Zalia explained.

"*That does indeed sound like a unique memory to experience. To the ruins, mighty steed,*" Delphi said.

Mighty steed? Zalia thought.

CHAPTER FIFTEEN

Cleansing

Zalia

Zalia looked at the pillar, stretching far up to the ceiling above.

"We're going to have to climb that," she said.

"*This is . . . acceptable,*" Delphi replied.

"Just think of it as a new memory to collect," Zalia comforted.

There was no reply for a few seconds.

"*Continue,*" Delphi said.

So she did, using the Structure Creation ritual to create a stairway leading up and around the pillar, ever upwards. This time, however, she was much less focused on her footing and more so on the surroundings. She was comfortable enough in her ability to climb without stumbling and wanted to keep an eye out in case she saw the demonic creature coming back this way.

They made it to the ceiling with ease, beginning the journey across the gap after a short rest in the little cubby she had made at the top. She even had the opportunity to test out her earth manipulation and made the cubby much bigger and more comfortable over the course of a few minutes. It wasn't anything super special or powerful, but the utility would definitely make her life a lot easier.

The trip across the gap was a lot shorter since her path was already set out with the marks she had made on the stone with her sword. She was starting to wonder if it were possible to create permanent effects with her rituals. It might be something she would get access to with a higher-ranked ability. Either way, for now she still had to resign herself to using the short-lived, vine-like structures she could make.

"Enjoying the experience so far?" Zalia asked Delphi.

"*Not falling has been pleasant,*" Delphi replied.

"Are you sure? I could drop you off if you would like," Zalia teased.

Congratulations! Herbal Magic has reached Iron 17.

"*I would not like to lose the memories I have gathered just yet. Maybe after I have transferred these to the collective, I could experience this memory too,*" Delphi replied.

"I wasn't being serious," Zalia said.

"*. . . I see,*" Delphi responded, sounding a little confused.

"Do you have jokes or sarcasm in the collective?" Zalia asked.

"*I do not understand these words,*" Delphi said.

"I . . . nevermind. You and your little collective can figure it out once we go back," Zalia replied, rolling her eyes.

"*This aura may be the reason none have ever returned from the surface,*" Delphi said.

"It might be. I have to constantly heal us all to keep it from overcoming us," Zalia explained.

"*Ah, that is what the other strange experience is. This explains why the sight sees no danger coming to the surface with you, when every other time it has,*" Delphi pondered.

The crow was flying back and forth between Zalia and the pillar they were heading towards, keeping an eye out across the land below.

"*Do you know how that crow has survived out here?*" Zalia asked Delphi telepathically.

"*I do not. They are a curious specimen, I cannot see any rank. I would love to see the memories this one holds,*" Delphi replied.

Boreal was in the middle of jumping back and forth, batting at the disintegrating edge of their bridge.

"Be careful back there," Zalia called.

Boreal stopped and came to walk up alongside Zalia, still looking extremely bored.

"We can clear out some of the undead once we get down there, if you're really that bored," Zalia said.

Boreal seemed to perk up at that, excited at the prospect of a hunt. Hopefully if they stayed to the edges of the city they would only face some of the weaker ones.

They finally reached the opposite pillar and Zalia made a similar cubby there that was bigger and deeper. She had considered making a bridge spanning the gap using her earth and stone manipulation powers but didn't want to make a direct path back to her island just yet. She would need a good, protected footing on this island before she thought about linking them up like that.

"Do you have any combat-oriented skills?" Zalia asked Delphi.

"*Some, though I would not measure up to the likes of either of you outside of the collective,*" Delphi replied.

"So you wouldn't really have any memories of combat, then?" Zalia asked.

"*No, some from the ancient ones, but none from recent times. Will you be taking part in combat?*" Delphi asked.

"I think I will. Boreal is itching for a fight, and I must say I'm feeling the same," Zalia replied.

"*I would like to observe this,*" Delphi said.

"That's fine with me," Zalia said.

She began the descent, not so worried this time about being seen. They were closer to the edge of the island, and the ruins beneath would hold fewer undead Bathar of lower ranks than there would be closer to the centre. Sure, making sound would draw some others closer, but she could probably hold out for a while. Besides, she had an anti-death measure now and despite not particularly wanting to test it out, she wouldn't mind seeing how exactly it worked.

She felt bad for the undead below. From what she could tell, they had once been normal people, twisted and forced into undying bodies. While she didn't enjoy the idea of massacring an entire people, releasing them from their torment would be a mercy. As she reached the ground, she quietly moved through the city with allies in tow until she found a somewhat clear area. It was a small square with three entries and plenty of shadowy areas for Boreal to take advantage of.

Zalia got to work setting up traps that she materialised with her new Trapper passive ability. She created poisoned tripwires, spring-activated wall spikes, poisoned caltrops, and even managed to make some spring-loaded bear traps. Each trap was magically hidden and enhanced by her passive. The tripwires would magnetically pull towards whoever tripped them, wrapping around and digging into flesh. The wall spikes were already enhanced by their nature; the spring activation was a magical enhancement. The poisoned caltrops would extend their spikes when stepped on, digging into flesh and stone, holding whatever triggered them still. The bear traps would clamp onto the offending limb and then release an acid that would eat through it with ease. All of this did take some time to set up but would greatly increase her survivability for what she was about to do next.

"*What are you doing?*" Delphi asked.

"*Preparing some traps for our enemy,*" Zalia replied mentally.

"*How do you know they will come this way?*" Delphi asked.

"*Because I am going to draw them into the traps as we fight,*" Zalia explained.

"*Interesting, this is not how I would expect combat to happen,*" Delphi said curiously.

"*Usually it wouldn't happen like this but I don't do things normally,*" Zalia said.

While she had been at work, Boreal had actually managed to find a use for Zalia's shared Trapper passive as well. She had created icy replicas of herself hiding in the shadows that crouched down with a grinding sound before sitting still. It was a simple concept and Zalia had a feeling they would pounce on enemies that walked near. She was surprised that Boreal was able to make use of the passive at all, yet an ambush was as much a trap as anything else so, why not?

Satisfied with her work, Zalia memorised where she had laid each trap so that she could use them to her advantage in the combat to come.

"All ready?" Zalia asked Boreal.

Boreal replied by slinking into a shadow and hiding. Zalia counted through her rituals, and began by using a Dodge-vine ritual on all her allies. That would protect them from attacks by minorly redirecting them away. She also applied the frost armour ritual to Boreal and herself, knowing that it could come in handy. That would give her two layers of armour for a minimal reduction in Mobility. Not wanting to use too much of her limited herb supply for this battle, she held back on preparing any rituals. Most of them she could cast in the moment if needed.

With all that set up, she quickly ran off to find some of the undead Bathar. Before she attracted their attention, she thought about what she was doing. When she had gained her Druid class, it had said she would protect the balance of life and death by her own methods, or something along those lines. She hadn't really known exactly what that meant but seeing the undead roaming around these streets, she knew it was wrong. Something like this simply shouldn't exist.

So, as she ran across two Bathar, she shot one in the head with her bow, killing it instantly. The other let out the screech that she knew would attract more so she ran back towards her trapped area, turning momentarily to let off another arrow, which killed the other Tin ranked Bathar.

As she ran, she turned every now and then to kill off or cripple another undead, letting them catch up a little before continuing on the chase. It wasn't long before she reached her little square and she set up in the centre, letting off arrow after arrow.

Many of the Tin ranked undead fell in the opening volleys, some of the arrows having enough force to punch straight through a Bathar's head before changing course slightly to punch through another's. For the moment, they were only coming from one direction and Zalia made quick work using Hunter's Mark and Kill Shot where necessary to take down the quickly appearing Iron ranked undead.

Despite her incredibly fast shooting, the undead coming through the entrances started increasing dramatically in number. Soon, Boreal had to get into the fray, appearing from a shadow and freezing an enemy's legs to the ground or bowling them off their feet with astounding force before vanishing into another shadow. She made good use of her short-distance shadow teleport, appearing and disappearing, always where she needed to be. Despite that, the undead started reaching Zalia's traps when the first Bronze rank arrived.

The undead ran ahead, catching two arrows to the chest and a spring-loaded spike to the arm before running over a bear trap that clamped over and dissolved half its leg. The undead crawled towards Zalia before a Kill Shot–enhanced arrow flew through its head and ended its life. It hadn't lasted nearly as long as Juniper had, maybe due to its extended time in the corrupting and corroding aura, or maybe due to the traps. Either way, it still managed to make room for its allies, who began sprinting through the traps as a horde.

Dozens fell to arrows, tripwires, bear traps, wall spikes, and caltrops as they approached. Soon though, Zalia had to switch to her sword as the first few broke through. She quickly dispatched the Iron ranked undead with quick strikes, following through to the next coming through. A few undead were now making their way down one of the other paths, setting off traps of their own.

Zalia realised she was in trouble when two Bronze ranked undead broke through to the front lines. She quickly activated Nature's Wrath, tying down all of the nearby undead and summoning two elementals. Two large stone elementals ripped free of the wall and floor nearby and began pummeling all the undead coming from the first path as Zalia began dealing with the two in front of her. She applied Hunter's Mark to both and began dueling them. They were easy enough to put off, quick moves and efficient swordsmanship sending one stumbling as she made three quick strikes at the other.

Each sword strike left glowing gashes in their bodies but they kept coming with a mindless fury. She didn't stop to think about how much their fighting style reminded her of the mindless soldiers back in Endaria and kept up her assault. She was forced to use Fight or Flight as the first undead came back at her, and she used her increased perception to perfect her dodges, ducking backwards under a swing and bringing her sword about in a circular motion, half severing one's neck and continuing the motion into a deep cut through the other's torso.

The half-decapitated undead stumbled backwards and Zalia used the advantage to push the assault on the other. Three quick moves had its arm hanging by a thread and one leg entirely gone. She turned the momentum on the somehow still alive, half-decapitated one by turning her spin into a strong Kill Shot–enhanced cut downwards that split it in two. One of the undead dealt with, she turned back and finished off the other with a sword point impaled straight through its head.

She was about to turn around but felt a heavy impact from behind, sending her sprawling across the square. She sat up, dazed from the hit, to see Boreal launch from the shadows to grab the offending undead by the neck and drag it down to the floor, where an icy replica jumped from the nearby shadow and crushed its head into mush. Boreal swung her head side to side like a dog, ripping part of the undead's spine out and tossing it away as she jumped back into the shadows.

Zalia stood up and got back to work, shooting the undead that were making their way through the second path—some had apparently made their way through the traps.

CHAPTER SIXTEEN

Road to Bronze

Zalia

Zalia finished off the last undead with a quick step back to avoid a blow and a simultaneous downwards strike that neatly bisected her enemy. Looking around for any remaining enemies and seeing none, she stabbed her sword into the ground and collapsed against the wall, sliding down to a seated position. She let out a long, slow groan, stretching her aching muscles as her healing took care of the remaining wounds. She had been stabbed in the side by a particularly sneaky undead Bathar with a dagger, the point managing to penetrate her icy armour and heirloom armour. She had also received a strongly worded fist to the head at one point and had needed to quickly retreat to recover from the ringing in her ears.

Despite it all, she had managed to win the fight, with only one more Bronze ranked Bathar coming out of the horde to challenge her. After that, it was just a cleanup of the lower-ranked enemies, most taken down in one or two strikes. While they might have been of similar ranks, they definitely were not as powerful as even a normal person of their rank, let alone a match for Zalia. She had noticed these Bronze rankers were less powerful than Juniper had been as well, a result of their long slumber maybe.

Still, she had managed to accrue various scratches and bruises over the course of the fight, though those were negligible at the moment. Her healing usually would have been able to take care of all of that almost as soon as it happened, but the constant fight it needed to put up against the corruption severely impeded it. She checked over the other side of the clearing where Boreal was cleaning the undead muck off herself. Seeing that she was alright, she looked around for Delphi. Zalia had put him on top of a nearby roof to watch the fight and only now thought to check if he was alright.

Her question was answered when the nimble little frog landed on her knee and inspected her.

"*You're injured,*" Delphi stated.

"What gave it away, was it the blood?" Zalia replied sarcastically.

"*Yes, the collective has no memories of your kind, but I believe the red substance is meant to stay in your body,*" Delphi replied, no sarcasm noticeable in his voice.

"Do you not have blood?" Zalia asked.

"*No, we have no need,*" Delphi said.

"Good for you," Zalia said.

She ignored Delphi for a moment, checking her ability level ups from the fight.

Congratulations! Kill Shot has gained two levels, reaching Iron 13.
Congratulations! Hunter's Mark has gained
two levels, reaching Iron 13.
Congratulations! Fight or Flight has gained
three levels, reaching Iron 12.
Congratulations! Hunter's Sight has reached Iron 11.
Congratulations! Hunter class has gained
two levels, reaching Iron 11.
Congratulations! Flora Identification has reached Iron 9.
Congratulations! Stasis has reached Iron 9.
Congratulations! Herbal Magic has gained
two levels, reaching Iron 19.
Congratulations! Herbalist class has reached Iron 9.
Congratulations! Nature's Wrath has gained
three levels, reaching Iron 11.
Congratulations! Protection of the Wilds has
gained three levels, reaching Iron 9.
Congratulations! Druid class has gained
three levels, reaching Iron 9.
Congratulations! Mobility has reached Iron 20.
Congratulations! Mobility has reached Bronze 1.
This ability will gain no further levels until
all classes have reached Bronze 1.
Mobility - passive

> **Tin - Your speed is increased. Your stamina
> is less affected by movement.
> Iron - You may step on air one time before
> stepping on a solid surface.
> Bronze - You are able to step on air three times before resetting this
> ability. Additionally, you may perform a short-range teleport with a
> long cooldown. Finally, when travelling long distances, you are able
> to maintain a fast pace while maintaining your stamina indefinitely.
> Congratulations! Weapon proficiency - Bow
> has gained two levels, reaching Iron 17.
> Congratulations! Weapon proficiency - Sword
> has gained three levels, reaching Iron 12.**

She eyed the Mobility rank up ability, a little surprised by the extensive upgrade it had received. Most of her other passives had only small additions or increases, but Mobility appeared to be different. Maybe it had something to do with the fact that a lot of her other passives were from the Survivalist ability. Were there such things as minor and major passives? She didn't really know but would find out eventually.

"*—ay you stepped back to follow through at the end was a particularly impressive display*," Delphi was saying.

"Thanks," Zalia said.

"*The collective shall enjoy inspecting these memories, I'm certain of it. It is something much outside of our experience despite the many cycles of memories we have*," Delphi explained.

"I hope they do," Zalia replied.

She was having a hard time gathering the energy to hold a proper conversation and Delphi must have finally caught on to it because he fell silent. Looking to the air above, Zalia could see the crow flying in a wide circle, keeping an eye out.

"What about Benjamin," Zalia said.

"*What?*" Delphi asked.

"Benjamin. We could call the crow Benjamin, or Benji for short," Zalia explained.

"*If you wish*," Delphi said.

"You don't think it's a good name?" Zalia asked.

"*The collective is not used to . . . names*," Delphi replied.

"Right, forgot about that. Boreal, what do you think about calling our friend Benjamin?" Zalia called out.

"Mreow?" Boreal said, looking up from her cleaning.

"Yeah, then we can call him Benji for short," Zalia added.

Boreal looked at Zalia flatly.

"Alright, not Benji then," Zalia grumbled.

"*What about . . . Ro-ak?*" Delphi asked.

"I thought you didn't do names," Zalia said.

"*It isn't a name, it's my best translation to your language of 'seer,' or one with sight,*" Delphi said.

"Ro-ak. Ro for short?" Zalia said.

"*That's not how our lan—*" Delphi started.

"What do you think, Boreal?" Zalia asked.

"Mow," Boreal replied.

"*—ks, you can't just shorten words,*" Delphi finished.

"It's decided," Zalia announced.

"*Decided,*" Boreal agreed.

"Alright," Zalia said with a groan as she stood up. She stretched, ignoring the pang in her shoulder. "Want to go round two with some undead or something else?" Zalia asked.

"*New memories are always sought,*" Delphi replied.

"I'm gonna take that as a yes," Zalia said.

So she set off with her small group of animal friends, looking for a new place to set up.

Many hours and a few fights later, Zalia lay on a rooftop exhausted. After each fight she recovered slowly but the constant fighting over the course of the day drained her mentally too. That, unfortunately, was not something she could quite heal yet.

During the fights, however, she managed to push two of her abilities to Bronze.

Congratulations! Kill Shot has gained two levels, reaching Iron 15.
Congratulations! Hunter's Mark has gained
two levels, reaching Iron 15.
Congratulations! Fight or Flight has gained
two levels, reaching Iron 14.
Congratulations! Herbal Magic has reached Iron 20.
Congratulations! Herbal Magic has reached Bronze 1.
Herbal Magic will not gain further levels
until all classes reach Bronze 1.
Herbal Magic - passive
Tin - Minor herb-based rituals are a keystone of magical

> **herbalists. You gain an instinctual understanding of herbal rituals of your rank or lower. Herbal Magic of your rank and lower has slightly increased potency.**
> **Iron - You may emulate the effects of herbs you have used in rituals of a rank lower than this ability.**
> **Bronze - When applying an Herbal ritual effect to a target marked by Hunter's Mark, all other marked targets are also affected. In addition, you are able to combine certain herbs to gain a new base effect.**
> **Congratulations! Nature's Wrath has gained two levels, reaching Iron 13.**
> **Congratulations! Protection of the Wilds has reached Iron 10.**
> **Congratulations! Druid class has reached Iron 10.**
> **Congratulations! Weapon proficiency - Bow has gained three levels, reaching Iron 20.**
> **Congratulations! Weapon proficiency - Bow has reached Bronze 1.**
> **Weapon proficiency - Bow will not gain further levels until all classes reach Bronze 1.**
> **Bow - Weapon proficiency**
> **Tin - Arrows shot from a bow you are using have increased speed based on rank and level of this skill.**
> **Iron - Arrows shot from a bow you are using have increased penetrative power based on the rank and level of this skill.**
> **Bronze - Bows you use will now shoot entirely silently. Additionally, when you draw the string back, you will gain insights into the weak points of your target.**
> **Congratulations! Weapon proficiency - Sword has gained four levels, reaching Iron 16.**

During the most recent fight she had definitely noticed the silence of her bow and the effect it gave her. She hadn't noticed, however, that her Herbal Magic could now affect each enemy that was marked by casting a ritual on only one of them. That would be cause for a lot of testing, especially around applying a mark to a creature when tracking them. That would mean she could theoretically cast a ritual on someone hundreds of kilometres away, kind of like a curse.

She kind of loved the idea.

It would also push her to make more use of her Herbal Magic in combat, where usually she only really used it in the set up before a fight. She had also tested out her short-range teleport during the fights, and being able to reposition herself out of danger was another small improvement to her survival here. She was also having ideas about how she could use it in a more utility-based way, maybe to get past those Silver ranked guards blocking her way forwards. She had yet to test how exactly that worked with her intangibility but was quite keen to try.

She watched as Boreal pounced across the room again and checked the ability description for her Pounce, thinking it may have levelled up after seeing some of the new effects.

> **Tin - When charged, pouncing on something will cause it to be coated with a layer of ice and snow.**
> **Iron - When charged, your pounce will have greatly increased strength and weight behind it.**
> **Bronze - When charged, your pounce will now grant you a body-tight, magical, icy shield that will protect you from one attack, no matter its strength. This can only trigger once every so often.**

"Wow, Boreal. You have your own extra defences now too!" Zalia said.

She was over the moon that Boreal had gotten something that would make her more durable. She often almost had a heart attack when Boreal pounced into the middle of a bunch of enemies.

"Maybe we can have another try at that keep, wanna see it, Delphi?" Zalia asked.

"*New memories are always sought,*" Delphi replied.

Zalia rolled her eyes.

"I should have known you'd say that," Zalia replied, a bright smile on her face.

CHAPTER SEVENTEEN

Murder Kitten

Zalia

They had made their way to the keep the same way that Zalia did last time, sneaking over the rooftops until they reached their destination. Entering the same way as before, Zalia closed the keep tower door behind her, breathing out a sigh of relief. She felt some of the background tension leave her as she entered what she knew to be a space safe from whatever vision that monster had.

"Do you have any memories of this place?" Zalia asked.

"*I do not, though the architecture is something I recognise. From where, I do not know. I will have to ask the collective,*" Delphi replied.

Zalia thought about that as she explained to Delphi what she knew about the keep so far, where guards were waiting and their ranks. She felt confident in being able to take down the Bronze ranked ones, knowing their strength. Though, the ones she had fought outside were only civilians; maybe these ones, having been guards in life, retained some form of skill or ability. Either way, she couldn't fight them in groups of one or two anyways due to the sound that would be made. She thought about the little addition to Herbal Magic's Bronze effect, the ability to create new base effects from some herbs. She kind of knew what that meant but would need to do some experimentation to figure out which herbs she could actually do that with.

The thought only came to mind because she wanted to see if she could make some sort of sound-dampening ritual. That would allow her to fight some of the enemies without potentially alerting the entire keep. Maybe she wouldn't need to go as far as using sound dampening, and her vine-like Structure Creation would be able to block the sound well enough.

"Hmm," Zalia hummed.

"*Speak your memories, Zalia,*" Delphi said.

"Thoughts," Zalia corrected.

"*Thoughts are just memories of the present, are they not?*" Delphi asked.

"No," Zalia said, "I might be able to create a space quiet enough to fight the Bronze undead in, but being limited to such a small area might get me killed."

She summoned a section of viney wall, pressing her hand against it. Strangely, her hand passed straight through.

"I thought I couldn't pass my body through magical structures," Zalia murmured.

Maybe because the structure was made by her, it didn't have any type of protection against her. That was definitely something she could use. She formed a large dome over herself, trying to make the surface as bumpy as she could. She knew a little bit about how sound worked from her education and was hoping that this would be enough to stop the sound travelling through the entire keep.

She stepped through the dome.

"Hey, Boreal, Delphi, let me know if you can hear anything, ok?" Zalia asked.

She stepped back into the dome, trying to get used to the odd experience of walking through a wall, and summoned her sword. She raised it up and slapped the flat of the blade against the floor. It produced a loud ringing sound as the metal vibrated slightly.

"*Heard the ringing,*" Delphi said.

"Hmm," Zalia said.

She thickened the walls a bit until she thought they might be good enough and tried again.

"*Barely heard it that time,*" Delphi said.

She tried stepping through the wall and found it was still thin enough, barely.

"It will have to do," she said.

"*Loud,*" Boreal said in her mind.

"You just have really good hearing," Zalia replied, "and besides, the undead have terrible hearing, they're still asleep even though we walked straight past them."

Zalia let the dome disintegrate, not bothering to renew it now that she had done her testing. She made her way down the stairs to the little bedroom-study combination holding the first Bronze rank undead she had found. She walked through the jammed door and inspected the space inside. The undead was still unconscious, slouched over with its head on the desk, so Zalia began building a dome there.

She wouldn't be able to kill the Bathar instantly, but with a good set up she might be able to seriously injure it before the fight even began. Once the dome was up, she stepped inside and very carefully set up a few traps around it. The put spring-loaded spikes in the floor all around it, a few tripwires across the length of the dome that it would get caught in, and even went so far as to summon a bear trap to put on the floor. Once that was all done, she summoned her sword and swung it down onto the leant over undead's neck. It was as good a strike as you could ask for but she still didn't manage to cut all the way through.

The undead woke up and burst into motion with a screech. It instantly got caught as three tripwires jumped on contact, wrapping around its body at speed, spikes appearing along their length. The undead managed to take one stumbling step as its head wobbled around on the last part of its neck. It stepped onto one of the spikes, which stabbed straight through its foot into its lower torso. Zalia took one last swing, taking off its head before it tumbled to the ground and landed on a few more spikes, with half its torso falling into the bear trap—activating the trap's flesh-melting acid.

"Hear anything?" Zalia asked Delphi.

The frog was waiting outside the door with Boreal.

"A very faint screech, barely audible even to us," Delphi replied.

Breathing out in relief, Zalia stepped out of the room, straight through the door.

"That worked like a dream!" she whispered excitedly.

It wouldn't work so well when she was facing two of the guards at once, but it was a pretty well-done job so far. She only had to take down two sets of the Bronze guards before finding some way around the Silver ones. She mostly wanted to get these Bronze ones gone so she didn't have to worry about having them in the way on her path of escape, if it came to that.

She carefully made her way down the second stairwell towards the lower floor. She skipped past the door she knew held two Silver ranked guards behind it and arrived at the bottom. Peeking around the corner of the doorway to the stairwell, Zalia could see the two Bronze ranked guards slumped against the wall opposite the keep's entrance.

"Wanna help me with these two, Boreal?" Zalia asked in a whisper.

"Help," Boreal confirmed.

Zalia very, very slowly began building the vine dome around them, making sure to block off the entrance to the keep as well. She had to build this one much bigger, and by the end it was a strain to keep the entire structure together without the magic collapsing. She walked into the dome, Boreal following with a short shadow teleport. Then, she began setting up her traps, as Boreal did the same.

Before long, they had a maze of dangerous traps, from tripwires to icy Boreal clones. To start the fight off, Zalia marked both undead and then started using rituals, unhesitant now that she could duplicate all her Iron ranked herbs. She started with the spreading ice curse that used Bitterbalm and Snow-leaf. That was quickly followed by an attack-slowing debuff ritual using Dodge-vine and Snow-leaf, an attack magnet debuff using Bitterbalm major and a Dodge-vine additive, and finally, a vulnerability debuff using Dodge-vine major and Bitterbalm minor.

The last two rituals she discovered were actually different things; her deep study into how the Herbal Magic ability actually worked helped her come up with them. Applying one herb as an additive to the major element in a ritual could create a different effect than the opposite combination. In this case, the attack magnet debuff brought attacks towards the affected individual, where the vulnerability debuff made them more susceptible to damage.

After the onslaught of ritual debuffs were applied to them, the Bathar finally began to wake up. Boreal wasted no time in pouncing on the first enemy, while Zalia finished applying the beneficial rituals to herself and Boreal, the same ones she used in most fights. She quickly summoned her bow and got to work, but the undead were faster. She was definitely right about the guards being stronger or more skilled than the undead civilians outside the keep, as they immediately split into two groups, one keeping Boreal busy while the other charged Zalia.

She got off one shot as the undead weaved between the traps towards her, the arrow striking it in the shoulder and passing straight through the armour without resistance. It seemed surprised at the ineffectiveness of its armour, and the impact pushed it slightly off balance as it stumbled into a tripwire. The tripwire wrapped around its legs, making it fall sideways where a Boreal clone jumped on its shoulder, freezing it to the floor.

Taking a brief moment of respite, Zalia shot an arrow at Boreal's enemy, which slammed into the undead's head as it tried to strike Boreal. For her part, Boreal was running circles around the guard, slashing out and tele-porting between shadows, leading the enemy into various traps laid about the room.

Zalia had to refocus on her own enemy as it finally broke the ice holding it to the floor. She shot it once in the chest as it got up but had to quickly switch to her sword as it reached her.

She was barely able to keep the undead's sword from impaling her on the first strike, its speed uncanny compared to the others she had fought. Quickly, she had to start backing up, blocking strikes and trying to land a few of her own. It seemed unable to figure out how she was striking straight through its armour and she was able to get off a few lucky hits due to that, thankfully. She received a stinging blow to her arm as she barely managed to deflect a hit and swung wildly in its direction.

As she managed to push the creature back for a moment with her swing, she summoned an icy wall using an ice creation ritual—Manifest major with a Snow-leaf additive. The undead paused for a moment as if considering what to do, but Zalia didn't hesitate, running straight through the wall and slashing at its neck. Surprised by the move, the undead only managed to get its sword up in time to deflect the blow, having its shoulder severed rather than its neck.

Seeing an advantage and having taken back the momentum, Zalia pushed forwards. She got in a smash with the pommel of her sword that forced the undead to stumble backwards. Zalia took advantage of that and aimed low as she ducked its wild swing, managing to slice its foot off. As it tried to put its leg back down, it fell once more, landing on a spring-loaded spike that impaled it, holding it to the floor. It managed to block two of Zalia's strikes before she severed its arm at the elbow, and finished the fight by plunging her sword through its head.

She stood up as she summoned her bow, the sword vanishing as she did so. Boreal currently had the other undead pinned with its leg frozen to the ground. She was on the undead's back, mauling it with her claws as her jaws were clamped onto its spine. Using its immobility, Zalia let off three silent shots that hit it with force, one after the other. Two more arrows to the head and one to the chest seemed to finally do the trick as the undead fell. Boreal didn't let go, ripping a piece of its spine out as it fell and throwing it across the space with a toss of her head.

Zalia let out a few panting breaths as she relaxed from the fight, releasing all her concentration from the magical constructions she had been focusing on. The dome, armour, and traps all began disintegrating into dust as she did.

"*Two down, two to go,*" Zalia mentally said to Boreal.

"*Mreow!*" Boreal replied in excitement.

Little murder paws, Zalia thought.

CHAPTER EIGHTEEN

Sound

Zalia

Zalia stood quietly as she built a new dome over the two unconscious undead lying before the door to the armoury. She was feeling pretty exhausted and knew she should probably sleep before even attempting to get past the Silver ranked guards further down. Not only were they a much higher rank, they were also awake.

As the dome finished, Zalia stepped inside and prepared much the same as she had last time, creating traps and performing quick rituals. As the undead woke, the battle began once more.

Much the same as last time, the two guards split and focused on one target each. The fight went well up until the guard Zalia was fighting sidestepped her strike and shoulder-rushed her, throwing her backwards through the dome wall into a roll. She nimbly rolled to her feet using the momentum of the fall and moved forwards, but she was too late—the guard broke through the wall and rushed her.

Frantically, Zalia started building a wall in the doorway towards the rest of the keep with her ritual, knowing that a whole horde of undead lay just metres away in the kitchen. As she did that, she jumped inside the reach of the undead in front of her, grappling with it. They wrestled back and forth, Zalia managing to slam the undead against the wall with a clatter, and its sword dropped to the ground with a loud clang. Quickly acting as she stunned it momentarily, Zalia literally threw the creature back into the dome, beginning to repair the structure straight away as she strode back through the wall.

She summoned her sword and made quick work of the disarmed undead, disarming it literally before she took off its head. Boreal had already killed her own, and was now calmly cleaning herself as she waited for Zalia to finish.

"Could have helped me," Zalia whispered.

"*Warm one strong*," Boreal said.

"Yeah, yeah, still could have helped," Zalia replied.

At that moment they heard the clattering of boots coming down stairs, just one set from what Zalia could tell. It could only be one thing: the Silver ranked that waited at the door upstairs.

A moment of indecision passed through her as she debated holding her ground, hiding or running. Both her and Boreal were able to take down a Bronze ranked with relative ease due to their reduced strength so together they might be able to take down a Silver. That was assuming these were reduced in strength as well, something she didn't know whether it was true or not considering they seemed to play by different rules. These guards were awake unlike most other undead in the city before she arrived.

Her moment of hesitation cost her the luxury of decision as the Silver rank undead came around the corner in a flash. She had already let go of the magic holding together the dome and wall, though she still had the protections on herself and Boreal. Acting quickly, Zalia applied Hunter's Mark to the undead and began trying to cast her ritual rebuffs on it. Unfortunately, the undead was fast enough to step out and away, dodging everything she threw at it.

She added her arrows to the mix as the undead avoided the ritual circles she was mentally commanding into existence between them. She used ice creation to block off the hallway, and Boreal began charging her pounce, the shards protruding from her back glowing a soft blue. Boreal pounced at the creature, appearing from a shadow behind it and landing with a crash. The undead didn't even miss a step as it ripped its feet free of the ice and slammed its sword into Boreal, throwing her across the room.

Zalia let out a choked cry in alarm but Boreal was safe due to her Bronze ranked Pounce ability. Zalia managed to activate the spreading ice curse ritual in its moment of stillness to strike Boreal, so she decided to go on the offensive to protect her friend. She rushed through the wall and engaged the undead in armed combat, finding herself thoroughly out-matched immediately.

Within seconds, she received a cut down her right side, from shoulder to hip. As she stumbled from the blow, her healing activated but it didn't stop the blade that impaled her through the chest. She let out a gasp of pain as the Bathar pulled the blade out and struck at her neck.

The blade hit, but in the last moment, a green glow emanated from within her, shrouding her in a skintight shield of magic. She could feel the healing energy from her anti-death ability, and the shell normally created by Protection of the Wilds covering her. It was enhanced by the wind element granted by Zephyr, pushing the undead back.

I would have died, Zalia thought.

Pushing her thoughts aside and focusing on the moment, she made the best use she could of the temporary invulnerability she received from the ability.

She stopped worrying about blocking and blows and went completely on the offensive, landing not a small number of strikes as she brutally assaulted her enemy. Despite the relentless nature of her attack, the undead managed to gradually respond to the momentum of the fight as her invulnerability ticked down.

Searching desperately for an advantage, anything she could do to win the fight, Zalia thought about the nature of the corruption that caused these undead to exist. She thought about the effect her healing previously had on the corrupted soldiers and the way it fought with the aura in the very atmosphere around her. With a desperate thought, she pushed her Healing Aura into the undead and it stumbled as if hit by a tangible force.

It slowed, no longer able to outfight her as she regained the upper hand and got in hit after hit. Gritting her teeth, she slammed the blade out of its hand and began methodically dismembering it as it tried to protect its head and body. With lethal efficiency, she finally destroyed the Silver ranked undead Bathar with a brutal strike to its head, cutting all the way through into its body.

The body slid backwards off her blade, falling to the ground with a clank. Zalia ran over and picked up Boreal, scooped Delphi off the wall where he waited, and sprinted up the stairs as the remains of her magical constructs turned to dust behind them.

She took the stairs two at a time on silent feet until she reached the top of the tower above. She gently closed the door behind her and sunk to the floor with her back against it. She gently laid Boreal on the floor and pushed her healing into her, then brought out a little bit of Frozen Heart and fed it to the still breathing feline. She had been protected from the initial strike but had hit the wall pretty hard. She wouldn't be in any mortal danger, but it seemed like Boreal had a few cracked ribs, maybe some broken.

"Death comes."

Ro-ak had said so and she had thought it forewarning of the monster she had seen flying across the land. Maybe it had been, but she had a feeling that this was what he had meant. Death had come for her but she had denied it.

She felt dizzy, the ghost of the blade impaled through her chest sitting cold in her heart. She put her hand to the skin, now fresh and healed due to the nature of the counter-execute healing her Protection of the Wilds ability provided. Her whole body shivered as a tear made its way out from her eye. She sat there petting Boreal for a while until her friend woke up from her unconscious state.

"Mreow," Boreal complained.

"You're lucky to be alive," Zalia told her, "we both are . . ."

"*That memory is not one I would wish to repeat,*" Delphi added.

Zalia gently pulled Boreal close into a tight hug, making sure to be careful of her still-healing ribs.

"You gave me a little bit of a scare there, little one," Zalia whispered.

They were still sat on the floor by the door some thirty minutes later. Their combined healing abilities had taken good care of their physical injuries but the mental strain of the day's events weighed heavily on them. They were lucky that the sound made by their conflict had not awoken the many undead unconscious in the kitchen area.

Despite the mental exhaustion, and the knowledge that they would both be dead if not for their recently acquired abilities that prevented such a fate, Zalia felt hope. Through the pain there was light in the information she now had, the knowledge that her healing could stop the undead. Just the use of Healing Presence alone had been enough to allow her to take down a Silver ranked undead. The ability that had been one of her most powerful from the start, as all her Druid abilities were, and could be used as a weapon against her enemies here.

She would also now be able to explore the section of the keep that was blocked by at least one of the Silver ranked guards on the second floor. She didn't know what was in there but was looking forward to finding out. The last sections of the keep were the only places she realistically thought she would be able to find anything of use on this island. If she didn't manage to then she would need to begin exploring other islands nearby for anything she could use to make her way out of here.

The only other option she really had was staying in Cormaine for such a long time as to rank up and hope she got an ability that would allow her to return home. She didn't think anything of the sort would be possible until much higher ranks, Emerald or Diamond even. Possibly as far as the mysterious further ranks above those.

Still, she didn't resign herself to that future just yet. There was still hope within her, a belief that she could find some way out of Cormaine if she only tried. She had the ritual that Juniper used, which had sent them both here in the first place, after all.

Finding herself nodding off to sleep, Zalia morphed the stone into a small cot for herself and Boreal. It wasn't comfortable per se but she was used to sleeping in trees and on the ground, so she wasn't bothered. She quickly drifted off to sleep and found herself in a dream.

She was floating through the sky of Cormaine amongst countless shades doing the same. Below, an endless dune of red sand swept across the horizon broken only by the sight of dozens of stony islands held aloft by pillars reaching to the ceiling above. It was undoubtedly the same world Zalia now slept in within the waking world, but it was not the same place. She didn't recognise the islands below, though they weren't the biggest discrepancy. Floating between the islands on air alone was a monolithic structure made of a pitch-black stone.

It was shaped like a huge, three-dimensional deltoid, like a kite, only with the top flattened. Flying around the large structure were many of the creatures that now apparently haunted her dreams, the four-legged monstrosity flying on bat wings lit with a dark flame. Amongst them were many other horrific creatures she didn't dare describe, turning her gaze away lest the vision of them be burned into her mind forevermore.

"*Find the prison.*"

The voice spoke within her dream, the entire vision distorting as if it were painted upon a vibrating mirror.

She awoke with a gasp for the second night in a row, managing to avoid throwing Boreal across the room this time. Her thoughts turned as the voice echoed within her mind.

Find the prison.

CHAPTER NINETEEN

Behind the Door

Zalia

Zalia mulled over the dream in her mind as she went through the motions of her morning routine. She had no sense of time anymore, what was day or night, whether it was morning or evening, but since she had just woken up, it was morning in her mind. The voice had sounded much like that of the voice spoken by Ro. While that seemed to imply that the dream had come from the god who Ro represented, she couldn't rule out its source being something more malevolent.

She had already decided the dream was something magical, sent by someone or something as a message. She rarely had dreams she remembered, and even then only fuzzily, yet this one lingered in detail within her mind. That was the main reason but it also stood out as something less like a dream and more of a message in the way that it held images she'd never seen. There were monsters that her own mind could never have come up with and a large prison ship floating through the sky that she'd never seen let alone heard about.

One of the sources she suspected of sending the dream was actually Zayes, the old leader of the Morning's Shade and Juniper's husband. It was one of the logical choices, considering she knew him to be trapped in Cormaine somewhere and most definitely powerful enough to be capable of sending some sort of message like that. Obviously, there could be a whole host of things at play she didn't know about. It wouldn't be out of character for her after all.

Deciding to put the dream to the back of her mind for the moment, she focused on her plans for what to do next. The now unguarded door to the second floor of the keep was her main plan for today, but who knew where that would lead. She could run into another Silver ranked guard or two in the process and was tempted to wait until her anti-death ability came back up for that very reason. Now that she knew about the damage her healing did to them, though, she could attack with a few more abilities that didn't require anything but sight, and sometimes not even that.

Two of her Druid abilities would be useful in that regard, both Healing Presence and Protection of the Wilds, since they were healing abilities that, together, would probably be able to incapacitate a Bronze rank quite quickly based on how much it affected the Silver rank ones. In fact, her ability to clean up the city would be increased significantly by this discovery. She had a feeling that if a creature didn't want her healing, they could deny it or at least fight against it in some way. It was an intuitive feeling, like many others she had about her own abilities, and what that meant for the undead was they must have some inkling of their original self inside them that wanted out. If they didn't they would fight against the healing magic rather than seemingly accepting it.

This only reinforced her determination to clear the undead in the city—to release the souls trapped in their decaying bodies. Initially it had been more so that she could level her abilities but that was now a dot point under the main text.

"Alright, Boreal, want to look around a bit?" Zalia asked.

Boreal hopped up and walked to the door, waiting for Zalia to open it. Taking that as an affirmative, Zalia opened it up and they walked down the two stairwells to the second floor. They stepped through the destroyed door, pushing bits of splintered timber aside, and entered the hallway beyond. Moving quickly to the end, Zalia peeked around the corner to see that the door was now unguarded as she had thought.

They walked up to it and Zalia stuck her head straight through the wood to see the other side. She only put her head through to catch a glimpse before pulling it back, the sensation odd, but less so than the sight. When she passed through the wood with her eyes open it was like looking into a void she couldn't understand, the emptiness was such that her eyes caught on nothing.

Inside the other room appeared to be a sitting area with a few small tables dotted around the space, each with comfortable looking couches. Leading off from the space were two doorways and most importantly, there were no guards. Opening the door and entering, Zalia noticed the other details, like the lush carpet covering the stone floor and the wall decorations spanning from banners to paintings. One wall had a small cabinet that looked to house bottles of liquid within its bottom compartment, fronted with a glass door. The top of it had a few jars with what once may have been appetising snacks but now contained tiny ecosystems within.

Checking around the well-preserved space but seeing nothing immediately of use, she moved on and stuck her head through the rightmost door. It led into another small hallway with a few doors leading off, and finding no guards there either, Zalia opened it up. She moved through the hallway and checked the first door on the right. As she stuck her head through, she had to quickly retreat as a sword came flashing towards her. She summoned her sword, trying to ignore her quickly beating heart and stepped to the side before walking through the wall. She had been able to identify her attacker as only Bronze ranked and so wasn't too worried as she reached the other side.

Having caught her enemy unawares by her strange usage of the wall as a door, Zalia pushed her healing into the undead as she impaled it straight through on her sword. She forced all of her healing power into it, ignoring Boreal and her own health for the moment. She watched as the very flesh and bone making up the undead began disintegrating into chunks and even further into dust before her. It didn't take long; the undead was easy to dodge and almost unable to move, before it turned entirely to dust in front of her eyes.

"That was significantly stronger than I expected," Zalia thought.

Obviously it wasn't something she could do in an extended fight, as she had to keep enough healing focused on Boreal and herself to ensure they wouldn't succumb to the corruption themselves. Being able to quickly focus down an enemy or two that were particularly hard to get rid of while still being able to fight normally would be a large boon though.

She looked around the room and realised it was a bedroom much like the one in the tower, only a little larger and much better decorated. She saw nothing of use and so quickly moved on. The next room was similar, though with no undead in it, so she moved towards the door at the end of the hall. This turned out to be a much larger room that looked fit for a king. She soon realised it was exactly that as she noticed lush decorations, some of them paintings that depicted two royal figures with kindly eyes. In one corner sat a writing desk and Zalia went over to peruse through the papers but found her ability to translate apparently didn't stretch to whatever language this was.

Frustrated, she gathered a few of them to take back with her to her cave. Delphi told her that he couldn't read them either but maybe one of the collective held the memory of the language. Hoping it were true, she moved on to the rest of the room but found nothing of value there either. The items were mostly personal belongings of the apparent royal couple, keepsakes and things whose only value was in the sentiments of two long dead people.

She left those rooms and that corridor and returned to the sitting room, looking towards the other door. Checking that one in a similar manner, she found that there was another corridor with doors splitting off. At the end of the hallway before a door, however, stood another Silver guard, in armour this time with a halberd at their side. She quickly ducked her head back and prepared for a fight. She didn't know if it had seen or heard her, but she wasn't about to wait and find out. She quickly summoned a few traps and placed them around the door, nudging Boreal to do the same.

As Boreal followed her instruction, Zalia summoned her bow and prepared to shoot at whatever entered the room. There were a few moments of silence before two footfalls sounded and the guard exploded through the door with shocking force. It immediately twisted in the air to land, avoiding a bear trap but snagging a trip wire. Zalia put on Hunter's Mark and activated both Nature's Wrath and Protection of the Wilds, pushing Healing Presence into it at the same time. She released arrows and began casting rituals on the creature as it struggled free of its cage.

It managed to break free but was severely wounded by the time it did, its flesh stripping away at the power of her healing magic. The nature of the counter-execute healing provided by Protection of the Wild's protective shell meant it had taken constantly scaling damage from the ability. Summoned by Nature's Wrath, two wind elementals locked down the guard with lassos made from the very air around the guard, holding it even further immobile as Zalia continued letting off shots.

Boreal joined in with a full power Pounce, freezing its legs to the floor and climbing up its back to assume her usual tactic of savagely assaulting its spine. Zalia had to readjust her aim to avoid hitting Boreal but the damage-over-time left by her heirloom bow's abilities was beginning to stack enough to do some serious damage.

It didn't take long before the guard slumped to the floor, lifeless, unable to escape the grasp of Boreal's ice, Zalia's spreading ice curse, and the wind elemental's lassos while weakened by the focused attention of Zalia's Healing Presence. Against any other Silver rank she would probably die within moments, but the stacked advantages in number, abilities that countered, and its weakened state allowed them the easy victory. Those factors helped Zalia win, along with her immediate use of her two long cooldown abilities—now that she knew just exactly how strong these undead were. She wasn't about to volunteer for being impaled again anytime soon.

She stepped past the disintegrating body of the undead and moved into the hallway, passing through the exploded door. There was an open door on the right that held a war room with maps, though no troop placements stood on the central table. The maps made her pause, though, as she expected them to be of the lands near Endaria, the place she thought the Bathar to have come from. The landscapes were nothing like she expected, however, with the land looking more like a chain of islands than a landmass amongst the ocean. It was nowhere she remembered seeing on her own map of Endaria that she'd left back in the other world.

So was this city not brought here from Endaria? Zalia wondered.

If that was true then Ember was entirely wrong about what had happened with the Bathar in Endaria; it was possible they weren't even from there in the first place.

CHAPTER TWENTY

Frog Flight

Zalia

Putting her ponderings as to the origin of the Bathar aside, Zalia checked the other room and found it was a library of sorts. It had many odd shelves with storage spaces in a diagonal square pattern with scrolls filed away in them. Despite the quite well-preserved interior of the castle, many of the scrolls were in a decayed state, bad enough that she didn't touch them. There might be some magical way to preserve or refurbish them that she didn't know about and destroying ancient knowledge wasn't really on her list of things to do today.

While many were in a bad state, possibly as a result of being ancient even before the fall of the city they resided in, some were still good. Unfortunately, much like the rest of the writing she had found, it was unreadable for her. Annoyed at her inability to understand the possible information she had found, Zalia exited the room, leaving everything in its place. She wanted to go hit something but knew it was unwise to try the two Silver guards until her anti-death and long cooldown abilities were back up. That meant she had almost an entire day to kill.

She could have tried to get past the guards with her new teleport ability but deemed the idea unwise, the risk too great. She had a look over her ability level ups from killing the couple of high-ranked guards.

Congratulations! Hunter's Mark has reached Iron 16.
Congratulations! Nature's Wrath has reached Iron 14.
Congratulations! Protection of the Wilds has

> **gained two levels, reaching Iron 12.**
> **Congratulations! Druid class has gained**
> **two levels, reaching Iron 12.**

She'd ignored the messages since they didn't hold anything exciting and quickly cleared them away. Some of her Hunter abilities were getting quite close to a rank up but her Herbalist abilities were falling far behind. Then she realised that, hey, maybe that was something she could spend her day doing. She had quite a few plants now that she didn't need, as well as the Water Lily she had already planted. Maybe starting a garden near her cave and searching some other islands for herbs would be a good idea.

With that in mind, Zalia went back up to the tower and using the ritual for her wings, she gave a set to Boreal and Delphi too.

"*This will be a new experience,*" Delphi said nervously.

"Don't worry about it, you'll be fine," Zalia comforted.

"Mreow," Boreal said.

"Yeah, exactly, Boreal will catch you if you fall," Zalia translated.

"*Comforting,*" Delphi replied deadpan.

They took off from the balcony, Delphi flying around near the ground experimentally for a moment. The flying frog was an odd sight to see, but it would be the fastest way home and Zalia definitely wanted to spend the least amount of time as possible out in the open. They eventually made it across the city, up a pillar, and back over to the island they all called home. Delphi was quite wobbly to begin with and both Boreal and Zalia had to slow down to make sure he didn't fall, but the little frog eventually got a handle on it.

When they arrived back, Zalia left the few pieces of parchment she had collected near to the pond edge of their cave home while Delphi dove into the water to meet up with the collective. It would take a while as they sorted through and thoroughly investigated each memory so Zalia and Boreal had some time. She started with pushing some healing energy into the Water Lilies, watching as their slightly withered stems came back to full life and slowly grew.

She definitely needed to stay around or at least come back to the pond often enough to keep them alive, otherwise the corrupting aura, which was somewhat fainter down in the cave, would wither them much like the trees outside. Looking over at the small wooden shrine dedicated to the nameless god that spoke through Ro, Zalia had a thought. Even though the shrine was ancient and the tree it had been made from was long dead, she had been able to make it grow roots with her ability. When she had pushed her healing into it, she had thought that was the doing of the god but now considered it differently.

It was very possible her own Druid ability was just capable of "healing" a plant to that degree. She left the cave to head outside and walked over to the nearest tree. She started pushing her healing into it, and to her surprise the tree began untwisting with a cracking sound, leaves sprouting from its dead branches. Within a few minutes, a healthy-looking, though still otherworldly, tree stood in front of her. It had strange blue, glowing leaves that released a light pollen coating as the wind blew through them, with the pollen dissipating soon after it left the leaf. She stopped funneling her healing into the tree and watched as the leaves slowly wilted and died, the trunk twisting in on itself once more with a horrid creaking sound. Before long, it matched the forest around it, dead and corrupt.

Zalia began using her earth and stone manipulation provided by the Physical Resistance passive to funnel a good chunk of dirt into the cave. Over the course of the next hour or two, she dug an extra cavern space shooting off from the pool room and filled the floor with a thick coating of dirt. She got some more of the purple, glowing mushrooms from the entrance cave, using the stone manipulation to help plant them into the walls of the new room as her healing provided them with a boost to get settled.

Then, she began planting a few of the bits and pieces she still held within her Stasis storage. Bitterbalm was the one she started with, despite it being replicable with her ability now. It was still a good herb to use with any cooking she would need to do, though it didn't make the grey creature any more pleasant. She pushed some of the pieces containing more stem into the dirt and focused her Healing Presence onto them. She watched in awe as small Bitterbalm plants slowly grew out of the stems, branching into the little bush shapes they took naturally. Granted, it was only an Iron rank herb and one of the most common herbs she had that grew everywhere, from what she knew, but it was still amazing.

She was kind of irritated that she hadn't thought of trying this before, as she had been focused mostly on the healing that the ability provided to people.

"*Infinite herbs*," she thought.

And it was true, to a degree. She would probably be able to farm herbs using the combination of her Herbalist class and Druid class. In fact, she was a little surprised that her Herbalist class hadn't come with any ability to grow herbs in the first place. Well, she wasn't complaining either way, though she would have to test if it worked on Bronze or even Silver herbs. Her guess was no. At least, not as effectively.

She tried Snow-leaf next and found it was significantly less effective. It only managed to get the herbs to spread a few small roots into the dirt, barely turning it from an herb into a plant.

Still need the right growing conditions, I guess, Zalia thought.

Well, that was significantly less useful than she was hoping but still good. She wouldn't be able to grow herbs like Flame-root or Zephyr without first replicating their natural growing environments. That wasn't impossible to accomplish in the short term, but making it a more permanent effect would be harder.

That brought her thoughts to her ritual lifespan. Nothing she knew how to make yet was permanent in any way and barely lasted for longer than a few minutes to a few hours. What if she could make something a little more permanent?

CHAPTER TWENTY-ONE

Planting

Zalia

Fiddling around with her rituals for a while, Zalia found that by forcibly extending how long it took to activate them, and by pushing more material into them, she could actually make ritual effects last longer. Usually she only used the rituals in combat, but with this she could use them in the way they were traditionally used. She found the rituals that she pushed a lot of Manifest into seemed to last a much more significant amount of time as well, some even reaching the point where she didn't need to maintain her concentration on the magical structure anymore.

Wishing once again that she had played around with it more earlier, she tried something a little more complicated. Digging a tiny room big enough for only a few plants off from the main nursery, she dug out a pit in the floor and began performing a long ritual. The main component was Snowleaf with a Bitterbalm minor to convert the element to lava. She also began funneling Manifest into the ritual for as long as she could manage. Once a small pool of lava filled the pit she stopped funneling the two main components in and continued with Manifest for as long as she could concentrate.

She was there for maybe an hour before her mind finally wandered off, her concentration breaking and the ritual circle fading. In front of her sat a pool of lava that radiated heat into the small offshoot room. The temperature of the liquid hadn't seemed to cool since she had started the ritual, but the moment of truth was whether it would maintain that without her constant attention and magical input. Concentrating for that long had funneled almost all of the mana out of her.

She watched happily as the lava bubbled away quietly, never cooling and not yet dissipating. Now it was just a matter of how long the lava would stick around for. Deciding to hedge her bets, she still planted one of her few Flame-roots and started pushing healing into it. Much as she expected, it started growing only significantly slower than the Bitterbalm. What it didn't do, however, was stagnate, continuing the slow growth as long as she pushed energy into it.

She repeated the process only using ice and snow for the Frozen Heart and Snow-leaf, creating a tiny icy biome in one corner of the main room. It was far enough away from the lava room to hopefully not interact too much and cancel out the temperature in between. With both her Bronze rank herbs now planted, she left the nursery and came out to find Boreal and Ro playing a game of chasey while Delphi watched intently from his perch near the pool.

"*This is a new memory. Boreal would normally be a predator of such a creature as Ro, would she not?*" Delphi asked in Zalia's mind.

"Yes, though I don't think Boreal ever would attack Ro for real. They're friends," Zalia explained.

"*Hmm, like a strange dysfunctional collective. Interesting,*" Delphi hummed.

"Which you're somewhat a part of now, aren't ya, little guy," Zalia said.

She laughed as Delphi turned to her and managed to convey a put-upon emotion in his stance. Zalia realised she had been thinking of Delphi as male but had never asked. She wasn't a frog professional.

"*Are you a male of your species?*" she asked mentally.

"*Our gender changes based on the needs of the collective. I am both and neither,*" Delphi replied.

Oh, interesting.

"*Would you describe yourself as a typical female of your species? The collective has deduced this as your gender and believe you are stuck with one throughout life. The reason we have made this deduction i—*" Delphi asked before being cut off by Zalia.

"*I wouldn't say there is really any typical example of a female, and we aren't necessarily stuck with one gender. There are ways for people to change their body if it doesn't fit their mind. I don't really know much about my own people, I'll admit. I am kind of a . . . solo type of person. Not really a fan of being in a collective—with my own race at least,*" Zalia explained, interrupting before the frog explained its assumptions about her biology.

"*Hmm, understood. What are these methods you speak of? We don't believe you have any biological method of doing so, but we may be wrong,*" Delphi asked.

"Not an expert, couldn't tell you. I just know it's possible," Zalia replied.

Boreal stopped chasing Ro, and Ro turned right back around to start chasing Boreal. She quickly took off with a slight scramble on the ice, running around the room and taking the chase to the air as she began running up the walls.

"She's still a child," Zalia pointed out to Delphi.

"*Yes, our young are much the same,*" Delphi replied.

"Boundless energy right? It's exhausting sometimes. I don't even need to sleep much anymore and yet it still makes me tired," Zalia said.

"*You need not sleep?*" Delphi asked curiously.

"Nah, a passive drastically reduces it. Still need some every now and then though," Zalia explained.

She mentally dismissed the slowly intensifying notification that declared her Low Light vision had increased by four to Iron five and sat down on a stool she fashioned quickly from the stone floor. She watched as Boreal ran upside down across the ceiling as icy holds appeared in front of her.

"I don't really know what I'm doing," Zalia admitted.

"*What do you mean?*" Delphi asked.

"Well, neither Boreal nor I are from this world. Hell, I'm not even from the same world as Boreal. I've just been kind of swept from place to place trying to survive but otherwise I don't really have any . . . goals," Zalia explained.

"*What do you need goals for? There is not much more to life than collecting memories and passing them on to the next generation,*" Delphi said.

"For you that may be true. I have no plans of having a future generation and many of my people do live for such lofty goals. Most of the time I'm alright, just living, surviving off the land and my own hard work, but sometimes . . . sometimes I feel lost. Lost in the hell of an unknown world," Zalia replied.

"*I understand, I guess. You are unable to pass on the memories within your mind much as we do. When you die, the memories die with you, something our species considers one of the greatest tragedies,*" Delphi said mournfully.

"That kind of covers it. I'm also quite lost on how to get out of Cormaine. Your people don't know anything about rituals, do you?" Zalia asked.

"*Rituals are not one of the subjects we have many memories about. We would not be able to help in this, most likely,*" Delphi replied.

Delphi perked up, standing from their sitting position.

"*The collective believes it has found the translation for this language. Our memories of it are old, very old, yet remain intact. The few pieces of paper you have collected here are messages directed towards various people. Many talk of evacuation plans to a place called Endaria, which resides within the sister lands. We cannot figure out what that means from the context, though reading more may provide further details,"* Delphi said.

Evacuation to Endaria?

"Endaria is where we came from before arriving here. It's on another world as far as I'm aware," Zalia said.

It felt like she had been handed a piece of the puzzle, but it was a middle piece that she didn't have any of the connecting parts to. She knew there was some significant information there, she just didn't know what it was yet. At the very least, it disproved Ember's idea that the kingdom of Endaria had stolen the land the Bathar lived on. Zalia had just found it.

"Thank you for the help. Think you'll be able to read the rest of it now without the collective?" Zalia asked.

"Certainly, the right memories have been sent to me," Delphi said.

There was a deep rumbling sound, the ground beneath them vibrating as a crack resounded from far away. Zalia dashed to the surface as she heard another crack and the sound of stone falling. It took her a moment of searching around, but she saw off in the distance a mass of shades around an island in a frenzy. A tumbling pillar slowly fell, knocking over another, and within moments, the entire island began to fall from the sky.

It tumbled end over end as debris and the remains of pillars fell through the sky with it, eventually hitting the ground with an ear-splitting boom, a cloud of dust exploding into the air. Glad it wasn't the island with the ruins on it that had fallen, Zalia quickly retreated back into the cave while the cries of torment from the shades above turned to angry whispering.

"What was that?" Delphi's question came to her mind.

"An island fell," Zalia replied, sending her memory of it to Delphi.

"A precious memory, to be certain. We have no memories of this occurring before," Delphi said.

That was a little concerning. Now that she thought about it, that had been the direction she had seen the monster flying. She was torn between waiting for her cooldowns and going off to search another of the islands, though that one having fallen from the sky made her a little less keen to be outside at that moment. She'd have to wait until the shades settled once more.

So Zalia did what she did best and started practicing. She used the ritual for her wings and began trying to float as stably in place as she could, going so far as to sit cross-legged in the air as her wings flapped. It was hard work on her back, but with her increased strength and apparently unchanged weight, Zalia managed to hold the position with her body just fine. The trouble was with the wings but that was what she was here to practise.

After that, she went through the motions of her sword practice, keeping form and focus as Boreal fell from the ceiling, bowling into her legs. Despite the annoyance at Boreal's shenanigans, Zalia knew it was good training to keep her focus, so she let it go. She wished she had some moving targets to train her archery with because she realistically couldn't accomplish anything without them.

Despite that, she dropped into her focused-yet-absent mindset she often took when training. She spent the next remaining hours hard at work as she waited for the abilities to come off cooldown.

Eventually, two levels in sword proficiency and five in flight later, Zalia felt her abilities come off cooldown. She put Delphi on Boreal's back, and together they exited the caves. Outside, under the power of Zalia's rituals, they flew up, across, and back down to the island holding the ruins of the Bathar city. They reentered the keep and made their way to the bottom floor, ready to fight.

CHAPTER TWENTY-TWO

Translation

Zalia

Zalia peeked around the corner of the hallway towards where the two guards stood vigilantly in front of a door. The sparsely decorated hall would have been an excellent fighting location for Zalia due to its straight and narrow path if it weren't for the fact that there was an entrance to the kitchen on her left. The horde of Bronze and Iron rank undead in there was a risk she had been willing to take when she was fighting only two Bronze guards, but in a fight with these two she wouldn't be able to hold them all off. She wasn't entirely certain that trying to take down these two guards was a good decision in the first place.

One solution she had was to bring the fight to the undead kitchen staff herself, running in there with the Silver guards following and using her big area of effect spells to lock them all down. It would certainly have helped if she was able to choose the location of the fight herself rather than needing to play around, trying to make as little sound as possible to not wake them.

First though, she had to get into the room those two guards were standing at the door of so she could see what rank they were inside. Her solution to that was quite simple. Using her stone manipulation, Zalia dug at the wall until it was thin enough that she was able to simply step through into the room beyond. The way the corridor turned left then right once more allowed for this as she stuck her head through the wall to look inside. The room was the one she had seen from above through the glass ceiling and it sat exactly as she remembered.

Along the sides nearest the entrance sat two tables that were equidistant from each other and their closest walls. Lining the walls on either side sat sixteen banners, eight on each side. Nearer to the end of the long room was another large table with seats facing the entrance and a huge thorny throne against the far wall. Zalia thought it looked something like a throne room set up for a meeting of nobles from across the lands. She could see the one banner she recognised from her place as half a head stuck through a wall. It was the Y-shaped imagery with tree-like growths coming from the top of each prong. From this angle she could also see that it appeared to be slightly stylised in the manner of a crow's foot.

Did the Bathar revere whichever god was the one who had spoken to Zalia through Ro?

Remembering her conversation with the starlight wolf back in Endaria, Zalia did recall the wolf had said the Bathar once revered the old gods. She scanned the other banners and saw one that looked like it might be a starry sky with a howling wolf on it. As she looked at each, they all appeared to represent a type of animal with an element of nature alongside it. She didn't recognise any of the other animals but did identify them as such.

She turned her attention away from the banners momentarily to check the rank of the undead in the room. From this viewpoint she could see another two guards that stood at attention towards the end of the hall on either side of the throne, and paying closer attention, she saw another figure. Masked amongst the thorny throne sat a figure with its head resting upon a leaning arm. The king.

A similarly themed crown sat upon the monarch's head and two green glowing eyes peeked out from a fleshless, grinning skull. As Zalia looked at the monarch, her eyes tried to slide off the undead as if they were being compelled not to see him. She couldn't identify any rank from here, but seeing as he was awake, he must have been at least Silver rank, maybe higher.

She pulled her head out of the wall and slowly backed away from the throne room, throwing aside all plans of fighting the Silver guards. An extra room of undead containing at least another three Silver rank Bathar was something she was very much not ready for. Maybe if she came back when she was fully Bronze rank or even Silver she could manage, but as it was, this was an unwinnable fight for her.

She left the bottom floor entirely and went up to the keep's tower, trying to decide on her next course of action. The list on the wall of her cavern had marked into it the objective of finding a way of harming, killing, or hiding reliably from the shades in the sky but she wasn't really in the mood to be swarmed by shadow-wielding ghosts at the moment. Instead, she decided to go and search another island.

The closest one was, if facing towards her island from here, towards the right. It was unfortunately much further away than her home island and the Bathar ruin island were from each other, but with her flight it wouldn't be so tedious bridging over.

"*I think we best search another island*," Zalia mentally told Delphi.

"*What did you see in that room?*" Delphi asked.

Zalia sent the images from her mind to the memory-obsessed frog and cast her air wing ritual on each of them. Ro came flying in through the open door from the balcony and landed on the ground, looking at Boreal.

"I think there is a banner dedicated to your god downstairs, Ro," Zalia said.

Ro-ak looked at Zalia and tilted his head, letting out a quiet croak. As he did that, she saw a shiny object held in his beak.

"What's that?" Zalia asked.

Ro-ak hopped over and dropped the metallic object to the ground with a soft clatter. She looked at the twisted metal for a moment before recognising it as what might have once been a spoon.

"Where did you find this?" she asked.

Ignoring the question, Ro-ak hopped over to Boreal and began cleaning her fur.

"*I believe we may have some information regarding these banners*," Delphi said.

"Oh?" Zalia said questioningly.

"*I do not have the information with me but I believe one of our members does. I shall ask when we go back*," Delphi explained.

"So . . . you know that one of the collective knows something, but you don't know what they know, you just know they do?" Zalia asked.

There was a pause before a reply came.

"*Yes*," Delphi said.

"Wonderful," Zalia said dryly.

"*I would like to go and read some more of the texts in this keep before we leave for another island*," Delphi said.

"Oh right, forgot about that. Yeah, that would be good, maybe we can translate that map of the city we found," Zalia suggested.

Most of the city was completely worn down or rubble but it would be good to get an idea of where any bigger or central structures may have been. Searching each and every building would take forever but some of the more important places may have been structurally sound or enchanted.

"*That would indeed be a good memory to have*," Delphi replied.

"So, library, then another island. Any problems with that, you two?" Zalia asked, looking at Boreal and Ro-ak.

Boreal and Ro-ak stopped cleaning each other and looked at her blankly.

"I'll take that as a no," she said.

They moved to the second floor and made their way to the library where Delphi asked Zalia to open and display various pieces of parchment. Zalia even held Delphi up so she could see them clearly. They also went and gathered the other scrolls and notes from what Zalia thought to be the king's bedroom. It took quite a while to go through everything but Boreal and Ro-ak weren't bothered; they played in the corners of the room and searched the ancient dust for secrets.

Delphi managed to translate the central map of the city, finding the locations of a town hall, central market, barracks, a magic research facility, and many other locations. A few of them were mediocre, boring things she didn't care about but some of the former were quite interesting to her. The magic research facility was one of those things and she hoped that it had remained intact at least somewhat.

Delphi also translated quite a few of the scrolls in the library room but most of them were reports of various kinds about income, production, and other managerial points.

There was one thing they did find that Zalia was instantly interested in for various reasons. It was a report they had found on the desk of the king that detailed locations of newly discovered rituals in their own kingdom. The descriptions of the rituals eerily matched what Zalia had seen firsthand in Endaria and what she remembered from the in-depth ritual sheet she had taken from Juniper. That disturbed her greatly.

It seemed like, for one reason or the other, the same rituals that had been happening in Endaria had also taken place here, and based on the fact that they had found the report on the king's desk, as well as the larger list and map they had found in the library, it had been happening right as the kingdom fell.

She knew what that meant, logically thinking. It meant that the same rituals happening in Endaria had caused the destruction of this region, and was likely the reason for the Bathar peoples' downfall. She didn't know if it had transported the city here to Cormaine from the world Endaria sat upon, or if it had somehow managed to transform Cormaine into the hellscape it now was, but either idea was terrifying.

"Do you have any memory of my race?" Zalia asked Delphi.

"*Hmm, some of our most ancient memories from when the collective lived on the surface have images of other races, yes. There was a race much like yours, but much shorter and with significantly less weight to them,*" Delphi explained.

"A shorter race? I don't know about an— Oh wait, what did they call themselves?" Zalia asked.

"There were a few different types of their kind that we had interactions with. The ones we most commonly interacted with were Those Born of the Watery Depths. There were a few other kinds, such as Those Born of Wind and Sky an—" Delphi replied.

"And Those Born of Heat and Stone," Zalia interrupted.

"You know of them? We have not seen their kind for many a cycle," Delphi asked.

"Yeah, a good friend of mine, Glemp, is one," Zalia said.

The fact that Delphi knew of Glemp's people and even knew of some types that she had never met gave life to the theory that this city, named Hetheir, that they had discovered, had been sent here from the same world as Endaria. They had found no mention of Endaria within the reports of ritual discoveries, the only mention being that first piece they had translated. Though she supposed that much like the Bathar people, the Nature Born, as she decided to call them, could have fled this world to the other.

"I don't suppose you remember where those people lived, do you?" Zalia asked.

"No, they always came to us asking for hints of the future. To a degree, they revered us, as is expected," Delphi explained.

"As is expected?" Zalia asked in disbelief.

"Of course, our powers have helped many different peoples in their times of need. Through our long memory and sight of the future we have gathered much wisdom over the cycles. We even knew you would come to us," Delphi replied.

"Then how come you didn't come talk to me the few times I came down to observe you before I reached out?" Zalia asked.

"We were observing you also," Delphi said simply.

Wonderful.

"Well, oh wise frog of the deeps, what shall I find upon the next island I visit, then?" Zalia asked sarcastically.

"You shall find that which grows, and remnants of a god," Delphi said.

"Funny," Zalia told him, looking over to Boreal giving her a look like, can you believe this frog?

"Not at all. My words hold no humour," Delphi told her.

"Wait, you're serious?" Zalia asked.

"Quite," Delphi said.

CHAPTER TWENTY-THREE

Bread

Zalia

Boreal, Zalia, Delphi, and Ro-ak stood side by side at the edge of the new island they were here to explore. They had left the keep and the ruins of the Bathar city, Hetheir, soon after Delphi had pronounced that they would find not only "that which grows," which Zalia had taken to be some type of herb or plant, but also the remnants of a god. Both were things that Zalia definitely wanted to find.

Why Delphi had not told them about this earlier, they would not say. Either way, Boreal wasn't much bothered. She knew that she could trust Zalia to lead them, the feeling even stronger after Zalia had taken a blade through the chest for her. Her cracked ribs had long healed now, but the feeling of Zalia's healing pushing away the throbbing pain only leant to further her love of the tall one.

The island before them was forested, much as the one that held their cave home was, only it was much thicker. As they began moving into the woods, Zalia strode through the thick undergrowth with barely a hint of effort, her long legs lending her greater mobility. Boreal on the other hand, struggled somewhat more with her short legs, having to jump up and down over obstructions that Zalia could simply step over. Boreal used her shadow teleport to keep up but couldn't help but be envious of Delphi's place on Zalia's shoulder.

"Does the collective have any memories of bread?" Zalia asked into the air.

She had been doing that a lot as of late, but she knew that Delphi was having a conversation with her. Boreal had had her own mental conversations with Delphi as well, though their topics strayed far from the worries on Zalia's mind.

Jumping over a log, Boreal crouched behind it and looked back, waiting. When Ro hopped over, Boreal pounced, causing her friend to jump back in alarm before realising it was her. Meanwhile, she sat nonchalantly, cleaning her paw. Ro gave her a look that she knew meant she would receive payback for that one later but she didn't mind. Their little games definitely made the days much less tedious. She loved Zalia but she could be awfully serious sometimes.

"It's a pretty basic food that my people very commonly eat. I just realised I haven't had it in quite a while and am kinda craving it," Zalia said.

Ignoring the half conversation she could hear, Boreal peered into the woods around herself, trying to find something interesting. She saw a little plant pad sitting on the ground and padded up to inspect it. She gave it a sniff but couldn't identify anything weird about it. It looked squishy, soft like a nice patch of grass. She lifted one paw and poked at the pad, and it instantly snapped closed around her front leg. She was about to give a loud meow of alarm when she was pulled off her feet and got the breath knocked out of her.

"I wish I could, but I don't really have the ingredients to make it here. I'd need some kind of raising agent and a type of flour," Zalia continued saying.

The pad-turned-trap started being pulled through the woods, dragging Boreal with it. Recovering her breath, she managed to start struggling and began furiously scratching at it.

"*Help!*" she mentally said to Zalia.

"Maybe I could make Bitterb—" Zalia said, interrupting herself. "Boreal, whatever you and Ro are doing, ba— Oh shit!"

She cut off as she noticed Boreal being dragged away by the leg. With a sound like a drop of water hitting a pool, Zalia appeared right next to Boreal, already swinging her sword.

Zalia swung a second time at the vine holding Boreal and finally cut through. She quickly checked their surroundings to see if there was any threat and seeing none, levered off the pad that was firmly wrapped around Boreal's leg.

"What the hell is this?" Zalia asked.

Boreal sent an image of her prodding the pad with her leg, a feeling of shame attached to it.

"Your curiosity is going to get you killed some day, I swear," Zalia reprimanded.

She held up the piece of plant and inspected it.

> **Living Trapvine - Bronze rank - Use in a
> ritual to add an element of Mind.**

"Element of Mind, that could be cool," Zalia muttered.

She glared at Boreal once more, who, for her part, looked regretful—regretful, yet too damn cute.

"It's alright Boreal, it's bound to happen. You just have to be a little more careful, ok?" Zalia said.

"Mreow," Boreal replied softly.

"I know it looks comfortable but there is a lot of danger here. We don't know anything about this island," Zalia explained.

Boreal let out a quiet mew.

"It's alright, you don't need to apologise, just take care of yourself," Zalia said with a sigh.

Zalia turned away, inspecting the plant, but she didn't miss Ro-ak hopping over to comfort Boreal out of the corner of her eye. Unfortunately her Herbal Magic ability wouldn't be able to tell her the uses for the new plant until she reached Bronze rank, but the element of Mind could be super useful to her. Even just considering the two herb combinations, she might be able to perform with it made her excited. Something such as mixing Frozen Heart and the Trapvine could possibly provide a type of mental healing. Something that might even be able to heal the trauma those men in the army camp suffered from.

She put the thought aside and stored the piece of plant in her Stasis ability's storage and looked back to their surroundings. After she had chopped the vine, it had simply fallen to the floor inert, as if she had cut off its head. It felt off to her that the plant would keep its mind in the part of it that was the trap. It had also been dragging Boreal off somewhere else, which made her think it might be a smaller part of a whole. Maybe whatever it was actually had a bigger central part to it.

She explained her thoughts to her companions and began carefully following the vine limb. It led down a winding path for a few hundred metres until Zalia saw where exactly it was headed. She didn't know what lived in this forest that the monstrosity before her fed upon, but there must have been something for it to have grown this large. Growing out the top of a large stone structure sat a bulb with flowering leaves spiralling outwards from the central hole in its top. Coming out of the hole were perhaps six dozen different vine lengths, each spreading out to a different section of the forest.

She observed it quietly before retreating into the forest to think. The stone structure that the bulb was growing out of had a symbol that she recognised from the city ruins back on the other island. It was the Y-shaped crow's foot stylised like a tree, only this one was a metal fascia that sat upon the wall above the entrance to the building.

As they retreated, Ro-ak spoke for the first time in a long time.

"*A piece. Find the piece,*" Ro-ak croaked.

"A piece?" Zalia said questioningly.

"*A piece,*" Ro-ak agreed.

"A piece of what?" she asked.

There was no response as Ro looked away and went back to his normal self. She was momentarily frustrated by the vagueness of the words but remembered Delphi's own. The remnants of a god. Might she find a piece of whoever the god was that spoke through Ro?

She already had the altar dedicated to the god back in her cave, but a remnant may mean something else. With that in mind, she decided she would definitely need to find a way into that building. The best chances of that happening unfortunately lay in the killing of this sentient plant. Something about that didn't quite sit right with her, however, an instinct told her that doing such a thing would be wrong.

Alright then, maybe she could remove it from the building or at least befriend it. If it could even move. Or be befriended.

"Know what this thing is?" Zalia asked Delphi.

"*This is that which grows,*" Delphi replied.

"No way—do you know what it *is,*" Zalia repeated.

"*The collective has never come across this plant life before but we have seen that a peaceful arrangement is possible,*" Delphi said.

"Why don't you tell me these things before I ask you?" Zalia asked with frustration in her voice.

"*I already told you that knowing what is to come may change the very future that was seen. Unless what we see is disastrous, there is no need to change the memories to come,*" Delphi explained.

"I guess that is fair enough," Zalia admitted.

Delphi was silent though she could tell they wanted to say more. Maybe there was something they couldn't say lest it break the future they deemed to be 'non-disastrous.' It seemed like a terribly frustrating way to live now that she thought about it, knowing the future yet unable to voice it lest the new future be worse.

"Didn't you say that Those Born of the Watery Depths often came to the collective to see their futures?" Zalia asked.

"I did, and that was the truth. Only rarely would we tell them anything and only when deemed important to do so by the collective. If I were to deviate from what I'm allowed to say without the collective wisdom of thousands of cycles to guide my words, I may cause a tragedy. It has happened before," Delphi explained.

"So you could tell me more if you were with the collective?" Zalia asked.

"Maybe, the importance is in knowing what is safe to say and what is not. Separate from them, I do not know," Delphi replied.

It . . . made sense. As much as she would like to know the future she would just have to trust that Delphi and the collective knew better. Hell, they definitely knew better considering just how long they must have been peering into the future and preserving those memories in the minds of their next generations.

"Right, you said that a peaceful arrangement is possible?" Zalia asked.

"Yes, though I cannot say how. This you must figure out yourself," Delphi said.

Well, that was great. She would just have to trust in her Druidic instincts, they had gotten her through similar trials before. She would just need to figure out what she could offer to a large, possibly carnivorous, living bulb that lived in an ancient temple to a long dead god. How hard could that be?

"Got any ideas, Boreal?" Zalia asked, turning to where Boreal was politely sitting and waiting for her to think.

"Mreow?" Boreal asked questioningly.

"Oh, right—any ideas about what we can give this giant plant thing that will make it friendly towards us?" she amended.

"Friend?" Boreal said questioningly.

"That is the plan, yes," Zalia said.

Boreal looked down at the floor for a moment before looking back up. Despite Zalia knowing Boreal was quite intelligent, this was obviously not something she was good at.

"Feed?" Boreal suggested.

"That's certainly an idea, yes," Zalia replied dryly.

Boreal looked up at her expectantly.

"Alright, we'll try it," Zalia conceded.

CHAPTER TWENTY-FOUR

Don't Forget to Water Your Plants

Zalia

Zalia had a few thoughts about what exactly she would feed the giant plant. It definitely ate meat as showcased by its attempt to eat Boreal, but that didn't necessarily mean that it wouldn't eat plant matter too. Zalia also knew that eating things that were a higher rank usually tended to . . . not taste better, but had an energy to it that was invigorating. She could feed it some of the grey creatures but those tasted horrible and she doubted it would enjoy such an offering.

Neither did she want to feed one of the undead to it for obvious reasons. So, the first thing she decided to try was one of her higher rank herbs.

"How do you think we can get close to it without it trying to eat us?" Zalia asked the others.

"*You don't have to get close to it, you could try placing something on one of its pads,*" Delphi suggested.

"Hmm, that is an idea, but how will it know if it came from us? We don't even know it will attack us if we approach though, to be fair," Zalia added.

"*Try!*" Boreal said mentally, sending an image of Zalia placing herbs onto a pad.

Boreal was getting much better at sending mental images that weren't things she had seen before. Zalia had quite the little artist on her hands.

"Alright, I'll try it," Zalia conceded, thinking about what herbs she had.

Bronze rank was the highest rank of herb she currently had and out of those the Water Lily was most likely to be well received. Even when Zalia ate it she felt a nice refreshing wave pass through her body, presumably from the water element it contained.

They followed one of the vines out, thankfully not being nearly as far away as the first one they had encountered. Pulling a little bit of the Water Lily out of her Stasis, Zalia quickly placed it on the pad and jumped back. The herb just sat there idly on top with absolutely no reaction from the pad.

"Maybe it doesn't like to eat plants?" Zalia questioned.

Boreal picked up a big stick in her mouth and pressed it down hard on the pad. It immediately shut closed around the herb and stick, dragging them off into the forest at speed. Zalia glared after Boreal as the feline sprinted off into the forest after the retreating limb.

"Can't take you anywhere," Zalia muttered, following after.

They chased it through the woods until they arrived back at the building hosting the bulb of the large Trapvine. The vine limb coiled into the bulb's mouth at the top and the entire thing closed shut in a rotating motion.

They waited for a while, watching the bulb sit idle before it opened up once more, the vine slowly extending back out again with its pad empty. As far as Zalia could tell, the plant had absolutely no reaction to what it ate.

"Hmm, what rank do you think it is?" Zalia asked.

Normally she could just say that it was Bronze since she had harvested a piece of it that was that rank, but she knew from the Water Lily that different parts of a plant could have different ranks. There was no reason to assume this plant wasn't the same.

"*Silver, possibly Gold,*" Delphi said.

"Are you saying that or do you know that?" Zalia asked.

"*An assumption based on its size and the rank of its lesser parts,*" Delphi explained.

"I suppose walking up to it would be a stupid thing to do," Zalia said, entirely considering doing just that.

"*Probably,*" Delphi replied.

There was a moment of silence.

"*You're going to do it anyway, aren't you?*" Delphi asked.

"Yeahhh," Zalia said, stepping towards the building.

The ground sloped downwards towards the central structure forming an almost caldera-shaped area remotely free from trees. Lining the slope were the many vines, but Zalia just avoided those, stepping closer. As she moved towards it, she noticed that the shades were avoiding flying close to the bulb—avoiding it more so than they usually avoided the ground. Their new flight pattern created a dome-like structure as the group kept their distance.

"*Hmm*," Zalia thought.

She didn't really know what the shades were or if they were even tangible, but she had seen one form from Juniper's death. To her, that said the shades were either some sort of soul or they were the latent consciousness of the person, kept in existence by the corruption in this place. Maybe this Trapvine had somehow come to exist in its current state—alive, and possibly even sapient or sentient since Delphi thought an agreement with it was possible—by eating the shades.

She stopped moving towards the bulb as the beginnings of an idea began to form in her mind. It was possible that she could lead some of the shades towards the plant as an express delivery meal. She knew she would be able to do that, she just wanted to make sure she wasn't completely off about the idea.

She turned around and shooed Boreal back towards the edge of the forest, following behind her.

"Alright, new idea. We're going to try to feed shades to it," Zalia said quietly as she knelt down next to the others.

Three sets of eyes stared at her.

"Alright, well, maybe I'm not sure if it actually eats them yet, but look at the way the shades avoid it," Zalia explained, pointing towards the sky.

Ro-ak, Boreal, and Delphi turned to look into the sky simultaneously, turning back one by one to look at Zalia. Boreal looked unsurprised but a little disappointed, and Ro looked entirely confused, but Delphi looked contemplative.

"Look, if it notices us bringing a whole host of floating shade snacks towards it, I'm sure it will be grateful. It was your idea to feed it Boreal!" Zalia explained defensively.

"*How would we test your theory?*" Delphi asked.

"By attracting a bunch of shades and running at the bulb," Zalia said.

"*That sounds like a distinctly bad idea, even with your anti-death ability up,*" Delphi said.

"It should only be a few more hours, you're probably right, and I should wait for that," Zalia conceded.

She sat down and summoned her wings, maintaining the flow of Manifest into the ritual as long as she could whilst simultaneously concentrating on holding steady in a cross-legged position as she floated with the wings. The exercise was a little mentally straining but that was the point, to train her ability to concentrate on her rituals for as long as possible.

They spent a few hours waiting like that and Zalia only had to reset her ritual once in that time which she was proud of. Boreal, on the other hand, wasn't playing around with Ro for once and was making ice sculptures for Delphi, which Delphi took pleasure in as a new and strange memory. Being used to mentally sending memories to others, they seemed to revel in the novelty of a more traditional method of communicating memories.

After that few hours, she felt her ability come off cooldown and she gently unfolded her legs to a standing position in a smooth movement.

"Alright, I'm ready," Zalia announced.

Boreal looked up from where she had made an ice sculpture of a small kitchen, featuring a tiny Boreal fleeing the scene with some food in her mouth as a chef chased her.

"I don't remember that," Zalia said, looking down at it.

"*Imaginary*," Boreal said in Zalia's mind.

Zalia narrowed her eyes at Boreal.

"So you didn't steal food from the kitchens in Endelbyrn?" Zalia asked.

Boreal shuffled her feet.

"*No?*" Boreal blatantly lied.

"You're a menace," Zalia said.

Boreal looked at her with wide, sad eyes.

"An admittedly cute menace," Zalia added.

Boreal seemed to take that as forgiveness and went about jumping all over her sculpture, shattering some of the more fragile parts. Menace.

Zalia stretched a bit, rolling her stiff shoulder and looked up into the sky.

"Alright, let's get your attention, shall we?" Zalia said quietly.

She decided the easiest way of getting their attention was to just shoot at them.

"Want me or Boreal to carry you?" Zalia asked Delphi.

"*If you will be taking most of the attention I'd prefer to be carried by Boreal,*" Delphi said.

"Fair enough," Zalia said, lifting them up onto Boreal's back.

Delphi sat between Boreal's shoulder spikes, holding on to each with a hand like a tiny cowboy frog riding a cat. Ignoring the absurdly cute duo, Zalia looked up to the sky again and summoned her bow.

"Let's do something stupid," she muttered before shooting an arrow at the nearest shade.

The arrow flew straight through the shade but left a glowing line where it passed. Its cry of torment changed to one of pain, and all the nearby shades began uttering angry sounds. Seeing they were definitely building up their darkness to make an attack, Zalia took off out of the forest edge towards the bulb.

The shades chased her for a while but slowed and eventually stopped as she approached the bulb. She shot a few more arrows towards them but despite the pain the glowing damage of her arrows dealt, they would not approach. Apparently, they had a stronger sense of self-preservation than she had thought.

"Why do my plans never work?" Zalia asked as the others came back over to watch the stopped shades.

"*Sometimes,*" Boreal said, sending comforting emotions with her words.

Zalia frustratedly considered her ritual options mentally. A mix of Manifest major and Bitterbalm minor could create a spiritual manifestation element she could potentially use. In her frustration, Zalia began that ritual, simultaneously starting a Zephyr major and Bitterbalm minor ritual too. She combined the two to form an Earth spiritual manifestation ritual that she mixed with a Bitterbalm major to turn it into a curse.

Throughout the ritual she continually pushed Manifest into it and targeted the shades. Tagging three with Hunter's Mark spread the curse to a few more as five shades were suddenly grappled by spiritual limbs made of earth that shot up from the ground and dragged them down. Zalia mentally controlled the limbs to start pulling the shades towards the bulb, but they fought back, hard.

The spiritual earthen limbs started to crack and crumble but it was too late—she had pulled them just close enough, and the shades suddenly stopped struggling and became compressed as if crushed into a giant hand. It seemed like the shades knew the exact distance they could safely stay from the bulb and when she had dragged them over that line, they broke out of her summoned limbs and disappeared into the top of the bulb.

A humming reverberated through the air that Zalia could almost describe as . . . grateful.

CHAPTER TWENTY-FIVE

Remnants

Zalia

'll take that as a good sign," Zalia muttered.

The group stood very still, watching the bulb that now appeared to be digesting the shades.

"My instincts appear to have been correct again," Zalia pointed out to Boreal.

"*Luck*," Boreal replied.

"That wasn't luck, that was . . . kind of my plan. I had to do some improvising but it worked, didn't it?" Zalia argued.

"*Worked*," Boreal grumbled.

"Why *are* you so grumpy?" Zalia said, poking Boreal.

Boreal let out a quiet, disgruntled meow.

"Come on, out with it," Zalia prodded.

"*Eat*," Boreal complained.

The complaint came with an image of the shades as Boreal looked to the sky. Zalia not-so-gently dragged one of her hands down her face as she let out a groan.

"You're grumpy because the bulb can eat the shades and you can't!?" Zalia asked incredulously.

"*Tasty shadows!*" Boreal whined.

"You don't know that they're tasty," Zalia replied.

"*Bulb likes!*" Boreal argued.

"You're not a plant, you might not enjoy them as much as it looks like the bulb does," Zalia tried to calmly explain, only managing somewhat.

"*Worth a try,*" Boreal replied stubbornly.

Zalia's mind had completely forgotten about the bulb for the moment, her eye twitching a little at Boreal's continued stubbornness.

"Will you feel better if I promise to try and find a way that you can eat one of the shades?" Zalia asked, giving up.

Boreal immediately perked up, looking at Zalia.

"*Snack!*" Boreal exclaimed.

Great, another thing for the list, Zalia thought.

Despite her irritation, she was glad to have found a way to affect the shades, even if it was only minor. The fact that she could reverse Manifest's element to cause spiritual manifestation rather than physical was one of the many things she had learnt from her deeper study of Herbal Magic. The way she had used it only had minor effects but she was sure some other combinations could provide better uses. That ritual had been one of her most complicated so far, including two rituals combined to create the major element for a third ritual. Despite its relatively low power—because of the rank most of the herbs were—its complexity had made it quite hard for her to maintain concentration.

Just as she was about to ask Delphi what she knew about the shades, the humming vibration of the bulb changed to form what were two words.

"*Thaaaaaaankkk youuuuuuu,*" the bulb said.

The hum was almost deafening, with the sound pressing down on her. It wasn't mental communication like she was used to hearing from Boreal and Delphi, but actual words created somehow.

She waited for more to come but the humming dropped down until it became a sound within the background, no more intrusive than the cries of the shades above.

"*We may enter now,*" Delphi said.

"You wouldn't care to explain further, would you?" Zalia asked.

"*No,*" Delphi replied.

"Figures," Zalia said in acceptance.

If she was to get along with Delphi and the collective, she might just have to accept that despite them knowing a lot about the future, they didn't seem inclined to talk much about it. Whether that was a warning passed down from their ancestors or just wisdom gained from memories of the past, she didn't know. Either way, she had found no reason to distrust the friendly collective as of yet, so the reward of working with them outweighed the risk.

She slowly approached the building, noticing finer details as she did. Parts of it were definitely crumbling due to the continued exposure to the elements and the corruption of Cormaine. What she couldn't see from afar, however, were the small fine vines intertwining between the stone blocks, holding the whole structure together.

Strangely, it looked like the finer vines were grown from plants placed along the walls of the building, yet she could see places where they attached to the larger bulb above.

I'd love to know the history of this place, Zalia thought.

The aesthetic of rough cut stone held together by living vines was a pleasing one to Zalia, reminding her of nature not so much conquered as befriended.

They stopped before the small door to the temple, looking at the sigil above.

"One of your churches," Zalia said to Ro.

"*Find the piece*," Ro-ak said once more.

"Yeah, yeah, I get it," Zalia muttered.

Damned crow didn't have much else to say. She had only *just* had the thought about trusting Delphi with their future-seeing abilities, but the two of them together were getting on her nerves. She was getting the feeling of being on a predestined path and she really did not like that.

Maybe being brought to Endaria wasn't a mistake, she thought.

It was a disturbing thought and she *hated* it.

With no reason to back down now, she stepped over the boundary and into the temple. Her eyes quickly adjusted to the darker space and she saw a long, low room, and on each side, placed in small alcoves, were wooden altars similar to the one she had found earlier. The central path was clear and led to a wide, circular chamber ahead that housed the large bulb that occupied the building. Scattered around the entire place were vines and roots growing in and around pillars, altars, walls, and the floor. If the vines outside looked like artfully grown roots designed to hold the building together, the ones inside looked like a chaotic forest. She had a distinct feeling that if the bulb so wished, she was in more danger inside here than out.

Looking at the bulb, her aura identified it as being Gold rank—expected, yet scary. She had seen a few Gold ranks in her time in Endaria but this was the first one she faced without similarly powerful allies or a great number advantage.

"What now?" Zalia whispered to Delphi.

"*Find the piece*," Delphi replied with what Zalia could have sworn was a mocking tone.

Even the damn frog was messing with her now.

"Savages and bullies, all of you," Zalia muttered.

Boreal took a few steps ahead, avoiding stepping on vines and sniffing at the air carefully. Zalia followed, going further in than Boreal but moving just as carefully. She thought they could probably escape the immobile bulb if they really tried but underestimating it was not a smart move.

"Um, hello? We're just going to have a look around for . . . a piece of a god if you don't mind," Zalia explained to the bulb.

She was met with absolute silence.

"I'm just going to walk around you so I can see what's further in, don't mind me. I'll avoid stepping on you as much as I can," Zalia added nervously.

Still receiving no response, she gently moved forwards again and started walking around the edges of the space. Reaching the other side from the entrance, she found a doorway with stairs leading down into the ground below. Not exactly where she expected to find a crow god, but who was to say where they did or didn't like hanging out.

"I'm just going to go have a look down here if that's alright," Zalia said.

She hoped if she just explained everything she was doing, the bulb wouldn't take offence to her presence. She glanced nervously to Boreal and then back towards the stairs leading down.

"Here I go," she announced.

She started walking down the stairs, fully aware that each step took her further from a potential escape. Boreal followed her, with Delphi riding atop the feline, and Ro-ak close behind. The crow was looking more and more energetic, excited almost, which was a good sign.

The stairs led down for quite a ways before reaching the ground, with a long hallway now ahead of her. Down here the room was entirely earthen, still riddled with roots and vines draping across the ceiling and walls. Despite that, as she walked through the hallway the vines and walls formed what she could have sworn were the shapes of animals. Crows were the main ones she saw appear but there were also wolves, something that looked like a badger, and a few others.

The experience was one of an ever-changing natural art exposition, pieces of vine, root, and wall lining up in only a single spot to form the images.

"You seeing this too?" Zalia asked Delphi.

"*Indeed. This will be a memory preserved for many cycles.*" The mocking tone was gone from their mental voice, with only a very slight hint of awe in there. At the end of the hall, they reached a door made of wood that depicted a giant crow hidden in the shadows of a forest, its eyes glinting with wisdom and knowledge. There was no colour of paint used in the depiction, yet she could see the glint as clear as day. Slowly, it grew brighter and the magic she felt briefly surge from the other side of the door was almost palpable. It swung open just a little as the surge died down and Zalia pushed it further open with apprehension.

Through the entrance was a small chamber, more overgrown than the rest of the building, with vines and roots so thick as to almost coat the walls. As she pushed through the door, having to slide sideways around it and shoving root and vine out of her way, Zalia found what she had come here to find.

Hanging suspended from the centre of the room was a large crow, held aloft by vines with its wings extended out to either side. Its two clawed feet looked exactly like the symbol of the temple stamped above the front door: crow's feet that looked like they were almost grown out of trees. The two bulky limbs hung loosely from the body of a crow, its feathers made from various types of leaves, forming an autumn pattern. From its head a cowl made from vines hung loosely, the piece of clothing growing from the crow's neck. From within the cowl a large, sharp beak, much the same as Ro-ak's jabbed out, a silvery glint of eyes visible within.

As she looked closer, she could see that the vines suspending the remnants of the god were not just holding its body but growing from it. The large bulb above was linked to or grown in some way from the god below.

Zalia cleared her throat.

"H-hello?" she said.

Ro-ak hopped forwards past Zalia and began closely inspecting the suspended god. Suddenly, Ro-ak stopped and turned to Zalia with the same silver glint in his eyes.

"*You have found the piece,*" Ro-ak said.

"As you asked," Zalia replied. "What do you want me to do with it?"

"*I cannot tell you what you must do, since I am not truly alive. Wisdom and faith, Zalia of the Druids,*" Ro-ak croaked.

Not truly alive? Zalia wondered.

How could the god be talking to her, yet not alive? Hanging here in front of her, yet unable to explain?

Wisdom and faith. Was that what it wanted from her?

She remembered something the starlight wolf had told her, that its power had decreased much since the days of its prime, since the days when many more had worshipped it. Did the gods' survival and power depend on the faith of their believers?

Maybe, and maybe since this one had no more believers, it no longer had power, and thus was not truly alive. Wisdom and faith it had said.

Zalia knelt down and gently laid out some of her herbs. A piece of Dodge-vine for the vine-like appearance of the god. A piece of the Glowing Cavern Fungus for the element of shadow associated with the god. A piece of the Living Trapvine for the element of mind, the host of all wisdom.

Unsure of herself but trying to keep faith in her plan, she pushed her Healing Presence into the herbs in front of herself. Mentally, she made a link from them to the god as she closed her eyes, making the healing flow from the herbs to the god to herself, then back to the herbs again in a circulating movement.

And so she sat in focus, pushing the Healing Aura around in constant motion, trying to keep faith in herself and in the last vestige of the god before her.

CHAPTER TWENTY-SIX

God . . . Kind of

Zalia

Time passed without meaning as Zalia knelt before the suspended remnant, only half conscious of her surroundings. Her mind melded between present and not, her only focus that of the undulating wave of power building in the loop of her magic. The slow build of the magic grew stronger as she pushed it through yet another circuit. Herbs, god, Zalia. Herbs, god, Zalia.

She was broken from her reverie as the built up power was vacuumed out from the air in a silent torrent. She felt it enter the god as the cycle was disrupted at that point, the sudden interruption of the rote push and pull startling and disorienting.

She opened her eyes and looked to Boreal, who was asleep at her left. Delphi was nowhere to be seen but she could feel them in the hallway outside inspecting the walls. Ro-ak was staring intently at the suspended body in front of him.

"Boreal," Zalia croaked.

She cleared her throat, surprised at the dryness she felt.

"Boreal," she repeated, clearer this time.

Boreal opened her eyes and blinked at Zalia.

"*Zalia awake!*" Boreal exclaimed in her mind.

Zalia winced at the volume that Boreal managed to direct into her head.

"I wasn't out that long, was I?" she asked.

"*A cycle and a half,*" Delphi mentally informed her.

"That can't be right," Zalia muttered, frowning.

A glint caught her eye, and she turned to the god remnant before her. It was now looking at her with its silver eyes as the two large wings twitched in an attempt to take flight.

"Hello," she greeted nervously.

"It has been long since I felt the presence of one with faith. Too long . . . I was dormant for . . . how many . . ." the god said confusedly.

Its voice was an exact replica of the one Ro-ak spoke with, in fact it *was* the voice that Ro-ak spoke with. This was definitely the god she had talked to in the past.

She felt drained, hollow, like the water had been pulled from her body. She summoned a Water Lily stem and chewed it before trying to speak once more.

"How did you come to be down here?" she asked.

"Here . . . where is here?" it asked.

"You're in Cormaine, land of the dead or something. Do you have a name?" she tried asking instead.

Coming back from the dead was probably a disorienting experience.

"Cormaine . . . dead . . . a name, I had a name once," it replied, its gaze leaving Zalia as it oh-so-slowly turned to inspect the room around it.

Zalia frowned. This was a much different conversation than the one she had with the starlight wolf. That god had seemed powerful and in control, wise and ancient. This one seemed . . . lost.

"Do you remember calling me to find the piece?" Zalia asked.

"A piece . . . a small, tiny piece of what once was. Even now so, so small," it said mournfully.

Seeing the conversation was going nowhere, she stood and stretched her pained legs and began gently pushing her healing into the god. A likely centuries-long death sleep wouldn't be shaken off so easily it seemed.

"*Might want to come in here,*" Zalia said to Delphi mentally.

As she said it though, she realised that Delphi was already sitting calmly on the floor by the door. Definitely not one to miss such a unique memory.

Zalia could see the god gaining strength by the minute and resigned herself to waiting just a little bit longer. Despite the thirty-six hours she had just spent gathering enough faith, mana, and energy to wake the god, it was more like a shot of coffee than a shot of morphine for the deity.

Personally though, she was feeling the effects of it, and checking her status page, she could see that reflected there.

Profile - Zalia Taori
Health - Excellent

Mana - Near empty
Stamina - Half

Class One - Hunter - Iron 11
Linked Attributes - Strength, Dexterity
Active Skills
Kill Shot - Iron 15
Hunter's Mark - Iron 16
Fight or Flight - Iron 14
Passive Skills
Hunter's Sight - Iron 11
Survivalist - Bronze 1
Class Two - Herbalist - Iron 9
Linked Attributes - Vitality, Resilience
Active Skills
Flora Identification - Iron 9
Preparation - Iron 10
Stasis - Iron 9
Passive Skills
Harvester - Iron 10
Herbal Magic - Bronze 1
Unity Class - Druid - Iron 12
Linked Attributes - Wisdom, Intellect
Active Skills
Nature's Wrath - Iron 14
Protection of the Wilds - Iron 12
Passive Skills
Healing Presence - Bronze 1
General Passives
Heat Resistance - Bronze 1
Cold Resistance - Bronze 1
Aura Observation - Iron 2
Low Light Vision - Iron 5
Poison Resistance - Iron 7
Mobility - Bronze 1
Stealth - Bronze 1
Trapper - Bronze 1
Teaching - Iron 7
Flight - Tin 6
Physical Resistance - Bronze 1

Mental Resistance - Bronze 1
Weapon proficiencies
Bow - Bronze 1
Sword - Iron 18
Throwing Knives - Tin 17
Bonded Items
Druidic Bow, Blessed by Starlight (Blessed
Heirloom) - Deeply bonded Iron rank.
Duskwraith Armour (Heirloom) - Bonded Iron rank.

The bonded items section was a neat little addition she had received upon bonding her second heirloom.

She watched the god a little apprehensively, hoping that what she had done was actually enough to keep it alive and that she hadn't just temporarily jumped a body soon to be dead again. Even that thought passing through her mind had a visible effect on the god as it drooped once more.

Scolding herself, Zalia cut that line of thinking and focused all her attention on having faith in its survival. This god was entirely dependent on her dedication to it at this moment, a thought that was scary enough in itself.

The god slowly recovered from Zalia's lapse in faith, leaning back straight once more. She breathed a sigh of relief and tried to keep her mind focused this time.

"Hey, Boreal, you believe in this god, right?" Zalia asked.

"*Friend?*" Boreal asked.

"Uh, yeah, friend. Friend that really needs you to believe in them right now," Zalia replied.

Boreal looked thoughtful, slightly tilting her head before walking up to the god and purring loudly. Then she sat next to it and continued doing so, and Zalia swore the purring had a visible effect on the god.

"What about you, Delphi, believe in the god?" Zalia asked,

"*The collective believes in the memories it keeps. This will be one such memory,*" Delphi said.

"Alright, that's good. Hear that god, it's not just me that believes in you. There's your little buddy Ro-ak here as well; he has more faith in you than the rest of us combined," Zalia explained emphatically.

She . . . wasn't really one for this kind of thing but didn't know what else to do. Having a god on her side would drastically improve her chances of getting the hell out of here, so, proving to a dead god that she believed in it was on the table.

"See. You're also attached to a giant Gold rank plant that has been protecting you for an eternity. I'm sure that plant has believed in you, if not kept you ali— " Zalia said, cutting herself off at a thought.

Boreal looked up at Zalia.

"Maybe you just need to eat something tasty to get your energy back," Zalia suggested.

Boreal caught on and stood up in excitement.

"*Eat!*" Boreal exclaimed.

She also let out a few excited mews at the same time.

"We're feeding the god first, Boreal, but if you get a chance, yes. Eat," Zalia promised.

Boreal excitedly did a few laps around the room before zooming out through the door. With a tired sigh, Zalia followed.

She chased after the faintly glowing footprints left behind by the quick pitter-patter of small feline paws. She still gave the bulb a respectful distance, though it looked like Boreal hadn't bothered, simply sprinting the fastest route out of the building. She was usually excellent at hiding her footprints and the sound of her movement but at that moment, Boreal simply *didn't care.*

Zalia exited the building to find Boreal had actually climbed the wall and was sitting on the half-collapsed ceiling held together with vines.

"What, are you going to try and catch them?" Zalia asked in amusement.

"*Tasty shades,*" Boreal demanded.

She was beginning to wonder if Boreal had something against shades. Their first shade, the Hidden, had betrayed them, so it may not have been completely inaccurate.

Or, Boreal simply wanted something to eat that wasn't the bland, if not foul, taste of grey creature.

Rather than rushing, Zalia laid out the herbal components required for the ritual she was about to undertake. The methodical nature of the action was calming and would help her maintain concentration by eliminating the need to summon the herbs in the moment. Three piles formed, one containing Bitterbalm and Zephyr, another containing Bitterbalm and Manifest, with the last containing just Bitterbalm.

Zephyr major and Bitterbalm minor would create an element reversal ritual on Zephyr changing the resulting element to earth. Manifest major and Bitterbalm minor would have a similar effect changing the resulting element to spiritual manifestation. Those two together would form a spiritual manifestation of earth targeted as a curse by the third and final ritual using the new combination and Bitterbalm major.

It was the same ritual she had performed earlier, only this time in a calm manner rather than a frustrated and expedited one.

Each of the piles dissolved as a large circle formed around Zalia, depicting many runes she could not read. The ritual formed from the dust remains of the herbs lit up a dull earthen brown and purple mix. Tendrils formed from the earth in the circle and as Zalia used Hunter's Mark on a few of the shades, even more sprouted. Once more, the shades were dragged unwillingly into range of the bulb's power and were crushed into small shadows before being dragged by a different power towards the bulb.

Boreal stupidly jumped over top of the bulb's large mouth to try and catch one of the shades in midair and landed only a hair's width from the edge of the mouth.

"Get down from there!" Zalia yelled.

She was willing to tolerate a lot, but that had been foolish of Boreal.

Boreal sulkily climbed down as the bulb digested the newly fed shades.

"I told you I would try to catch one for you, but we need to take care of the god first," Zalia scolded.

She hoped . . . no, she knew that the shades' power would help heal the god below.

Boreal sat down on the ground with a soft *thump*, still looking upset.

What am I going to do with you, Zalia thought.

The answer to that was probably find a way to get a shade for her to eat. With determination, Zalia began preparing a new set of herbs for the next ritual feeding. It was going to be a long day.

CHAPTER TWENTY-SEVEN

Frog . . . s

Zalia

Zalia ran out of steam after another fourteen— . . . or fifteen?— rituals. The shades also very quickly caught on to what was happening and began staying further and further from the bulb. Very soon, she had to focus her entire attention and the power of the ritual onto a single shade in order to drag it far enough to be caught and even then they moved further.

At this point, she could no longer drag them far enough to be caught in the bulb, but that was ok with her. The strain of concentration and mana flowing, especially so soon after the initial revival of the dead god, was building to be too much.

Boreal had left after Zalia failed to bring a shade for her to eat, going back inside the building to concoct mischief no doubt. Zalia half-stumbled, half-walked back into the temple and downstairs to the god below. She entered, finding Boreal innocently sitting next to the god with Delphi standing on its face and Ro-ak looking somewhat annoyed. All three were frozen, staring at her.

"What happened down here?" Zalia asked, looking at Delphi who was suctioned to the half-dead god's face.

"*I . . . was discovering new memories,*" Delphi said, a little self-consciously.

"You're meant to be the responsible one," Zalia reminded them.

Ro cawed once in an annoyed manner.

"And you're standing on the face of Ro-ak's god," Zalia pointed out.

"*Boreal said it would be alright and was the one to throw me up here,*" Delphi explained, throwing Boreal under the bus.

This caused a mew of outrage from Boreal that was followed by an accusatory croak from Ro. An argument broke out between the two as Zalia stared at Delphi, who was trying really hard to be invisible.

She gave him a stare with narrowed eyes that meant "I'm blaming you for this" before walking over and picking up Boreal. The argument stopped as Boreal loudly complained, but Zalia just walked over to a corner and set Boreal down, lying next to her. Despite the argument she had noticed the god was looking much better already. Its leafy feathers had taken a certain sheen to them, and it hung in a less . . . dead manner.

"I'm going to catch a few hours of sleep—refrain from killing each other or something important while I do," Zalia said, pointedly loud enough for Delphi to hear.

She closed her eyes and the combined exhaustion, both mental and physical, quickly took her to a deep sleep.

Zalia's eyes opened to see the same room she had fallen asleep in, yet none of her companions were present. She rolled over and looked over the rest of the room but nothing seemed out of place.

"Boreal?" she called.

There was no response, so she stood up and stretched lightly.

"Delphi?" she called, a bit louder.

No response.

She walked over to the door but stopped as she saw a glint of light in the periphery of her vision.

She looked over her shoulder and saw the god was twitching slightly, an indistinct whisper coming from it.

"*Delphi,*" Zalia called out mentally.

There was no response so she walked up to the god to hear what it was saying more clearly.

"*Find the prison,*" it whispered.

"What?" Zalia asked, unsure if she had heard right.

The vines holding up the god began writhing and morphing. Their shape became chain-like, taking on a metallic sheen as the room about her began melting. The god, its wings replaced by arms and now suspended by chains from the ceiling, looked up at her in a sudden flash of movement.

"*Find the prison,*" it whispered.

She jolted upright in her bed, launching a small shape across the room.

She looked about wildly, but all was normal and Boreal looked down at her in concern. The god was the same as it had been when she had fallen asleep.

She shook her head gently, trying to break the confusing visions floating around her mind. She was getting really sick of random powerful creatures whispering for her to find things, whether it be in her dreams, mind, or through a crow.

She looked across the room to where Delphi had landed after being launched by her jolting awake.

"Were you on my face while I was asleep?" Zalia accused.

"*I was trying to wake you,*" Delphi explained.

"What for?" Zalia asked.

Boreal mreowed, conveying a sense of concern and an image of Zalia curled into a ball with her entire body tensed.

"Ah, just a . . . nightmare," Zalia assured them.

"*A nightmare? I don't fully comprehend this word,*" Delphi asked.

"It's like when you have a dream but it is a bad one," Zalia explained.

"*Ahhh, I sometimes forget that some less-established life-forms dream,*" Delphi said in understanding.

"Less-established, what does that mean!?" Zalia asked, a little insulted.

"*Your biology has not grown to be the least restrictive version it can be. Many creatures still require things such as breathing, sleep, and blood. That kind of thing,*" Delphi explained.

Zalia just stared at the tiny frog on the floor that was dictating to her what a perfect life form was.

"And you have reached such a state, I assume," Zalia said dryly.

"*Of course, the collective has had a long time to perfect their form,*" Delphi replied.

Zalia narrowed her eyes at the frog and stood up. She walked over and tried to pick Delphi up, but the form shimmered and then shattered at her touch. An illusion.

"*A good but unsuccessful attempt at proving a valid point,*" Delphi said.

Zalia looked around and found the damn frog standing where she had just gotten up from.

"*That one weakness is why we usually stay within the strength of the collective,*" Delphi added.

Rolling her eyes at the ridiculous and dramatic frog she had befriended, Zalia walked over to the god to inspect its health.

"Are you awake?" she asked.

The body twitched and its head turned to look at her.

"Awake, yes, after so long. Memories . . . memories return," it whispered.

She took that as a good sign and left it to its recovery.

"I have a feeling that our friend's recovery may take some time. I believe the god needs either a dramatic increase in true faithful or a long time to sort its memories. Maybe you can help it with that, being all about that kind of thing?" Zalia asked Delphi.

"*I have already been in contact with it. I believe a few more members of the collective would be beneficial here,*" Delphi replied.

"Alright, we can do that. Anything else you can think of?" Zalia added.

"*Not at this moment in time,*" Delphi said.

"Let's go, then," Zalia said.

They left the temple and Zalia gave them all Zephyr wings so that they could fly back to her home island. She wasn't worried about the god, knowing that it had been protected by the bulb for a long time and would be much better defended by it than she ever could manage.

It took a while for them to arrive at their destination and she was relieved when they did. Flying over the open ground was definitely a freeing activity, but the memory of the twisted monster she had seen would linger in the back of her mind forever more.

While Delphi went to talk with the collective, transfer memories, and pick some more members to accompany them back to the god, Zalia checked up on her little herb garden. All the plants were looking a little bit wilted but, overall, doing well. It was nothing a short time of her Healing Aura couldn't fix up.

The zones of ice and lava she had made with her rituals were still going strong, unfettered by the corruption or lack of her presence. Encouraged by their success, she stayed there for a time, enjoying the refreshingly clean air. Boreal joined, lying calmly next to her, the lack of shenanigans probably her version of an apology for her recent behaviour. Ro-ak wasn't there, having opted to stay with the god.

"Want to go search some of the rest of the city once we drop Delphi off, just the two of us?" Zalia asked.

That made Boreal perk up.

"Oh, so you've been missing spending time together, have you?" Zalia asked teasingly.

Boreal gave a mreow of denial.

"Explains the behaviour," Zalia said, pretending to think hard about it.

Boreal jumped at Zalia and bowled her over, and they went rolling as Zalia let out a laugh. Their mock battle rolled over a Snow-leaf before they came to a stop, Zalia holding Boreal up above her out of reach.

"Oh please, have mercy mighty Boreal," Zalia cried out in feigned distress.

Boreal gave out a sound that was somewhere between a hiss and a meow yet conveyed the word "never!"

Zalia pushed Boreal up into the air and used her teleport to blink to the other side of the room, standing and preparing for the next attack. Boreal prowled towards her and got low, giving a little wiggle in preparation to pounce. Using a sneaky tactic, Boreal used her shadow teleport at the last moment to come at Zalia from the side, bowling her over once more and freezing her to the ground.

"Yield, yield!" Zalia called.

Boreal stood on her chest in victory, letting out a tiny, cute roar that would no doubt turn into something much more terrifying once she was fully grown.

Zalia grinned and broke free from the ice with some quick manipulation, standing and brushing the rest off.

"You're such a little shit sometimes," Zalia said warmly, scratching Boreal behind the ears.

Boreal gave a little chirp like, "yeah, I know."

Rolling her eyes, Zalia left the little side cavern to see if Delphi was done yet. She came out of the doorway to find not one but five frogs standing next to the pool staring at her.

"*We are ready*," Delphi said.

Zalia could barely tell the difference between them, though they each had a slightly varied pattern in their colourings. A little unnerved at the simultaneous stares from the five sets of wide frog eyes, Zalia waved.

"Hello, I can see that, yes. Want to leave now?" she asked.

"*At the earliest convenience*," Delphi replied.

Before they left, Zalia marked off the entire list from her wall, all the objectives having been completed. She had explored the flying island; found a way to defend against, harm, or kill the shades; and had investigated the immediate area. Now she just needed a way out of Cormaine.

"Rrright, easy enough. Let's go then," she said, quickly leaving the chamber towards the cavern exit.

They quickly made their way to the surface and Zalia picked up all the frogs, with their permission, and placed them on her shoulders.

"It'll be a little windy, so do your best to hold on," Zalia informed them.

"*They have my memories, Zalia, they are aware of what is happening,*" Delphi reminded her.

"Right, right, collective and all that. Here we go, then," she said before casting the Wind Wings ritual and taking off. Boreal was close behind on wings of her own.

They travelled back to the god island and Zalia dropped off the frogs in the temple, hoping they would be able to help in some way.

They then flew back to the island containing the ruins of the Bathar city, as there were a couple things she wanted to tie up there. Firstly, she wanted to release as many of the Bathar from torment as she could, something she could now do in relative ease from the sky. There was always the fear of attracting the shades above, but she thought she had a way around that now. Secondly, there were the buildings they had seen on the map that she wanted to explore, one of them hopefully holding something of interest.

If there was nothing there, well, a shame, but if there was it might be useful and worth the time invested. She had to wait for the god to recover either way.

CHAPTER TWENTY-EIGHT

Field Clearing

Zalia

The first location on her list that Zalia wanted to explore was the barracks. It was closest relative to the direction she was coming from and one of the more likely to have had something magical enough to survive its time down here. Most everything that wasn't stone or steel had degraded to the point of misrecognition, even then most metal had rusted. Most of the pieces in the keep's armoury were intact but really not of use to her.

After the barracks, she wanted to go to the research facility next. It sounded like the kind of place that some powerful, magical artefacts would have been kept.

First though, the barracks. She flew with Boreal quietly over rooftops in the direction of the compound that had been marked on the map. She spotted it from above as a walled area with multiple buildings within. It looked like it had suffered quite some damage at the hands of whatever had assaulted the city to bring it to this state. They landed some thirty metres away on a rooftop to observe the compound through sections of wall that had been brought down.

As expected, many undead roamed around, yet these looked like they had seen battle. Most of the undead she had cleared so far were normal citizens or guards that had been hidden away in the keep when the city was taken, but many of these had injuries such as missing limbs, broken bones, and other similar wounds.

"Think there will be any Silver ranked Bathar down there?" Zalia asked Boreal.

Boreal meowed in affirmation.

The chances were high, with this being the central barracks for the city's armies. The king himself was possibly Gold rank and it was likely that some others in the city were as well. She highly doubted there were any of a higher rank here, finding it hard to believe that something of that rank would be turned or even defeated. The gap in power between each rank became bigger and bigger as they went up, with the difference between Silver and Gold being quite large. She remembered the absolute destruction the fight between Larel and the Gold rank elemental had wrought and couldn't imagine what a fight between two Emerald or even Diamond rank creatures would be like.

Shaking herself free from idle thoughts, she refocused on the compound before her. The easiest way of going about this would be to simply fly to the centre and make some noise, attracting all the undead to pick them off from the sky. However, she would gain levels quicker if she was in the rough of things. She decided on a good balance between the two, aiming to stay in the air until she could confirm no Gold rank undead were there, and then would land to fight. She could always fly back up if it became too much to handle without some preset traps. Though, she now had the knowledge that her healing ability could degrade the undead, so it shouldn't be a problem.

First, she needed to test a theory.

She had concocted a little ritual on the way here, a way of hiding herself from the shades. It was based on a few assumptions, like the shades seeing in a non-physical manner, but it was worth a test. So far the shades hadn't intervened in her fights with the undead, but if she stayed up in the sky it might prove to be a problem.

She mixed Manifest major and Bitterbalm minor to create the element of spiritual manifestation, then used that as the minor with Dodge-vine major to create her final ritual. The final ritual settled over her and she moved around testing it, finding it had no effect on her movement.

The purpose of the ritual was a slightly altered version of one of the first rituals she had performed with Dodge-vine. That ritual had used the Dodge-vine to protect her from being seen, and this one did the same, but as protection from spiritual senses. That was where her assumption about how the shades saw or heard came in, but it was worth a try. She performed the same ritual on Boreal as well.

All set, Zalia informed Boreal of her plans and flew over to just above the centre of the compound. Deciding that testing her ritual immediately would be the best move—as attracting the shades' attention mid-fight was a bad idea—Zalia screamed. It wasn't particularly loud but it definitely got the undead's attention. They began swarming to the open centre of the compound, many leaving buildings. Thankfully, the shades above had no reaction whatsoever. Zalia quickly sent a prayer of thanks to the crow god, who was being watched over by Delphi. It couldn't hurt.

She began letting off arrows at a quick pace, each one punching through a head and dropping the targeted Bathar. She also began applying Hunter's Mark in batches, and applying various harmful rituals to each set of three marked Bathar before repeating the process, even as her arrows flew. She also started pushing her healing through all the undead and they began dissolving under its power. Boreal hovered nearby, waiting for her signal to be allowed down.

Eventually the stream of undead from the nearby buildings and streets slowed down, and without a single Silver rank in sight, Zalia signalled the ok to Boreal.

Boreal dove down in a flash as her Pounce ability charged, hitting a Bronze rank undead in the head. The force of the strike threw her target to the ground, its skull exploding across the courtyard from the impact. Zalia turned away from Boreal, trusting her to stay safe, and dropped to the ground herself. She entered in a far less dramatic manner, landing in a soft crouch with a precise and efficient diagonal swing that cleaved a poor Tin rank undead in two.

She burst into motion, making good use of her Healing Presence to heavily weaken a few enemies and keep them at bay while dispatching others with her blade. Rituals popped up in various places as walls were summoned to funnel or block even more undead. Now, using a new effect she had discovered—one that reminded her of a dear friend—she summoned patches of lava across the field, and as unwary undead stepped through, their legs began to melt.

As things got a little overwhelming, Zalia activated Nature's Wrath and the entire field came to a sudden stop. Every single undead in the yard was caught up by thin, rock-shard spikes slamming up from the ground through torsos, arms, and legs. The stone slowly turned red-hot, melting to leave patches of burning lava within their bodies.

The ability summoned two elementals as well, one being a large canine-shaped lava elemental that began immediately tearing into the nearest enemy. The next was a stone elemental with two huge shields on its arms, which it slammed together to form one giant wall. Zalia used the space generated by the rooting ability and the two elementals to back up and begin quickly taking down some of the lower-ranked enemies with arrows that flickered through the air, changing directions to pierce two, sometimes three, heads.

There was another change in pace as she had to switch focus to a Silver ranked undead that exploded through the wall of a building behind her. She immediately activated Fight or Flight, time slowing as the full power of her healing ability was focused on the new danger. Boreal appeared out of nowhere, incredibly fast despite Zalia's slowed perception of time. Propelled on wings of air, Boreal slammed into the Silver undead hard enough to throw it back into the building it had just left, bouncing back safely due to her abilities' damage mitigation.

Zalia took advantage of the distraction and applied Hunter's Mark as well as a myriad of harmful rituals to the Silver Bathar. Sword in hand, she engaged it as it left the rubble once more, this time much slower due to the combined weight of her debuffing effects.

She deflected one fist down the length of her blade, stepping her right foot back to turn the deflection into a quick diagonal slice into its right shoulder. She had to twist her body to lessen the impact of the other fist as it crashed into her left shoulder, using the motion to jump back a few steps for space. It quickly closed the distance and she took a full step back to slash at the oncoming fist, cutting halfway through the Bathar's arm.

Boreal jumped from the shadows, freezing one of the undead's legs to the floor, and Zalia bull-rushed, shoulder-bashing the Bathar into a stumble. It broke the ice but didn't catch its balance as it tripped to the floor, and Zalia took quick advantage, getting in another slice, this time severing the already cut arm.

She had to step away as some undead finally broke apart the defender elemental behind her. While Boreal was busy trying to tear the undead's last arm out of its shoulder, Zalia fought back against the swiftly dwindling horde. Still focusing her Healing Presence onto the Silver undead, she was beginning to feel some of the corruption aura's effects, and her right shoulder began to ache. She quickly flew up, mentally telling Boreal to do the same as the tide of undead, in addition to the Silver one, became too much. Boreal disengaged and flew up beside her, and Zalia focused the healing back onto the two of them.

She could have activated Protection of the Wilds onto all the undead to very likely end them but wanted to save the second of her long cooldown abilities for a rainy day. Pulling her bow back out, she swiftly released two, then three, arrows into the Silver undead and it finally stopped struggling.

With the tables turned in their favour once more, Zalia dove down to get back into the fight.

* * *

Zalia stood looking through her notifications about five minutes later, the battle finally finished. No more Silvers had appeared so it had been a quick cleanup of the remaining lower-ranked undead.

> **Congratulations! Kill Shot has reached Iron 16.**
> **Congratulations! Hunter's Mark has reached Iron 17.**
> **Congratulations! Fight or Flight has gained**
> **two levels, reaching Iron 16.**
> **Congratulations! Hunter's Sight has reached Iron 12.**
> **Congratulations! Hunter Class has reached Iron 12.**
> **Congratulations! Nature's Wrath has gained**
> **two levels, reaching Iron 16.**
> **Congratulations! Weapon Proficiency - Sword**
> **has gained two levels, reaching Iron 20.**
> **Congratulations! Weapon Proficiency - Sword has reached Bronze 1.**
> **This ability will gain no further levels until**
> **all classes have reached Bronze.**
> **Sword - Weapon Proficiency**
> **Tin - You can wield a sword faster and hit harder**
> **with it based on the rank and level of this skill.**
> **Iron - The durability of a sword wielded by you is**
> **increased based on the rank and level of this skill.**
> **Bronze - When you successfully parry, you gain a burst of**
> **speed for a short time. Additionally, you can gain slight**
> **insights into the movements of your enemies when engaged.**

As usual, only her abilities used in the fight had gained many levels. Her Herbalist ones were *really* falling behind, but she was working on an herb garden just for that reason.

The Bronze rank effect of her sword proficiency looked like it would most definitely lead to a different style of fighting, though it was sort of in the direction of how she fought anyways. A more defensive style that used her damage-over-time and various Herbal Magic effects to wear the enemy down or trip them up before she struck.

Gently stretching her arms, she looked around the courtyard full of re-dead Bathar and moved towards the closest building.

"Let's find some goodies!" Zalia said to Boreal.

"Mreow!" Boreal replied.

CHAPTER TWENTY-NINE

Battle Cat

Zalia

Zalia pushed a rock off the remains of a table and it fell to the floor with a thud.

"Not much in this building either, looks like," Zalia muttered.

They had searched many of the complex's buildings, finding nothing but bunks, a mess hall, offices, and other utility structures. The reason Zalia was still hopeful was she hadn't found anything akin to a storage room or an armoury of any sorts. She was, of course, assuming that anything like that even existed and wouldn't be completely degraded. She looked over to Boreal.

"Want to check the next building?" she asked.

Boreal was busy dashing through the rubble of the room, playing cat and mouse with the shadows, as far as Zalia could tell. At the question, she stopped sprinting around.

"*Next!*" Boreal exclaimed.

She had far too much energy. Zalia remembered her cat when she had been growing up had been something like this, but Boreal had the added power of a magically enhanced body and didn't require much sleep. The combination of the two resulted in a restless bundle of fluffy energy incapable of focusing on any one thing for too long.

As they were leaving the building, Zalia had to smoothly catch her balance by stepping to the side as a piece of the stairs crumbled and fell away. Moving a little more carefully, they made it down and out, looking towards the other buildings in the complex.

"Do you want to pick one this time?" Zalia asked.

Boreal ran across the field of dead skeletal Bathar, most of which had patches of fur sticking to their bones, until she arrived at one of the other buildings. As Zalia followed behind, she couldn't help but notice again just how much Boreal had grown since they had found her. Once barely reaching Zalia's mid-calf, she was now almost up to her waist. As they entered the low, inconspicuous building, Zalia was surprised by a message popping up in her vision.

> **Congratulations! Your passive "Feline Eyes" shared through your Beast bond with Boreal Taori has reached Bronze.**
> **Feline Eyes - passive**
> **Tin - The sharpness of your vision is dramatically increased.**
> **Iron - When activated, you may see heat in addition to your normal vision.**
> **Bronze - You are now able to see vibrations in the air and ground around you to a much more significant degree.**

Immediately, Zalia could see the vibrations. It was like when she used to be able to see the heat waves coming off roads in the summer. It was similar, yet so different. The waves were directional, each of Boreal's steps letting out vibrations so small as to be barely noticeable, while each movement pushed the air in a visible yet almost indistinct manner. In fact, if she wasn't looking in Boreal's direction with the knowledge that she was there, the vibrations would have been so small as to be invisible. The same applied to her own steps, and she realised that the Iron rank of the Stealth passive was most likely the cause. It inhibited other forms of senses and it turned out this counted as one.

While the new sense was disorienting, she quickly grew used to it and began experimenting with ways she could walk to minimise her own impact, even as they entered the building chosen by Boreal.

"Nice new ability," Zalia said.

"*Wavy*," Boreal replied.

"Wavy," Zalia agreed.

They moved into the low building and found themselves in what was definitely a storeroom. There were severely degraded boxes that were close to dust, their contents mostly in similar shape, yet she was surprised to find a small piece of parchment squared off with leather edges in perfect shape. The reason for its survival soon became apparent as she picked it up, shaking off the dust and decayed wood that lay atop it.

> **War Map - Bronze rank.**

Surprisingly, it wasn't an heirloom item, and had managed to survive this entire time without falling apart. She was more than certain that there had been many more magical items in a city this large, but most of them had likely fallen to pieces by now. She carefully unfolded the map and was met by a detailed image of the military compound and the surrounding area. What was initially most surprising about it was the fact that all the damage done to the surrounding buildings showed up on the map. That meant it either updated itself automatically by some sort of divination magic, or it had been made quite recently.

The answer to that soon became apparent when a small, translucent, red dot appeared on the map. Looking closer, Zalia could see it was an undead. It was odd, the quality of the drawing was as if it were a drone video streaming from above. She watched the undead shamble slowly towards the military compound, measuring the map to show maybe one hundred and fifty metres in each direction from where she stood.

Oddly, she couldn't see herself or Boreal on the map, and walking outside, found it to be the same. Not only did one of the translucent dots not show up, neither did their image. Once again, she remembered her Stealth passive's ability to inhibit other senses from seeing her. It was a war map after all, probably more for seeing the surrounding terrain and general troop movements than watching for stealthy rogues or spies.

She folded up the map and slipped it half under her waistband, covering the other half with her shirt. It would stay there alright if she didn't jostle around or fight too much but she was really missing her spatial bag. She stepped back inside and searched the rest of the building with Boreal. They found only one more item which both of them now stood over, inspecting it.

> **War Harnsh Plate Armour (Heirloom) - Unbonded Iron rank.**

"What is a Harnsh, do you think?" Zalia asked.

From what she could tell, it was some sort of a four-legged beast that the Bathar must have used for war. She hadn't seen any undead versions of that in the city yet but was definitely not looking forward to finding any based on this armour. It was a set of full interlocking plate armour that would cover the creature's entire body, leaving only slits for the eyes. The mouth section looked like it was designed to attach to the lower jaw to allow for full movement so that whatever wore it could still bite.

Each section looked to be fitted in such a manner that they would not hinder movement; the pieces were so well-made that as she moved it around, they soundlessly slid past each other. The entire set was coloured in a matte grey, a perfect colour for Boreal. Thinking back to the way her armour had shrunk and moulded to her form, Zalia turned to her.

"Want to try?" she asked.

Boreal hopped up excitedly.

"*Try!*" she yelled in Zalia's mind.

Zalia nodded, considering whether it was entirely a good idea to give Boreal a set of Heirloom plate armour.

"Alright, my little bowling ball, let's try then," Zalia agreed.

What followed was probably an hour and a half of Zalia trying to figure out how to put the armour on Boreal. Much as she suspected it would, the armour did shrink to fit Boreal's form, but that wasn't the issue. The issue was that plate armour was incredibly difficult to put on—not that she had ever tried it herself. It was much harder because she was entirely unfamiliar with how it should work for what was essentially a cat, and the pieces only shrunk when she tried to put it in the right place on Boreal. Luckily, the set had all been assembled before she had started, so she had a vague idea of what to do and they eventually got it equipped.

"Alright, try it out," Zalia said, hands on her hips as she admired her handiwork.

Boreal started moving slowly before speeding up until she was sprinting around the place like a madwoman. The plate itself didn't make much sound but it definitely had a very noticeable effect on Boreal's ability to sneak, as she walked and landed a bit heavier. Through the vibration sight, Zalia could see the difference in a more definite way.

"Feel good?" Zalia asked once Boreal had finally stopped sprinting around.

"*More heavy,*" Boreal replied, panting heavily.

"Damn, I was hoping it would be good for you to use in combat," Zalia muttered.

"*More heavy good,*" Boreal exclaimed.

The statement came with an image of Boreal hitting an undead at high speeds wearing the armour.

"More heavy good," Zalia agreed, smiling a little.

While a work of art, the mental image wouldn't compare to seeing it happen for real. With a mixture of flight and a charged Pounce, Boreal would most likely explode even a Bronze undead on impact.

They left the long, low storeroom and searched the rest of the complex's buildings but didn't actually find any kind of armoury. Maybe it was in another part of the city, or maybe the soldiers all kept their own gear, she didn't know. Giving up, Zalia got a bearing on where she was and mentally recalled where the other places she wanted to search were located.

She was getting much better with that as her rank increased, and could recall and remember things accurately with less time needed to memorise them. The two closest places to them were the central market and the magical research facility. She definitely knew which she wanted to go to more but asked Boreal her opinion anyways.

"We can either go to the central market or a magical research facility. The latter is most likely to have some interesting things, but I don't know what type of facility it is or what kind of markets they had here, so it's anyone's guess," Zalia informed Boreal.

Boreal looked intently at Zalia with her piercing blue eyes glowing from beneath the plate armour. In addition to how big she was now and the trail of glowing prints she still left behind despite the armour, Boreal was actually starting to look less cute and more . . . scary.

"*You*," Boreal replied, relaying a sense of trust.

"Research facility it is, then," Zalia said with a smile.

Despite how much of a little shit Boreal could be sometimes, when it came down to it, she still trusted her, and it kept a small flame burning in Zalia's heart that had been so frozen over from years spent in the snow.

They left on wings of wind, with Boreal slightly quicker now despite the extra weight because she was somewhat streamlined and had less drag from her thick fur due to the armour. They arrived near the designated location and Zalia frowned at what they saw before them. She had been expecting a large, tower-like structure similar to a wizard's tower with a fanciful design, but instead was met with the sight of what was essentially a bunker. The central part of the bunker was a pit that led far into the ground with windows watching out, lending it the appearance of a reverse tower.

She could have just flown down to the bottom of the pit and into one of the windows but once again wasn't so keen on the idea of getting stuck down there surrounded by enemies, so she decided to take a little bit of a different route. She landed atop the roof of the circular bunker on the surface and prepared her ritual against being seen by the shades above. Looking forward to yet another fight, she activated the ritual and let out a loud yell.

CHAPTER THIRTY

Research

Zalia

Zalia looked out on the field of no longer undead corpses strewn in front of the bunker. The fight had been short and brutal, only very few were even Bronze rank. With only one shot required for her to kill the Tin, and not much more for the Iron, Zalia was able to take down the undead from afar. Annoyingly, the undead within the bunker had not come outside for a reason she was about to discover. First though, her ability levels: Kill Shot, Hunter's Mark, and Fight or Flight had all received only one level each, probably due to the ease of the fight.

Hopping down from the roof and lightly stepping past the half-disintegrated skeletons of Bathar, Zalia moved up to Boreal, who was sitting perfectly still by the door like a statue. She frowned at the door, finding it quite sturdy-looking. Realising she probably should have had a closer look *before* she had decided to fight half the neighbourhood, she tested the handle.

Frustratingly, it didn't budge more than a slight movement informing Zalia that it was indeed locked. She gave a test kick but it didn't move in the slightest. It was unfortunately magically protected in some manner because she couldn't just walk through it either. It made sense, having survived this long and being a magical research facility and all. She tried a few other things like slashing at it, jabbing her sword into the gap to cut the lock, manipulating the floor and door with her stone manipulation, and even a ritual meant to target the lock mechanism with the spreading ice curse to try and shatter it. She finally gave up on it.

Instead, she would have to unlock it from the inside, leaving Boreal behind for a short moment.

"Wait here," Zalia told Boreal, flying back up to the roof of the donut shaped bunker and walking towards the deep pit at its centre.

She dismissed the notification that was tallying her Flight passive up another eight levels to Tin fourteen so far and tried to fly down into the pit. She could see the windows leading into the building and thought the lack of protection here with such a strong door at the front was a silly design— until she felt a wave pass over her as she flew down. Her flight turned to a fall as her ritual was dispelled.

In a panic, she tried to quickly recast the ritual but found the magic wasn't working as she plummeted to the floor below. Luckily, it seemed her passives still worked, and she managed to slow her fall three times with the Mobility passive air step until she safely reached the ground. Her greatly enhanced body did a lot of the work to lessen the impact. Now at the bottom of the pit, she quickly inspected her surroundings for danger.

The near area was likely a once beautiful garden, now decrepit and twisted by the corruption permeating the air. The feeling of corruption was thankfully lessened probably due to whatever magical protections lay built into the structure, yet panic, just a little bit, crept into her mind as she realised her healing was not working. The defences were suppressing all her class abilities; only the general passives were available.

She desperately searched around the ground level for an exit but found only another door, locked and sturdy against her efforts. Feeling a fool, she got a run up and using her three air steps, managed to get high enough to catch the bottom of one of the windows. She hauled herself up quietly and checked both directions, not wanting to get stuck down here with no abilities and a bunch of high levelled, very awake undead.

Thankfully, the moment she stepped over the boundary of the window, she could feel Healing Presence activate once more. She hadn't been aware that power muting or disabling effects were even a possibility, and her first experience with it was horrible, to say the least. She had grown used to the feeling of power, the constant healing flowing through her body, and its absence had been nothing short of terrifying.

Trying to calm her nerves and only half succeeding, she began softly padding through the curved corridor she found herself in. There were many doors leading off it, but her goal for now was to reach the top. Once she was safe with no undead behind her, the more dangerous part of exploration could begin.

Sensing no vibrations of movement, she explored the entire corridor and found that there were no easily visible exits. If she wanted to find a way out she would have to start opening doors and hope to find the right one. She moved towards the nearest door but had a better idea. She went over to the window and had a look outside and up, seeing that there were indeed more windows lining the next floor up. She had seen that previously, of course, but wanted to make certain of their location before attempting the idea.

With a run up, Zalia vaulted out of the window, used one step to push herself into a sideways motion, a second for height, and the third to slow herself as her hands caught the next window's ledge. It was a difficult maneuver to pull off that a less dexterous Zalia wouldn't have managed. At this height it was mostly harmless, but as she looked up, she dreaded how many times she would have to pull it off to get to the top. Another . . . sixteen times by her count.

She managed another twelve floors before she slipped up. She screwed up the final step and almost flew straight past the window, barely catching on with one hand. She managed to get her momentum under control and hauled herself through the window, standing in silence as her heart beat loudly in her chest. She had thought of and tried passing through the floors but found them magically protected as well.

"*Boreal?*" Zalia asked, projecting her thoughts.

She had tried to contact Boreal on each floor but was met with silence each time. A few of the floors did have undead unconscious or strolling about but none had taken notice of her as she quickly ascended the floors. This floor had no more undead on it, so she took a moment to rest and relax, considering her next move. Statistically speaking, she could probably make it to the top, but she wasn't much of a statistics person anyways. The risk of falling the entire way to the ground with no air steps left was much too high for her. She loved flying but falling to her death didn't sound so fun.

With a gentle, almost silent sigh, she pushed off the ledge she had been leaning on and looked down each side of the corridor. Much like the rest of the bunker, it was a single corridor with many doors leading off it. She was starting to wonder if they even had any stairs at all or if they had just somehow floated between levels via the windows. What were the chances that a magical system controlling travel between levels was broken when the magical system in charge of defending wasn't?

Thinking about it, she realised it would probably be likely.

She remembered that in her world, before she had moved to be more solitary, methods of travel tended to break down quite often.

Her mind made up, Zalia stepped up to the closest door and inspected it closely. It was definitely magically guarded, given her inability to step through it, but testing the handle, she found it unlocked. She released the handle gently and observed the vibrations coming through the door and floor beneath. She couldn't identify any signs of movement from the other side of the door and so turned the handle and pushed it open slowly. Inside was a bare room with the remains of various instruments on a desk, and seated in front of the desk was an undead slumped in a chair.

In the centre of the desk was the focus of the instrument's attention—a single object. A glove.

CHAPTER THIRTY-ONE

Ascending

Zalia

Zalia quickly checked the undead's rank and was shocked to see it was Silver. It was Silver, yet it was not awake like the guards in the keep had been. She paused in thought, inspecting the glove as well.

> **Ethereal Vault Gauntlet (Heirloom) - Unbonded Bronze rank.**

"*Oh damn,*" Zalia thought.

A Bronze rank heirloom item, and it looked like it might be a storage item of some sort as well. The only issue being that a Silver rank undead lay between her and the heirloom; the guard's face on the table was mere centimetres from the glove. She could *probably* take out the undead before it made enough noise to attract others, but she was not certain of that fact. She was also uncertain whether Silver was the highest rank she would find in this bunker either.

Her curiosity almost got the better of her; the temptation to try and take the glove right there and now was strong but not quite stronger than her survival instincts. Taking it now with no path of retreat was a risk with a strong chance for death.

So, she left it there. She marked it in her mind as being on the fifth floor and left the room, managing to carve a tiny scratch into the floor in front of the door as a marker for later. She walked a circle around the floor she was on, trying once more to discern any visible difference in the doors, yet finding none at all. Questioning if she would have to use the floor-jumping method to climb the rest of the way anyways, she decided to try opening one more door.

Picking somewhat randomly, she tried to see if there were vibrations of movement coming from under the door, and this time she saw some. She wasn't an expert at deciphering the meaning of the vibrations by any means but it looked like something was either walking around in a circle or continuously walking into the wall.

Deciding to move on from that door rather than risk it, she moved to the next on her right. Once more, she was met with slight, repetitive vibrations. She found another two doors with similar patterns and skipped those too, with the third after those finally bringing change. Much like the first door she had opened, it held no vibrations, and so she lightly pushed it open, peering inside.

Within was a room that had the appearance of a weapons-testing range. The walls, floor, and ceiling were very easily distinguishable as having been fortified with magic—they had a light sheen that could have been described as a glow. Further down the hallway-like room, a solid block of stone protruded from the ground. As she had hoped, there were no undead in here, but it was not the exit she was looking for so she left the door open and went to the next.

She stood before three more doors before finally finding something different. She was about to leave the current one when she noticed that the vibrations were fading, their centre moving upwards on the wall rather than remaining on the ground. She waited for them to fade entirely before opening the door, revealing a stairway that led up, rotating leftwards.

Relieved that they did actually have stairs in the building, Zalia thought for a moment before coming up with a plan. Leaving the door open, she went back into the corridor and down to the door that held the weapons-testing room. She peeked around the door, looking towards the staircase and waited. Just as she hoped, the undead came shambling out of the stairway door and began walking towards her.

Quickly pulling her head back behind the door and slowly closing it, she waited. She heard and saw through the vibrations as the Bathar moved past the door she was hiding behind, beginning the first of many loops around the circular corridor that was the fifth floor. Once it was far enough past, she left the room and went to the stairway, closing the door behind her and ascending to the next level.

The moment she was at the door of the fourth floor, she tried contacting Boreal again.

"*Boreal?*" she projected.

"*Zalia!*" The reply came shortly after.

She breathed a sigh of relief at finally making contact.

"*Are you ok?*" she asked.

"*Ok. Zalia where?*" Boreal asked.

The tone her mental communication relayed was tinged with concern. Zalia chewed on her lower lip a little.

"*I might have fallen all the way to the bottom,*" Zalia explained.

There was a moment of silence.

"*Zalia fly?*" Boreal asked.

"*No, no, there is some type of magic that stops abilities from working. Don't try to come down here,*" Zalia replied.

Once more, a moment of silence.

"*Zalia ok?*" Boreal asked.

"*Zalia is doing just fine, I'm almost all the way up now,*" Zalia said comfortingly.

She began explaining what she had seen so far, sending images along with her explanations. Boreal didn't ask her to, but it was as much to distract Boreal from Zalia's current situation than anything else. Once Boreal caught up to where she was, Zalia began explaining what she was doing.

"*I'm about to open the door to the fourth floor. It looks like there are some vibrations coming under the door so I'll have to time this right,*" Zalia said.

"*Zalia careful,*" Boreal insisted.

Giving a mental affirmative, Zalia waited until all the vibrations had faded and opened the door. Seeing that there were undead all over this level, she quickly slid to the left and entered the door there, hoping it was the stairwell. Luckily, it was. Unluckily, she slammed face-first into an undead that was standing unconscious right in front of the door.

With a reaction speed born of training and bonded physical and mental stats, her sword was summoned and slammed point-first through its face before it could react. Its skull began disintegrating from the blue light applied by the blade, and she closed the door behind her with one hand as she still held the undead upright by its skull. She caught the dead Bathar just before its head completely disintegrated and slowly lowered it to the floor.

"*Zalia careful?*" Boreal asked.

In a moment of panic, Zalia had stopped transmitting.

"*Just a little Iron rank undead, nothing to be worried about,*" Zalia replied, sending an image of her blade through its head.

"*Zalia bad sneaking,*" Boreal said, sending a tsking sound.

"What? I'm great at sneaking. When did you learn to tsk?" Zalia refuted.

"Cook would catch already," Boreal insisted.

"What does that mean?" Zalia asked.

"Camp cooks would catch," Boreal explained.

"No, they wouldn't, they would give the food to me. You would only be at risk of getting caught because you're bad at asking," Zalia retorted.

Boreal was silent for a moment.

"Cook never catch Boreal," she explained.

"How many times did you steal from them?" Zalia asked incredulously.

"Just . . . few," Boreal lied.

"Klepto-cat," Zalia said.

"I like name," Boreal replied proudly.

Zalia sighed, quietly, and focused back on what she was doing. The stairway before her was empty and she couldn't see any vibrations coming from it so she ascended.

She made it all the way to the top floor with no more trouble, though each level had more undead than the last. The issue she ran into was that while the top floor was relatively clear of undead, the one part that wasn't was the corridor leading to the front door. Some lay unconscious against the walls while others stood still like statues. It looked like they had all died where they stood, clumped up against the door.

She had assumed the death of many of the Bathar in the city had been instantaneous based on where she had found the undead in the keep, but the sight before her told a different story. It was like they had died as they tried to escape the building in a panic, pushing towards the door as they tried to open it.

The reality of the horror that had befallen the city here finally settled in as she looked at the clump of undead pushed into the hallway. She had seen more of the Bathar here as undead than people that had once been alive, yet they had been, hadn't they?

She shook her head, thinking about the massacre and enslavement of an entire city via undeath could wait until she was safe. Her issue now was getting past the undead to unlock the front door, something easier said than done.

Now that she was near to the entrance, she could possibly begin releasing the undead from their eternal slavery. She decided it was a good idea to do just that as she realised she did actually have a route of escape if absolutely necessary. Being on the top floor, she would be able to jump through the window onto the roof above if it came to it.

Mind made up, she started summoning various traps and placing them around. The tripwires wouldn't work as she couldn't plant them into the walls but bear traps and the extending caltrops both would work just fine.

Satisfied with her preparation, she decided to start the fight off with a giant ritual seeing as they wouldn't respond until she did so. Knowledge she had courtesy of the Bronze guards back in the keep.

Using the Bronze ability of Herbal Magic, she combined Bitterbalm and Snow-leaf to make it create the lava element rather than the ice it originally did. She did the same with Bitterbalm and Dodge-vine making the base element vulnerability. She began laying down a ritual using the altered Snow-leaf and Dodge-vine as minor elements to a major Bitterbalm base. The entire thing put together would apply a lava and vulnerability-based curse to the whole clump of undead. Simultaneously, she used an ice creation ritual to begin summoning a wall in front of her.

She summoned her bow as both rituals activated at once. The undead were woken immediately as their bodies were riddled with deep red glowing lines that began smoking. A wall of ice with holes for her to shoot through appeared in the start of the hallway, entirely blocking it off. Traps went off left, right, and centre as the horde charged towards her and the wall. Used to the terrifying sight, Zalia let off arrow after arrow into the approaching mass, trusting the various stacking abilities of her bow proficiency and heirloom weapon to do most of the work. Blue lines joined the red as the bodies of the undead were burnt up from the inside and out.

Trying something a little different, she cast the spreading ice curse on the wall in front of her so as the undead began impacting it and trying to break through, the wall started growing over their bodies, encasing them. The undead behind them began pushing and ripping at the ones stuck in front, some even starting to tear each other apart in their rush to reach Zalia.

The fight was quick and brutal; the combination of Zalia's preparation and the confined area reducing the numbers advantage brought a swift end to the Bathar. Once more, they died in droves, none of them releasing the dark shade Juniper had when killed.

Once the work was done, with most of the bodies completely burned away due to the curse she had inflicted upon them, Zalia let go of the rituals and walked through the mess. She had not gained a single level on any ability from the fight, the numbers too small and the fight too easy to grant any.

Stepping over the last body, she pulled back the bar built into the door and clicked the small lock on the handle. For such a small lock, the amount of effort she needed to put in to reach it annoyed her, but it was what it was. She pulled the door open and was greeted by a flying Boreal landing right in her arms.

"*I missed you too, little one,*" Zalia comforted.

She gently put Boreal down, having finally calmed the now large feline. Boreal was getting much too big for Zalia to comfortably hold anymore, which was a sad reality, but the truth of it. She looked back towards the bunker, towards disintegrating corpses and the heirloom glove she knew to lie far beneath the surface.

"There is something down there I really, really want to get," Zalia said.

"*Glove!*" Boreal exclaimed.

"Yes, young one, glove. It might solve some of our more carrying-based issues," Zalia explained.

She stepped back into the bunker and began the long process of making her way back down.

Now that she had a clear escape route, a lot of the stress and unnecessary sneaking was eliminated. She began slowly clearing out, room by room, floor by floor, as they descended towards the layer she knew to have the glove. Along the way she had to kill many of the undead and searched many rooms, and while she found many interesting bits of instruments and artefacts, she didn't find anything particularly useful until reaching the fifth floor.

Finding the door with the small marking she had made, Zalia gently pushed it open for Boreal to see. Killing the Silver undead would be easy; the thing was asleep and definitely was not on the level of the guards in terms of combat skills. She assumed.

They made quick work of the undead, finding it indeed didn't have much skill in fighting at all. They had noticed something similar on the way down, as most of the Bathar here were incredibly weak in comparison to the guards at the keep. It made sense, if the undead retained some of the same skills they had when alive, then the researchers wouldn't be the best at combat.

And so, with a blade impaling it to the desk, a violent cat, and an unhealthy dose of magic later, the Silver researcher lay dead in its chair. Zalia let her sword fade away to mist, pushed the undead's remains out of the way, and picked up the glove.

> **Ethereal Vault Gauntlet (Heirloom) - Unbonded Bronze rank.**

She had a slight feeling that this would be much harder for her to bond than the other two had been. Since it was Bronze rank already, whereas she was not, it only made sense. She slipped the glove onto her right hand and flexed it, testing her mobility. She had to take off her armour's gauntlet to do so but it would be worth it if she could get the thing working.

"*Any ideas?*" she sent to Boreal.

"*Feed it?*" Boreal asked tentatively.

Zalia looked at Boreal incredulously.

"*That's really all you can ever come up with, isn't it?*" she asked in response.

"*Food works,*" Boreal retorted.

Annoyingly, food had worked for the most part so far.

"*Let's get out of here,*" Zalia said.

They left the bunker and started flying back to the island holding the god. Maybe Delphi would have some insight into bonding heirloom items.

She inspected the glove as she flew. It was a supple leather with metal rods extending above where the tendons on the top of her hands were. They went all the way to her fingertips and strangely didn't seem to inhibit her movement at all, shrinking or growing to fit the movement of her hand. The bottom side of the glove had an intricate design inlaid in a pale blue metal.

After having defeated a whole bunch of undead on the way down into the bunker, she checked her profile for the level ups.

Profile - Zalia Taori
Health - Excellent
Mana - Full
Stamina - Full
Class One - Hunter - Iron 13
Linked Attributes - Strength, Dexterity
Active Skills
Kill Shot - Iron 18
Hunter's Mark - Iron 19
Fight or Flight - Iron 18
Passive Skills
Hunter's Sight - Iron 13
Survivalist - Bronze 1
Class Two - Herbalist - Iron 9
Linked Attributes - Vitality, Resilience
Active Skills
Flora Identification - Iron 9
Preparation - Iron 10

Stasis - Iron 10
Passive skills
Harvester - Iron 10
Herbal Magic - Bronze 1
Unity Class - Druid - Iron 12
Linked Attributes - Wisdom, Intellect
Active Skills
Nature's Wrath - Iron 17
Protection of the Wilds - Iron 12
Passive Skills
Healing Presence - Bronze 1
General Passives
Heat Resistance - Bronze 1
Cold Resistance - Bronze 1
Aura Observation - Iron 2
Low Light Vision - Iron 5
Poison Resistance - Iron 7
Mobility - Bronze 1
Stealth - Bronze 1
Trapper - Bronze 1
Teaching - Iron 7
Flight - Tin 15
Physical Resistance - Bronze 1
Mental Resistance - Bronze 1
Weapon Proficiencies
Bow - Bronze 1
Sword - Bronze 1
Throwing Knives - Tin 17
Bonded Items
Druidic Bow, Blessed by Starlight (Blessed
Heirloom) - Deeply bonded Iron rank.
Duskwraith Armour (Heirloom) - Bonded Iron rank.

A few abilities had gone up by one, and Hunter's Mark was swiftly approaching Bronze. All of her Herbalist abilities were still far behind, but she could work on them later. Her combat abilities would be much more impactful in her current activities anyways.

She still hadn't managed to bond the item by the time they arrived back at the island, so she left it for the moment as she walked into the temple. Going downstairs, she found Delphi and the other collective members arrayed in a semicircle facing the god. While no sound came from them, she was surprised to see that the god was speaking clearly.

"*Welcome back, Zalia, we have a bit to talk about,*" Delphi greeted her.

CHAPTER THIRTY-TWO

Door Thoughts

Zalia

What do you mean by 'a bit to talk about?'" Zalia asked, looking warily at the god.

"*We have managed to help this god get its fractured memories under control. It does not remember much—anything at all, to be frank,*" Delphi explained.

Zalia stared at Delphi. Sensing the gaze, Delphi turned to Zalia.

A moment passed.

"*Don't yo—* " Delphi started.

"Anything to be Frank?" Zalia interrupted innocently.

"*Zalia—*" Delphi said, trying to speak again.

"Oh, I know, I know. It was a stressful few hours I just had, give me a break," Zalia said, waving her hand.

She now had all five frogs staring at her with eerie eyes.

"I've got some questions!" Zalia said enthusiastically.

"*About?*" Delphi asked.

"Well, see this glove here? I was wondering if you knew anything about bonding heirloom items?" Zalia asked.

"*You appear to have quite a few now, Boreal even has one as well. Have you not bonded with these?*" Delphi asked.

"Oh, I have, but I thought since this was a Bronze rank one it might be harder," Zalia explained.

"*Not at all. All heirlooms have different requirements to be bonded. I'm sure those that you have bonded with have told you as much. The difficulty you have with bonding an item increases depending on whether it is a fit to you.*

All can be bonded, of course, you just need the right mindset and actions to do so," Delphi replied.

Zalia thought about that and saw the truth in the words. Her bow had been quite easy to bond, only needing her to go about her life while using it, as she would with a normal one. The armour had been similarly easy, just requiring her to wear it in what was deemed as a ritualistic manner. That had just been her carefully putting each piece on as it resized to her dimensions, yet with that requirement, the armour itself must have had some link to rituals or religion of some sort.

The armour currently equipped to Boreal was bonded, as far as she knew, though she didn't deign to ask. Her best guess, based on it being the armour of an animal used in war, was that it either bonded by being equipped by Boreal's 'handler' or by her fighting with it on.

"So what do you need to be bonded with?" Zalia muttered to her glove.

She . . . didn't really know anything about it other than it *might* be a storage device of some kind. With a name like Ethereal Vault Gauntlet, it just had to be, right?

Well, if it was a storage item, maybe she could try to bond it by holding things with it. It sounded a little goofy but it was kind of all she could come up with at the moment.

So, she took out her map and held it. She tried to think really hard about storing it too, keeping the feeling of taking things in and out of Stasis in her mind. She thought about how it felt to take her weapon in and out of its storage space.

She stared at the glove and the map held lightly in its grip. Nothing happened.

"It's not working," Zalia said.

"*You may take a while to bond if it is not something suited to your personality or mindset. Some have been known to take many, many cycles,*" Delphi informed her.

"How many cycles is many!?" Zalia asked.

"*Many,*" Delphi replied mysteriously.

Zalia put the map back and squinted her eyes at the glove.

"You will not be taking many, many cycles. Whatever that means," Zalia told it.

She finally turned to the god that was watching her with interest.

"Have you remembered your name?" she asked.

"My name, I do not remember," it replied.

Its voice was croaky, light yet gravelly. It wasn't deep, yet it had a certain resonance to it that gave it a quality of power all the same. This was what she was used to when speaking to gods, its voice now clear, yet full of mystery. Similar to the starlight wolf but with its own uniqueness.

"Do you remember how you ended up here, in this condition?" Zalia asked instead.

"Exactly, I do not. It happened slowly, ever so slowly across many, many years. Lost, forgotten, cast aside to fall down where those who die go to live. Above, I am forgotten, yet here a temple of mine resides, and so I live just as I am not alive," it explained.

"It doesn't sound like a pleasant fate. I met someone you may have known, a large wolf cast in stars, glowing amidst its pack," Zalia told it.

"I do not have memories of this person you speak of, yet I know them by the very essence of my being. They are one of the few left truly alive," it said.

"I think I might know what happened to you, based on what the starlight wolf told me. It said that its power had diminished over the long years, as it had been forgotten by most. I fear what has happened to you will happen to it too, should it be truly forgotten," Zalia explained.

"Yet, by your very thought of it, so too does it continue to exist. Much as I do now," the god told Zalia.

A light shiver ran down her body at the words. It confirmed the idea that the gods did indeed live off the faith or belief of their followers.

Ro-ak was staring up at the god with what Zalia could only think of as awe. She personally had no idea how a crow could just be chilling alive down in hell without any abilities that she could see, but she had a feeling it was the power of the god before her that kept him alive.

"Is there anything you can tell me that might be helpful or important at the moment? Maybe there is some way that I can help you recover?" Zalia asked.

"I . . . there is something. Something I cannot remember, yet it is important. I . . ." it said falteringly.

Its eyes went cloudy and the look of confusion appeared once more. Its voice slowly lost its power and went back to how it had been before as it struggled to remember.

"*You should cease questions now, Zalia, we will work to help it remember,*" Delphi told her.

"Alright, sorry for pushing. It seems so . . . fragile," Zalia commented.

"*It may be a god, but it is one that has been dead for a very, very long time. This will take much patience,*" Delphi said firmly.

"Not always so good at that with everything," Zalia murmured.

"*Just think of it as one of your hunts, you have patience aplenty for that,*" Delphi replied.

She snorted a laugh and moved away, turning her focus back to the glove on her hand. She walked over to the door and pushed it open before pausing. She took her hand off it and opened it the rest of the way with her gloved hand.

"A vault, hey?" she muttered.

She hadn't considered it before, but what if it was quite literal about it being a vault? Would it be possible it opened an actual ethereal vault she could walk into, rather than storing items directly like she was used to with her bow?

Keeping that thought in mind, she left the small room to go get some air. Ro-ak and Boreal had started dueling again and the sound of metal clanking as Boreal threw herself bodily at the walls was a little grating.

She slowly walked up the stairs, keeping her thoughts open to . . . doors opening. If there was not necessarily a limitation to her bonding a higher-ranked item, then she should be able to manage it. Though, maybe higher-ranked items tended to be a little more complex and thus naturally were harder to bond.

She stepped out of the temple and sat on a rock. Staring at the glove she flexed her hand a few times, imagining a door opening. Then, she reached out to the air and pulled on it like she was opening a door. Nothing happened.

She dropped her hand with a sigh.

Congratulations! You have given up trying to understand the 'Ethereal Vault Gauntlet' and your mind has now finally opened to it. This item is now bonded to you.
Ethereal Vault Gauntlet (Heirloom) - Bonded Bronze rank.
Tin - You may tear open space to access an ethereal vault. The ethereal vault is a limited extradimensional space that you may enter and store objects within.
Iron - You gain the power to store and retrieve information within the ethereal vault. By concentrating on a specific topic, memory, or piece of knowledge while wearing the gauntlet, you can mentally "record" it into the gauntlet's vault. This information is then stored in an abstract, ethereal form, like a shimmering light. When needed, you can access the gauntlet to "read" the stored information, allowing you to quickly recall facts, details, or instructions you have previously recorded.
Bronze - Your control over the ethereal vault extradimensional space becomes more

> refined. You gain the ability to manipulate the spatial dimensions within the vault, allowing you to efficiently organise and stack stored items without regard to their physical sizes. This ability enables you to store a larger quantity of objects within the same limited space.

"Well, I'll be damned," Zalia murmured.

CHAPTER THIRTY-THREE

Vault

Zalia

Zalia flexed her hand, now very aware of an intangible feeling coming from the glove. The contradicting idea of a feeling she could not feel was somehow impossible, yet the best way she could describe it.

Wanting to try out the ability immediately, she stood up from her rock and took a few steps away from the temple. Reaching out, she pushed her hand *through* something. A glowing amber outline grew from the empty air, wrapping around her hand like a hold on a piece of reality. When she pulled to the side, a gentle sound akin to wood groaning could be heard as an oval was cut out of the space in front of her.

The opening reminded her of the blurry portal she had seen when first discovering the rituals taking place in Endaria, back in the mine. The main difference was that this one didn't look into the very hell she now inhabited, but a bland room with untarnished white walls and rows of grey shelves.

She stepped through the portal and into the space beyond. The corrupting aura faded, though didn't disappear entirely, and the sulphurous taste and smell to the air changed to clean and clear. She breathed deeply, having been completely unaware of how much she missed breathing clean air until that moment.

She stepped back out.

"*Hey, Boreal, I just bonded with the glove if you want to come see what it does. Bring Delphi and Ro if they're interested too,*" she projected towards the room below.

With that done, she stepped back into the vault.

Looking around the small room, there wasn't really anything else to see. It was pretty basic, no obvious lights of any sort, yet a gentle light permeated the space, and no furniture other than shelves. There were a total of ten shelves, and each shelf contained two smaller shelves with five small half-sphere shapes cut out equidistantly across their surface.

The two rows of five shelves lay to either side of where she had entered, and she stepped up to the closest right-side one, reaching out to touch the small indent. She felt a light tingle of energy run down her arm as she ran her fingers over the smooth surface. An understanding of what its purpose was entered her mind and she got out her map, her only other possession at that moment.

Touching the indent with her glove as she held the map, it floated out of her hand, shrinking as it moved. Now fitting in the indent, it gently came to rest and a clear dome formed over it.

Boreal burst through the vault doorway with Delphi hanging on to her neck for dear life, Ro-ak flying through close behind. Boreal slowed down, checking out the vault as Ro settled lightly on top of a shelf. Ro-ak saw the map now protected by a dome and took flight again, leaving the vault.

"What do you think?" Zalia asked.

"*Can eat?*" Boreal asked.

"No, you cannot eat the shiny new vault I just got," Zalia replied flatly.

"*It will be a good tool for one such as you who needs to store many physical items,*" Delphi admitted.

"Ahh, now, now, oh high and mighty frog lord, so ascended as to need nothing but the strength of his mind. This here vault can store more than just physical things," Zalia said, a little happy she got to show off.

Before she got a chance to, Ro-ak flew back through the door with a shiny object in his beak. He dumped what she recognised as the damaged spoon at her feet, looking up at her with a cocked head.

"We are not using this as a storage for your shiny things, Ro," Zalia said.

Ro looked down at the floor and gently picked the spoon back up, turned about and started walking back out in a slow and dramatic fashion. Zalia rolled her eyes.

"Fiiine, give it here," she said.

Ro spun back around and hopped over joyfully, dumping the spoon at her feet again. Zalia picked it up and walked over to the first left shelf and put it into the first spot there.

"Happy?" she asked.

Ro bobbed his head up and down in a gesture not unlike a nod.

"Right, as I was demonstrating," Zalia said, turning back to Delphi.

Unsure how exactly it worked but giving it a try, she touched the glove to the next open spot and focused on a memory. Thinking about the name of the Bathar city, Hetheir, a wispy stream left her eyes and flowed down her body to her arm and around the gauntlet, accumulating in the indent. A clear dome grew over it and the mist swirled slowly within.

"It can store memories too," she said proudly.

"*Well, now I'm interested,*" Delphi replied, a little bit of awe peeking through the usual scholarly tone.

"As far as I know, it can store them indefinitely too. Cool, hey?" Zalia added.

"*It is certainly a good tool for one unable to do this naturally,*" Delphi said, blinking his eyes at Zalia.

"You're telling me you have perfect memory recollection? What about the memories you said you've lost?" Zalia countered.

"*Memories lost on purpose. The sheer volume of memories within the collective simply cannot be held with our current population. Every new thing we learn must have a space made for it if we wish to keep it. The memories even I hold would simply overwhelm this space's ability to contain them,*" Delphi answered patiently.

"Yeah, alright, I get it, memories are your thing. Still, it could come in handy for me," Zalia said, still happy with it.

She tried to remember the name of the Bathar city but it was simply gone from her mind. She knew that she knew the name, she just didn't know the name. Focusing, the name popped back into her mind. Hetheir. As soon as she stopped focusing on it, the name vanished once more.

It was exactly like Delphi had explained to her previously about knowing what the collective knew, just not knowing exactly what that was himself.

She touched the glove to the wispy memory and collected it, the mist flowing back into her eyes.

"Right, I'll have to play around with that some more, but it seems I can access the memories I store here even without collecting them back directly. It might be worth storing some of the more tedious things I learn here," she thought out loud.

"*Anything that has fine detail is good to keep within your long-term memory storage; it will be less affected by your mind's ability to warp details that way,*" Delphi explained.

"Like, maps, for instance?" she asked.

"*That would be a good example, yes,*" Delphi confirmed.

Zalia walked to the back of the room and touched the first spot of the right-hand shelf's top shelf. Focusing on the map of Hetheir she had memorised, she pushed the wispy memory into the indent.

It was then that she noticed another wispy memory sitting on the bottom of the shelf a few spots in.

"Hey, Delphi, come check this out," she called.

Delphi hopped over and looked at what she was pointing to.

"*A memory—you did not put it here?*" Delphi asked.

"No," she replied, eyeing the wispy dome, "think I should absorb it?"

"*That . . . would be a risky decision. I am interested as to what memory could have possibly been stored in here,*" Delphi pondered, "*tell me, where did you find this item?*"

Rather than retell the story, Zalia simply played back the events before and after finding the glove in Delphi's mind. Kind of like a fast-forwarded mental movie beamed directly from her mind to his.

"*I see. My best hypothesis is a memory placed in here by the person you saw lying on the desk. The one you brutally slaughtered, I might add,*" Delphi said.

Zalia winced. While she felt it was a good deed to release the Bathar from their undead soul prisons, it did take a level of . . . disconnection or coldheartedness to do what she was doing. The ability to disconnect emotion from the kills she made came from a long time as a hunter. It was both a good and bad thing, allowing her to survive without guilt, but saying that, she did also need to remain careful of walking that line lest she lose touch with her morality.

"Yes. You have seen me killing the other undead, why does this bother you more so?" Zalia asked, having not missed the slight anger in Delphi's tone.

"*The knowledge and memories that such a person would have held are invaluable. A Silver rank researcher, and everything they knew is now just . . . gone,*" Delphi said, anger turning to sadness.

"It is an unthinkable nightmare, what happened here. An entire city just gone. From what I've seen, it happened in just a few moments as well," Zalia said.

Her vivid memory of the monster flying over the city returned, as did the feeling of panic at the strength of the corrupting aura it emitted. What would it feel like to experience the aura of even two of those beings? What about ten of them?

She shuddered at the thought.

"But saying that, the knowledge these people hold is already gone, Delphi. All except this one little orb and the few pieces of parchment preserved in the keep," Zalia finished, looking at the stored memory.

"*Despite that fact, I still think it is a great risk. We don't know how some-one else's memory will mesh with your brain when put in directly like that,*" Delphi said.

"I'm gonna do it anyway," Zalia told him.

"*Yeah, I know,*" Delphi replied.

Nodding, Zalia leaned down and touched her hand to the clear dome with the Vault Gauntlet. She prepared herself as the mist trailed up her arm and entered her eyes.

CHAPTER THIRTY-FOUR

Memories

Zalia

A burning sensation flowed through Zalia's mind as the memory took hold. Unlike the memory of the city name that slotted neatly back into the place it had left, this one felt incongruous, disconnected even. Knowing that she had a master of memories next to her relieved her stress as her consciousness was transported to the memory now dominating her mind.

Zalia blinked lightly, looking around at the city before her. She was in Hetheir, only it was not Hetheir as she remembered it. The city was a hive of busy movement, Bathar clothed in vibrant strips of colour with thick fur underneath, going about their day. No, they weren't going about their day. This was just one of many days filled with an unusual level of activity as they prepared the city for evacuation. Everyone had a job to do, people to watch out for, and preparations to make. Everyone except for her, of course.

She—no, he was a researcher. His work had been deemed more important than the possible manpower he could provide to the evacuation efforts. He looked down at his fur-covered hands, turning them over. What had he been doing?

That was right. He quickly set off once more, heading towards the research facility he called home for most of his waking hours these days. The time and freedom to research whatever he deemed most important for a reasonable number of hours a week were a thing of the past. No, now he worked far too many hours in the hopes of discovering anything that could help.

He arrived at the research facility, and as the guards saw his vibrant orange sash trimmed in Silver, he was let in. He passed through the entrance corridor and moved towards the stairs, nodding towards workmates and friends alike as he descended. Reaching the fifth floor, he entered his own little research room, something akin to a cell these days.

Honestly, though, that was how he liked it. Most of his kind scoffed at the lack of reverence he held towards nature and the gods who oversaw it, but neither had ever really been his thing. No, the quiet, simple, and comfortably solitary confines of his study were the place for him.

Sitting down at the desk, he pulled out his notes from the desk and ordered them neatly before him, tuning the aura reader onto the glove on the desk. He began by reading over his notes from the previous day, cementing in his mind the measurements taken and reactions observed.

Despite the fact he had been assigned to research the glove's potential to reveal knowledge about portals and the connection between two different planar spaces, it was still interesting work. In addition to that, this particular item had some very unique properties that would make it useful to him, now that he had bonded it. Its ability to store memories that were easily and perfectly recalled at any moment provided an excellent tool for any sort of research he would undertake in the future.

A few hours later as he was about to begin some more in-depth tests of the glove's ability to open portals directly, he felt a . . . wrongness in the air. A ripping sound, loud as anything, deafened him as the world shook, the bunker thankfully magically reinforced. From out of nowhere, a powerful force slammed into him.

It was like a . . . corruption within the very air around him was pushing him down to the desk. He felt his body decaying, the flesh withering and his mind fading. Desperately, he reached out for the glove and touched his hand to it. He could feel his death approaching as the aura pressed into his body, wearing it down. So much knowledge, so much time spent gathering, taking notes, writing, remembering. Surely the glove would take some of it, keep a piece of him alive even as he died.

His last sight was that of the mist leaving his eyes and entering the glove as he felt himself die.

Zalia came back to, breathing in sharply. She stood in the same place she had been, breathing heavily as the memory finally settled in her mind. She sat down heavily against the wall, a sob wracking her body.

She . . . he had died. She had felt it, the panic, the desperation as his body fell to the corruption. The final desperate actions of a body pumping adrenaline to keep itself alive. The eventual peace.

She shuddered, tears flowing freely now. A calming presence laid itself over her mind and she focused her own healing on herself, taking comfort in the feeling of healing circulating through her body.

"*That was hard to experience, yet an important memory indeed,*" Delphi said tiredly.

"Y-you saw it too?" Zalia asked, her breathing evening out as the combined effects calmed her.

"*I was guiding the memory in a way that would stop it breaking your mind,*" Delphi explained.

She remembered the gradual shift from the memory being her in perspective to the Bathar's own.

"Thank you, I see that. It was so sudden and that aura . . . so strong. There is nothing we could do against that if it were to happen. We would be dead in moments, just as that Bathar was," Zalia murmured somberly, another shudder racking her body.

". . . *Yes,*" Delphi said.

"I don't want this in my mind," Zalia said.

She reached out to the nearest indent, the bottom right of the furthest shelf in the room, and focused the memory in her mind for a moment. She pushed it out and the mist gathered before being closed in once more. As long as she had the glove on she wouldn't be able to be entirely rid of the memory but she definitely didn't want it just . . . sitting there in her mind.

"Thank you for your help, Delphi, I appreciate it. I'd probably still be a huddled mess without you here," she added, looking towards the little frog on the ground.

"*No need to thank me. I . . . the collective didn't see this. We had no idea of this place, or of these happenings. That is concerning,*" Delphi replied.

"Not so all-seeing after all," Zalia said, allowing a small smile onto her face.

At that moment, Boreal decided to bury Zalia in a decidedly uncomfortable metallic hug. She had to hold Boreal still as the flailing, metal death-machine smacked her head into Zalia's with a dull *clank*.

"Yeah, that's one way to get rid of the memory," Zalia groaned, holding her head.

"*Zalia sad?*" Boreal asked.

"No, no, just . . . tired," Zalia told her.

"*Should hunt,*" Boreal said.

"I'm . . . a little tired of death right now, Boreal," Zalia explained.

"*Then should grow,*" Boreal countered.

"That's actually a good idea," Zalia said.

Boreal jumped off her and dashed through the vault, only smashing into one set of shelves as she took the turn too tightly. For an incredibly dexterous and stealthy feline, she could definitely be chaotic, clumsy, and loud sometimes.

"Do you want to go back to our island? I'm going to go stare at plants for a little while," Zalia asked Delphi.

"*No, we will stay with the god and see if we can heal their mind any more than we have. Please do not stay away for too long, however. The aura is weak enough down there that we can mostly take care of ourselves, but we will not be able to leave,*" Delphi replied.

"I won't be too long," Zalia promised.

She left the vault with the others, Delphi and Ro going back into the temple. Zalia mentally let go of the portal and the vault closed once more, but she could feel the contents in the back of her mind. She knew that the memories, her map, and the damaged silver spoon were all still in there.

She summoned wings for both her and Boreal and they began the long flight back to their island. Along the way she received another two levels of flight, bringing it to Tin seventeen. She could definitely feel the effect the rapidly increasing passive had on her flight, allowing her control and speed to both increase dramatically.

Before long, they arrived at the island and made their way into the cave, past the few traps and into the small chamber she had for growing plants.

Quickly reinvigorating the plants, she closely observed the rituals and power flowing through the room and found something weird. Now that the plants were grown and established, there was an almost cyclic feel to the power in the room. In the snow area, for example, the rituals she had set up were cooling the area and that was allowing the plants to grow. The odd part, she discovered, was that the plants had begun fueling that ritual with their own power, as if they knew their survival relied on it or . . . like they had become a part of a natural ritual.

She stared at the plants for a few minutes, considering what this meant for her powers. Could she set up natural, self-cycling enchantments or ritual emplacements in the form of living plants?

Inspecting the plants, she could tell it wasn't accomplishing what it was trying to do very efficiently. So, she decided to try to fix that.

She carefully dug up some of the plants and placed them in a shape that roughly copied the very ritual she had used to create the small snowy biome. She dismissed the original ritual and overlaid the plants with the ritual and watched as they immediately took hold, the ritual becoming a part of the Snow-leaf plants.

Now doing so in a much more efficient manner, Zalia felt like the plants would be able to sustain the ritual almost indefinitely if they didn't require her to come by every now and then to ensure they didn't die to the corruption aura permeating the place. What if she could set something up to counter that though?

Her healing was able to prevent the plants from dying and even grow them, should she wish, and she had a feeling that a ritual born of that power would be able to accomplish a similar thing. That was one idea for something she could set up to stop the aura from killing the plants. The other idea was that she could set up some sort of protective dome to stop them from dying.

That would obviously include Dodge-vine, which she could very easily use to create a form of protective dome, but she didn't really have anything to target the aura specifically. The only source she knew of that the aura came from was that creature she had seen flying across, very obviously so due to the massive increase of the aura coming from it. All she could really think the aura could be coming from otherwise would be . . . the shades.

The shades that stayed away from the solid ground, the ground where it seemed to be safer from the corrupting aura—because there it was further from the shades. Feeling like an idiot, not for the first and probably not for the last time, she started a new ritual.

It was very similar to the one she had done with the altered Dodge-vine ritual intended to protect her from their senses. This time, however, she tried the original one, the one intended to protect her from attacks. This was a Manifest major and Bitterbalm minor ritual that created the spiritual manifestation element, which she mixed with Dodge-vine to create the protection from spiritual manifestation ritual.

As soon as the ritual was complete, she could feel the corrupting aura fade significantly to more of a background noise.

"*What that?*" Boreal asked.

"I just found a way to block a hell of a lot of the aura," Zalia said happily.

It wasn't perfect, and even down there still let a bit of it through. It wouldn't have much of an effect against that monster, but it did set a precedent and took some of the strain off her healing ability. Most importantly, it would allow her to set up some protection for her plants.

It took her about half an hour of hard work to place Bitterbalm, Manifest, and Dodge-vine in an array that would work. For each point of the spiritual manifestation she required in the larger ritual, she had to make a smaller one from both Manifest and Bitterbalm, and form the ritual over it. Then those parts worked as the larger one took form with the Dodge-vine added in, mostly growing around the edges of the room as a vine, but with some central parts also needed.

Eventually, she finished the large array and stood back to admire her work. It wasn't an exact replica of what the ritual was like when she used Herbal Magic to create it, but it was pretty damn close. The smaller rituals were all already going, maintaining themselves and outputting what she could feel was the element of spiritual manifestation. That was maybe not so good of a thing to just have floating around, but she was quickly putting it to use as she activated the larger ritual.

A dome of semi-visible energy formed around the perimeter of the room and closed upwards, blocking out the corrupting aura coming from above. As she felt the rest of the aura fade away, she smiled brightly. Maybe things weren't so bad after all.

CHAPTER THIRTY-FIVE

Nearing Bronze

Zalia

Dropping the ritual applied to herself, Zalia realised the corrupting aura was still gone entirely. It seemed that the ritual powered and incorporated into the plants themselves was actually more powerful than the temporary ones she made herself. It made sense; the time and effort required to make the more permanent one was considerably higher than the other.

Many ideas popped into her mind as she admired her handiwork. She didn't see any reason this same thing wouldn't work for the island in its entirety. She could spend days, weeks, or even months setting up sections of the ritual across the entire island and protecting it from the aura that way. Considering that, though, she didn't know if the shades or the larger creatures would notice or get upset at that. Probably not such a good idea.

Still, this was something she could theoretically apply to many different areas of her life. When camping in the wild, some quickly set up protective arrays over the campsite would be invaluable. If she ever had a proper home again, a complex set of protective arrays could provide an excellent means of defence.

She could also set up greenhouses with biomes inside that helped grow and were fueled by the plants inside. Maybe, once she reached Bronze rank, she could even use the mind element from the Trapvine to create some sort of elemental protector that was fueled by an array of plants.

The possibilities were endless and she had trouble containing her excitement. She could set up magically protected areas all across Cormaine now too, no longer necessarily reliant on finding underground spaces to hide in. That was assuming the shades wouldn't attack her for trying to do that, however.

Imagining what she could do when she had the instinctual knowledge of Bronze rank herbs, she had a yearning to reach it as soon as possible. That would mean doing a lot of work with her Herbalist class, though. While her Hunter class wasn't far off, Herbalist would need a lot of work.

So, for the next two weeks, Zalia did just that. She started off with a few more fights in Hetheir just to get her Hunter class abilities to Bronze.

> **Congratulations! Kill Shot has gained two levels, reaching Iron 20.**
> **Congratulations! Kill Shot has reached Bronze 1.**
> **Kill Shot will gain no further levels until**
> **all classes have reached Bronze.**
> **Kill Shot**
> **Tin - Enhance an attack, go for the kill. This ability deals**
> **a tiny amount of damage. The damage of this ability**
> **scales exponentially with the target's missing health.**
> **Iron - Kill Shot deals increased damage based on how**
> **many separate effects you have active on the creature.**
> **Bronze - Kill Shot becomes Enhanced Shot. You are**
> **able to infuse arrows with an element created by your**
> **Herbal Magic ability, or execute a Kill Shot, putting**
> **this ability on cooldown for thirty seconds.**
> **Congratulations! Hunter's Mark has reached Iron 20.**
> **Congratulations! Hunter's Mark has reached Bronze 1.**
> **Hunter's Mark will gain no further levels**
> **until all classes have reached Bronze.**
> **Hunter's Mark**
> **Tin - Marked by the hunter, there is no escape. This ability**
> **marks a creature you can see. Marked creature takes a**
> **small amount of extra damage when damaged by you.**
> **You know the general direction of the marked enemy.**
> **Marking a second creature removes the first mark.**
> **Iron - You may apply Hunter's Mark to three creatures at once**
> **Bronze - The three-creature limit increases to ten, and**
> **a small amount of damage a marked creature takes**
> **is applied to other marked creatures as well.**
> **Congratulations! Fight or Flight has gained**
> **two levels, reaching Iron 20.**

> **Congratulations! Fight or Flight has reached Bronze 1.**
> **Fight or Flight will gain no further levels**
> **until all classes have reached Bronze.**
> **Fight or Flight**
> **Tin - Choose one:**
> **When used, your perception increases greatly for five seconds.**
> **Remove all slowing and restraining effects and prevent further**
> **slowing and restraining effects for the next five seconds.**
> **Iron - Option one now grants the ability to sense**
> **if you're going to be hit by an attack and where the**
> **attack is coming from within the duration.**
> **Option two now grants you increased speed and dexterity.**
> **Bronze - Fight or Flight now grants both options at**
> **once rather than having to choose between them.**

The ability level ups for her Hunter class abilities were . . . ridiculous. Her ability to take down larger groups of enemies increased dramatically with the Hunter's Mark upgrade. Not only could she apply harmful rituals to ten enemies at once now with Herbal Magic's Bronze rank effect, but when one took damage, all the others would take a small amount of that damage too. She figured it didn't also reflect that extra damage, otherwise it would lead into an infinite spiralling damaging effect.

Still, when she marked ten creatures and applied something like the lava curse to them in addition to her starlight arrows, they very quickly died. In fact, when it came to higher ranks, she could now kill things quicker in groups of ten than she could individually.

The Kill Shot upgrade meant she could infuse an element into each of her shots as long as it was replicable by Herbal Magic. She found that Bitterbalm was actually the best option she had at the moment because it seemed to enhance the debuff the arrows applied, starlit.

Finally, Fight or Flight was now a single option that allowed her to act quite quickly while her perception was sped up as well, meaning her body caught up to the speed she was seeing at. There was no longer that disconnect as her body slowed down to her own perception, the two now in sync.

All in all, it was a set of very good upgrades that allowed her to move through the city a bit less carefully, now able to take down quite a few enemies at once.

The next abilities to upgrade shortly after that were, of course, her Druid ones.

Congratulations! Nature's Wrath has gained
three levels, reaching Iron 20.
Congratulations! Nature's Wrath has reached Bronze 1.
Nature's Wrath will gain no further levels
until all classes reach Bronze.
Nature's Wrath
Tin - You invoke the wrath of nature. Nearby enemies are
bound by vines, sinking sand, or other area-related hazards.
Enemies are also subjected to a damage-over-time effect
relevant to biome that lasts until the restraint has ended. The
damage-over-time effect deals moderate damage per second.
Iron - When used, Nature's Wrath now summons two short-lived
allies of nature. The allies are one rank lower than this ability.
The allies are of a type based on the surrounding environment.
Bronze - Upon using Nature's Wrath, you gain temporary
control over the natural elements within the area. You
can manipulate the environment to your advantage,
causing vines to entangle enemies, rocks to rise as
barriers, or water to surge forth and sweep foes away.
Congratulations! Protection of the Wilds has
gained eight levels, reaching Iron 20.
Congratulations! Protection of the Wilds has reached Bronze 1.
Protection of the Wilds will gain no further
levels until all classes reach Bronze.
Active Two - Protection of the Wilds - spell - area - counter-execute
Tin - You call upon the protection of the wilds. You and
nearby allies are protected by a biome-specific shield and
are subjected to a moderate heal-over-time effect. The heal-
over-time heals exponentially more based on how low the
target's health is and remains until the shield is broken.
Iron - Protection of the Wilds now has a more ethereal and
moving visage. You and allies within a shield created by
this ability may still see and move as normal. Additionally,
you may enhance this ability with a single effect
replicable by the Iron rank ability of Herbal Magic.
Bronze - Upon activating Protection of the Wilds, you
and your allies within the shields are not only healed over
time, but the healing effect becomes more potent as the
shield absorbs damage. The shield's resilience increases
with the amount of healing it provides, creating a symbiotic

> **relationship between protection and restoration.**
> **Congratulations! Druid class has gained**
> **eight levels, reaching Iron 20.**
> **Congratulations! Druid class has reached Bronze 1.**
> **Druid class will gain no further levels until all classes reach Bronze.**

In line with each other ability rank up, her Druid class abilities were the most potent. The Bronze rank upgrade of Nature's Wrath gave her what could only be described as a temporary control over the elements on a scale much larger than her passives allowed. She was used to doing minor things with her passives, like taking a while to dig a cutout into the tops of the pillars or playing around with ice with Boreal.

This ability took it to another level, though. She was able to pull walls out of the ground or whip the wind into a temporary storm. She could form large stone hands that crushed the undead or held them fast as she killed them in another manner. Unfortunately, despite the wisdom and intellect attributes increasing to Bronze with the abilities, she could no longer use both at the same time without running out of mana. She could feel it instinctively; if she tried she would pass out immediately.

Previously, it used a significant chunk of mana to do so but she could manage quite well despite it, since most of her other abilities were quite low in how much mana they used. Now she would have to be careful.

The new effect of Protection of the Wilds actually made it useful to use at higher health as well. As the shield took damage it would heal a greater amount and as that amount increased, so too did how much damage the shield could take. It actually became something that could be used as a long-term effect rather than an emergency button.

All those level ups happened within the first week. Each ability that reached Bronze meant the others would level faster, as the experience from killing the undead was split between fewer abilities.

Unfortunately, because her Herbalist class didn't have much use in combat outside of Herbal Magic, its progress was much slower. At the end of the first week there were a few levels in some of the abilities, but it was the second week, when she spent most of her time gathering herbs and tracking creatures, that brought out the biggest results.

She had travelled to another island and found quite a stealthy creature there, living off a plant she had discovered. Somehow both the creature and the plant were resilient enough to survive the corrupting aura. When she discovered the element that the plant yielded, she realised how both the creature and plant had survived the aura.

> **Adastem - Bronze - Use in rituals to add an element of adaptability.**

She, of course, harvested as much of it as she could get her hands on to take back to the other island. She even got Boreal to hold some on the way back.

> **Congratulations! Hunter's Sight has gained
> four levels, reaching Iron 17.
> Congratulations! Hunter Class has gained
> four levels, reaching Iron 17.
> Congratulations! Flora Identification has
> gained five levels, reaching Iron 14.
> Congratulations! Preparation has gained
> six levels, reaching Iron 16.
> Congratulations! Stasis has gained five levels, reaching Iron 15.
> Congratulations! Harvester has gained
> seven levels, reaching Iron 17.
> Congratulations! Herbalist has gained five levels, reaching Iron 14.**

In addition, as bad as she did feel for killing the odd one, the strange, ever-changing creatures she found on the island tasted significantly better. Boreal agreed.

They took on a roughly canine shape, yet when fighting them, Zalia often had to change tactics as they adapted to her style. Whether it was forming a carapaced shield to block her arrows despite their armour ignoring properties, becoming more lithe to match her speed, or growing in density to match a full-on charge, they were a hard task to take down, even at the average Iron and Bronze ranks.

She did see a Silver ranked one but decided to avoid engaging with that entirely.

It wouldn't be long until her last abilities and classes ticked over to Bronze and she could begin the even longer journey to Silver. And so, as she arrived back at the cave, she started planning what to do next.

CHAPTER THIRTY-SIX

Bigger Boreal

Zalia

Zalia sat on a chair she had summoned from the ground, staring at the now blank wall that used to hold her list. The list she had made when first arriving here had pretty quickly become pointless as the circumstances of her situation evolved, yet it had lent her some direction—so here she was, making another.

First, she wrote down "find the prison?"

Something in her dreams, twice now, had told her to find the prison, whatever that meant. She had seen a vision of what exactly that prison might look like, a large, flat-topped, actually floating platform surrounded by a large number of the flying monsters. Under that she wrote a few things:

"Bad idea."

"Twisted aura monsters"

"Zayes??"

It was an exceptionally bad idea to follow that as any kind of plan at the moment. The serious number of—as she decided to call them— aura monsters alone would spell her death long before she even got close to the prison. Her suspicion was that Zayes was being held there, and she hadn't even yet decided if she was alright with letting that guy out yet. His wife had turned out to be backstabbing and manipulative. If he was anything like her, Zalia wanted nothing to do with it.

The only reason that one went on the wall at all was the fact that as a known high-rank person, Zayes might offer a chance to escape from Cormaine if she could free him. If.

The next thing that went on the wall was "find a way to make the ritual work."

The ritual in question was the one that Juniper had used to bring them here. Another avenue for escape, it could possibly be a way out if she could just learn how to reverse it. Under that point she drew an arrow leading to Zayes, as well as "god."

Under "god," she wrote "god's name?"

The god was the other idea she had at the moment for reversing the ritual, or at least finding another method of escape. For that, though, she would have to help bring back its memory and trying to find its name could be a good start to that, if it had one.

As she stared at the daunting list, another idea came to mind. She knew that Zayes could control Hidey by using his true name, but what if his true name was really just his name before he died?

Well, she had a shade in Cormaine whose name she knew and who was quite knowledgeable when it came to the ritual she had—the shade being the very person who Zalia took the ritual from in the first place.

"Juniper?"

At that, she circled the ritual section and then put both that and finding the prison under a bigger circle that she named as "finding a way out."

Moving over, she wrote something new on the wall that simply read "get to Bronze." She wasn't far from it, only needing to grind through those last few levels on her Herbalist class and the last ability for the Hunter class. Once she made it there, her Survivalist and Healing Presence skills would hopefully begin levelling once again, albeit slower, and she could start the road to Silver. She also knew that her heirloom items could rank up as well and wanted to find a way to get that done for her armour and bow. Boreal's too.

Thinking of, she checked out Boreal's ability rank up that had happened just as they arrived back in the cave.

Blending Shadows
Tin - You are able to blend into shadows,
using their darkness to hide yourself.
Iron - When blended in a shadow you can move
directly into a nearby shadow as you move.
Bronze - While blending into a shadow, you can now
manipulate the shadows around you. This enables
you to stretch or extend shadows, as well as creating
shadowy movements that mimic your shape.

With her new ability, Boreal was manipulating shadows now just as well as she often manipulated ice. It was quite something to experience, seeing shapes out of the corner of her eye only to turn and see nothing there. Boreal would be quite good at scaring the hell . . . Cormaine out of people with it.

That left only two other abilities to rank up, Cute Convincement and Frost Adaption, meaning Boreal was pretty close to Bronze too.

Zalia's own Flight skill had also ranked up the past week.

> **Congratulations! Flight has gained three levels, reaching Tin 20.**
> **Congratulations! Flight has reached Iron 1.**
> **Flight - passive**
> **Tin - Your maneuverability is increased and your air resistance is reduced while in flight. This scales based on the rank and level of this passive.**
> **Iron - Your ability to perceive your surroundings while flying becomes exceptional. You can spot distant details and potential threats with remarkable clarity, allowing you to anticipate and counteract aerial assaults effectively as well as see threats on the ground.**
> **Congratulations! Flight has gained four levels, reaching Iron 5.**

It was mostly a utility upgrade, and nothing that special, but still useful all the same.

Zalia was looking forward to seeing which of her abilities would be the last to rank up and what change would be wrought from it. Last time it had been her old skill Escape that had changed to Fight or Flight. This time it looked likely to be one of her Herbalist skills, and she was tempted to manipulate her actions a little to choose which it would be. Stasis was the only one at the moment that had any sort of extradimensional effect, and anything she could get that would help in that regard would be good. The researcher from her memory had been looking into extradimensional stuff to try and discover something when he had died after all, maybe there was something to it she could use to escape.

Standing from her sitting position and sinking the chair back into the floor, Zalia looked around to try and find Boreal. The shadows were all contorting and moving, some Boreal-like shapes flickering within a few before disappearing and reappearing in other shadows. The room being filled with many different light sources didn't help. Even her thermal sight didn't help as Boreal's natural, now mastered ability to hide from that type of sight was much better than her own.

Trying to use the vibration sense to find Boreal, Zalia spun around as she saw a light tap on the ground, only to be jumped from behind by a large, metal feline. She was thrown to the ground under Boreal's weight, letting out a gasp of air as she did.

"Boreal," Zalia groaned.

Boreal jumped off her back and, for lack of a better word, pranced around in triumph.

Flipping over, Zalia sat up and rolled her shoulder with a wince.

"You're getting much too big to be ambushing me like that anymore," Zalia complained.

Over the past two weeks, and with her approaching Bronze, Boreal had grown even more. She now stood as high as Zalia's stomach and was becoming quite . . . terrifying. She was certain that the speed at which Boreal was growing was unnatural, having gone from a kitten to almost fully grown in the space of . . . a month or two?

Zalia wasn't quite sure how long it had been since she had found Boreal. It felt like much longer than a month or two, though. Standing up, Zalia patted Boreal's fluffy head a little. Somehow, Boreal had managed to bond deeper to her armour before Zalia had, now able to summon and dismiss it much as Zalia could with her bow. Zalia was still working on her own armour, not quite sure how to go about bonding deeper to it. With her bow, she had learnt about its past a little and that had been all it required. She really didn't know anything about her own armour, who the previous wearer had been, what kind of order it belonged to, or what its origin was. How Boreal had bonded her armour, Zalia could not figure out, nor would she tell.

Summoning and dismissing her armour would be quite useful, though she needed to bond deeper to her gauntlet as well. She had a feeling that it wouldn't be summonable and dismissible like her other heirlooms. Something about putting an item responsible for an extradimensional space into a different extradimensional space felt like a bad idea.

"If only I had a god to bless either of the items for me," Zalia muttered, glaring at Boreal with narrowed eyes. "You didn't manage to get that god to bless your armour, did you?"

Boreal turned away innocently, licking her paw and cleaning her face. Damned cat.

Boreal was now probably as heavy if not heavier than Zalia herself, and a fiend in a fight. No undead stood a chance against this battle cat.

With a sigh, Zalia moved off towards her herb garden. It was always nice to relax there with the fresh air and nonexistent aura of corruption.

Though, she had planted another herbal array in the main chamber to block the aura as well, she still enjoyed sitting with all her plants.

She moved the dirt in the centre of the room around to form a little nest for herself and sat down in it, allowing the dirt to spill over her a little. She closed her eyes and focused on the tide-like feel of her Healing Aura, letting it wash over the plants around her then spill back into her body. As the healing nurtured the plants, she carefully used Preparation to harvest sections of each, trimming the plants just as she let them grow. It was a calming cycle, allowing the plants to grow as they wished yet limiting them to stop overgrowth. A balance.

She let her conscious mind fade away as she almost instinctively played the game of balance with the plants around her.

> **Congratulations! Preparation has reached Iron 17.**

After a while, she stopped and stood up, instinctively settling the dirt so that there was no trace of her presence in the room. Another level in Preparation reached, she needed to get some in Flora Identification and the only way to do that was to carefully study something.

Her herb of choice today was Adastem, the new one she had found on the fourth island she had explored. It was somewhat close to the island containing the god, so going back and forth between was relatively quick.

Thinking of the god, she was a little frustrated with the lack of progress it had made over the last two weeks. Delphi and the other four from the collective were still there, trying their hardest to help it recover, but the going was slow. It might not even be possible for a few creatures of their rank to single-handedly resurrect a god like they were trying to do.

Sitting back down in the main chamber, she retrieved a piece of Adastem from Stasis and studied it closely. It was an excellent piece of plant for her to study as a method of levelling Flora Identification. Unlike all the other plants she had that would completely freeze when Stasis was applied to them, Adastem didn't really seem to care. Its element being adaptability, it was constantly shifting form from vine to bush to tree. Of course, it wasn't an entire plant, only a piece of one, so it looked more like stem to twig to stick. The larger plants were truly something to behold though, ever shifting between different states and forms.

She had been a little perplexed when first encountering the plant but was definitely looking forward to seeing what types of effects she could bring about with it. Adaptability was just so, well, adaptable. She imagined a type of adapting armour or even an adapting curse, the potential combinations were endless.

Studying the Adastem for another hour, she was aptly rewarded.

> **Congratulations! Flora Identification has reached Iron 15.**

The past week she had taken to developing Stasis by taking things in and out of the extradimensional space and observing the effect it had on the plants. But she decided she did want it to level last after all. So, she would level Hunter's Sight next.

"Alright, Boreal, tracking time," she said.

She and Boreal had taken to a game, one that was probably the reason for Boreal's Blending Shadows skill levelling. Boreal would run out into the forest and try to hide her tracks as well as she could and Zalia would follow shortly, doing her best to track her feline friend. Zalia always found Boreal in the end, of course, but the odd fifteen years difference in Zalia's tracking experience and Boreal's hiding experience made that an expected outcome.

Boreal sat up alert and dashed out of the cave at her call, more than prepared for this. Zalia quickly followed, sprinting after her, slower to get through the tunnels yet having a teleport to skip the hardest part. Just before she got out of sight, Zalia managed to get off the ritual that kept them both hidden from the shade's sight. Better safe than sorry.

She made it out some ten seconds after Boreal did, and the feline was already gone. Zalia quickly sorted through all the information she gathered from her perceptive gaze and locked on to Boreal's tracks quickly. The hunt was on.

Forty minutes or so later, Zalia found Boreal. After not three but four backtracks, a few purposefully misleading tracks, and five split tracks, Zalia found Boreal hiding up in a tree. Boreal didn't quite see Zalia coming, though, so she got payback for earlier as she teleported behind Boreal and grabbed on. The two of them tumbled out of the tree as Boreal lost her footing, and they crashed through the withered branches to the ground below, a mess of limbs.

"Gotcha!" Zalia exclaimed, Boreal wiggling out of her grip and getting up.

"Mreow!" Boreal complained as Zalia grabbed her and wrestled her to the ground again.

"You might be stealthy as all hell when you're right in front of me, but you have a long way to go with hiding your tracks," Zalia scolded, jokingly.

"Mow mreow meow, mreow," Boreal replied, sarcastically imitating Zalia. Badly.

"You little—!" Zalia said with a gasp, tickling Boreal.

Boreal let out what could only be called a scream before finally escaping again and sprinting off into the forest. Zalia quickly got to her feet and followed.

Only one month earlier she would have been able to keep up with Boreal with no effort at all. Now, she couldn't. Boreal sped off into the forest on long legs, far outpacing Zalia.

Congratulations! Hunter's Sight has reached Iron 18.

Hunter's Sight finally levelled as she had to resort to tracking Boreal once more to follow.

She reached the cave just in time to see Boreal launch herself at some creature with a yowl.

CHAPTER THIRTY-SEVEN

New Dangers

Zalia

Zalia summoned her bow, alarm flashing in her mind just as adrenaline pumped through her veins. Boreal, in full armour, was attached to the back of a . . . demon. It stood at twice Zalia's height, still smaller than the aura monster, yet just as hideous. It had six large wings that looked more blade than limb, each with sharp metallic edges. The humanoid creature spun in alarm, trying to grab at Boreal as she mauled its back.

An aura much like the aura monster's yet weaker burst from the creature and Zalia responded in kind, pushing her own aura towards it. As that happened, she had already applied Hunter's Mark and was in the process of casting three simultaneous rituals. One was an extra layer of armour for Boreal in the form of the ice armour, as well as the Dodge-vine basic ritual. The third was the lava curse on the demon.

As the rituals went off, Zalia began firing, but the demon was faster. Feeling her aura, it whipped around in her direction and took off into the air, dragging Boreal up with it. Its flight was somewhat disturbed as Boreal had her jaws clamped over one of the top wings.

? - **Bronze rank.**

It was definitely stronger than the undead, but hopefully, nothing they couldn't handle. The real problem came when the shades above took notice and swarmed towards Zalia. They either really didn't like Zalia's focused aura or they were being directed by the demon above. She liked neither option.

Deciding Boreal would be fine for the moment as the shades ignored her, Zalia cast the ritual to evade their sight, dropping Hunter's Mark on the demon, and applying it to herself and Boreal so that she also got the effects of the ritual. As that happened, she ran.

While the ritual would hide her from their senses, they would still swarm where she had been. Dashing off into the forest, Zalia began using her air steps to jump, twist in midair, and let off a shot before using her remaining steps to stabilise and land. The demon was flying towards her in an unstable flight, somewhat less focused on her and more on trying to get Boreal off.

One, then two of her arrows landed as she ran—the shades had lost her in the forest. Applying her air wing ritual to both herself and Boreal, Zalia dropped Hunter's Mark on them both and placed it back on the demon. She flew up above the treeline to take a few more shots but was surprised as the demon vanished in a puff of smoke, leaving Boreal hovering.

She felt a push of air behind her and quickly dashed to the side, but was too late as the claws of the demon caught her left hand and tore her arm free below the elbow. Muffling a scream of pain, her healing automatically focused onto her arm and she spun about, summoning her weapon as a blade to fight back.

She wasn't good at airborne combat but held her own as Boreal flew at high speed through the air on a collision course. Zalia held back from using either of her Druid actives as her arm slowly grew back, using her other arm to defend against the extremely quick enemy before her.

While she was close to Bronze, both her Herbalist and Hunter classes were still Iron, and the difference in stats was definitely noticeable. If she was to guess, the creature had both mental stats, and had both strength and dexterity bonded. Its body was already showing some damage from being riddled by the lava curse, in addition to the few glowing starlit arrows sticking out of it. Not to mention it probably had a severely mauled back from Boreal's initial surprise attack.

There was a pause in the battle as they regarded each other warily, but despite the rank disparity, the biggest difference in this fight was the fact that she had allies. Not waiting for her arm to fully regrow and ignoring the pain for now, she used her own teleport to pull the same maneuver it had just pulled on her. She appeared behind it already swinging, but it predicted that and swiftly moved to the side as it spun. What it didn't see was Boreal, who had been diving from above at that very moment with a fully charged Pounce at the ready.

Boreal's armoured form enhanced with the impact-increasing effect from Pounce hit the demon like a truck, the two of them shooting down towards the ground. Zalia quickly followed suit, dropping into a dive as she saw the two of them impact the ground with a loud *slam*.

Boreal was on top, mauling the creature's face as its claws tried to get through her armour. Unfortunately for it, in the disadvantaged position, it simply couldn't get the force or leverage to do any real damage.

Zalia soon landed next to it and got to chopping.

Pinned under the heavy form of Boreal, the demon no longer stood a chance as they finished it off. It had some type of regeneration that grew stronger the more they hurt it, but it too was soon overwhelmed. Unfortunately, she was unable to force her Healing Aura into the creature as she had predicted previously. This thing was obviously a lot more conscious than the undead and fought back against her aura with its own, not allowing hers to come into contact.

With a final yank of her whole upper torso, neck, and head, Boreal managed to rip the demon's head off, tossing it aside. Looking away from the gruesome sight towards her own injury, Zalia flexed her newly grown arm with a wince.

There was a phantom pain in her arm, an ache that wouldn't leave. It was an odd feeling and one she didn't feel like experiencing again. The thought made her chest ache, the memory of being impaled surfacing once more.

She shook her head and focused again on her now unarmoured and unclothed arm. The shirt would hopefully grow back but she would need to go find her . . . missing pieces.

"Drag that thing back to the cave, would you?" Zalia asked Boreal.

Boreal looked up with a maw dripping with black blood, her icy blue eyes a sharp contrast to the red and black surroundings. She gave a little chirp.

"Yeah, I'm alright, thanks for tearing its head off for me," Zalia said gently with a smile.

She had bigger concerns than having her arm torn off.

She found her missing arm not far from where they were, stuck in the V of two twisted tree branches. She flew up and picked it up with a grimace, taking her armour off it and equipping it back on her new arm. With a shudder, she threw the rest of the limb away and flew back to where Boreal was.

She helped drag the body back to the cave and they dumped it in the entrance chamber. There were a few reasons she had in mind for why it had come sniffing around her home. One was she had been seen killing the undead or flying back and forth between the islands, and it had followed her here. Two, and she only considered this due to the possible control it had over the shades, was that the shades had informed it of her location.

Three was the worst: that it had somehow been able to sense the ritual arrays she had set up under the ground. If that was how it had found her, she would be in trouble wherever she set them up and she really did not like that.

She quickly went down to the cave she called home and set about setting up another ritual array. Using the same plants, she spent the next two hours setting up the ritual that hid her from the shades' senses, or rather, any form of senses that were spiritual. She didn't stop there, however. The smart thing to do would be to abandon the caves entirely, and she definitely considered that. One issue was the fact that she lived just next to the collective and would feel horrible about bringing attention to their hiding place then abandoning them.

So, she set up another ritual array. This one was to hide from normal senses, a third layer of protection around the two rooms. With that one done, the rooms were positively packed with plants, almost like her own private cave forest. The air had a tangible feeling of magic to it, so full of power that she could feel it when she breathed it in. She instinctively felt that if she decided to do something like this with clashing ritual arrays or more varied plants they would most likely interfere with each other. The good news was that all of the rituals had the same few plants in different patterns to form the different effects so it wasn't an issue here.

After almost five hours of hard work trying to get the three ritual arrays to fit into the two separate rooms, Zalia sat down and exhaled deeply. She had sent Boreal off to watch the entrance up above and was considering setting up these same ritual arrays up there too. It felt like things had just gotten a lot more dangerous. Encountering a new type of demon, one that she could at least defeat, wasn't such a bad thing but the fact that even such a low level one had found her was concerning.

The image of the aura monster flashed through her mind—four spiked legs, flaming bat wings, the twisted torso covered in thousands of eyes.

She was almost tempted to go into her vault and deposit that memory into one of the storage slots but held back. Getting rid of that memory might seem like a good idea, but preserving it for as long as she lived in all its horror—not such a good idea after all.

Instead, she ripped open the doorway to the vault and dragged the demon body in, depositing it in one of the indents. Much like the map, it shrunk until it fit nicely into the indent and a clear dome formed above it. She closed up the vault and left it in there, unsure as to what to do with it entirely. She didn't want to eat it, that was for sure. Maybe it would make a nice gift for Glemp if she ever made it back to Endaria.

"See anything up here, Boreal?" Zalia asked.

"*Nothing,*" Boreal replied.

She manipulated the floor into a small stone stool and sat down next to Boreal.

"Do you think we should leave the caves? They might come back here," Zalia said.

"*Leave with collective?*" Boreal asked.

"If we can convince them, maybe. I doubt they would and we would have to find a way to transport their little jellyfish homes too. We could probably use a ritual array to create a self-reliant water biome they could live in but where would we go? We could go to the temple with Ro's god in it but I don't want to bring attention there," Zalia explained with a sigh.

This was annoying.

"Maybe it just followed us back here after we went to that fourth island with the adapting beasts," Zalia said hopefully.

"*Maybe,*" Boreal agreed.

"Want to go to the temple and tell Delphi about it?" Zalia asked.

"*Delphi! Ro!*" Boreal replied excitedly.

With that decided, and the best hiding rituals she could make at the moment set up, Zalia performed the air wing ritual on them both and they took off towards the god temple.

"*Probably should have put that demon into my vault before dragging it all the way back to the cave. That was stupid,*" she thought.

Oh well, what was done was done. She focused her mind back to her destination and took flight.

CHAPTER THIRTY-EIGHT

Damn Prophecy

Zalia

The flight to the god's island was a tense one. Zalia was a little stressed about leaving her cave home and the rest of the collective unprotected, though she was sure they as a group were significantly more powerful than she was. She wasn't really certain what kind of abilities they had other than Delphi's ability to see some of the future.

The way Delphi had spoken of that though, she was certain that it wasn't something that every member of the collective got. They had told her of the cycle keeper, a member of the collective who counted the cycles across their entire lifespan, keeping count from the very moment that the collective went underground in the first place.

She had never learnt just how long ago that was but maybe it was something she should talk to Delphi about. Another day perhaps. Today, she had to talk about relocation.

She arrived at the god island, flying down in a curling path around one of the pillars. Landing in a crouch in front of the temple, Boreal soon landed just behind her. Her thick fur was ruffled and messy, having been blown around by the quick flight. They went inside and down to the room below.

"Delphi?" Zalia called out as she entered the room.

"*Zalia,*" Delphi replied.

"I've got some . . . bad news," Zalia said, getting straight to business.

"*And?*" Delphi asked.

"We found some creature hunting around the cave entrance, a

humanoid figure with six wings. We killed it, but the cave might be com-promised," Zalia replied, frowning a little. Shouldn't Delphi already know? Or was this something they didn't foresee?

"*That is . . . concerning. Are you certain it knew the cave entrance was there?*" Delphi asked with a hint of worry.

"Not entirely. We came back from the game of hunting Boreal and I have been playing, and Boreal attacked it immediately. I was a little behind, can't keep up with this terrifying furball much anymore," Zalia explained.

"*Smelling the air! Feeling, corrupt, enemy. Not tasty,*" Boreal added.

The sentence, long for Boreal's standards, came with images of what she saw before attacking. The creature had its face up in the air in an action that looked like smelling the air.

"Definitely hunting for something. I'm afraid that the ritual arrays I put up were felt or seen somehow. I've just put up a few to block more senses but I don't know if that will work or not," Zalia finished.

"*What do you suggest we do?*" Delphi asked.

Zalia was taken aback again.

"I don't know, I thought you would have an idea. Can the collective move?" Zalia asked back.

"*. . . We will discuss,*" Delphi replied.

Delphi hopped away from Zalia back towards the other four members and they sat in a little circle.

Zalia looked towards the god who had been observing them through the conversation. Ro was right there, hopping around the god's feet as if trying to perform some kind of dance for it.

"Have you ever met these creatures before?" Zalia asked.

"I have no memory of them. Delphi has shared images of the world above with me. It was . . . not like this when I was previously alive. There was no ceiling above us, only open sky. This much I remember. The for-ests . . . the forests were so much more *alive,*" it replied.

"I found a map of the Bathar kingdom and the surrounding lands in the keep, on another island. Do you remember the Bathar people? Tall, fur-covered, long arms. Anyways, they had a kingdom that is on another island now and it had a map that shows a very different surrounds to what we see now. Maybe I can get it for you, to jog your memory?" Zalia said.

"The Bathar . . . yes, they are . . . were believers? Once, maybe. A map is no replacement for a memory but maybe it would help. I would appreciate that, Druid," the god said.

"Druid—how did you know that?" Zalia asked.

"I . . . I just do, it is part of you, is it not?" the god asked in kind.

"It is, yes. The other god I told you that I met also referred to me in this way without being told. Is it something you can see?" Zalia asked.

"See? No. It just is," it explained.

"I won't pretend I fully understand," Zalia admitted.

"Neither do I," it replied calmly.

"*I believe we must go talk with the collective,*" Delphi interrupted.

"I figured as much, want to go now?" Zalia asked.

"*As soon as possible. This is an important decision,*" Delphi urged.

"Let's go, then," Zalia said.

She collected the collective of frogs and placed them on her shoulders. Small as they were, they fit with one of them placed on Boreal's back. Leaving the temple, Zalia and Boreal once again took flight towards the island they called home.

After the short flight, Zalia landed back at the cave and deposited the five frogs to go talk with their collective. She promised to be back soon and took off again with Boreal towards the ruins of Hetheir.

She flew near the ceiling across the gap before dropping by a pillar to the ruins, flying low towards the keep. She arrived, landing on the tower balcony and quickly made her way down the now familiar stairs. First, she entered the second floor that held the royal family's quarters, gathering as many of the maps as she could find and storing them into her Vault Gauntlet.

Going to the bottom floor, she also decided to grab the large sword she had found deposited in the skull of the body she had taken her armour from. The details surrounding that whole situation were still very much hidden to her. All she knew was that the person must have died before the corruption had come to the city, as the person was dead, not undead. Unless sword-through-skull-itis was a chronic condition that stopped one from being raised from the dead.

Either way, with both sword and maps in the vault, she left the keep once more, not wanting to bring the attention of the possibly Gold ranked undead in the other room. Deciding to fly back to the collective first, they took to the skies and quickly crossed the gap between once more.

They arrived back in their icy cave home just as Delphi exited the pond in the room.

"Decided?" Zalia asked.

"*The collective will not leave,*" Delphi replied.

"Care to explain why?" Zalia asked, though not with surprise.

"*It is safe for us to remain,*" Delphi explained.

"It is safe for you . . . and for me?" Zalia questioned.

". . . *Yes*," Delphi said.

"I don't like the sound of that," Zalia replied, a little wary.

"*You have nothing to fear*," Delphi said calmly.

"You say that, Delphi, but I have a distinct feeling that doesn't mean the same thing to you as it does to me," Zalia retorted.

"*We cannot explain what will happen. You must trust in our sight*," Delphi replied.

"Trust in your sight?" Zalia asked in exasperation. "What the hell does 'trust in your sight' mean? What, am I living on some kind of predestined path? No, I won't trust your sight. My instincts tell me that we need to leave this place or we are going to end up having to protect it with more than sense-blocking ritual arrays and a well-hidden location. I will not fight an unknown enemy for no reason."

"*Zalia*," Delphi warned.

"What do you want me to do?" Zalia said in frustration, throwing her hands up. "I do not want to live by your prophecies and warnings, trusting my entire future to your hands. I have lived independently for a long, long time and I'm not about to throw away my years of learning and hard-earned wisdom because you say it will be fine!"

"*The collective will not leave*," Delphi repeated.

"That is your choice to make, I will not make you leave but I also do not wish to stay here. Not without knowing what is coming," Zalia replied, holding her ground.

"*Telling you may be dangerous. We do not know what will happen by our intervention*," Delphi explained.

"Could it be worse than me leaving you all here?" Zalia asked.

That was met with silence.

"Go talk to your collective, I'll be back," she finished, turning on her heel.

She left the cave, Boreal close on her heels. She had decided early on to trust in Delphi's visions despite how much it got on her nerves to do so. She had always been one for freedom of decision and making one's own path. Hell, she had even moved by herself to an uninhabited land so that she would be the only one with a hand in her future, amongst other reasons. The fact that Delphi was very obviously hiding knowledge of a future encounter that was possibly harmful to her or Boreal did not sit well with her.

Hiding things was one thing, hiding possible dangers from her was another.

So, she took off and flew towards the god's island.

Throughout the flight she turned the conversation over in her head.

She knew she was being slightly hotheaded about it but had come to the conclusion that she *really* did not like having her future . . . planned out for her.

She landed at the temple, hoping showing the maps to the god would be a little less of a frustrating experience. Ro hopped out of the temple to greet her, hopping a circle around Boreal before heading back inside. Following along, Zalia carefully stepped past all the roots growing across the floor.

Arriving in the god's chamber, she opened the vault and collected the stack of papers from the storage indent. Picking the largest scale map she had found, she walked over to it.

"So, this is the map the keep held that shows the lands all around the city. It looks like it used to be surrounded by rivers and forests," Zalia explained, holding the map up for the god to look.

"Yes . . . this is—this is it. I remember the rivers, the trees. The way the birds sang and the Esebers dug in the dirt. The sounds of nature, now so quiet. So, so quiet," it said in a sing-song voice.

"You are the god of the forests, aren't you?" Zalia asked.

"Yes, that was one of my titles. I remember it now as you say it, as if I never forgot. The god of the forests, the god of mysteries. Those were my titles, yet my name still eludes me," it said in agreement.

"Were you . . . tied to nature? Is that how you died, the sudden destruction of all you stood for?" Zalia asked quietly.

"Yes, yes I think it is. One moment it was all there and the next, shattered. Torn apart. Torn apart and eaten," it whispered, a visible shiver going through its leafy feathers.

"I'm truly sorry for what happened to you," Zalia said.

She used her manipulation to move the earth into a small patch and then grew a single stone pole out of it. She planted some Dodge-vine at its base and funnelled her healing through it until the plant grew up the stone pole.

"This plant is protection. It both protects what it grows on and is protected by the very same thing. Like a symbiotic relationship between the plant and what it grows upon. I leave this here as my promise to you, a promise to protect you just as you once protected nature. One day, you will be strong enough to do so once more," Zalia explained as she worked.

The god watched her silently, closely watching the plant grow.

"I have to go talk to Delphi, but I'll be back as soon as I can. Ro will keep you company," she added, standing up and making to leave.

"Druid," the god said.

"Yes?" Zalia asked, looking back over her shoulder.

"Be prepared," it said.

"Prepared for what?" she asked.

But there was no response as the god focused back on the Dodge-vine she had grown before it.

CHAPTER THIRTY-NINE

Some Protection

Zalia

Zalia's mind was too full of thoughts as she flew back to the island she called home once more. The god's plight, Delphi's inability to explain what the collective knew, the new type of demon she had killed. Boreal was flying silently beside her, thankfully much more peaceful than her usual chaotic flight pattern.

"*Do you think we should trust Delphi with this one?*" Zalia asked Boreal mentally.

"*Zalia trust instincts,*" Boreal replied.

Zalia was inclined to agree.

"*What if something bad happens to the collective because we leave, though?*" she said.

"*Choices are made,*" Boreal answered.

Boreal's handle on language wasn't excellent but the way she expressed emotion and images with her words lent the usually short sentences a deeper meaning. In this case, Zalia caught on to her intended one. Everyone must make choices as they see fit, there is no point taking responsibility for the decisions of others.

"*Maybe we can take advantage of this situation,*" Zalia mused.

"*Advantage?*" Boreal asked.

"*I feel like since I've arrived in Endaria, and now here, everything I have done has felt reactive in one way or another. Maybe we can take advantage of this and actually take the upper hand for once,*" Zalia explained.

"*Still reactive,*" Boreal said.

"Well, I guess that is true. Still, we could set some kind of trap or . . . I don't know," Zalia replied, trailing off.

She had many, many ways of setting traps and preparing for a fight before it happened but that usually took into account knowing what the enemy was. Maybe . . . maybe Delphi would tell them that much.

Keeping the question in mind, Zalia fell back into silence as they flew.

Once they arrived back at the cave, they walked into the icy central section with purpose. Delphi was nowhere to be seen, but Zalia was alright with that for now. Instead, she decided to do something she hadn't done for a while and stepped right up to the pool and jumped in.

With her addition of the sight that allowed her to see vibration, the visual experience of moving in water was an extremely disorienting one. It took her a good while to adjust to the freedom with which energy moved through water—in comparison to stone—though its similarity to open air helped.

She pushed forwards once her mind had caught up to the unexpected input, moving towards the collective's home. As the small passage widened to the dimly lit underwater space filled with the floating jellyfish homes and waving plants, she sent her thoughts out.

"Collective," she called.

"Zalia," the reply came.

Unlike talking with Delphi, the experience was more like the many-voiced one she had spoken with when meeting the collective for the first time.

"I have questions," she said.

"Ask, though we make no promise to answer them," the collective said.

"Alright. From what I understand, you are not able to tell me how, when, or why there is a danger. You tell me to trust that if I stay, everything will be fine, yet I don't know what your perception of fine is. If you can't tell me when this danger will be, are you at least able to tell me what it will be?" Zalia asked.

"No, the effect telling you anything will have on the future is uncertain," they answered.

"Yet me knowing you have seen the future and have seen something bad coming will have an effect on the future in its own right, will it not?" Zalia retorted.

"That would be right, assuming this very conversation is not something we have already experienced," they replied.

"So you will tell me nothing?" Zalia asked.

"We cannot reveal more," they said.

Zalia stopped there, turned around, and left. There was no point continuing that conversation.

Fucking seers, she thought to herself.

She really didn't know what to do. She knew that everything would be fine if she just trusted their judgement, or rather, experience of the future. Well, everything would be fine by their measure of the word. The issue lay in that she didn't know exactly what that meant for them.

She came up out of the water, not even bothering to breathe in as she simmered in anger. Pacing around the room, she considered her options. Boreal, for her part, sat quietly waiting.

"We can only prepare as much as we know how to," Zalia said to Boreal, finally taking in a breath.

"*Delphi friend,*" Boreal reminded her.

"I know they're our friend. I won't leave them to die alone," Zalia said with a sigh.

"*Prepare?*" Boreal suggested.

"That's all we can do, isn't it? They won't leave and they won't tell us more. Let's get to it then," Zalia replied, pushing her anger aside and steeling herself.

As much of a bitter taste it left in her mouth, she wouldn't abandon the collective, especially since she was most likely the one to bring attention to their hiding place. She doubted it was anything they did, since they had lived there for countless—well, counted—cycles. So, her only option was to set one hell of a trap for whatever came their way. She doubted it would be one of the aura monsters or the collective wouldn't deem their circumstances as alright.

Unless, of course, they had some way of negating the aura themselves. That would just leave a probably Gold rank monster to kill. Easy.

The first thing Zalia did was begin setting up more of her ritual arrays. She left the cave and moved into the forest. With a little worry, she decided to carefully test how much of an effect the arrays would have on the shades above. They were pretty mindless and more reactive, if anything, so they would be a good test for how much the creatures of Cormaine could actually sense her powers.

The first array she set up was the one she used to block the pervasive aura. She had to work extra hard to keep the plants alive as a war between her aura and the aura of Cormaine was waged within each plant. Eventually, with a little extra work, she managed to set up the array, and the plants were immediately a significantly smaller strain on her healing. In fact, they barely needed it at all, almost able to maintain themselves on their own.

There was no reaction from the shades to the array forming, thankfully.

That sort of eliminated one of the theories she had for why the demon had come here. Unfortunately, there were still a few more and all of them pointed to her as the reason. Maybe she hadn't been stealthy enough when exploring the nearby islands, or flying between them, for that matter.

Well, whatever the reason, she could at least set up some of her rituals without worry.

Within the protective dome of the plants, setting up further arrays was quite easy. The plants, now protected, grew as they normally would and before long she had set up the two additional arrays that protected from both normal senses and spiritual based senses. The three together would provide a little safe haven for her outside of the cave.

Next, she worked on the entrance to the cave. Previously she had set up some trip wires within the actual caves themselves but wanted to do a little more than that if she could. Using her Trapper skill, she summoned and set up bear traps, extending spikes and further tripwires. Using her own skills, she started digging pits in the ground and filled them with stone spikes. Each of those pits she covered with a mesh of vine she gathered and dried from the Dodge-vine. Those vines were intertwined with Bitterbalm to prevent any of the protective element from the Dodge-vine interfering with the trap.

Once the Trapper passive magic was done with it, the result was a perfectly hidden trap that she could walk across. She knew if something other than her tried, though, they would find themselves on a short fall towards a sharp fate.

She was also able to use Preparation to turn the vine into a more rope-like material. She used this to set up traps hanging from the trees. The inconspicuous vines hung from branches but would whip out and grab something if it walked too close, pulling it up.

All of this, of course, was only possible because of the Trapper passive she had and its ability to magically hide and enhance all traps that she made. As well as its ability to create traps from nothing, of course. Those ones were a little less permanent though.

With the forest and immediate area in front of the cave entrance thoroughly trapped and now very dangerous to walk through, she focused back on defences. She had worked almost ten hours straight now to get as much as she had done but wasn't about to stop now. She would need to be as ready as possible. Thankfully, due to the amount she was using them, both Preparation and Harvester gained a level, reaching Iron eighteen.

She wanted something a little sturdier in front of the cave entrance to serve as a barrier. She could, of course, summon a variety of walls into being when she wanted through a few different methods. Her manipulation of stone and earth could, her rituals could, and Nature's Wrath now could as well.

However, she was certain there must be a way to create a barrier without having to be consciously focusing or actively doing so. Her ritual arrays were the perfect solution to it but she was having trouble coming up with something that would both create a barrier and still allow her through.

Her first idea was to make it a spiritual barrier but that would only keep out things such as the shades, or so she thought. She didn't think the demons were quite the same thing in that regard.

In the end, she decided she would just have to make something that could be activated quickly but wasn't necessarily active at all times. To do this, she had to create a ritual using Snow-leaf and Zephyr to create a small biome in which the Zephyr could live. Inside the larger entrance chamber, she was able to fit in the extra plants on top of the three needed to provide protection from the corrupting aura, as well as spiritual and normal senses.

With Zephyr now able to grow properly in a space where the air was a bit thinner and much colder, she was able to form the array for a ritual using Dodge-vine and an altered Zephyr. The altered Zephyr was changed by Bitterbalm to have the earth element rather than the air element. All in all, the ritual created a protective earth wall that would cover up the entrance should she ever place the initial ritual overtop.

Finally, after another three hours working on that particularly complex and very new ritual array, she decided to get some rest. She was dead tired from the past thirteen hours of preparing, the fight against the demon before that, flying not once but . . . many times between islands, playing the hunting game with Boreal, and so on, so forth. It had been one long day.

She stepped carefully through the forest of plants that now inhabited the caves, walking through the passage she had widened, around, and down to the icy cave much further in. Stepping around the plants there, she found Delphi sitting next to the pool.

"Hey," she greeted.

"*Hello, Zalia,*" Delphi said.

They stood awkwardly in silence for a moment.

"I'm sorry for going off at you," Zalia said.

"*No need to apologise. I am sorry for my part in the collective not being able to tell you what is to come. I wish I could,*" Delphi replied, sadness in their tone.

"I only need to know one thing. Whatever else happens, will Boreal be safe?" Zalia asked.

"*I cannot say,*" Delphi said after a short pause.

"Know this. If she comes to harm and you could have prevented that outcome, I don't care how strong your collective is, I'll find a way to pay you back for it," Zalia said matter-of-factly.

"*I wouldn't expect anything else,*" Delphi replied.

"Good," Zalia said.

CHAPTER FORTY

Getting in Touch with Nature

Zalia

Zalia woke to the gentle sounds of Boreal purring. She was curled up in a patch of slush, her face tucked away under her paws. While Zalia was used to sleeping in all kinds of conditions, the slush was a new one to her that probably wouldn't be super comfortable. Boreal seemed to really enjoy it, though, and the healing effect she received from the cool, soft ice was probably quite relaxing.

Zalia stretched, letting out a quiet groan. She felt refreshed, having slept well for a good two hours, somewhat longer than her usual these days. She did feel a kind of strain, a mental pressure that came from living in hell. She rarely had time to properly relax, almost always under the decaying effect of the corrupting aura that permeated the entire place. Her garden was the only place she could really, truly be at peace amongst the plants, with the corrupting aura suppressed there to the point she could barely feel it.

She had a few things she wanted to get done, mainly levelling her abilities as quickly as possible now that she had some defences set up. Those included a small fallback position in the woods, defences for the caves, and a hell of a lot of traps around the place—they had a calming effect on her. Whatever may come.

She had actually come to the conclusion that dealing with whatever was coming as soon as possible might be a good idea. While she was a hunter herself, and quite used to the game of cat and mouse that a hunter and its prey undertook, she was very rarely on the prey side of it. She didn't really like the idea of spending an indeterminate amount of time running from an unknown threat.

So it came to them fighting whatever it was and hoping it wasn't some Emerald or Diamond rank creature from the depths of Cormaine that wanted to eat her soul. It probably wouldn't be. Hopefully.

Besides, she and the collective would be stronger together. She didn't necessarily disagree with the idea of them standing their ground; it was the lack of information about what was coming that irked her.

Not wanting to wake up Boreal, as she was being way too cute at that moment, Zalia decided to work on her two Herbalist abilities instead. Stasis could wait for the moment but levelling Preparation and Harvester could very well be quite useful in the near future.

She went and sat down in her little earthen-floored garden, breathing in the fresh air. Much as she had done not so long ago, she began her slow rotation of harvesting using Stasis and Preparation. Harvester would naturally level through the use of the others.

She also had the ability to grow a plant from herbs that she had harvested from them. Something she'd learnt from this was that the ones that became potent from the Harvester ability actually grew into plants that were themselves more potent. Her instincts told her that this was one of the reasons that the ritual arrays she was making worked as well as they did. That didn't work on the Bronze ranked herbs, those she couldn't really use to good effect just yet anyways, but it would in due time.

The feeling of approaching Bronze was intoxicating in a way, knowing that a ledge for a large increase in power was just around the corner, one that would increase her chances of survival drastically. So she sat for a few hours, her trance only interrupted by Boreal coming down to see what she was up to and then leaving her to it.

Slowly, her abilities levelled one by one.

> **Congratulations! Preparation has reached Iron 19.**
> **Congratulations! Stasis has reached Iron 16.**
> **Congratulations! Harvester has reached Iron 19.**

Her heart gave a little jump with each level, knowing that the next would be an upgrade. It took two more hours before another message dinged in her mind.

> **Congratulations! Stasis has reached Iron 17.**

Still, she sat in focus, circulating her healing through the plants, into herself, and back through the plants. Carefully trimming and storing pieces of the plants that she could feel with the Iron rank ability of Harvester. That feeling had evolved from sensing their location to sensing their shape as well.

Three hours of her trance later, another message floated in front of her.

> **Congratulations! Preparation has reached Iron 20.**
> **Congratulations! Preparation has reached Bronze 1.**
> **Preparation will gain no further levels until all classes reach Bronze.**

Despite her wish to read through the description of what the ability did, she waited. Shortly after, another message appeared.

> **Congratulations! Harvester has reached Iron 20.**
> **Congratulations! Harvester has reached Bronze 1.**
> **Harvester will gain no further levels until all classes reach Bronze.**
> **Preparation - spell - targeted**
> **Tin - The careful preparation of herbs, poisonous or healing, can enhance their effects. You may magically dry, cut, or otherwise prepare various foods, herbs, and other similar items that are plant-based.**
> **Iron - Preparation can now be used to magically harvest plants. All bonuses from harvesting manually are still applied. You may also dry, cut, or otherwise prepare foods that are not plant-based.**
> **Bronze - You may harvest entire plants in their healthy form to be transplanted later. These can be stored directly in your Stasis ability or bonded item 'Ethereal Vault Gauntlet' under those abilities' normal conditions.**
> **Harvester - passive - skill enhancement**
> **Tin - The Herbalist harvests herbs and other flora, with which they do what they will. You gain an instinctual understanding of how to harvest flora of your rank and lower. When harvesting flora of your rank or lower it has increased potency.**
> **Iron - You are able to sense nearby herbs and flora of a type you have already harvested before.**
> **Bronze - Plants you harvest of a rank lower than yours are granted additional potency to match your rank. Additionally, plants that are transplanted by you have increased resiliency.**

Zalia read over the changes a few times and once more was pleased with the results. Originally, she had thought the abilities were changing to encompass how she was using them but she could see now that they were changing to match how she *wanted* to use them. The difference was minute but distinct.

She also didn't miss that one of her abilities actually referenced a bonded item now, this being the first time any of them had done so.

She tested Preparation and found that she could take an entire Bitterbalm out of the ground and into her Stasis. She re-dug the hole she had just taken the plant from and summoned it from Stasis right into the hole.

> **Bitterbalm (Potent) (Resilient) - Iron rank - Use
> in a ritual to add an element of Curse.**

The new tag told her it was now resilient, meaning it would survive better. She smiled brightly at the little plant, happy with her ability. Her other classes' powers that allowed her to survive and kill with efficiency were all well and good, but the simple joy of being able to treat her plants well was pleasant.

She tried the same thing on a Dodge-vine, except when she took this one out, something very fundamental had changed about it.

> **Dodge-vine (Potent) (Resilient) - Iron rank - Use
> in a ritual to add an element of Protection.**

Zalia froze. She knew that Harvester said it would increase the potency to match her rank but she hadn't thought it meant it would raise the actual rank of the plant to match hers. That . . . actually raised some issues. Herbal Magic allowed her to reproduce the effect of an herb she had used in a ritual of a rank *lower* than her own, whereas this would increase the rank of herbs to her rank. She would have to be careful about using any herb at its current rank first before harvesting it lest she be unable to reproduce its effects at all.

Nevertheless, the effect was still powerful and would allow her to upgrade the herbs she already had to the same rank as she was. Not wanting to waste any time, she immediately got to it.

It was another four hours of work to go through and transplant each of her Tin rank plants in such a way that they didn't disrupt the ritual arrays they were a part of. As she finished the first room, though, she could feel the effects as the ritual grew stronger until the pervasive aura of corruption was nowhere to be felt. Underground, at least.

The small hideaway she had made up in the forest was significantly improved by the rank up of the Dodge-vine plants there, but it still did not entirely block out the aura. It was now more comparable to how it had been underground previously. Not entirely gone, but still a background afterthought.

Once that was all done, she returned to the cave to try and find Boreal. Finding Boreal nowhere inside, she went to the cave entrance to see if she could track her friend at all. As usual, it did take her a little while, but her combination of abilities and experience overtook Boreal's natural stealthiness.

She followed the tracks for a short while before noticing one of Boreal's icy clones hiding up in the boughs of a tree, a trap made by the shared Trapper passive Boreal and Zalia shared. She smiled at the icy clone hidden up above and continued tracking, realising what Boreal had been up to while she had been busy.

As she thought, there were many more of the Boreal clones hidden under roots, up in trees, and within viney plants. She found Boreal after a short time and saw her forming another icy clone with her own abilities, the clone crouching down under some undergrowth and sitting perfectly still.

"Boreal!" Zalia called out.

Boreal spun about.

"*Zalia!*" Boreal answered, dashing forwards.

Zalia braced herself and caught the fluffy missile in a tight hug.

"I see you've been busy out here," Zalia commented.

"*Traps for the corrupt ones,*" Boreal explained.

"I can see, I fear anything entering these woods should be quite scared by now," Zalia replied.

The comment wasn't entirely untrue, they had turned the forest in the immediate area around the cave entrance into a death trap for anything Iron rank and even possibly a Bronze rank if they weren't careful.

Zalia frowned at Boreal.

"Did one of your abilities rank up again?" she asked.

"*Frost!*" Boreal exclaimed.

"I didn't even notice, sorry. Congratulations!" Zalia said.

Zalia checked it out.

Frost Adaption - passive - body enhancement
Tin - You have incredible resilience towards snowy and icy terrain

> **and environments. This includes ignoring the majority of cold and cold-based magic damage and walking easily on ice and snow.**
> **Iron - You have a passive healing effect based on how cold the temperature is.**
> **Bronze - The passive healing effect is increased. Additionally, you may now receive a small amount of nourishment from cold temperatures, reducing your need to eat. Finally, you may emit an icy aura that creates a severely chilled area around you.**

She gave a low whistle.

"Now, that is a nice upgrade. Do you even need to eat anymore?" Zalia asked.

"*Need, no. Want,*" Boreal explained.

"And how about that chill aura, want to show it off?" Zalia prompted.

Boreal did just that, emitting a chill that permeated the air around them, frost crackling on nearby surfaces. She then manipulated the frost into icy spikes and shapes, controlling it with incredible skill.

"Aren't you one fancy cat," Zalia said.

"*Cat?*" Boreal asked.

She realised she had never really called Boreal a cat; the large feline with semi-translucent icy spikes sticking from her shoulders, back, and tail had a quite fantastical look compared to your regular house cat.

"It's like you, but small with no magic. No cool shoulder spikes either," Zalia explained.

"*Weak, but still friend?*" Boreal asked.

"Well, kind of. For my world, no magic is normal. They're actually quite successful hunters," Zalia replied.

"*Strong friend!*" Boreal corrected herself.

"Yeah, not anywhere near as strong as you though," Zalia said.

"*Boreal strong, Zalia stronger,*" Boreal said, bobbing her head down a little.

"Phhh, you've beat me in a fight before," Zalia replied.

"*Zalia very gentle,*" Boreal said.

"I'm sure you could hold your own. Besides, you're so close to Bronze now!" Zalia retorted.

She could see with Aura Observation that Boreal was on the cusp of reaching Bronze. Her last ability to rank up would be Cute Convincement, which meant it would most likely receive a big change, if her tier rank ups worked the same as Zalia's.

She was a little sad at that and hoped it wouldn't remove Boreal's cute powers. She liked those.

"Come on, let's finish these traps of yours and head back shall we?" Zalia said.

Boreal responded by forming her icy aura into another of the trap clones.

CHAPTER FORTY-ONE

Flora Facts

Zalia

With all of Boreal's clones now in place, Zalia wanted to talk to Delphi once more. They were in the cave waiting for Delphi to surface after Zalia had called out mentally. While they waited, Zalia opened her vault and took out the war map she had taken from the ruins of Hetheir.

She unfurled it, laying it on the ground and looked over the depiction of the surrounding lands. A large section was blacked out where the pillar rose up into the sky, but the rest of the map was like a satellite image of the forest from afar. She could actually see many green dots on the map where the collective lived within the pillar, though she and Boreal did not appear due to their stealth.

She heard a little splash and turned around to see Delphi had surfaced.

"You called?" Delphi said.

"Yeah, I have an idea. How far can the collective communicate?" Zalia asked.

"Quite far if we put our mind to it, why?" Delphi replied.

"Because I have this map. It should show where any enemies are if they show up. It only stretches a couple hundred metres, but any warning is good warning. I was thinking, if it does come to a battle then you could watch the map and tell me where the enemies are," Zalia explained.

"An interesting proposition. There is a slight issue in that we cannot seem to see you on this map," Delphi pointed out.

"I know, but Boreal or I should be able to show you where we are through a connection, if you make one," Zalia said.

"*It . . . could work, yes,*" Delphi replied.

"What's the issue?" Zalia asked, noticing the hesitation.

"*. . . Nothing. This should work, we can keep one of the collective watching the map at all times, if you would like to leave it here,*" Delphi said.

"Fine by me," Zalia said.

Zalia watched Boreal trying to slap around a small ball of ice.

"Look, I'm sorry if I have been a little upset recently. I want you to know I'm not so much upset at you as I am at the collective. I know you can only do so much," Zalia apologised.

"*Zalia, there is no me. I am simply a part of the whole, one piece of many,*" Delphi replied.

"Isn't there any part that is just you?" Zalia asked.

"*No,*" Delphi insisted.

"And yet, when we met you spoke out to me, not as the collective but as yourself, a single voice," Zalia mused.

"*I had memories that many others did not. I was simply the piece of the many that had seen that moment,*" Delphi explained.

"What more does it take to be oneself than the memories you hold, the voice with which you speak, and the manner in which you act?" Zalia asked.

Delphi stayed silent at that, as if actually considering the words. Zalia wasn't really the best at turning her thoughts into words but she felt like she did an alright job with that one.

"Boreal and I are very close to Bronze, I wish to be there before whatever danger arrives. Is there anything you need?" Zalia asked, breaking the silence.

"*No, I . . . we will contact you if required,*" Delphi replied.

Zalia did notice the slight slip in language. She felt a little bad for making Delphi question their individuality and it probably wasn't her place to destabilise an extremely old culture with her attempt at depth of thought, but Delphi was her friend, or so she thought. She was not upset at them individually, just the collective as a whole. It was a hard sentiment to get across when Delphi did not see any difference as she did.

Either way, she had to focus on levelling her abilities now lest they mean the difference between life and death later. The quickest of her abilities to level would be Hunter's Sight.

"Hey, Boreal, time to play the game!" Zalia called over.

Ever ready, Boreal took off.

It took the next ten or so hours for her to finally reach Bronze in Hunter's Sight. Despite the fact that Boreal was getting quite good at hiding from her, and hiding her tracks too, it was quite a push to get the level over that final threshold.

> **Congratulations! Hunter's Sight has gained
> two levels, reaching Iron 20.
> Congratulations! Hunter's Sight has reached Bronze 1.
> Hunter's Sight will not gain further levels
> until all classes have reached Bronze.
> Hunter's Sight - passive - body enhancement
> Tin - The Hunter tracks their prey. You can track creatures more
> easily. When tracking, you learn very basic information such as
> number of legs, number of creatures, and general size of creatures.
> Iron - You now learn how long ago a creature left tracks and may
> apply a Hunter's Mark if tracking it for more than an hour.
> Bronze - You are now able to discern finer details
> from tracking your prey. These details include things
> such as maturity stage, general health, and even the
> individual who left the tracks if they are known to you.
> Additionally, you gain an innate sense of direction.
> Congratulations! Hunter class has gained
> two levels, reaching Iron 20.
> Congratulations! Hunter class has reached Bronze 1.**

Zalia felt the surge of power in her body as the Hunter class finally reached Bronze, with both her dexterity and strength attributes stepping over the threshold. While the Druid class had been an exhilarating feeling, the Hunter class threshold rank ups were always the most immediately noticeable. She stopped her tracking of Boreal to test her body's strength, feeling its new speed and power.

The feeling was intoxicating, a very palpable result to her continued survival despite the odds. Her mind had been quicker than her body before, but now her body had caught up, finally able to harness the speed at which she could use it to its fullest.

She withheld her exhilaration for a moment to check over her profile.

> **Profile - Zalia Taori
> Health - Excellent
> Mana - Full
> Stamina - Full
> Class One - Hunter - Bronze 1**

Linked Attributes - Strength, Dexterity
Active Skills
Kill Shot - Bronze 1
Hunter's Mark - Bronze 1
Fight or Flight - Bronze 1
Passive Skills
Hunter's Sight - Bronze 1
Survivalist - Bronze 1
Class Two - Herbalist - Iron 15
Linked Attributes - Vitality, Resilience
Active Skills
Flora Identification - Iron 15
Preparation - Bronze 1
Stasis - Iron 17
Passive skills
Harvester - Bronze 1
Herbal Magic - Bronze 1
Unity Class - Druid - Bronze 1
Linked Attributes - Wisdom, Intellect
Active Skills
Nature's Wrath - Bronze 1
Protection of the Wilds - Bronze 1
Passive Skills
Healing Presence - Bronze 1
General Passives
Heat Resistance - Bronze 1
Cold Resistance - Bronze 1
Aura Observation - Iron 7
Low Light Vision - Iron 9
Poison Resistance - Iron 7
Mobility - Bronze 1
Stealth - Bronze 1
Trapper - Bronze 1
Teaching - Iron 7
Flight - Iron 5
Physical Resistance - Bronze 1
Mental Resistance - Bronze 1
Weapon Proficiencies
Bow - Bronze 1
Sword - Bronze 1

> **Throwing Knives - Tin 17**
> **Bonded Items**
> **Druidic Bow, Blessed by Starlight (Blessed**
> **Heirloom) - Deeply bonded Iron rank.**
> **Duskwraith Armour (Heirloom) - Bonded Iron rank.**
> **Ethereal Vault Gauntlet (Heirloom) - Bonded Bronze rank.**

Aura Observation and Low Light Vision had both been passively levelling as time had passed but she mostly ignored those now, happy to let them advance at the rate they would. They as well as the other low Iron passives would speed up once she reached Bronze anyways.

Other than that, her profile was looking beautiful, with only two more abilities to reach Bronze. Those were Flora Identification and Stasis, both of which were quite hard to rank up in any easy manner.

No, Stasis she could probably level up with a day or two of filtering things in and out of it using Preparation. She wanted to get Flora Identification to Bronze first though, just in case a change to Stasis gave her some sort of dimensional ability.

To do that though, she would most likely have to go explore other islands. She could probably get it in three or four days by spending most of her time inspecting the ever-changing form of the Adastem. That would be incredibly boring, though.

In the end, she did decide on that path. As boring as it would be, she didn't want to get caught out on another island while she knew danger was coming this way. She also didn't want to drag any more attention to the island she now inhabited by being seen travelling.

So, her mind made up, she settled in for the long haul.

Each hour stretched into eternity as she focused her mind on simply pushing to level this one ability. She only slept once during the entirety of the four days, her only other distraction the occasional break to level Stasis a little bit. In the end, however, it paid off.

> **Congratulations! Flora Identification has**
> **gained five levels, reaching Iron 20.**
> **Congratulations! Flora Identification has reached Bronze 1.**
> **Flora Identification will gain no further**
> **levels until all classes reach Bronze.**
> **Flora Identification - spell - targeted**
> **Tin - Poison, cure, or food, you'll know. You may identify whether**
> **targeted flora is poisonous, helpful, nutritious, or all of the above.**

Iron - You may now identify what elements different flora contain. Bronze - Your ability to identify flora extends to understanding their role within ecosystems, including their interactions with other plants and animals, aiding in ecological preservation efforts. Additionally, you gain knowledge about the historical uses and significance of the identified flora, allowing you to uncover hidden cultural or magical insights related to them. Congratulations! Stasis has gained two levels, reaching Iron 19. Congratulations! Herbalist class has gained four levels, reaching Iron 19.

The new effect was actually very interesting. She spent a little time after the four long days inspecting a few plants to test what it actually meant. Identifying her own plants yielded a few key pieces of information. Firstly, if they were a part of one of her ritual enchantments, the permanent ones made from the live plants, it actually told her of the plant's role in that enchantment.

The more interesting facet of the ability came when she identified Bitterbalm. It told her of its common use as an herb used in cooking, as well as an old use it had in a certain type of religious ritual. It didn't tell her exactly what that ritual was or what its purpose was, only that it indeed had once been a thing.

It also better described the element that Bitterbalm encompassed, curse. She already knew that the curse element in fact caused a reversal of element when used in a minor ritual with another, but the new ability stated that for her explicitly.

She used the ability on all the other herbs she had on her, quite interested in what she could learn.

Snow-leaf had historically been used by northern-dwelling people as a form of cooling to preserve food and was still used in that way by the people more in touch with nature. There were no magical insights for the herb, unfortunately.

Frozen Heart had a similar history in that it was often used by a tribal people in Endaria as an herb to help the sick and wounded recover. It didn't tell her who those people were or where they lived, unfortunately, maybe she could find them one day.

She learnt something quite cool when inspecting Flame-root. There were no magical insights, but it told her how it was used in a ceremony by Those Born of Heat and Stone to create more of their race. She hadn't really known how they reproduced as she hadn't seen any young, and the information made her even more curious. Were they somehow actually created from heat and stone?

She had a few questions for Glemp if she ever made it back.

Dodge-vine didn't have much to say other than it was often treated as a weed by people, yet had a very symbiotic relationship with many other plants in any given ecosystem it was found in.

Manifest didn't have much history, but she did find out that it was actually a result of a large density of magically invested creatures living in close confines. She remembered that it was found anywhere that a large amount of construction was found but apparently due to the large population, not the buildings themselves.

Each other herb had interesting little bits of information about how they functioned in their natural ecosystems, but the one that caught her attention next was the Glowing Cavern Fungus.

According to her ability, it was actually commonly used in a religion focused around a god. A god in particular that she got the sense was one she knew. Once again, it didn't explain the religion or the specific use of the fungus in the religion, but it was just another piece of the puzzle that she was trying to solve around that crow god of hers.

She put the little tidbit of information to the back of her mind as she stood up from where she had been inspecting various plants. She had one last ability to level up and she was just about ready to reach Bronze.

CHAPTER FORTY-TWO

Bronze

Zalia

Congratulations! Stasis has reached Iron 20.
Congratulations! Stasis has reached Bronze 1.
Active 3 - Stasis - spell - targeted
Tin - Can put a small amount of herbs into stasis.
Iron - Herbs in stasis may now be put into a spatial storage.
Stasis becomes Druid Grove!
Active 3 - Druid Grove - spell - targeted - realm
Tin - You may place herbs in stasis. Additionally,
you are able to establish a small Druid Grove.
Iron - Herbs in stasis may now be put into a spatial
storage. Plants and friendly creatures within your
Druid Grove are constantly affected by the base effect
of Healing Presence separate from your aura.
Bronze - The spatial storage effect of this ability is now
linked with 'Ethereal Vault Gauntlet,' creating one larger
space. This space is considered part of your Druid Grove.
Druid Grove Added Effects
Healing Presence.
Druid Grove Base Effects
The protective energy of your Druid Grove extends to ward
off harmful magical influences and creatures, providing
an added layer of defence to those within its bounds.
Your Druid Grove changes with the seasons, adapting its

> **flora and effects accordingly. In spring, it might emphasise growth, while in winter, it offers protection from the cold. Your Druid Grove becomes a haven not only for plants but also for animals. Creatures within the Grove may form a bond with you, aiding you in various ways.**
> **Mana - low / N/A**
> **Cooldown - N/A / N/A**
> **Congratulations! Herbalist class has reached Iron 20.**
> **Congratulations! Herbalist class has reached Bronze 1.**
> **Congratulations! All of your classes have reached Bronze. Would you like to ascend to Bronze?**

Zalia was overwhelmed as her consciousness was flooded with a surge of messages and the feeling of another two linked attributes. When she was feeling a little better, she accepted the ascension.

> **Congratulations! You have ascended to Bronze.**

The sensation to begin with was one of disconnection. She could feel her three classes, each with their two linked attributes at Bronze level. The attribute pairs were linked to each other as well, she could see that now. It wasn't something she had noticed last time around, but now it was clear as day.

As the ascension clicked into place, she could feel the disconnection between those attributes . . . not quite disappear, but lessen. It felt as if they were closer, more in sync with each other.

She could feel it too, she knew the strength and speed of her mind and body, she had felt the *health* that had flowed through her when the Herbalist class had reached Bronze, but they now complemented each other in a much better way. The speed of her mind lent further speed to her muscles, even as they were kept in one piece by her resilience.

Her instinctual knowledge, granted by her intellect, perfectly applied strength and power to her body, the very same body that was kept in peak condition with the health provided by her vitality.

She could feel the two new connections, the link between dexterity, wisdom, and resilience, and the link between strength, intellect, and vitality.

Those were the links that bridged her three classes, the links upon which her abilities evolved to better complement each other. No longer were the classes separate, they were closely connected.

Yet, she could still feel there was much to learn, much room to grow.

She had reached some checkpoint in her advancement, the threshold of Bronze making her now more supernatural than she was human.

It took a while for her to finally come back to her own body, the sensations dying down to a new normal. She was laying on the floor with Boreal curled up against her. She had a few more messages now as well.

> **Congratulations! Your ability Stasis has evolved to Druid Grove and formed a bond with 'Ethereal Vault Gauntlet.' 'Ethereal Vault Gauntlet' is now deeply bonded.**

She breathed out and read through the new ability, Druid Grove. Much like when the previous ascension had changed Escape to Fight or Flight, the upgrade was substantial. It added an extra effect at each previous level of the ability as well as the additional one granted by Bronze.

In this case, it was this Druid Grove.

Reading through what it actually did, she was ecstatic. It would be a powerful addition to her defences, depending on how far it actually stretched. Another overlaid Healing Presence alone, making it extremely powerful, though the effect was only the base one, which she took to mean it would not provide things such as the anti-death ability.

She started testing things one by one. First, the melding of the two spaces was a little confusing. She couldn't store just anything through the old Stasis ability, it was still limited to herbs and plants only.

The look of the Ethereal Vault Gauntlet had also changed dramatically. It was now like an exoskeleton wrapped around her hand and wrist, and made of wood. It had Druidic-looking runes carved into its surface with imagery of what she could only describe as Boreal and various starry depictions.

She summoned her bow and realised it too had changed. It now had some minor ethereal-looking imagery to it, like vapour. She also found that the gauntlet had melded to her skin.

That was somewhat alarming to begin with, but she didn't mind how it looked and it was actually quite comfortable to wear. It had become a part of her, in a way. She opened her vault and was taken away by the changes inside and out. The portal itself was no longer a tear in the air but a nice archway grown from two intertwined vines with leaves shooting off them.

The clean and sterile environment inside had changed to one of natural beauty. The same ten shelves were there, five on each side, yet they were now made of wood, flowing in a way as if grown naturally.

The floor had become earthen and tiny pinprick, warm lights floated around in the air giving it a nice atmosphere. Rather than a wall at the back, there was now an open space with sun shining in from above. In that space were all the herbs and plants she had stored within her Stasis Druid Grove ability. The whole plants were planted in the centre of the space with the harvested herbs stacked neatly in ordered piles on a long bench that stretched around the circumference of the half circle.

Each of the items stored in her gauntlet were still there, kept safe by golden domes that held them to the wooden shelves. She also noticed that there was another warm Healing Presence in the room, the origin of the effect being her Druid Grove. With it came a sense of safety that wasn't just in a metaphorical way. She could feel that it actually strengthened her a little, increasing her resiliency.

She left the vault, having to be quite careful with her newfound strength, as she had yet to adapt to it. Closing the vault, she tried shaking Boreal awake.

"Boreal," she said gently.

Boreal rolled over in her sleep.

"Boreal!" she said a little louder.

Boreal let out a quiet mew, still asleep.

Rolling her eyes, Zalia started poking her finger in between Boreal's feet pads. One paw twitched. She poked it again. It twitched more violently. After poking them once more, Boreal finally awoke, looking around in confusion.

"Wakey, wakey," Zalia said.

Boreal slumped her head back into the pile of slush she'd been asleep in.

"Oh no you don't—look I'm Bronze rank!" Zalia exclaimed.

That finally got Boreal to wake up.

"I've got this cool new ability called Druid Grove and my gauntlet changed to look like this!" Zalia said proudly, holding her hand up.

Boreal examined the gauntlet, looking a little smug when she saw the depiction of her carved into it.

"Oh yeah, go on and gloat. Just because you're a big old meanie doesn't mean I don't love you," Zalia said, rolling her eyes once more.

She got up and opened the vault again for Boreal to explore. While Boreal sniffed around, Zalia explored the bounds of her new ability internally. There were usually a few things not stated that she could determine instinctually. For instance, one of her biggest concerns was immediately wiped away as she discovered she would be able to move the Druid Grove if she so wished. The process wasn't easy but it was doable.

Establishing a Grove seemed to require a fair bit of work, which involved becoming intimate with the area, changing it to her liking, and taking care of the plants there. She could only have one Grove at a time, which made a lot of sense.

She also realised something that hadn't occurred to her immediately: her chances against any serious corruption aura just increased massively. Two Healing Presences stacked on top of each other as well as the aura dulling enchantment by the living plant ritual would provide quite a lot of protection.

With that in mind, she started doing what she did best. Planning.

CHAPTER FORTY-THREE

Druid Grove

Zalia

The first thing Zalia did was set up her Druid Grove. She had an intuitive feeling of exactly what it required, though said requirements were not listed under the ability. Thankfully, they seemed to all be things she had already done, so all she had to do was perform a small ritual.

The ritual itself didn't require any materials, simply needing her to walk from one end of the caves to the other before sitting down in the main chamber cross-legged. There, she closed her eyes and felt a presence growing outwards from herself.

The feeling was strange, like it wasn't some magic expanding to fill the cavern but her very being. She could sense each and every plant, not just by the Harvester Ability but by the Druid Grove. She could feel the little warm, pinprick lights spreading through the caves, filling each chamber with a warm glow.

She could feel when they stopped at the T-intersection, going towards the entrance but not heading further towards the grey creatures. She could feel as a system of roots slowly grew out from beneath her as well. The room she was inside transformed, a large trunk growing from the centre of the room and splitting into many branches that spread across the ceiling. She could feel the decorative wooden edging grow around the pool in the room, turning sharp rock edges to soft wooden ones with depictions of Boreal and the starry night sky.

A bench formed along one side; the altar to the crow god became a part of the root system quickly growing underneath. Her herb garden grew a system of roots through it that formed gentle paths more like the sideways grown branches of a tree than the constructed paths of a city.

The tunnel leading towards the surface was turned from a treacherous and narrow path into a gently curving passage with wooden walls decorated similarly to the pool edging. A large, reinforced door grew at the T-intersection, blocking the direction to the grey creatures, and the passage continued towards the entrance chamber.

There, another bench grew from the floor and a patch of soft vines dropped from the entrance, blocking sight to the outside.

She could also feel the Healing Presence that grew with the Grove, the plants within all looking immediately healthier upon its contact. The feeling of safety that she had felt within the vault followed soon after.

All of this she felt before she even opened her eyes. When she did, it was a space transformed. Gone was the purple light, replaced now by the warmth of the pinprick lights. While the purple glowing mushrooms still grew on the walls, their light was significantly dimmed. The caves were now warm and inviting with surfaces now made of soft wood that looked grown, not constructed. Various coloured flowers bloomed from the branches overhead and the floor was transformed to a soft loam with a comfortable mossy surface.

Zalia breathed out, looking over to Boreal, who was looking around at the transformation in wonder. Zalia felt like she had an extra limb or an extra pair of eyes as she sensed and felt everything that was happening within the Grove.

She hopped up from her seated position and went about exploring the new space. She found the newly transformed sleeping chamber above with a nice moss bed; the ceiling was covered with the depiction of a sky with Boreal chasing the stars.

The herb garden was just as she had imagined it, the plants all looking healthy with a beautiful splitting path winding through the complex living rituals. She went up the passageway, now much nicer to walk through and built as if for her height. The wooden door blocking off the grey creatures' section was sturdy and locked, and was even able to block her ability to move through solid objects.

She went to the entrance chamber and checked out what it looked like from the outside, finding that the vines covering the entrance camouflaged the whole thing to look like solid stone, and the crack was no longer visible.

She also noticed that the corrupting aura had a significantly lessened effect on her even outside of the Grove. That was probably due to her resilience and vitality attributes having reached Bronze. She wasn't certain if

Juniper had had either of those bonded, though if she had, she might have actually survived much longer against it. Thinking that though, she had been in a terrible state before coming here in the first place.

Zalia went back into the Grove and walked through the comfortable space back to the central chamber. Something she had noticed was that the large trunk that grew up in the centre of the chamber had a doorway shape built into it that was extremely familiar. Without even needing to raise her hand, she commanded the vault to open, and the portal came to life.

Inside was the rest of her Druid Grove just as she remembered it.

Unfortunately, she didn't want to spend too much time dawdling around inspecting every facet of the new Grove. There would be time for that later; at the moment she had some learning to do. Her Herbal Magic ability would now be able to provide her insight into an additional *six* herbs and their uses in rituals. The elements of healing, fire, water, shadow, mind, and adaptability were all available to her in their variety of uses with rituals. She had a lot of thinking to do.

First though, she needed to do one other thing. She was now able to transform all of her plants into their Bronze forms, thanks to Harvester. That would hopefully increase the strength of the living rituals even more, which would in turn make the Grove a safer place. She also had an idea for the entrance defences that Herbal Magic was already telling her was possible.

It took her a good while to upgrade all the plants, but once it was done she could move on to her new idea. She altered the ritual that would create the defensive wall to include some Adastem. When she activated it, it created a defence that instead of being earthen, having taken out both Zephyr and Bitterbalm, was now adaptive.

She wasn't quite sure how the Adastem knew how to adapt, maybe it was part of the plant, maybe a part of the ritual itself, but it immediately started changing until it was a sense protection. She knew that if they came under attack, it would change itself to become a physical defence. It slightly weakened the overall defensive capability of the ritual as a whole, but it meant that no matter what type of attack came, it would be able to protect from it.

Next, she used Frozen Heart, an herb she had gathered on her very first day in Endaria, to set up a small living healing ritual in each room. They weren't much but were also mixed in with some Adastem to create an adaptive healing ritual, adding another layer of healing to the Grove.

She was very happy to have found Adastem and started by inspecting it and all its possible uses once she was done with those few ideas she'd had immediately. It had . . . a stunning variety of uses in conjunction with all of her other herbs. Basically any ritual she could create, Adastem could be added to. It would slightly weaken the resulting ritual, but in turn would make it significantly more complex and varied in what it could accomplish.

She spent a few hours delving into the possibilities with the Bronze rank herbs she had on her, and tried to come up with some unique things, the types of rituals that Herbal Magic wouldn't instinctively tell her about until she basically asked whether they were possible or not.

She came up with a few stealth and light-oriented rituals that used the glowing purple mushrooms and a variety of utility and combat focused rituals using the others. She did feel like a combination of the Living Trapvine and Frozen Heart would have a healing effect on trauma, something she was excited to show to Ember when she got back.

Some of the combinations between the new Bronze herbs and Bitterbalm were . . . disturbing. The Water Lily would cause a desiccating curse, the cavern mushrooms would cause blindness, and even Frozen Heart would cause, well, essentially cancerous growth in the target.

None of those would have much of an effect on the undead, or so she thought, but they were still terrifying to consider. Unfortunately, she had no new ideas for traps that she could make with the living rituals. She would have to find something with an element of trap or something of the kind. Of course, there were a myriad of harmful rituals she could set up, but those she would have to activate herself.

She was interrupted by Boreal coming up and nudging her.

"What's up?" Zalia asked.

Boreal looked up at her with wide eyes, looking oh-so-bored.

"I know, I know. Zalia sitting here thinking about plants isn't interesting. Would you like to go see the god, maybe? I'm hoping I can use some of this Living Trapvine to maybe heal the god's mind, though I'd like to talk to Delphi about it first," Zalia suggested.

Boreal perked up, bouncing around in victory.

Then, she froze in place.

Your bonded ally, Boreal, has reached Bronze rank.

"Boreal!" Zalia exclaimed.

Boreal started looking woozy and out of it, presumably having just accepted the ascension immediately without thought. Zalia, though, wanted to check out the new ability transformation she would have just received.

Predator and Partner
**Tin - You can use your cuteness to make others less aggressive
towards you. Alternatively, you may instil a primal terror instead.
Iron - You're able to slightly affect the actions others take in
regards to you. Additionally, you can cause others' bodies
to betray them, causing them to freeze or run in terror.
Bronze - You become the embodiment of fear in the animal
kingdom, radiating an aura of dominance and terror that
can influence even the most ferocious of beasts. Wild
animals will instinctively avoid confrontation with you,
and you can call upon them to aid you in times of need.
Additionally, particularly cowardly enemies may turn on
their allies when confronted by your presence in battle.**

Zalia raised an eyebrow, looking at the admittedly large but still very cute feline friend she called Boreal. The subject of her gaze was also currently stumbling around like she was drunk.

"Boreal?" Zalia asked.

Boreal tripped over with a weak "mreow."

Zalia just shook her head, looking at her in wonder.

She started pushing healing into Boreal, hoping it would help with the adjustment. Thankfully, a few minutes later she seemed more or less back to normal.

"Your new ability is interesting," Zalia commented.

Boreal turned to Zalia and she did have to admit, there was something . . . different about her.

"*Boreal strong!*" Boreal exclaimed.

"Yes, you certainly are. You are also apparently a prime example of a terrifying beast, if your ability has any truth to it," Zalia replied.

"*Am scary,*" Boreal proclaimed.

"Maybe to the chopped meat in a kitchen under the gaze of a distracted chef you are," Zalia said.

Boreal managed to look a little offended.

"Look, all I'm saying is you're going to have to work on your intimidation with an ability like that. Sure, you are quite scary when you fight, but outside of it, you're a little bit of a goofball all the time," Zalia explained.

Boreal looked hesitant but didn't argue.

"We can work on your scary face another time, maybe," Zalia promised.

That seemed to satisfy Boreal.

"Now, should we go see Ro?" Zalia asked.

"*Ro!*" Boreal shouted into Zalia's head.

She then bounced around a little bit on the mossy floor.

Zalia raised an eyebrow.

"My point stands," Zalia told her.

"*Delphi, we're going to go see Ro and the god. Want to come along? We have both just reached Bronze and I have a new ability I'd like to test. It might help the god heal,*" Zalia projected her thoughts towards the collective.

"*I'll be up soon,*" Delphi replied.

Zalia sat down on her newly grown bench to wait, finding it remarkably comfortable. What a life.

CHAPTER FORTY-FOUR

Light Flight

Zalia

Delphi had come up and Zalia had explained her idea with the Living Trapvine to them. They had said it wasn't such a bad idea and it might possibly work, considering the Trapvine seemed to be a part of the god in the first place. With that dealt with, they had gone up to the surface to fly across to the god.

Zalia still felt . . . a little unsafe flying across, but this time decided to be a little more careful. She applied a few rituals to herself, Boreal, and Delphi before they left the cave. The first three were the trio that made up the protective rituals in the Grove. The ritual to protect against normal senses, the one to protect against spiritual type senses, and the one that blocked spiritual type attacks. Additionally, she used a new one that she had come up with using the shadow element from the Glowing Cavern Fungus.

It was . . . essentially a type of invisibility, or close to it. She used a Cavern Fungus major and Bitterbalm minor ritual to convert the element to light instead of shadow. Then, she used the light element as the major and Dodge-vine as the minor to give herself a kind of protection from light. Maybe that wasn't the right way to describe it, using light as protection might have been better. Either way, the effect essentially warped light in a weird way around her such that she didn't become invisible but semi-transparent, blurry almost. Unfortunately, it also did something weird to her vision such that the world became a little blurry.

It was still possible to see but it would not be usable in a fight, for instance. For a flight across a large distance where her destination was a giant island, it was perfect though.

They made the trip quickly, Delphi having gone back to a haphazard flight after the light-guarding ritual was applied. Fortunately for Zalia and Boreal, they both were able to see vibrations in the air and that particular sense wasn't affected by the light ritual. Due to that, as well as the flight passive and their mental attributes, they were able to fly without hindrance. With the stacks of stealth-based rituals, passives, and abilities, Zalia was unable to see Boreal whatsoever. The only reason she could sense that Boreal was near at all during the flight was due to the bond they shared, something she usually didn't use to locate Boreal unless absolutely necessary. It also didn't really work from a long range, but they were close enough in flight to keep together.

Delphi on the other hand, Zalia could still see, if barely. They didn't have any Stealth passive as far as she knew, probably having had no need to develop one. She didn't even know if it was possible for them to get one, she didn't exactly understand how gaining general passives worked entirely. Sometimes they just appeared and she was happy for it. She wasn't about to go around searching out every single resistance or utility passive she could get her hands on, after all.

Once they reached the temple and had entered, Zalia went over to greet Ro with a bop to the head.

"Finding yourself bored out here yet?" Zalia asked.

Ro led her over to a corner where there was a small stack of shiny objects. Something like a coin, a piece of . . . tin foil? A pebble that was startlingly reflective.

"What's all this?" she asked.

Ro looked at her expectantly.

"Don't tell me you expect me to store all of these in the vault too," Zalia said, aghast.

Ro bobbed his head up and down.

Zalia sighed.

She opened her vault and the god suspended by vines immediately turned and stared at the portal.

"W-what is that?" it asked.

"It's a vault that stores things. It is also part of my Druid Grove," Zalia explained.

"It feels like . . . nature," the god whispered.

"It is," Zalia said with a smile, "there is a larger one on one of the other islands too. Your altar, at least I'm pretty sure it is one of yours, sits right in the middle of it. Can you feel it?"

The god turned its head away from the portal and looked, by Zalia's estimation, directly towards the cave, through the wall, far off into the distance.

"Yes, I can feel it. Nature, such a small pocket, but it is there. Did you do this?" it asked.

"Yes, I've been cultivating a few plants, making them stronger. Forming a little ecosystem of sorts. Nature returns to your world," Zalia replied.

It didn't reply, still staring as if it could see through the wall. Maybe it even could, she didn't know how a god functioned.

She picked up Ro's small pile of shinies and went and stored them with the spoon she also had in there. Luckily, she was able to store them all as one item in the same spot so it didn't take up any more space. She would have to figure out how far she could stretch that particular function. How much of something could it hold, or how big of an item could it store?

She left the vault again, leaving it open so the god could feel the altar's presence.

"I have something that might be able to jog your memory a bit. Would you like us to try? It will be a simple ritual involving a piece of the Trapvine from above, the one you are connected to," Zalia explained.

"I would not say no to such a thing. Try what you will," it replied, still staring into the distance.

Zalia shrugged, then pulled out a piece of the Trapvine. She also deposited some of the Glowing Cavern Fungus and helped it grow onto the walls. Flora identification had told her it had relevance to this god so she thought it might help in some way. She had also used the ability on the Trapvine, but all it had done was confirm that it was indeed connected physically to the god. It had no religious significance, at least none that her ability told her.

Next, she pulled out some Frozen Heart, and Herbal Magic took the ingredients, each turned to fine-cut, dried pieces by Preparation. They floated into a ritual circle before Zalia, pointed at the god. She also added some Adastem to the mix, the ritual shifting to form a different pattern. It was a last-minute adjustment by her because she thought the extra comprehensibility when dealing with an unknown memory issue would be helpful.

She activated the ritual and a dim glow emanated from the circle as the ingredients began burning away. The god finally looked away from the wall towards her; Delphi was off to the side, ready to intervene in any way they could.

A pulse went through the god and it sat up a little straighter, a presence unlike anything it had previously displayed coming to the fore. It was, unfortunately, only momentary. It relaxed again, the strength fading.

"Anything?" she asked.

"There was . . . something. I remembered but it is gone. I don't think whatever you did was powerful enough," it replied sadly.

"Damn," Zalia said.

It was progress at least. If she could find some way to turn it into a living ritual, maybe?

The issue with that was she didn't know if she would be able to just grow one of the Living Trapvine like that. Unless she could somehow . . . make the huge one above into part of the ritual. That was definitely something to think long and hard about before making a rash decision. She didn't know how it would react to her doing such a thing, let alone if it would work. Maybe it would have an adverse effect on the god as well, who knew.

No, she thought this was good enough for now.

Boreal and Ro were sitting politely next to each other, Boreal practicing at not being an entire goofball.

"Well, any more ideas?" Zalia asked the room.

She personally had a few but wanted a little more confirmation that the living rituals weren't what had drawn the demon's attention. Though, the Gold ranked bulb above was very capable of defending against a lot that could come this way. Maybe not something like the aura monster, but if that thing cared at all about it, surely it would have found the bulb by now. How long this god had been down here, she had no idea. Sometime during the history of the Endarian kingdom, though how long that was, she had no idea.

It would have been a good time to have someone around who had studied a lot of history. Or knew any, at all.

"*The collective has no further ideas at this time*," Delphi said.

"Hmm, Boreal, no, feeding it more won't work," Zalia mentioned as she noticed Boreal looking at the god.

"*Wasn't thinking that*," Boreal complained.

"What were you thinking then?" Zalia asked.

"*. . . Could . . . give it water*," Boreal explained.

"I don't think gods get thirsty, Boreal," Zalia replied. "You don't get thirsty, do you?"

She asked anyway, just in case.

"I have no need for nourishment of the sorts you require. Something else entirely," it explained.

"What would that be?" Zalia asked.

"I do not know, at this moment," it said.

"Yeah, thought as much," Zalia replied with a sigh. "You have a temple in the city," she said, a memory surfacing.

She had seen the god's symbol above one of the crumbling buildings near the keep in Hetheir. She had even used it to secure the large metal object she had used to distract many of the undead. Far back, before she had any flight at all.

"I cannot feel the temple of which you speak. Not as I can feel the altar within your Grove," it said softly.

"You might not have been able to feel that altar at all before I . . . healed it? Maybe this one is the same!" Zalia replied, a little excitement in her tone.

"I do not know. If you would be kind enough to search it for me, I would appreciate your assistance," it pleaded.

"I will, I have a little free time now in which I can go check it out," Zalia said.

"Thank you," the god replied.

"My pleasure," Zalia said, giving a little bow.

CHAPTER FORTY-FIVE

Temple Two

Zalia

The flight across to the island that hosted the ruined city of Hetheir was much the same as the one to the god's island. Zalia was used to the strange, blurred vision now, able to direct herself with enough proficiency to not lose course. She did leave Delphi behind to keep an eye on the crow god and to ensure that no latent harm had been done by the ritual.

She and Boreal arrived at the temple before long, flying low to avoid the attention of the shades. There was a chance that they would be able to fly straight through them without harm but she didn't quite want to risk that just yet. Though, thinking that, she had been able to go unseen by shades that were actively trying to hunt her down during the fight with the humanoid demon. Still, a risk not worth taking anyways.

The temple was sitting just as she remembered it, somewhat broken down but still in one piece, the metal symbol above the entrance attached to the roof degraded at the top.

"*Think we should clear the undead out first?*" Zalia asked Boreal mentally.

"*Fight!*" Boreal exclaimed.

Of course she wanted to fight.

Zalia knew that the sound wouldn't enter the keep and get the attention of the Gold ranked undead king in there, so she wasn't super worried. Even if a Silver undead showed up now she might have an alright time fighting it, as she had already been able to beat one when she had been Iron rank. Not that she thought skipping two ranks in power was a good idea in any normal case, though. She was also definitely not going to try to "release" the king just yet; she didn't know if it would have powers or not. The Silver ranked undead didn't, but they did act differently than the Bronze and lower-ranked undead—maybe the Gold would act differently than the Silver.

Bringing her thoughts back to the task at hand, she looked down at the low-ranked undead milling about on the street. She had cleared out a good few chunks further out in the city but hadn't done any within the centre section just yet. Why not start now?

There were a few new rituals she wanted to try using, mainly with the Flame-root she could now utilise properly. There was a particularly nasty combination she had come up with using Flame-root, Zephyr, and Manifest that was, basically, an explosion. The herbs would yield the ritual elements of fire, air, and physical manifestation, the result of which would probably garner the attention of even the shades above. It was a risk but she just *really* wanted to test it out.

She also wanted to test the Flame-root and Bitterbalm combination that would create a cursed fire that should spread pretty quickly across the desiccated undead, especially if they were all grouped up tightly.

"*Want to be the distraction, or do you want me to?*" Zalia asked.

"*I get attention,*" Boreal said.

She didn't wait for any more questions, charging Pounce as she dropped from the sky at high speed. Zalia felt an aura of . . . predatory intent emanate from Boreal at the same time the very air around her dropped rapidly in temperature.

Zalia began preparing many, many rituals at once as Boreal did that, not wanting to waste the free time she would have to lay waste to the undead.

Boreal slammed into the ground, crushing the undead landing pad to dust as a swirl of icy crystals exploded out from beneath her. Immediately, the undead around her charged mindlessly. The swirl of icy crystals moved under Boreal's control, forming a few dozen small, spinning, spiked projectiles that shot outwards as more formed.

Without wasting time, Zalia had begun releasing rituals left, right, and centre as she also applied Hunter's Mark to ten undead spread at different points across the street. She applied her usual array of debuffing rituals, giving reductions to dodging, resiliency, movement speed, and a few others by use of her basic herbs such as Dodge-vine, Bitterbalm, and Snow-leaf. Once she was done with that, the fun began for real. She dropped the cursed fire ritual onto one of the marked undead, adding in Adastem to the mix of the ritual to provide it with that extra boost for its ability to spread.

Even as the dozens—if not hundreds—of undead charged at Boreal with varying degrees of speed, a riotous flame of red, green, and blue began spreading through their ranks. Some, such as the few Tin ranked undead this close to the keep, collapsed almost immediately. The Iron ranked ones didn't last much longer but were still quickly approaching Boreal.

The shades decided to finally pay attention at that moment, a dark cloud forming above and around them.

"*Get out of there,*" Zalia thought towards Boreal.

She began preparing the final ritual she wanted to try, the very explosive one.

As the Bronze and remaining Iron undead gathered in a giant flaming pile, with the shades swarming down in a large cloud that blotted out the light, Boreal shot away from the entire mess at speed, and Zalia activated the ritual.

She had purposefully waited a few seconds longer than needed to charge it up a little extra.

Flaming bones were sent flying as a large explosion rocked the streets, the shades not faring much better as their dark cloud was dissipated and they were shot off into the distance. The explosion only gathered the attention of more shades, but both she and Boreal still had the ritual that would block the shades' sight in effect from the flight. They had only swarmed due to the large flaming horde.

Still, she quickly moved away from the commotion, finding Boreal sitting on top of a roof nearby, cleaning her paw as she watched the mayhem.

"Like that?" Zalia asked in a whisper.

"*Very loud,*" Boreal complained.

"Phhh, and cool," Zalia retorted.

Boreal hesitated a moment. "*Yes, good for hunting,*" she admitted.

"Not the usual type of hunting, there wouldn't be anything left to eat," Zalia pointed out.

Boreal looked entirely offended at the mere suggestion.

"I won't do that," Zalia said comfortingly, rolling her eyes. Damn food-obsessed cat.

The undead had been entirely annihilated by the explosion, but the sound it had made only caused more to swarm. They charged through the alleys and streets towards where the shades were now confusedly milling about.

Seeing a chance to clear a few more out, Zalia began letting off some more rituals.

* * *

Zalia looked at the battlefield of still-burning corpses. The cursed fire had gotten, well, a little bit wild. She hadn't really expected it to go as crazy as it had, but the ritual was the culmination of three Bronze ranked herbs working together against an enemy that was essentially a group of undead, some of whom were as weak or weaker than normal people. Normal people who also happened to be susceptible to burning because their bodies were covered in kindling dry fur and had a zero percent water content.

"That was frighteningly effective," she said, looking at Boreal.

Boreal, for her part, looked pretty bummed out. She had really wanted to fight some more but it kind of became unnecessary after Zalia had started a wildfire. Even Zalia hadn't bothered to use her bow as the ritual magic played its part. It had occurred to her that she could probably set half the city alight by dragging the undead population on a long fiery chase.

Another day maybe, she had a temple to search.

She entered the temple first, Boreal close behind. They had to push a large piece of stone out of the way and step over another, though Zalia could have walked through both. Inside was a small room with a tiny wooden altar that looked more decorative than anything else. Zalia pushed through one of the two doors that led further into the building. Inside was the temple proper. It would have been modest if there wasn't a chunk of stone from a ceiling arch that had crushed through a set of benches to the left side of the room. The benches themselves were all but dust, mostly rotted away. Zalia did note that the small altar in the entrance was quite well-intact.

Further into the room she was in, however, there was another altar very similar to the one she had in her cave back at home. She stepped up to it and did the only thing that was natural. She healed it with her aura and watched roots grow from its base, very similarly to how they had with the one previously. Then, she used Druid Grove to store the whole thing in her vault. She wanted to properly set the altar in the room that the god was in, since the temple it inhabited didn't have one; there was a big bulb in place of where it might have once been. Or maybe the bulb had grown out of the altar, who knew.

The altar did have some text on it that was readable but she hadn't been able to decipher it. That would be a job for Delphi when she got back. Checking around the rest of the room, she found what may have once been banners, some remains of books or scrolls that were long since turned to dust, and a small pendant that had actually managed to survive the long time it had sat on the ground. It had been right behind the altar, making her think it might have belonged to a priest or worshipper of some sort.

It was definitely based on the symbol that was dedicated to the god in the other temple's basement, but this had a stylised twist to it. It must have been made by a particularly skilled craftsman or imbued with some magic to have lasted the stresses of time. It was the Y shape of the crow's foot, but the treetop-like design of the top was far more pronounced, having swirling decorations running down the length of the branches. The very top had two branches that made a small loop through which there must have once been a cord to wear the small wooden item.

There was nothing else of interest in the temple, which was a little disappointing, but there was still a chance that something good came of the altar she now had in her vault. On her way out, she also picked up the smaller decorative altar from the entrance chamber. She wanted to put it as a permanent feature in her vault just so the god would always have a connection to the nature that was her Grove.

With the temple searched, she and Boreal took off to fly back to the island that held the other temple.

CHAPTER FORTY-SIX

Origin

Zalia

Zalia arrived back at god island, making her way to the large living bulb that was the only landmark on its surface. It wasn't visible until she was close, but she knew where it was by now. She had travelled between the islands quite a few times during her relatively short time in Cormaine.

When Zalia entered the lower chamber in the temple that the god resided in, she didn't waste any time.

"I found a few things!" she announced.

She followed up the statement by summoning the big altar right in front of the god, letting her healing solidify it and spread its roots into the existing ones around the floor. Maybe such abruptness wasn't a good idea, but she was hoping to shock some memories into surfacing for the god.

Unfortunately, nothing really happened.

"*Another altar*," Delphi commented.

"Yep! This one you might be able to translate something from, though, wanna try?" Zalia suggested.

"*Right away*," Delphi replied.

That dealt with, Zalia opened her vault and took out the little pendant from the indent in one of the front shelves. She had tried just leaving it on the shelf without being stored, but when the vault closed, it popped out just before the portal vanished. She could use the herb- and plant-storing ability to store the smaller altar as well; the piece was now a permanent decoration on one of the benches at the back.

"This is a little necklace or amulet that one of your followers must have once had," Zalia started, holding up the piece for the god to see. "I found it in the temple in Hetheir, behind the altar. It's possible whichever priest it belonged to dropped it when the city fell, I suppose. I was wondering if it would be ok for me to wear it with me at all times, in your honour."

"The honour would be mine, Druid, if you chose to wear my symbol on your body," the god replied.

She still wasn't quite used to the way its voice sounded, somewhat melodious, yet croaky. Like the sounds of gravel somehow harmonised.

"Alright, I will make a loop to hang it from my neck. Did the altar bring back memories for you?" Zalia asked.

"I . . . no. I can feel it now that you have helped restore it, but I have no memory of it," the god said.

"*The altar tells a story, from what I can surmise,*" Delphi said, the thought sent to all in the room.

Zalia could tell because Boreal spoke up.

"*Story!*" she exclaimed.

"*I will do my best to translate,*" Delphi promised. "*It begins with a young spirit of nature.*"

Nateysta

The young nature spirit glided through the treetops, hopping gently from one overhanging branch to the next, listening to the sounds of the forest below. It could hear the creatures burrowing beneath the soil and leaves, the birds singing in the trees, and the many animals roaming the lands between. It had always been good at listening, hearing what others could not. It didn't understand why the others couldn't hear what it could.

"Do you hear that?" it asked a bird passing by.

"Hear what?" the bird replied.

"The animals burrowing beneath the dirt," it said.

"There are no animals burrowing beneath the dirt, silly," the bird said, laughing with a raucous sound.

The bird flew on, back to whatever plans it might have.

The nature spirit frowned. Of course there were animals burrowing beneath the dirt, how could the bird not hear?

So, it decided to go down and find out for itself.

It floated gently down to the ground below and found a little hole in the ground where it could hear the burrowing sounds originating. It squeezed in, its malleable spirit-like form adjusting to fit. It went down the small tunnel until it reached a little chamber in which a tiny furry animal scratched at the walls.

"Do you hear that?" the nature spirit asked.

The furry animal jumped in surprise, spinning around to face the newcomer.

"H-hear what?" the little animal asked.

"The birds chirping in the sky above," the nature spirit explained.

"C-chirping? In the sky? What animal in its right mind would be in the sky. No, there are no birds in the sky," the little animal scoffed.

"There most certainly are! You must come up to the surface and meet them," the spirit insisted.

"Bah, I am safe down here in my home. I have no need to come to the surface," the little animal said.

The nature spirit turned away, disappointed in the animal's narrow-mindedness. Couldn't it see that there was so much to see and hear in the world above?

It left the tunnel and looked around. Maybe those animals that lived on the land could hear both the birds above and the creatures below.

The spirit travelled far and wide, searching for the animals of the land as the sky above turned from day to night. Eventually, it saw a sparkling wolf, translucent with bright stars speckled across and throughout its form. Intrigued, the spirit went down to talk.

"Hello! What are you?" it asked.

"Greetings young spirit, I am the god of the stars above. What are you about at such a time of night?" the wolf asked.

"The stars above! I cannot hear those, they must be so quiet because they have to use all their energy to shine so bright," the spirit reasoned.

"Very few can hear them, young spirit. I think you might be able to, if you paid them enough attention," the wolf replied. "For what reason did you approach me?"

"Ah yes, you have keen hearing too, god of the stars. Tell me, can you hear the animals buried below and the birds singing above when the sun sits high in the sky?" the spirit asked.

"Of course young spirit, why do you ask?" the wolf asked in turn.

"I have spoken to the birds and they cannot hear the animals burrowing below, and I have asked those very creatures and they cannot hear the birds above. Why is that?" the spirit questioned.

"They are not interested enough to hear such things, young spirit. The birds above see only that which is before them and the animals below need not think of things such as the sky. That is the way of things. Does this strike you as odd?" the wolf asked.

"No, I am just curious about nature and all these animals who live in it yet experience so little of it," the young spirit explained.

"I see. Go forth and listen all that you can, young spirit, listen and learn all that you can about nature and when you are done, come back to me and tell me all that you have found," the wolf urged.

The spirit took the encouragement straight to heart and set off into the forest in search of the hidden truths nature kept within its boughs.

Zalia

"*That is all I can get. The rest is too worn near the base for me to read,*" Delphi said.

"Damn, I was hoping it would tell us the god's name," Zalia said in frustration.

"The—the spirit travelled far and wide, searching through every part of the forest and far beyond," the god started.

They all turned to it. Its eyes were wide, the silvery glint in them brighter than it had ever been.

"Over mountains and valleys, through oceans and storms it travelled. It met many a creature, those of the sky, the land, the sea, and the world below it all. Through its travels it learnt many things, not only discovering the nature of the world but the nature of those that lived in it. It came to understand why the little furry creature below did not care for the world above, why the bird did not care for the burrows beneath the earth. It learnt of the beauties of nature, the flowers of a blooming forest, the cute newborn of two creatures, still ponds and lilies atop. But, it also came to know of the horrors of nature too. Floods and storms, earthquakes and landslides, wildfires and volcanoes. The hunter hunting the hunted, disease and pain. It was horrified by the things it found, suddenly not so excited to be hearing all that it heard," the god continued.

It paused, shivering as if experiencing the very events as it remembered.

"It returned to that forest where the wolf, lit by the light of the stars, had told it to go forth and learn. It spoke to that very same wolf once more and asked it, 'Why? Why did you tell me to experience such things if you knew?' To that question, the wolf responded, 'You have done well to see and hear so much. Look closer, listen harder, see what you have not yet seen.' The spirit was dubious but despite all the horror it had seen, following the advice of the wolf had led it to experience much beauty, too. The spirit decided to trust the wolf once more and went out into the world. It saw much the same as it had before, the beauty and the horror. It took a very long time before the spirit saw what the wolf had been telling it to see. The beauty that came from the horror, and the horror that came from the beauty. That cute newborn of the two creatures went on to hunt and killed children of others, feeding upon them. Yet, that in turn allowed for the next generation of cute newborns to exist. The wildfires tore through the land and burnt all in its path, yet in its wake, new life thrived. An earthquake might tear the ground apart but that tear would become a river that hundreds would drink from in the future," the god continued, its voice growing ever stronger.

There was a tense silence in the room as the power of the god grew stronger. None of them, even Boreal, dared speak up.

"It finally saw what the wolf wanted it to see, heard what it wanted it to hear. It returned to that forest once more, and when the spirit found the wolf, it told the wolf of all it had learnt. That without the horror there was no beauty. It wasn't the beauty or horror alone that made nature so wonderful, it was the contrast between the two. The good and the bad that led from one to the other in the constant cycle that was life. That was the true beauty. The wolf congratulated the spirit.

"'What is your name, young one?' it asked.

"'I have no name,' the spirit told the wolf.

"'Choose one, then,' the wolf told it.

"'Choose one . . . I shall be named Nateysta, after nature, for my passion, and after the stars, for your guidance,' the spirit said.

"'Well, young Nateysta, tell me. Can you hear the stars now?' the wolf asked.

"'I . . . can, I thought the way they sparkled so brightly in the sky could not be matched, yet the voices with which they sing are beautiful. Thank you,' Nateysta replied.

"That is the end of the story," the god finished in a whisper.

They all sat in silence, watching the god with apprehension. It didn't seem any stronger yet it seemed to be able to see clearer. No longer looking around with confusion but watching them with intelligence.

"Hello, Nateysta. It is good to finally meet you," Zalia said.

"Me? I am not Nateysta, young Druid. That," it said, nodding its head towards Ro-ak, "is Nateysta."

"What?" Zalia asked in confusion.

"I am but a remnant of the power held by Nateysta, woken by your actions. It is now up to him to reclaim what is his," it replied, watching Ro- . . . Nateysta with a calm acceptance.

Zalia turned around and stared at her little crow friend.

He hopped up to the god—no, remnant of power, and looked up with wide eyes. He touched his beak to the remnant's foot and a surge of power flashed through the room.

CHAPTER FORTY-SEVEN

Nateysta

Zalia

As the flash of power rolled over Zalia, the form of Ro-ak slowly began changing, growing. Feathers became leaf-like; feet turned from small and thin to large, trunk-like limbs made of wood and bark, from which writhing vines formed toes. His form grew until it matched the size of the remnant just as the body of the remnant deflated like old grapes on a vine. It withered, turning from large and powerful to no more than a bunch of dried-out leaves hanging suspended from the vines across the room.

"Thank you, Zalia," Ro-ak said.

His voice carried power, like that of the starlight wolf. His voice was grating, like gravel being dragged across stone, yet it was melodic and full of mystery at the same time.

"Happy to see you returned to your former power Ro- . . . um, Nateysta," Zalia replied, bowing her head just a little.

"I am not as I once was; much of my former power is now lost. Yet, I remember now. I remember everything. You may call me by the name you have given, I see it as an honour bestowed by the one who has brought me back," Nateysta—Ro-ak—said.

Zalia tried to see his rank with Aura Observation but it simply returned a few question marks, much as the starlight wolf had.

Nateysta - ???

Well, he was most certainly a god of some type. The story had described him as a nature spirit, however, maybe there was something that her power lost in translation. Or, maybe whatever word the Endarians used to describe nature spirits was more akin to what a god was in her world, whereas the Bathar's version was akin to a nature spirit.

That was all too confusing for her, and thinking about the levels of translation—from Bathar, to Endarian via Delphi, then to her own language via whatever unspoken power she had—was enough to give her a headache.

"Do you have the power to take us out of Cormaine?" Zalia asked.

"I do not know how, though I might be able to find out just how to go about it now that I am partially restored," Ro explained.

"Are there more fragments of your power lying about in Cormaine, maybe? Can you feel any?" Zalia asked.

There was a lot she wanted to get answers to now that the opportunity was here.

"Not that I can feel. They may have been consumed already, unguarded as this one was. The shades would try to absorb such an undefended power," Ro replied.

"Damn. What about how you and Hetheir managed to find yourself in Cormaine, do you have any memory of that?" Zalia asked.

A thought tickled at the back of her mind but she ignored it for the moment.

"Yes, I do. Cormaine is a sister world to the one you are from, the world containing the place you call Endaria. While there are many worlds amongst the stars, these two are linked on a deeper level. Thus, the gap between the two is easier to bridge than most. I do not know how they managed to do it, but the creatures you see flying around in this place—not the shades but the others—took advantage of that weakness. Somehow, they latched onto that connectivity and . . . ate Cormaine. Yes, for lack of better words, they ate the world. Ripped it apart, took its parts, and assumed its place as the sister world of Endaria. I felt it happen, like the sundering of the land so often wrought by earthquakes, yet it was the whole planet that shook. Now, they seek to use this connection to consume Endaria too," Ro explained.

"You seem to know a lot about events, despite your almost-dead state previously," Zalia questioned.

"Dead, yet not. I hear many things, Zalia of the Druids. While I do not yet know how to escape Cormaine, I do know that your best chance is to use the weak barrier between the worlds as the path to your

freedom. No such thing as the ritual description you took from Juniper would be able to work without using that weakness," Ro said.

Zalia stopped for a moment, considering the new information. She also had an idea on how Zayes might have awakened the Hidden. The Hidden had never told her how it had happened, but maybe Zayes had found one of these remnants of power that belonged to Nateysta and used it to achieve the feat. Maybe, she didn't know anything about the subject, but it was a possibility. Thinking about the shades, she realised she might have one she could make use of as well. Juniper. Zalia knew her name, unless that wasn't her real one, and could probably use that to control her much as she had controlled the Hidden. She might even be able to learn the Hidden's real name through that. Now that would be helpful. She just had to find the right shade.

"Right, how strong are you currently? I can't seem to identify what rank you are, but would you be able to take on one of those big aura monsters?" Zalia asked, her mind switching to the issue she was soon to face.

"I believe I am able to fight one, but to kill one is a different matter. At the level of power we are at, death is not so permanent, as you have seen. It may take decades or even centuries to recover from such an injury but recover we most likely will. It takes a lot to put one of us in such a state that it requires outside interference for us to return," Ro explained.

"So . . . they are on the same level as you in power? Like the starlit wolf?" Zalia asked.

"The Divine, or the Demonic. Past Diamond rank, there is Mythical, then Ascendant and past that, Divine or Demonic. The range of power within this rank is greater than even the difference between Tin and Ascendant with the monsters you speak of. And I myself am of an equivalent of a high Gold or possible Diamond ranker, where some can far surpass even the Ascendant. The biggest difference for us is our inability to fully die," Ro explained further.

"Divine and Demonic, I see. Those would be the further ranks that no one really knows if they exist or not, then. I know you weren't around for it, but have you managed to hear somehow that we might come under attack? Delphi won't bloody tell me what danger exactly is coming but I have a feeling we might need you," Zalia said.

"I know. I will be there," Ro promised.

"Delphi, if Ro does manage to find a way to get us out of Cormaine and back to the world I come from, would the collective come with us?" Zalia asked.

"I do not know. We have not spoken of this. That future is . . . shrouded from our sight. I will bring it to the collective and we shall talk amongst ourselves about it," Delphi replied.

"Good. Do consider it strongly. Your once safe home here is not safe anymore, I think, and Endaria is a much, much nicer place to live. I actually know of a beautiful little pond where the Water Lilies I planted in yours first grew. It sits in a forest, under a small waterfall surrounded by a beautiful grassy clearing," Zalia urged, sending Delphi memories of the little pond she and Boreal had spent a few comfortable moments at.

"It does seem nice, Zalia. We will consider," Delphi promised, sounding just a little sad.

"I know it would feel bad to leave your old world behind, trust me, but there is nothing much left here for your kind. Imagine all the new memories your people could collect," Zalia added, trying to convince them.

There was no response to that.

"This is all assuming we can find a way out, anyways," she finished.

"A task for me to work on. For now, though, I wish to give you a blessing, Zalia," Ro said.

"What for?" Zalia asked, a little surprised.

"Drastically reducing the time I would have had to spend in that state, of course. You have done me a great service," Ro explained.

"I won't say no," Zalia said.

"Good, put your armour upon my altar," Ro directed.

Zalia did as he said, taking off the armour and placing it upon the altar delicately. She managed to fit it onto the relatively small surface and turned around.

"Alright, what now?" she asked.

"I give you my blessing, Zalia of the Druids. May nature guide and help you just as you guide and help it. May the power of nature's wrath flow through you in times of war and the beauty of nature's gentle times bring you peace," Ro chanted, his voice deepening, crackling with the sounds of earthquakes and storms, before softening to the sounds of a gentle river winding through a quiet forest.

Zalia brushed aside a host of messages as a deepness settled around the room, the vines above and trailing the floor moving with an energy and life they should not have been able to muster. The altar grew roots from its top that surrounded and grabbed onto pieces of the armour, a thin layer of wood growing over it.

Once the roots retreated and the deepness had risen once more, her armour was transformed.

> Congratulations! Your bonded item 'Duskwraith
> Armour' has been blessed by a god.
> 'Duskwraith Armour' becomes 'Druidic
> Armour, Blessed by Nature.'
> Congratulations! Your bonded item 'Druidic Armour,
> Blessed by Nature' has become deeply bonded.
> 'Duskwraith Armour (Heirloom) - Bonded Iron rank'
> has become 'Druidic Armour, Blessed by Nature
> (Blessed Heirloom) - Deeply bonded Bronze rank.'
> Druidic Armour, Blessed by Nature (Blessed
> Heirloom) - Deeply bonded Bronze rank.
> Tin - Wearing the armour applies Shadows' Veil to you.
> Iron - Shadows' Veil gains a new effect called Partial Intangibility.
> Bronze - When intangible, you may step through flora
> to move out of similar flora within a limited range.
> Shadows' Veil - Shadows' Veil suppresses the wearer's aura and
> magical signature, making it challenging for magical beings
> or entities with heightened senses to detect their presence.
> Shadows' Veil now muffles any sound you make while
> wearing the armour, making your movements silent,
> even when moving quickly or engaging in combat.
> Partial Intangibility - Shadows' Veil grants the wearer partial
> intangibility, allowing them to phase through thin barriers
> or objects, such as walls, fences, or closed doors, as long as
> the barriers are not too thick or magically protected.

The armour had taken on a more natural look, changing from its leather and slightly religious appearance to match what was her nature. It was still fashioned in dark colours, the full set made of smoothly carved wood that looked grown, not made. Where the helmet used to have two horns, it now had two small antlers. Carved into the surface of the armour were the depictions of Boreal, a starry sky, and now a wraith-like crow. The crow was on one shoulder plate, Boreal on the other, while linked constellations decorated in between and down the chest plate. It all curved and flowed in a very natural way, and once she had finished putting it on, she almost resembled a leafless tree more than a person.

She noticed a couple changes to the abilities of the armour. Firstly, Shadows' Veil now made her entirely silent, her movement making no noise whatsoever. She was used to hearing a tiny bit of sound when she moved, a slight scrape of the foot or bump as armour pieces connected, but now there was nothing at all. It also added the ability for her to step between flora of similar types when using the intangibility. Overall, a solid upgrade. It still didn't allow for her to store the armour in its own spatial storage which was unfortunate . . . or did it?

Stasis, now Druid's Grove, had allowed her to store living wood before, why not her armour?

She gave it a go, and much to her pleasure, found it vanished off her body straight away.

"Thank you, Ro, Nateysta, I shall treasure it for as long as I live," Zalia said, giving a deeper bow this time.

"May that be a long time indeed," Ro replied.

CHAPTER FORTY-EIGHT

Time

Zalia

The first thing Zalia did when their conversation was over was resummon her armour onto her body, activate the intangibility effect it granted, and walk confidently face-first into a large root that grew up the wall. She had been meaning to test out the ability that allowed her to step from one plant to another of a similar type but had forgotten that the roots in this room were actually a part of the large magical bulb growing above. No using that ability on overtly magical plants. Got it.

She ignored Boreal's mocking glance and left the room, allowing Ro to slowly walk back and forth, testing his new body. While he now had gotten back all of the memories from his previous life, adjusting to the new level of power would probably take a little bit.

She went up and left the temple, returning to the forest to try again. This time, when she stepped into a largish, withered tree, her perception shifted. For a moment, she was able to see as if from every tree within a hundred metres. A barrage of sensory information assaulted her mind but the newly Bronze attributes that helped it function allowed her to quickly sort through and comprehend the mess. She was seeing out of every possible location for her teleportation. It was just a moment, but during that time she chose a nearby tree and stepped out of it.

Her perception shrunk and returned to normal as she left the tree, now somewhat far from where she had been previously. She could feel that if she did not choose a place to move to during that short moment she would have simply been left where she was, sunk most of the way into a tree with her intangibility.

She turned about and tried stepping back into the tree but found the sensation did not repeat. At least, it didn't do so immediately. She stepped back out and waited five seconds before trying again, it didn't work. Another five seconds later and she was finally able to use the ability again, transferring back to the first withered tree she had stepped from.

"See that!?" Zalia exclaimed, looking at Boreal who was looking very confusedly at the tree. Like she hadn't been expecting it to swallow Zalia.

"Mreow?" Boreal said in confusion.

She had forgotten to explain the new ability to Boreal.

"Right, sorry. It lets me step into a plant and come out another one, kind of like what you do with shadows," Zalia explained.

An understanding seemed to pass through Boreal as she lost her confusion. She jumped up.

"*Chase!*" she exclaimed.

Zalia waited for Boreal to sprint off into the forest, but she just waited, staring intently at Zalia with pupils so large her eyes were almost black. She was in hunting mode.

"Other way around this time, hey? Alright, let's do it," Zalia said, immediately beginning to cast a few rituals. She applied her stealth and slow-fall rituals, forgoing flight to be fair about it. She also managed to cast a movement-slowing ritual on Boreal as she sprinted face-first through a tree. Even with the slowing, Boreal would still be faster than Zalia, especially so, considering the time between her shadow jumps was significantly lower than Zalia's plant one, though the range was much shorter.

Still, Zalia planned to give her a run for her money as she did everything she could to get a head start, using her other teleport as well, compliments of Mobility.

She sprinted through the forest, ignoring branches, bushes, and other smaller obstacles as she used her intangibility to pass straight through them. Doing so did apply some force to her, but it was so little that her strength and momentum allowed her to ignore it. She felt a little like a spirit of the forest, flitting through without a care for where she ran, quick and reactive enough to avoid anything big enough to be an issue to her intangibility.

Despite her speed and various advantages, it wasn't enough to escape Boreal. She was a natural-born hunter, enhanced by her own attributes and abilities. While she wasn't in what would be considered her natural habitat, it didn't really seem to bother her, as she eventually caught up and bowled Zalia over, again. She was doing that too much lately.

"Ow, you got me, you got me," Zalia groaned between deep breaths and the laughter escaping her.

Boreal jumped up and ran about in victory, obviously excited to be big enough and quick enough to catch Zalia like that. She supposed it was the turning point in any kid's life to become better at something than their parent. Was that what Boreal was to her, a child?

Zalia had raised her, so to speak. She supposed she hadn't been far off from being a parent to Boreal.

She smiled at Boreal running around, bouncing off the trees and sat contentedly in the dirt. That was, before she remembered that she had to be ready for whatever danger was coming their way. Stupid foresight, predicting the future. She much preferred being unaware of what the future held, it was kind of hard to enjoy the moment when you knew the death of you and your loved ones may soon approach.

With a sigh, Zalia picked herself up from the ground.

"Come on Boreal, we've got to get back and pick up Delphi. Preparations to be made still," Zalia called out.

She stepped through a tree and started making her way towards the temple. Boreal would probably get there before she did anyways.

As predicted, Boreal was waiting for her when she left the forest, the cheeky feline sitting innocently on the doorstep of the temple.

"Yeah, alright, alright. You're damn fast. No need to be so smug about it," Zalia grumbled as she stepped past Boreal.

They picked up Delphi and flew back home together. Ro said that he would be able to join them when he was ready. Zalia wasn't sure how exactly he would go about it, but he did have big wings and a tendency towards mystery and shadow. She was sure he could get here unseen.

When they were back, Delphi went off to tell the collective all about the story and Ro's awakening. It was certain to be a memory the collective would hold onto for a long time, of that Zalia was sure.

"Right, I've run out of ideas for any preparations we can make. Do you have any ideas, Boreal?" Zalia asked.

Boreal stared at the ground thoughtfully, like she was trying to discern the nature of the dirt beneath her feet.

"*Food*," Boreal said.

Zalia was about to roll her eyes but the idea that came with the thought stopped her. Boreal had sent the idea of . . . distraction?

"Do you mean we should set up something as a distraction from the cave?" Zalia asked.

Boreal bobbed her head.

Zalia thought about it, weighing the good and bad of the idea. On one hand, having something that brought attention away from the caves was an excellent idea. The issue she had with it was that it would have to be something very . . . visible. That would definitely drag attention to the island if there wasn't attention already. It might have been a good idea, but what if doing this was what brought the danger in the first place?

She stopped, uncertain. What were the chances that the demon had already told something or someone of what it found before coming to investigate further? Was there some force that already knew of her place here, or would she bring that focus by setting up something to distract that very same attention?

Once more, she found herself doubting and overthinking because of the damn foresight of the collective.

"I don't know, Boreal. Maybe we can find a way to do it without bringing too much attention to the island. I don't want to give away our presence if that demon we killed hasn't gone and revealed something about us. Maybe we can try to build an escape from these caves so we don't get trapped in here instead," Zalia suggested.

She would take the time to consider Boreal's idea. It wasn't a terrible one but it might serve to know more about the danger before trying something like that.

So, not waiting for Boreal's response, she moved over to the wall near to the pool holding the collective. The Grove responded to her thoughts and created a doorway in the wall through which she started using her passives to move the stone. It flowed like water, ever so slowly creating a tunnel that led away from the Grove.

It took some time but with Boreal's help, as she too had access to the Physical Resistance passive from Survivalist, they managed to create a path that led to the other side of the giant pillar their cave was built into. It was a relatively shallow incline, the distance much farther than the normal entrance to the cave system. They left a good few metres of stone there, knowing they would be able to remove it quickly if needed to escape.

The process really gave Zalia a good feel for how big these pillars really were. From the outside and compared to the scale of the island, they seemed somewhat small, yet while digging through them, it took her a very long time to reach the other side with her limited stone manipulation skill.

Despite that, it was done. She had still not come to a decision about following through with Boreal's plan by the time she arrived back in the Grove from the tunnel, though, when she arrived, she discovered that she wouldn't need to. Before the pool, in the middle of the room, sat a very large gathering of frogs. It must have been the entire collective, out of their little pool home with the jellyfish and now in her Grove.

"*It is time*," the collective said.

CHAPTER FORTY-NINE

Corruption

Zalia

Time for what?" Zalia asked, her heart beginning to beat heavily in her chest.

"*You know what,*" the collective said.

And she did. The "danger" Delphi had spoken of. She had a choice, at that moment. She could turn around and leave by the tunnel she had just dug, become the hunted in Cormaine, or she could face whatever lay ahead and trust in the collective's sight.

"What do you see?" Zalia asked, a little bit of fear tinting her voice.

While she was by no means a coward, with the whole damn collective sitting there, staring at her with those all-knowing eyes, and an unknown enemy at the surface—well, it was not something any sane person would find relaxing.

"*We see what must be done. It is time,*" the collective said.

Her fear, just a little bit of it, turned to anger. She was sick of their obscurity.

"Fine, let's go see what the hell is so important that you won't tell me about it," Zalia growled.

She turned on her heel, making her way towards the entrance of the Grove, Boreal close behind.

They reached the entrance and Zalia pushed aside the thick vines there just a little to peek outside. In the sky above, flying through the shades, Zalia could see three figures soaring through the sky towards them. She recognised the figures; they were the same race of creature as the previous demon she'd killed. The one at the front, however, was much larger than that one had been. The two behind it were smaller by a bit, not so calm as the central figure, and constantly striking out at each other like they were vying for power.

"And what else is coming?" Zalia whispered.

She couldn't see anything else, but even with the aura-blocking effect of her living rituals and Grove, she could feel the corruptive aura growing stronger. It wasn't as strong as the one created by the twisted monster she had seen flying over the island hosting Hetheir, but it was definitely something more than just the three creatures she saw before her.

She heard the little tapping of the horde of frogs approaching behind her and turned to see three of them were sitting watching the map she had left on the ground. She'd forgotten about that and walked over to see. Approaching from the same direction as the three flying figures were a large number of red dots. The shades were blinking to life on the map while the three figures moved closer to them, as if their presence was turning them from mindless parts of the scenery to creatures actively looking to kill.

"Well, that's certainly a lot more than three," Zalia said.

"*It certainly is. We will do what we can,*" the collective said.

"Are you sure we should even fight this battle?" Zalia asked.

There was a momentary pause, as if the collective was trying to decide what to tell her.

"*It is important that we do,*" they replied.

"Why? What will happen?" Zalia asked in frustration.

"*Since you have arrived in Cormaine, our visions have gone from ones of bleak and eventless future to ones of great change. We cannot tell you of those visions, only that this battle must be fought; what comes must happen for the future of Cormaine,*" they explained.

Zalia stopped for a moment, taking in the fact that they had even explained at all. Maybe what was to come was now no longer stoppable. She turned to Boreal.

"We'll fight down low, in the forest. That is where our strengths lie. Stay safe, do not take any risks. I don't want you dying today, nor any day," Zalia whispered, gently holding Boreal's head.

"*We will both live,*" Boreal said.

Her usual tone of humour and joy was gone, replaced by something more serious. An understanding of the stakes, perhaps a fear of losing another mother.

Zalia applied all the protective rituals she could apply to herself and Boreal, as well as the base Zephyr for slow-fall. She did not apply the flight ritual, thinking it would be unwise at any point to be flying up towards the three demons of unknown rank and the shades they controlled.

She gave Boreal a kiss on the head and sprinted out of the Grove, with Boreal following behind and overtaking her as they reached the forest edge.

She could see the three demons flying overhead as the trees and branches flashed past at speed. She ignored many of the obstacles, dashing straight through them with her intangibility. The aura out here was significantly stronger, especially so without the protections of the Grove. It only grew stronger as they found the first of the creatures running through the forest.

It ran on all fours, yet was humanoid with a snarling face filled with sharp teeth. Its back was hunched, large spikes coming out like those of a hedgehog. Its eyes were beady, filled with a hunger, a rage, a madness. It was unlike anything she had seen in the others so far, be it corrupt human or demon above. It was most comparable to the madmen that charged the rebels' camp yet was so, so much more. It was less mindless and more focused.

Fortunately, it seemed these were the lower-ranked of the demons above for as she saw more and more, they were all of Tin or Iron rank.

The first began dying as she released arrows from the treetops, applying Hunter's Mark and various rituals as their screams rang out from the forest. She saw one die to an icy approximation of Boreal that jumped out from under a root, catching it by the neck and ripping through it with ease.

Another died as a spike from a tree extended out, impaling it through the head to another tree nearby, which held the corpse up in a macabre posture of false life.

Dozens died as Zalia focused on spreading the lava curse through their ranks, others yet becoming blind as she cast a mass ritual of Bitterbalm major and Glowing Cavern Fungus minor. Many of those stumbled into various traps: there was a pit in the ground filled with spikes, and a tripwire that wrapped around the stumbling creatures, growing ever tighter in a death hold.

Far above, two of the demons dropped down, noticing the chaos that had begun within the ranks of their creatures below. The larger one hung above, frozen as if engaged in some kind of mental battle, most likely the target of the collective's attack.

Boreal appeared from the shadows, the dozen creatures immediately freezing at feeling the aura she emitted. She must have been holding back since Zalia had not felt it like this, a prey instinct within her yelling that there was a predator she must avoid. She quickly shook it off but the creatures facing her were not so lucky. Heads were bitten almost all the way through, bodies slashed apart. One creature was slammed with so much force from Boreal's armour that it flew back into a tree, impacting with a sickening crunch.

The two demons that were flying down swerved towards Boreal as she made an appearance, but Zalia wasn't about to let them team up on her. Ignoring the many creatures dying or wounded nearby, Zalia dashed through the treetops towards the two, releasing arrows. One of them caught an arrow to the leg and another two to the chest. Mortal wounds for the low-ranked below, but an annoyance for the Bronze enemy before her.

It swerved away, coming towards Zalia, and she sent a quick mental message to Boreal to watch out for the other creature that was still approaching her. Focusing on her own battle, knowing that Boreal would be saved by Healing Presence should she receive a fatal blow, Zalia released more arrows as she applied rituals to the quickly approaching enemy.

It vanished, leaving the rituals in empty air.

This time, Zalia expected the move, immediately using her own teleport to appear a few metres back, behind the enemy that had appeared behind her. Her weapon, already transformed from bow to sword, came down in a quick and brutal strike that clipped one of the demon's six wings off. It spun around in anger and pushed into an attack. This time Zalia was also Bronze rank, however, and she more than held her own.

Thanks to her sword passive, she could see and feel how the enemy would attack and reacted in kind, moving swiftly and sure of foot back through the treetops. She parried a strike, gaining a burst of speed that she put to good use, pushing the attack back.

A quick ritual had a vine grow from the trees underneath the demon wobbling in its unbalanced flight. Her sword struck true in that moment, cutting deep into its right shoulder. She ripped it out and dodged the desperate strike coming at her. Confident in her victory, she waited for a good moment to strike rather than pushing her advantage, knowing she would safely succeed in time as long as she was patient.

The other demon came hurtling towards her and for a moment she thought it was coming to defend its ally. However, the shades it was controlling were swarming behind it, and the thing held an expression of . . . fear?

As it dashed past, Boreal appeared from a shadow amongst the treetops and slammed into its side, her jaw clamping around its neck, the two dropping from the air immediately. Zalia heard a crunch but quickly focused back on her own opponent.

With a dead ally, and bleeding heavily from a wound that glowed with a burning light, the demon looked like it might try to flee as well. At that moment, the whole fight changed.

An aura that Zalia recognised all too well began pressing down on the battlefield, and upon feeling it, it was only the rituals she had applied to herself, her abilities, and Bronze rank that allowed her to stay standing. She thought it had been bad when she was in the keep but out here in the open it was something else entirely.

She was pushed to her knees, her opponent standing straighter as if bolstered by it. It felt hopeless, the aura of the thing alone enough to put an end to her.

The demon stood before her, arm raised and ready to strike her down. It might take it a while to rip her apart piece by piece with her healing keeping her alive, but it would do just that.

The collective had lied, this was the end.

The corruption ate her body.

The demon swung.

The attack ripped across her throat and she gurgled as blood flowed. Another hand punched into her chest and reached for her heart, but the life-saving ability of Healing Presence shoved the arm back out, covering her in a shimmering green light. The wounds began quickly closing even as the demon railed against the shield.

Just then, the aura disappeared.

Ro-ak, Nateysta, bigger than before, swooped in from far above and the aura was pushed back.

Zalia felt hope again, the emotional and physical crushing sensation gone as she used her teleport to get some distance from the demon before her. Its swing barely missed and she quickly looked up.

Above, the monster she remembered, feared, had nightmares about, flew on its fiery bat wings, a thousand eyes observing the battlefield. Slamming into it was Ro, her little crow friend turned god. His power matching that of the creature, a fight of gods above ensued as the smaller creatures fought below.

Zalia turned back to her opponent, no longer at any disadvantage.

She pushed forwards, taking an arm in a quick maneuver fueled by the speed of Fight or Flight. She could sense exactly where the creature's next strike would come from, parrying its sharp claws and using the further burst of speed to remove its head from its shoulders.

"Where are you, Boreal?" Zalia called out with her mind.

She could feel her direction and began making her way towards it.

Boreal had hopefully already taken care of her enemy, but she didn't have as much protection from that aura as Zalia did.

"*Safe*," Boreal replied.

Zalia breathed a sigh of relief, slicing a hunched creature in two while another got a leg slammed in a bear trap, and its head was caught by another as it fell with a screech of pain.

She found Boreal hiding within the little safe spot that she had set up in the forest, protected by the aura-blocking effect.

She didn't have long to be relieved as she saw another of the thousand-eyed creatures flying in from afar.

"*Oh no*," she whispered.

CHAPTER FIFTY

Lost

Zalia

As the winged form flew closer and closer, Zalia could feel the aura begin to overpower Ro-ak's power, penetrating both it and her own protections. It wouldn't be enough to be debilitating as long as she remained within the small protected area, but she feared for Ro-ak, who would now have two enemies to fight at once.

"*Can you feel that? How could you not tell me about this!?*" she mentally screamed towards the collective.

"*Fight . . . on . . .*" the reply came.

Zalia looked up and she could see the one remaining demon, the largest of the three, was starting to move now. No longer was the power of the collective holding it still.

Her attention was drawn away as Boreal let out a low growl and the first of the ground creatures began their assault. She didn't know how exactly they could tell where she was but with all the powerful creatures above, she didn't doubt one would be able to see her and direct the others towards her.

Boreal ripped through two creatures as Zalia quickly dispatched more with arrows. She fought on desperately, trying to find some way out of their situation. If she acted quickly, she and Boreal could escape, yet the chances of that plan working diminished with every passing moment. She didn't want to leave the collective and Ro-ak behind, yet this fight was so far out of her power.

"***Zalia, they . . . are . . . trying . . . to use my power. My power . . . to rip open . . . a portal. You must be ready,***" Ro-ak said in her mind.

The force of the mental words struck her like a physical blow, as if in using his power to this degree, Ro was unable to project his thoughts less vigorously.

"*Did you hear that? Be ready for the portal, come with us!*" Zalia said to the collective.

She quickly dodged a slashing claw, bringing her sword down on the creature's overextended arm as her legs shifted.

"*Keep our memory, Zalia of the Druids. Do not forget us,*" they replied, sadness lacing the thoughts.

"*What?*" she asked.

"*It is time,*" they replied.

"*You told me that I would have nothing to fear . . .*" Zalia trailed off.

She saw the demon begin flying down towards the cave.

Zalia rushed out of the protective area, stumbling a little at the strength of the aura outside the protective dome. She stepped into a tree, seeing for a moment through hundreds in the forest nearby. She could see countless creatures, possibly thousands, littering the woods, pouring through them like a disease. She stepped out near the Grove in time to see the demon, Silver ranked, slam through the entrance of the cave and into the room beyond.

"No . . ." Zalia whispered.

A memory entered her mind, a confusing jumble, something she couldn't decipher. It was like a million memories compressed into one. She immediately shoved the entire thing into her gauntlet, a large misty flow leaving her eyes, travelling down her arm into the heirloom wrapped around her hand.

She stumbled towards the Grove, sword out, the pressure of the aura too strong for her to think. She could hear someone talking in her mind, a loud voice. Ro-ak.

She ignored it, tumbling through the entrance to see the room littered with the bodies of the collective.

The large demon, with skin like cracked obsidian, held a small creature in its hand. Delphi.

The hand closed in a sharp movement. A crunch resounded.

Zalia was pulled from behind, a force ripping her out of the entrance. She spun wildly in the air, disoriented, spinning further still as she was slammed by something hard and metallic. Something with blue eyes, missing a piece of metal on her shoulder, fur peeking through. Boreal. They were flying through the air, pulled by an invisible force towards a giant gash in the world, through which she could see the dunes of a desert.

"Prepare the world for what comes," Ro-ak said.

Her last vision of Cormaine was of a large god fighting a desperate battle with two thousand-eyed monsters.

Everything blurred together, colours, sounds, smells, feelings. She was flung heavily through the air, the sound like the ripping of fabric, yet loud as an explosion. She looked up dizzily at the tear in the world as it rippled, then closed. It ripped open again before promptly closing once more.

This time, it stayed closed.

She stood up shakily, brushing off the sand covering her armour. She looked around desperately and saw Boreal also standing shakily atop a nearby dune. The sky above was clear and blue, the air fresh. She took a deep breath, feeling a relief flood her body, her healing no longer needing to fight the corruption.

Despite all that, the first thing that left her was a sob as she fell back to her knees. Her body shook as she cried, the memory of Delphi being crushed in a clawed hand sharp in her mind. She heard the patter of paws on sand as Boreal came up and curled around her, gently pushing her head into Zalia's hands.

"They're . . . they're gone," she said between gasps of breath.

They had known, known what would happen. They had seen it, done nothing about it, let that future happen because . . . because why?

She remembered the memory that had entered her mind but wasn't ready to think about that just yet.

She knelt there for a time, crying. She couldn't say for how long, only that the sun shining brightly in the sky was that much lower as to be noticeable when she finally uncurled from the position she had taken.

She hadn't known the collective for long, yet they had been one of her few friends in the hell that was Cormaine. For that, she had felt closer to them than many she had met in her life. Now, they were dead, sacrificing themselves for a future for their world that she could not see.

She almost gave up to lie back down, but the survivalist in her won out. She took the memory of the past hour and shoved the whole thing into her vault. She could feel it leave and was left with but a simple summary of what those memories had been. She knew Delphi was dead, a fight had happened, yet the emotions and specifics were swept away. She could take time to process that later; for now she had to figure out if she was safe or not.

She looked around herself, rubbing at her bleary and sore eyes. She didn't have much of an idea where she was but did remember that there was a large desert to the south of the Endarian kingdom. So, going by the assumption she was on the same world as Endaria, she began travelling north.

"Come on, Boreal, let's go find home," she said quietly, gently patting Boreal's back.

The sun was sinking towards the horizon as she began what might be a long journey. When she got back to Endaria, then, she would process everything.

Far above, she could see some type of winged creature flying about and decided to keep an eye out on them. She was certain they would be keeping an eye out on her too, some sort of scavenging creature like a vulture, maybe.

That night, she walked ever onwards. She could probably have kept on walking but decided after another three or four hours of trudging over the endless dunes that some sleep would do her good. She summoned the vault, a sandstone archway growing out of the desert below, and stepped inside. The interior was the same as she remembered, though two new memories sat in misty swirls within their clear domes. Just looking at them brought a flash of two eyes looking at her as a large hand crushed down.

She quickly averted her gaze, moving past it to sit in the little herb garden at the back of the vault. There, she lay down to sleep.

She woke up maybe an hour and a half later, though time was hard to tell. She was curled up with Boreal curled around her like a large, warm, breathing pillow. She let out a deep sigh, opening her eyes and staring at the ceiling. She watched the little lights floating about her Grove, following them with her eyes as they drifted. She steeled herself and sat up with a groan.

She had felt the connection to the other part of her Grove break when she had been thrown through the portal. Whether that was a result of damage done to it, her own subconscious, or some other reason, she did not know. It didn't matter, she would have broken the connection herself when she had found herself in a different world either way.

It occurred to her then that she probably could have flown the whole previous day; her speed would have been increased greatly. She had just been so wrung out and absent-minded that the thought hadn't occurred to her.

So, the next few hours were spent flying over the dunes, somewhat low to the ground to avoid entering the air space of the creatures above. She let her mind go numb, simply enjoying the feeling of the clean air on her face and the moon far above, lighting the dunes in a dim light that she could see perfectly by.

So her mind was jolted back to reality when her gaze was caught on a bright light amongst a stone outcropping jutting from the dunes. Atop the rocks was a little fire, shielded from the wind by an alcove formed from yet more stone—though, it looked to be magically created, a tell being the way in which it looked like water turned stone rather than some natural formation.

There was a single figure sat by the firelight, hunched in a light cloak.

"*Want to go check it out?*" Zalia said to Boreal.

There was no reply.

"*Boreal?*" Zalia urged.

"*Food?*" Boreal replied, seeming confused.

Had she been lost in thought too?

"*Want to go check out that fire over there?*" Zalia repeated.

"*New friend?*" Boreal asked.

"*Don't be hasty now,*" Zalia said.

Everyone always seemed to be either friend or food to her, though that one demon had been neither friend *nor* food. Not tasty apparently.

Thoughts of the demon Boreal had killed brought the eventual flash of cracked obsidian skin and large clawed hands around a dear friend. A crunching sound.

Zalia shuddered, pushing her mind away from the memory. She was really not enjoying the ability to recall the stored memories in perfect clarity.

She dropped swiftly, deciding to land on the outcropping some distance away. In a move reminiscent of her first meeting with the Hidden, Zalia crept towards the campfire, wanting to get a closer look at the person.

They were a small human with dark skin wearing a light cloth wrap with a hood pulled up. They had the same light cloth covering the lower half of their face and a strange ethereal material wrapped around their eyes. Leaning against the stone behind them was a spear with a leather flask hanging from the grip. As Zalia approached, their eyes jumped up and they grabbed their spear, holding it firmly as they stood.

"Who goes there?" the woman called out, her voice rough but whispery like the sand.

? - Iron rank.

Deciding she would definitely not be a threat, Zalia came out of the shadows with her hands up.

"*Stay hidden for a moment,*" she said to Boreal.

Boreal was definitely a lot more terrifying than Zalia was. Especially to someone who had probably never seen anything quite like Boreal before.

"I mean no harm," Zalia said.

"How'd you get up here?" the woman asked, eyes narrowed.

Zalia could see something weird happening with the vibrations in the stone underneath the woman. Kind of like . . . sonar, maybe?

Maybe she had some sort of tremorsense, too.

"My own two legs," Zalia said, deciding to keep her abilities a secret for now.

She supposed she did look very out of place, wearing armour fashioned after the forest.

The woman looked at her a little nervously, probably having seen her rank.

"I promise I mean no harm, may I sit? I'm a bit lost and would love directions if you have them," Zalia asked, letting some vulnerability through to help build trust.

The woman flicked the tip of her spear towards the stone opposite the fire from her, and Zalia walked over, using her manipulation to make herself a more comfortable seat.

"So, what's your name?" Zalia asked.

News

Zalia

Zalia sat waiting, warming her hands by the fire as the short woman opposite her still stood, spear at the ready.

"How'd you get up here?" the woman asked, having ignored Zalia's earlier question.

"Walking, as I've said," Zalia repeated.

"Well, that's real funny considering I've been stuck up here for two days due to the sand wyrms buried beneath the sand all around this rock," the woman said, glaring suspiciously at her.

"They must not have sensed me, I am quite stealthy," Zalia replied, pretending she had any idea what a sand wyrm was.

"They've got better sense for tremors than I do, and I felt you coming," the woman said.

"Maybe I let you," Zalia said. She definitely hadn't *let* her. She hadn't really tried to hide either.

"*Where do you think you're going,*" Zalia said to Boreal, sensing she had begun moving away.

"*. . . Sand wyrm tasty?*" Boreal asked.

"*Seriously? Now? We can find out later,*" Zalia reprimanded.

The woman was still standing with weapon ready.

"Look, if I wanted to harm you I wouldn't have walked up to you to do it. I've just not seen another human in . . . a little while and wanted to see what the people that lived in the desert are like. This is the desert to the south of Endaria, right?" Zalia explained.

"Well, we don't appear by a stranger's campfire in the middle of the night and most definitely do not appreciate you Endarians coming into our desert," the woman said.

She did let down her guard, just a little. Zalia also didn't miss that she had answered her question, indirectly.

"Well, I'm not Endarian if it helps. I suppose my approach was a little bit . . . untactful," Zalia admitted.

"Just a bit," the woman replied, letting out a tiny bit of a laugh. More of a sharp exhale really.

"So, what do I have to do to get your name?" Zalia asked.

"Tell me the truth, for a start," the woman said.

"Fine, fine. I flew here, I've got some magic that lets me fly. I've got no idea what a sand wyrm is either," Zalia admitted.

She really did suck at lying.

"Better. I'm Sazcha, you?" Sazcha asked.

"Zalia and my friend is Boreal," Zalia said.

"Friend?" Sazcha asked in confusion.

"Come out Boreal," Zalia called.

Boreal melded out of the shadows, padding up to sit beside Zalia. Sazcha's somewhat relaxed posture went straight back to guarded.

"Boreal is my friend, no need to be worried. She's quite harmless," Zalia said.

"She certainly doesn't look like she's harmless," Sazcha said.

"Looks can be deceiving. She would only ever attack you if she wanted to eat you, and she doesn't eat people. I think? Besides, she is way more interested in eating the sand wyrms you mentioned at the moment. Do they taste good, do you know?" Zalia asked.

Boreal opened her mouth slightly like she was ready to sprint down the rock towards the sands to try the wyrms immediately.

"Not the best, but they are good enough. The bigger ones taste better, though they're much harder to kill. So, what exactly are you doing out here, then?" Sazcha asked.

She was less guarded and more wary now, eyeing Boreal like she was expecting an attack. To be fair, Boreal had grown quite menacing in their time away.

"Well, I'm just back from a bit of an adventure, heading back to Endaria to see if any of my friends died while I was away. Heard any news from there, demon invasions, the dead coming to life, that kind of thing?" Zalia asked in kind.

Sazcha looked at her a little oddly.

"Where did you go on an adventure to have not heard the news?" she asked.

"A whole new world," Zalia said sarcastically, though it was closer to reality than she let on. Tried to let on, at least.

"Well, it must've been far off in the world. Yes, there have been people fleeing Endaria into the desert, which is incredibly annoying. They tell tales of war, corruption, monsters, and death."

Zalia's heart sank.

"How bad?" she asked in a whisper. Today was just getting worse and worse.

"There are still fights warring across the whole kingdom, from what the few refugees I've seen say. While people all tell different stories, one part seems to stay the same. Beams of light blasting into the sky and moments later, they all came crashing down, causing explosions. Some caused massive damage, from others came monsters, and yet others caused the surroundings to wither and die, with the air becoming toxic. If you've friends in Endaria, you have good cause to be worried for them at this time," Sazcha explained, her voice a little softer having caught on to Zalia's very visible misery.

"I didn't stop it, then," Zalia said quietly.

She had spent weeks, months even, in Cormaine. She had made that sacrifice to stop this very thing from happening. Maybe she had lessened the impact but she had not done enough.

She suddenly had a million questions flood her mind. She had thought Zen would have been safe in Ember's capable healer hands, but what if the ritual had caused an explosion and killed them? Worse yet was the possibility of the corruption or some of the creatures from Cormaine coming over. Was the Hidden now free from influence with Juniper out of the picture? Were General Faian and the rebellion one of the groups of people still fighting a war?

All the troubles she had put aside when she had gone to Cormaine came back to her now, layering on top of everything she had already experienced as of late.

"Thank you for telling me," Zalia added.

Sazcha shrugged. "Not like it wasn't something you'd have found out soon enough anyways," she said.

Zalia stood up.

"I have to go, every moment counts. It was nice meeting you, Sazcha, maybe I'll come back and find you one day when this is over. I'd love to see more of the desert you call home," she said, gently patting Boreal.

"And nice meeting you too . . . kind of. Hey, before you go, could you, um . . . give me a lift off this rock?" Sazcha asked.

"Oh, right. Yeah, of course," Zalia agreed.

She gave Sazcha a lift some distance to the west, past where she thought the sand wyrms were waiting. Waving her a farewell, Zalia and Boreal flew with haste towards Endaria, a two-day trip by Sazcha's estimate.

She had friends to save.

About the Author

Leif Roder is the author of the Hunting and Herbalism series, originally released on Royal Road. They studied both aeronautics and software engineering before quitting university and moving abroad, where they began writing books on their phone while on the bus on the way to work. This eventually turned into a full-time career as an author. Now, they write all kinds of fiction, from fantasy to sci-fi with a sprinkling of magic to short stories about cats. They also enjoy a little wall climbing and archery as a treat. Roder lives in New Zealand.

Podium

DISCOVER MORE

STORIES UNBOUND

PodiumEntertainment.com